Retribution

The Centurions: Volume III

ANTHONY RICHES

HODDER

First published in Great Britain in 2018 by Hodder & Stoughton
An Hachette UK company

This paperback edition published in 2018

1

Map illustration by Clifford Webb

A CIP catalogue record for this title is available from the British Library

Paperback ISBN 9781473628830

Typeset in Plantin Light by
Palimpsest Book Production Ltd, Falkirk, Stirlingshire

Printed and bound in Great Britain by Clays Ltd, Elcograf S.p.A.

Hodder & Stoughton Ltd
Carmelite House
50 Victoria Embankment
London EC4Y 0DZ

www.hodder.co.uk

For Helen

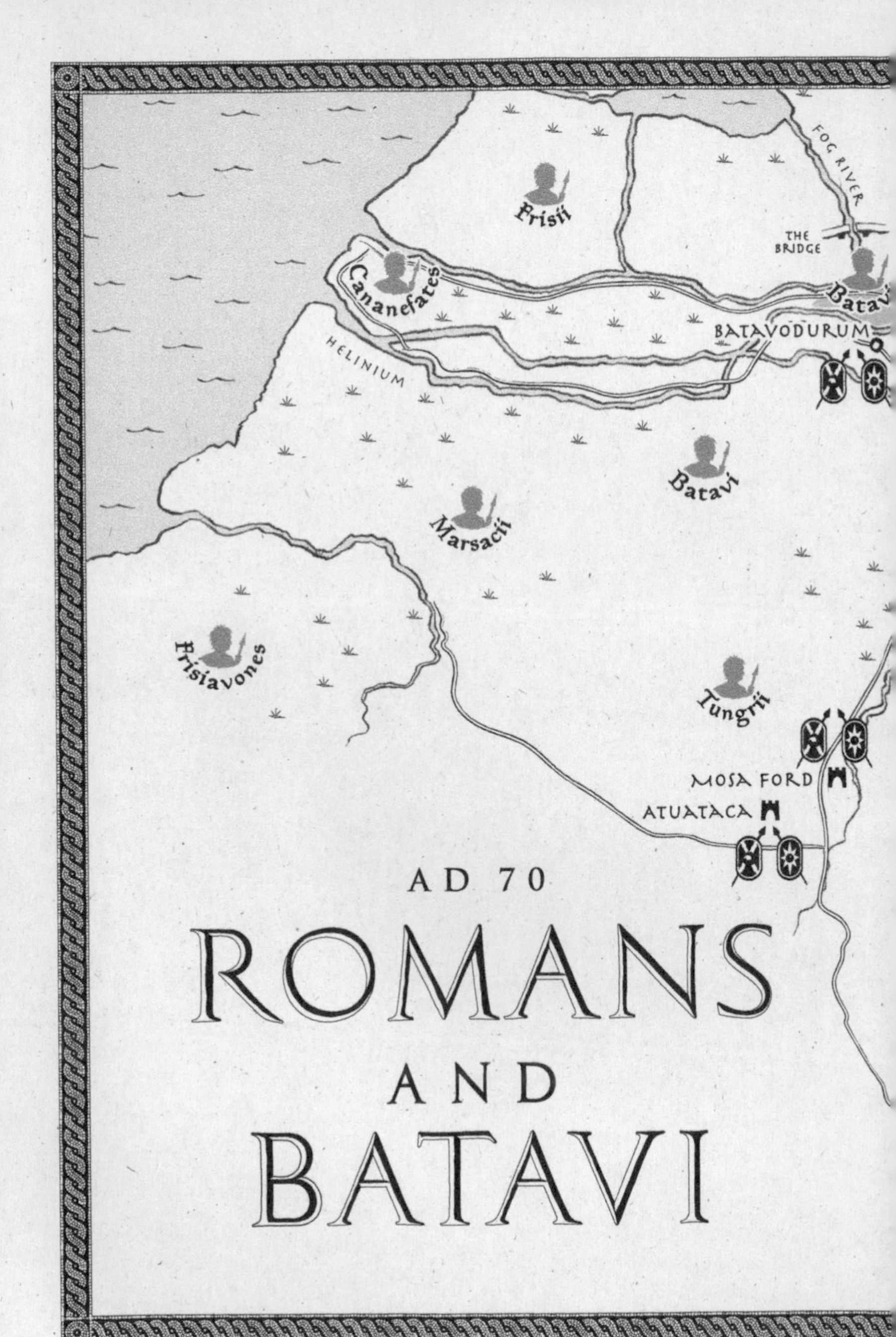

AD 70

ROMANS AND BATAVI

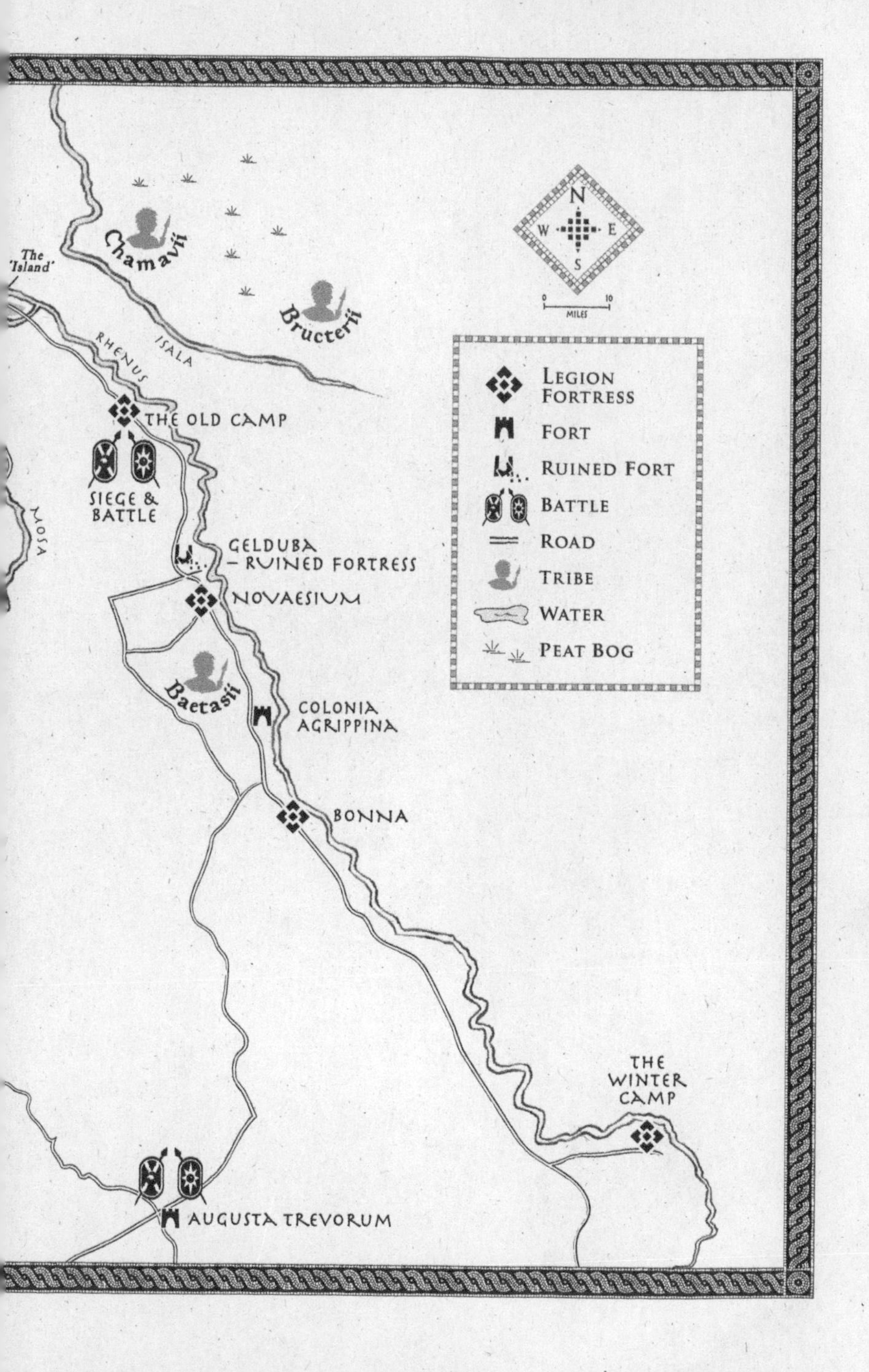
N
W
E
S
0
10
MILES
Legion Fortress
Fort
Ruined Fort
Battle
Road
Tribe
Water
Peat Bog
Chamavii
Bructerii
The 'Island'
RHENUS
ISALA
MOSA
THE OLD CAMP
SIEGE & BATTLE
GELDUBA – RUINED FORTRESS
NOVAESIUM
Baetasii
COLONIA AGRIPPINA
BONNA
THE WINTER CAMP
AUGUSTA TREVORUM

ACKNOWLEDGEMENTS

Over the course of this amazing, enthralling and occasionally surprising trilogy, I have never ceased to be indebted to the patience of my editor Carolyn and the invaluable assistance of her assistants Abby, Thorne and Madeleine, the ever-indefatigable publicity efforts of Kerry and Rosie, and the gentle but persistent encouragement – only very occasionally backed up with strong language – of my wife Helen. My thanks to all of you who helped, cajoled and generally drove me to deliver a readable story that still did some measure of justice to the amazing twists and turns of this episode in Rome's history.

Jona Lendering, the driving force behind the indispensible Livius website (*livius.org*), was kind enough to cast an eye over the manuscripts and point out any gross errors. His comments have been invaluable on more than one occasion ('There were no trees there so your character can't run off and hide in them', for example), and the series has benefitted hugely from his input. Thank you, Jona.

Ben Kane was instrumental in helping me mull over the choice of titles that eventually coalesced into the three that have proven so evocative, to the degree that they have tended to reflect each book's contents even better than I ever intended. The fact that we conducted part of that long-running discussion driving from Xanten (the Old Camp) to Kalkriese (the site of Arminius's momentous betrayal of Rome in AD9) only added to the enjoyment. And speaking of the Old Camp, Ben and I walked the site of the legion camp – now farmland – as the evening's last light faded into night, and came across the remnants of the fortress's amphitreatre, still in use for concerts. I can't tell you here the brilliant idea that he then spontaneously gifted to me, or it'd be a spoiler, but it typified the generosity of a man I'm proud to call a friend. Thanks Ben!

And, just as heartfelt as ever, thank you, the reader, for continuing to read these stories. Please keep reading. We were only ever taking a temporary break from the *Empire* series, and now that the story of the Batavian revolt as seen through the eyes of the men I've imagined fighting on both sides is done, Marcus and his *familia* are set to return in the tenth book of the *Empire* series. There's a murderous bandit on the loose in Gaul, an imperial chamberlain toying with our heroes' lives and . . . Well, wait and see, eh?

One last thing. There's a gold aureus from the time of Vespasian – yes, a real Roman gold coin – to be won by one lucky reader in my Centurions competition. All you have to do is go to my website and enter the answers to the three questions that you'll find there, the solutions to which are contained in *Betrayal*, *Onslaught* and *Retribution*. There's no restriction on when you enter each answer, multiple entries are allowed but the last answers given will be taken as your definitive entry, and all answers will be invisible to everyone except myself and my trusted webmaster (who's not allowed to enter). So don't hold back, get puzzling, think acrostically (and if that's not a clue then I don't know what is), and the very best of luck – someone's got to win a precious piece of history. Why not you?

LIST OF CHARACTERS

AD70
In Egypt
Titus Flavius Vespasianus – legatus, imperial 2nd Legion Augustan
Gaius Hosidius Geta – legatus, imperial 14th Legion Gemina
Sextus – senior centurion, imperial 14th Legion Gemina

AD70
In Rome
Gaius Licinius Mucianus – consul
Quintus Petillius Cerialis – legatus augusti, imperial Roman army
Tiberius Pontius Longus – legatus, imperial 21st Legion Rapax
Pugno – first spear, imperial 21st Legion Rapax
Alfenius Varus – former commander of the Praetorian Guard, emperor's emissary to the Batavians
Gaius Sextiliius Felix - legatus, auxiliary cohort
Julius Briganticus - commander of the Ala Singularium, Kivilaz's nephew
Appius Annius Gallus - legatus, commander of four legions in Gallia Lugdunensis

In the Old Camp (modern day Vetera)
Aquillius – senior centurion, imperial 15th Legion Primigenia
Marius – senior centurion, imperial 5th Legion Alaudae
Munius Lupercus – legatus commanding imperial legions 5th Alaudae and 15th Primigenia

Batavi warriors
Kivilaz – (known as Julius Civilis by Rome) – prince of the Batavi, commander of the tribe's revolt against Rome

Hramn – commander of his cohorts (formerly leader of the imperial German bodyguard), Kivilaz's nephew
Draco Bairaz – commander of the guard cohort, Kivilaz's cousin
Brinno – king of the Cananefates tribe, allies of the Batavi
Alcaeus – wolf-priest, centurion, 2nd century of the 1st Batavian cohort
Egilhard (Achilles) – watch officer, leading man, son of Lataz, brother of Sigu
Hludovig – Alcaeus's chosen man
Sigu – soldier, brother of Egilhard
Lataz (Knobby) – soldier, father of Egilhard and Sigu
Frijaz (Stumpy) – soldier, uncle of Egilhard and Sigu
Adalwin (Beaky) – soldier
Levonhard (Ugly) – soldier
Lanzo (Dancer) – soldier
Wigbrand (Tiny) - soldier

AD70
In Novaesium
Gaius Dillius Vocula - legatus augusti, legion commander
Antonius - senior centurion, imperial 22nd Primigenia
Herennius Gallus - former legatus, imperial 1st Germanica
Numisius Rufus - former legatus, imperial 16th Gallica

AD70
Germania Inferior
Julius Classicus - prince of the Nervii tribe and prefect of the First Nervian cavalry cohort
Montanus - Classicus's cousin

AD70
Gallia Belgica
Claudius Labeo - prefect, commander of army of allied tribes

Preface

It is January of AD 70, and Roman rule in northern Europe is teetering on the edge of disaster. Weakened by civil wars, first between Otho and Vitellius and then Vitellius and Vespasian, the legions whose fortresses safeguarded the Rhine frontier are either under siege or pathetic remnants of their former strength. The Batavi tribe of Germania Inferior and their tribal allies from both sides of the great river have moved decisively to defeat every attempt to contain their revolt, and the Gallic tribes to their south plot a similar rebellion, planning their own 'Gallic Empire'. At a point in the struggle to defeat the Batavis' revolt when every soldier is needed, two legions are bottled up in the Old Camp, present-day Xanten, while two more are on the brink of mutiny, having murdered their general for the crime of favouring the victorious Vespasianus. To the men charged with holding off a Batavi thrust to the south, defeat seems inevitable.

In Italy, on the other hand, preparations are well in hand for the re-conquest of the land north of the Alps, with legions under orders to march from their duty stations in Hispania and Britannia to join those returning north over the mountains to reclaim their fortresses and enforce Rome's will. First among them is the famed Twenty-first *Rapax*, at least to its officers and men, long the most infamous unit in the emperor's army, left bitter and in need of bloodshed by defeat at the Second Battle of Cremona whose loss resulted in Vespasianus's victory. And the Twenty-first is under the command of the emperor's son-in-law Petillius Cerialis, himself a man with a point to prove having been disgraced in the war against Boudicca's Iceni rebels. The rebels have yet to face such crack soldiers, or men with quite so much need for vindication.

And the Batavi cohorts themselves are not the force that marched north to join the rebellion less than six months before. Bled of much of their strength at Gelduba late the previous year, they are no longer pre-eminent in the rebel army led by their prince, Kivilaz, but in the fighting to come, the Romans are likely to learn the hard way that the most dangerous opponent is the one with his back against the wall – and with nothing more to lose.

Prologue

The Old Camp, January AD 70

'Once we are out on the field of bones you must all move in total silence.'

The grizzled chieftain looked around the circle of men gathered around him, staring at each of them in turn. His last remaining son, his brothers and his nephews. All of them were beloved to him, his blood and that of his father, all were men of whom he was proud. And there were a good number fewer than there had been at summer's end, when, with the harvest gathered, he had led them to war to answer the call of the Batavi prince, Kivilaz, and make fact the prophecies of the priestess Veleda in her prediction of a great German victory.

'If the Romans hear us out here then they will shoot their machine arrows out into the dark, and while we make small targets in a wide, empty night we have all seen the horror of a man killed in such a way. Death is certain, but it is not always swift. And their machines are not the only terror that awaits us out there, if the rumours of the *Banô,* the evil spirit that haunts this place, are true. So make sure your faces and hands are blackened with ashes, like this . . .' he gestured to his own face, striped with the lines left by his soot-laden fingers to break up its pale image, 'and leave your boots in our camp. We must be as silent as the mouse that hunts in the forest, knowing that the owl lurks above, waiting for a single sound to betray its presence. Now go and prepare.'

He waited patiently while they made ready for their night's work, content there was no sign that the heavy clouds that had rolled across the sky late that evening would part to admit the light of the moon and stars any time soon. Turning to contemplate the darkened fortress on which he and thousands of German tribesmen stood guard, its outline barely visible in the gloom, he spat softly into the dirt at his feet, muttering a curse on the Romans who had robbed him of two sons in the three months they had been besieging the stronghold that their enemy called the Old Camp. One had died instantly with a bolt in his chest, the other a slow, lingering death as a result of the horrific scalding inflicted on him by boiling water poured onto the tribe's warriors as they had flailed furiously but to no avail at the twenty-foot-high brick-faced walls. The circle of heavily battle-scarred grass around the fortress was a killing ground that had claimed thousands of men over the previous months, fallen warriors whose bodies had been left to rot for days before the Romans had finally allowed them to be gathered, painfully slowly by only a small number of men, and granted a suitable farewell. Already he wished he had never set eyes upon it, or heard the names Kivilaz, the Batavi prince who was the leader of the revolt, or Veleda, the priestess who had encouraged his tribe and several others to join it, but he kept such thoughts to himself. As, he suspected, did many other men of his rank, the hundreds of clan leaders who had led their families to this place of death and horror.

With all attempts at breaking into the Romans' fortress having failed, and now that the decision had been made to starve the defenders out, with the promise of a grim revenge to be extracted on that day, there was nothing for any of the besiegers to do but wait and take what opportunities for distraction and profit presented themselves. Only a week before a man had slipped back into the camp just before dawn with a gold brooch in his dirty hand, trembling both with the cold and the fear of the terror that was said to haunt the field of bones when darkness fell, but nevertheless undeniably rich. His find had been fit to grace a tribal king's cloak, heavy enough to buy a farm and cattle, and he had left swiftly, before word got round and attempts were made to claim its return by false and genuine claimants alike. The brooch would by now be on its way to Rome, where, it was said, authentic tribal jewellery was in huge demand. And so, in the absence of any better way of earning some recompense for sons lost and a wife left alone too long, the chieftain had finally decided to risk the various dangers inherent in roaming the battlefield after dark, and had agreed to lead his family in a search of the ground over which so many men had fought and died. His warriors gathered around him again, and after making a few last adjustments to their ashen camouflage, he nodded and turned back to the fortress.

'We go. From now, no sound.'

Climbing quietly up the timber steps out of the great fortified ditch that ran the full length of the perimeter around the Old Camp, a barrier that Kivilaz had ordered both as a means of keeping the legions inside the camp trapped, and to keep out any relieving force, they padded silently out onto the wide expanse of pitted and ravaged ground, their pace set by the man at the head of their line, the chieftain's youngest son and his only remaining heir, an irrepressible boy on the cusp of manhood whose eyes and ears were undoubtedly the sharpest among them. Advancing slowly out into the killing field of the fortress's bolt throwers they barely made a sound, their presence undetectable in the deep gloom of the overcast night.

A whispered command stopped them, and each man turned to his right and sank silently to the ground, the fortress barely discernible in the night except as a darker mass against the gloom. No lights burned on the walls, the Romans having learned early in the siege that to do so invited the attention of archers, who would creep in close and then loft speculative arrows at any torch or watch fire. The walls could have been empty of life, were it not for the fact that the sound of voices could be faintly heard in the night's silence, men talking to pass the long hours of their watch. Good, he mused, for if they were talking then they could not be listening. He whispered the order to begin the search, and with an almost imperceptible rustle of fingers combing through frost-rimed grass his men began to crawl forward. Doing the same, his hands feeling forward in the darkness, he inched his way across the freezing cold ground, probing the ice-crusted blades of grass with his fingers for any sign of the prize in whose pursuit he had led his kindred out onto the dark battlefield. His skin touched cold metal, and with a thrill of discovery he slowly and painstakingly freed it from the earth into which it had been trodden, but even as it came free from the ground's tight grip he knew that it was close to valueless, a piece of iron shield edging that would be worth next to nothing. Tucking it into his belt he crawled on, listening as the men on either side stopped and scraped at the soil as they chanced on items of potential value, only to breathe disappointed sighs as the truth of their discoveries became apparent.

'*It's an arrowhead.*'

His son's almost inaudible whisper was freighted with the despondency that followed the first thrill of a find, when the potential for wealth was dispelled by the certainty of what it was that lay on the discoverer's palm. He had, of course, warned them that their search was likely to end in disappointment. The men with the unenviable job carrying away the rotting bodies of their dead fellow warriors after each battle had routinely searched them for valuables, and combed the ground on which they lay, and the vast majority of gold and weapons had doubtless been found and carried away. There would be other groups of men searching the battlefield elsewhere, as there were every moonless night, and previous searches had already seen men come away with items that had evaded the eyes of men struggling with the horror of their gruesome task, but such good fortune was rare, and becoming less and less likely as the weeks passed.

A faint sound away to his right snatched the tribesman's attention away from his task, a hand snaking to his dagger, but no other noise broke the silence and, after a moment longer to assure himself that all was still well, he resumed the search, crawling slowly across the cold ground with the increasing feeling of having risked the battlefield's perils for nothing, not yet willing to admit defeat, despite the fact that he could no longer feel his fingers or toes. Only when he judged that the dawn was approaching did he hiss a quiet command, waiting while it was passed down the line before creeping away from the fortress with his family at his back. Once they had regained the safety of the earthwork he straightened and stood erect, stretching out the knots in his muscles and counting his men as they walked stiffly past him into the besiegers' camp.

'Twelve. There is one missing. Come here!' He looked at each of them in turn in the dim light of the torch that lit that section of the earthworks, quickly realising who was absent. 'My son. Where is my son?'

They looked at each other in growing horror, all having heard the stories told by men whose narrow escapes from death in the darkness had usually been purchased with the lives or, more chillingly, the ruin of their comrades or family members – men who had professed, with wide eyes, their hands raised to protest the truth of their words, that they had never heard or seen a sign of the *Banô*, of whoever it was who had killed or mutilated the man barely feet from them, the terror that was said to roam the night in search of blood, and the opportunity to inflict a lifetime of misery on his victims. Turning back to the battlefield, forbidding any of them to accompany him, he retraced his steps with less care than before, heedless of the danger that he might be heard in his increasingly desperate need to find his son before the sun rose, and revealed whatever had befallen him, praying that the boy had simply got lost in the dark and made his own way back across the fortified earth defence. Out on the field of bones the fortress's dark shape loomed a little larger, its outline fractionally clearer against the slowly lightening eastern sky, and he knew he only had a short time before the ground around him began to receive a portion of the impending dawn's feeble glow despite the Old Camp's brooding presence. Scouting across the bumpy, pockmarked surface, he cast frantically to his left and right, moving in an aimless hunt no less likely to reveal his son than a carefully thought out search. And then, just as he knew he would have to give up the hunt, he tripped, sprawling full length onto the hard ground with the breath driven out of him by the unexpected impact in a loud grunt that caught the attention of the wall sentries, who called excitedly to each other at the prospect of something to break their monotonous routine. Hobnailed boots were slapping at the stairs as the Romans ran for their arrow machines, but the chieftain's attention was riveted to the corpse over which he had fallen, lifting the dead man's head with the dread of certainty. He choked with the horror of his son's lifeless eyes, and the gash that had been torn in his throat to allow his lifeblood to soak the ground on which he lay in a slick of fluid made black by the absence of light. Shuffling backwards, away from the boy's cold body, desperate to escape the corpse's accusatory stare, he felt a hard grasp pinion the back of his neck, fingers clamping so tightly that he instinctively knew his chances of escape were infinitesimal, even before the point of a knife slid under his jaw to rest on the soft skin beneath which his veins awaited its cold iron kiss.

'You wish to live? Or die? *Quietly*.'

The words were spoken in fluent Latin, a language the German had learned a little of in his youth living in a village close to the great river, the voice brutally harsh even as a whisper, leaving him in no doubt that he was closer to death than he had ever been fighting under the defenders' spears and missiles.

'I wish to l-live.'

'Then I will let you live. In return you will wear my mark for the rest of your life. Do you agree?'

He nodded minutely, knowing that the smallest movement of the knife's blade could kill him, but his relief as the iron's cold touch left the skin of his throat was replaced by horror as he was pushed effortlessly back onto the frozen grass, a dark shape looming over him with one big hand covering his mouth and holding him down with a force he could never have hoped to resist. Looking up into the featureless face that loomed over him he saw the faint reflections of his captor's eyes, pitiless and without expression, a gaze that fixed him in place as effortlessly as the hand on his face. His knife was within easy reach of his right hand, and the man pinning him to the frozen earth was making no effort to prevent him trying to take it, but he knew without conscious thought that to do so would be to die before the blade had cleared its sheath.

'This will hurt. If you make a sound I will kill you. Understand?'

The German nodded, starting as the blade's point was suddenly touching his face, then stiffening with the first cut, feeling the iron scraping across the bone of his forehead in a line that curved down from one temple to the bridge of his nose and then up again on the other side of his head, red hot pain tensing his body as the knife descended again to peck at his face in a pattern that repeated half a dozen times above his right eye before the weapon's point was momentarily withdrawn.

'Nearly finished. But you can still die here.'

The blade came down again, repeating the same odd series of short cuts over the other eye, then withdrew.

'Done. When men ask you what it is, tell them it is the mark of the eagle. Tell them that's what happens when you pull Rome's tail just a little too hard without working out that the dog you're teasing still has teeth. Now leave in silence, without drawing attention to me, or I'll run you down in a dozen strides and leave the rope of your guts hanging out for the crows.'

Padding silently away with blood pouring down his face from a dozen deep cuts to his forehead, the German was almost back at the earthwork, the shock of his disfigurement swiftly being overridden by the memory of his dead son's corpse staring up into the blank sky, when the silence was broken by a sudden roar.

'*This! Is! Aquillius!*' Silence descended again, no answer call given, or, from the speed with which the Roman renewed his challenge, expected. *'Let down the rope and get ready to pull me up! And if I find out that any one of you so much as puts bolt to bow while I'm down here, I'll put that missile up your arse fins first!'*

I

Egypt, January AD 70

'Gaius Hosidius Geta! At last, a man I can talk to without bothering about protocol!'

Beaming with pleasure, the newly enthroned emperor Vespasianus greeted his visitor with the evident warmth of a military man for a former brother-in-arms, gesturing to the couches that had been set up for their meeting along with wine and an assortment of morsels should either Caesar or his guest find themselves in need of refreshment. Taking a cup poured for him by the emperor, Vespasianus's invited guest lowered his head solemnly in the universal gesture of respect. A man in his late middle age, he retained the razor-sharp intelligence that had characterised him as a legion commander over twenty-five years before, and which was one of the reasons the emperor had sent for him, summoning his old friend across the sea to Alexandria where the imperial court awaited favourable winds for the voyage to Rome.

'Caesar. Allow me to present the compliments of my senatorial colleagues. Those men not selected to join the official delegation you met earlier, after a selection process that exercised the best minds in Rome for days with the arcane methods by which the undeserving, uninspiring and those men known to have favoured Nero, Otho or Vitellius were excluded.'

Vespasianus barked a gruff laugh.

'Hah! I'd imagine Licinius Mucianus had a field day with that nonsense, it's just the sort of thing he's good at, smiling while he slides the knife in. Not like you and I, Gaius? The darker political arts don't come easily to soldiers like us!'

Hosidius Geta inclined his head with a slight smile.

'Indeed not, Caesar, you and—'

'And you can cut out all that imperial fawning! You and I are Gaius and Titus, fellow legates who both very nearly bought our farms one misty morning on a hill in Britannia, eh?'

Geta stared at the older man for a moment, the niceties of dealing with an emperor falling away at the older man's command.

'Indeed we did. And, of course, when your colleague Mucianus summoned me to the Palatine, I guessed at once what it was that he would request of me, given our shared near-death experience.'

Vespasianus laughed again.

'Did you now? You always were a smart arse, weren't you? You pulled off the near-impossible in Africa by defeating the Mauri at twenty-three, and you were victorious in Britannia against all the odds at twenty-four, so gloriously victorious and at such great personal risk that dear old Claudius made you walk with him through Rome on the day of his triumph to celebrate the conquest of the new province, even though you weren't a consul. And then?'

Geta winced.

'And then, Titus, I was reclaimed by my family. Glory won, honour more than satisfied, I was to run the family estates and allow my father a well-deserved retirement. Retirement from public life with a pretty wife chosen for me, not that they got that choice wrong in any way, but with that feeling that as a man of less than thirty I could have done more. So much more.'

The emperor smiled wryly.

'Such hardship! Whereas, with a legion centurion for a grandfather rather than a pillar of an old and well-respected family, I never had any alternative but to serve, or to trade mules when times were thin . . .' The two men exchanged smiles at his recounting of a story that had long since passed into legend. '*Mulio*, they called me. They won't dare do that again, will they!'

Geta laughed.

'No, they surely won't.'

The emperor was suddenly serious, tipping his head to one side in question.

'So come on then, Gaius, if you're so clever, tell me what it is I want with you?'

The younger man smiled slyly.

'The empire is still . . .'

'Shaken?'

'I was going to say "unsteady", but shaken will serve as well. Your son Titus will see to the Jews, that's obvious. He'll make a fine emperor when the time comes.'

Vespasianus grunted.

'Not too bloody soon, I hope. There's a good deal of life left to be enjoyed! But yes, he will, and yes, he'll put the Jews back in their place with the minimum of fuss. But these Batavians . . .'

'Exactly.' Geta nodded knowingly. 'You don't need a general, not with your son-in-law Petillius Cerialis breathing fire to be sent north, and you wouldn't have brought me all this way to appoint me commander of an army even if I were qualified for the task. But perhaps you need . . . counsel? The advice of a man who knows . . . shall we say *the individual* concerned?'

The emperor nodded.

'I thought you'd understand. So, tell me, why you? What special qualities do you possess that I couldn't find in any other man of our class?'

'That's easy enough to make out. It's my knowledge of the events of that morning we both almost died in Britannia. My memories.'

Vespasianus nodded.

'Yes, your memories. I'm becoming an old man, Gaius, and old men sometimes find themselves with a recollection of distant events that is less precise than might be desirable. I need you to remind us both exactly what happened that day, and then I need to ask you to help me answer a question that's been troubling me for a while now.'

'Ever since the revolt of the Batavians got somewhat . . . out of hand? I take it that the rumours that you incited our mutual friend to lead his tribe to war, so as to tie down the army of Germania and deny Vitellius the support of his own legions, are correct?'

'Yes. I had my son-in-law Petillius Cerialis and his friend Secundus Plinius woo Julius Civilis, Kivilaz among his own people, with exactly that intention. With the somewhat over-enthusiastic assistance of that poor fool Hordeonius Flaccus.'

'You've heard the stories of Legatus Augusti Flaccus's death then?'

'Yes. It seems he put his head into the lion's mouth one time too many, and his German legions obliged their commander's apparent death-wish in the bloodiest manner possible. And yes, partially thanks to Flaccus and partially our own miscalculation, I suppose, the Batavians are running amok across Germania Inferior. And the war threatens to spread south and consume the Gauls as well. Peace will be restored, of course, at some further cost in dead legionaries, and when that state of calm has been achieved, if our former ally Gaius Julius Civilis survives the pacification, we'll have to be clear what should be done with him. So, Gaius, remind me of what happened that day in Britannia.'

Geta leaned back on his couch and sipped from his glass.

'The battle of the Medui river. What a disaster that could have been.'

Vespasianus snorted.

'*Could* have been? What a disaster that very nearly was! And you're not the man who spent the most uncomfortable night imaginable waiting for the enemy to come down that hill one hundred thousand strong and erase any trace that we'd ever even been there!'

The younger man inclined his head, accepting his emperor's acerbic rejoinder.

'Yes. And then, the morning after, came that moment when the fate of an entire army rested on one tribe. On one man, it's probably fair to say. "Our" rebel Civilis.'

The emperor stared at him, his expression suddenly rapt as the younger man's words brought memories of the most desperate moment of his military career.

'Two men.'

'Yes. Your memory is as sharp as ever, Titus. I'd totally forgotten Prefect Draco's part in the matter.'

A slave approached bearing a platter of delicacies, laying it between the two men as he had been directed, and then backed away, never once having made eye contact with either of them.

'Ah, these are good.' Vespasianus pointed to a cluster of pastries. 'I taught the cooks here how to make them, to my mother's recipe. Try one.'

Geta bit into the proffered delicacy and tasted black pudding, a heavy scent filling his nostrils as the warm filling was exposed. The smell was redolent with the iron-rich scent of blood, and just for an instant he was standing on a corpse-strewn hillside with a hundred thousand enemy warriors baying for his head.

~

'We're cut off!'

Geta looked about him calmly, swiftly assessing the truth of his first spear's words. The legion's first cohort was embattled on all sides, his legionaries fighting with the desperate ferocity of men who realised that their only hope of salvation from the massed barbarians pressing in on them from all sides was their own strength and determination.

'The eagle! They're trying to capture my legion's eagle!'

His first spear nodded.

'They are! That, and your head. Legatus! The rest of us will be left to rot, but your life's journey will not end here!'

The perimeter around them was gradually but visibly shrinking, as wild-eyed tribesmen tore into his soldiers on all sides, their ferocity redoubled at the sight of the hated symbol of Rome's power almost within their reach. The Fourteenth's other cohorts were battling to either side of the isolated body of men, but the sheer strength of numbers being hurled down the hill and into their ranks at the enemy king's command was driving them back, step by laboured step, leaving their first cohort ever more deeply mired in the sea of their enemies. A sword rose and fell only a dozen paces from where he stood, and an iron helmet was smashed from view, the blade's victorious wielder staggering back as the fallen legionary's comrades took swift and bloody revenge, but in an instant another man was in the gap formed by his sacrifice, and fighting as if he had nothing left to live for. Geta drew his sword, looking down at its gleaming length of razor-sharp iron.

'I'll take more than one of them with me.'

His signifer grinned broadly at the sentiment, his sword already in one hand while the other held his eagle proudly aloft, exuding the sort of grace under pressure that, Geta supposed, was the usual reason for selection to the most honoured position in any legion.

'That's the spirit, Legatus! I'm planning on killing half a dozen of them before they prise my fingers off this standard!'

His legionaries were being crushed into an ever-constricting space by the sheer press of the enemy, the barbarians deliberately pushing into their shields and forcing them back against the men behind them, and the rate at which they were dying was getting faster, as fresh enemy warriors pressed forward to throw themselves at soldiers who were already exhausted.

'Not long now! This is where all those hours spent knocking the shit out of a wooden post with a wooden sword might suddenly prove to have been of some value!'

Geta grinned at his first spear's unfailing bullishness, even in the face of almost certain death, and offered the senior centurion his right hand.

'It's been a pleasure fighting with you, Sextus!'

'Likewise, Legatus! Perhaps we'll meet in the Underworld!'

Geta nodded, hefting the sword as the enemy warriors hacked their way into the line of men only two ranks from where he stood next to the eagle.

'Here! You're going to need this!'

The first spear was offering him a shield, but the younger man shook his head with a grin, shouting back over the battle's unrelenting angry roar.

'I'll be better without it, thank you, First Spear! It's not as if I've spent any time familiarising myself with the thing's use!'

Something caught his eye down the hill's slope, some sort of disturbance within the ranks of the enemy, but as he craned his neck to see what it was the man in front of him was suddenly under attack by a quick-handed swordsman clearly intent on the prize behind him. Geta waited, calculated, chose his moment and struck, driving his sword over the soldier's shoulder and deep into the Briton's chest, sending the dying warrior staggering back into the mass of men behind him with blood spurting across legionary and legatus.

'Good work, Leg—'

The soldier's praise was cut off before it could be voiced by a spear thrust into his throat from the baying press of men railing at the Romans' shields, and with a bubbling groan of agony he was gone, leaving Geta facing the horde with no more protection than his sword. A soldier stepped into the gap in the line from behind him, got a single stab of his gladius into the enemy and then fell, run through by a spear blade thrust with enough force to punch through a joint in his armour and sink deep into his body, grunting in pain as he sank to his knees. Geta snatched up his shield, realising that without it he was open to the enemy's long spear blades, raising the layered wooden board just in time to deflect a pair of strikes that rocked him back on his heels into the men behind him. A swift glance around him revealed that the fight had reached an end, or all but as good as, with less than fifty legionaries remaining within the circle around the Fourteenth's eagle, his attention returning to the men in front of him barely in time to punch the shield into their assault and momentarily avert the deadly threat of their swords and spears. Gathering themselves to pounce, all eyes fixed on the legion commander's richly plumed helmet and shining breastplate, the Britons suddenly found themselves beset from the rear by a wedge of men driving forward into them with scored and battered shields, their swords running red with the blood of tribal warriors who had failed to flee from their implacable advance. Two men formed the point of their formation, one the prefect commanding their cohorts, the other a centurion not known to Geta, both men's faces and bodies blasted black with the dried blood of their fallen enemies.

'Batavi!'

Smashing through the last resistance between themselves and the eagle, they parted to either side of the dumbfounded legatus, pushing through to the signifer and pulling him into the bloodied ranks of men pushing up behind them. The prefect ceded his place at the tip of the wedge to another man and staggered back to where Geta stood, resting his hands on his knees and fighting for breath.

'This is . . . a young man's . . . game . . . Legatus.'

'First Spear Sextus?'

'Dead . . . I saw . . . his body. We saved . . . your eagle . . . though.'

Geta nodded.

'And you will have Rome's eternal gratitude if I have any say in the matter. What now? Do we retreat?'

Draco straightened his body, dragging in a deep breath and shaking his head.

'Retreat, Legatus? The Batavi have retreated once already in this battle, and that is already once more than we are accustomed to turning our backs on an enemy! No. The Britons have spent their champions in the hope of reaping your eagle, and they have not only failed but lost their swordsmen in that failure! Now their king stands less than a quarter of a mile from here, and with no more protection than the men of his bodyguard and this hapless army of farmers. I command the Batavi, and the Batavi are determined to either have his head or send him away in shame. Unless you command otherwise?'

The legatus shook his head.

'My ancestors would never forgive me, Prefect, if I were to allow myself to be shown less courageous than even the empire's boldest allies.' He looked up the slope at the tribal banners clustered around a tight knot of men at its crest. 'I'm with you all the way to the top of that hill!'

★

'This man Draco was invalided out of the service as a result of the battle, if I remember correctly?'

Geta nodded, dragging his thoughts back to the emperor's question.

'I was fighting beside him when a spear blade pierced through his thigh, close to the top of that hill. He stood long enough to watch Caractacus leave the battlefield to save his own life, and to call insults after him in the manner of his people, then we had him carried back to the river to receive treatment. He was never able to run after that, and another man was voted into his place by the tribe's centurions.'

'He lives still?'

Geta looked at the emperor for a moment.

'Draco? He does, I believe. And still takes a keen interest in his tribe's politics, as an elder of the council, which in happier times provided the magistrate with guidance as to the tribe's feelings on matters of note.'

'You said there were two men leading their advance. The other was Civilis, of course.'

'The same. Even then he was a headstrong throwback to the men who ruled the tribe before the Divine Julius upset their applecart, unused to being told what he could and couldn't do.'

Vespasianus chuckled.

'Evidently. And, as you've already guessed, it's Civilis I wished to discuss with you.' The younger man stared at him in silence, and the emperor nodded. 'And there he is, the same old Hosidius Geta. You're still the most dangerous knife in the drawer, razor sharp and quite untroubled by any risk that you might end up cutting yourself. You do know that Claudius put you on a list of men to be watched, after your participation in his triumph after the victory in Britannia?'

'I did hear something to that effect some years afterwards.'

Vespasianus chewed on a spiced sweetbread.

'Delicious. Yes, he saw something of his brother Germanicus in you, it seems, and wanted to be assured that such a prime candidate for the highest office in the empire wasn't harbouring aspirations above his place in society.'

Geta shrugged.

'It's probably why my father made such a show of withdrawing me from public life. After all, what would be the point of climbing the cursus honorum if your reward for doing so was a knife in the back. Or worse.'

The emperor nodded.

'And that's why you will be serving my administration in whatever capacity I decide is best suited to your abilities. You are uncompromising in your intelligence, but always willing to be pragmatic when the occasion calls for it.'

'And on this occasion you wish me to apply my intelligence *and* my pragmatism to the matter of what you should do with this man?'

The emperor nodded.

'Who better? You know the rules we work by. The empire is all important. No insult to Rome can go unpunished, no matter who the perpetrator might be. And yet in this case . . .'

'The perpetrator is a man who has given twenty-five years of loyal and unstinting service to the empire. A man who saved my life in Britannia, and won Rome a battle, and quite possibly a province, in the doing of it. Who gave an eye to the empire. Who lost his brother to the empire's jealousies and insecurities. And who was asked to rise up in revolt by your own emissaries, as a means of weakening your enemy Vitellius.'

'Yes. And who has now gone too far in that revolt, but who may yet still lay claim to legitimacy in doing so, given my encouragement, and who may also yet still swear loyalty to my rule.'

Silence fell between the two men.

'So . . .' Geta stood, walking away across the room's wide expanse of marble. 'You wish me to advise you as to what is to be done with our former comrade Civilis. And will you follow this advice, or do you simply want to hear it and then make up your own mind?' He turned back to stare at Vespasianus. 'I'm happy enough to provide it, but if my words are no more than a means of you reflecting upon your own thoughts then there are dozens of good men in Rome who can fulfil such a role.'

Vespasianus raised his hands.

'Yes, you are assuredly still the same Hosidius Geta, bold enough to tell an emperor where he stands. And that's exactly what I need. So tell me, advisor, what should I do? What options are there for an emperor when the man he has asked to revolt on his behalf takes that revolt a step too far?'

Geta thought for a moment.

'By rights, Caesar . . .' He raised a hand to forestall Vespasianus's protest. 'You ask as Caesar, I'll answer you in the same vein. By rights, *Caesar*, you have every right to order him to be subjected to a felon's death. He has stepped outside the protection of his citizenship in taking his tribe to war against Rome, and in throwing a spear at Rome's fortress. He could justifiably be beaten, scourged and crucified, and no man could declare that to be anything other than reasonable punishment. However . . .'

The emperor nodded.

'His service?'

'More than that. More than just the time he has spent in Rome's service. Consider his bravery on Rome's behalf. It wasn't me that should have walked in triumph with Claudius all those years ago, it was Civilis and his countryman Draco. They won the battle of the Medui, firstly by destroying the Britons' chariot horses and then by pulling glory from the ashes of *my* defeat. That bravery, his fearsome reputation earned on a dozen battlefields across Britannia, that alone should act to at least partially excuse his more recent acts of betrayal. Especially given the way that Rome has single-mindedly undermined our relationship with both Civilis and the Batavi, and driven them to the insanity of confronting us in a war that they can never realistically hope to win. All of these facts demand that we exercise some degree of mitigation as to the punishment that Civilis must receive, once his revolt has been crushed.'

'I see.' Vespasianus took another pastry and bit into it, chewing the mouthful slowly as he thought. 'And your suggested mitigation?

If our former ally has earned something more honourable than a felon's death for his insult against Rome, what form should that softening of Rome's traditional vengeance on a defeated enemy take? What punishment is just when an ally with otherwise unblemished service rises up and sinks his teeth into Rome's throat? I surely cannot afford to ignore such an act of betrayal?'

Geta looked at him in silence for a moment.

'I find myself very much in two minds, Caesar. I am clear as to the necessary punishment required to deter others from the same course of action, and the threat it raises to Rome's empire, but troubled by my personal attachment to both the tribe and the man. If I might have an hour in which to reflect?'

Vespasianus rose.

'It's time for my afternoon sleep in any case. I find an hour at this time of the day allows me to work a long way into the evening, and trust me, dinner with your senatorial colleagues will be quite the hardest work I can imagine. I will return here when I wake to hear your verdict on the matter. And welcome to my world of intractable decisions, Hosidius Geta. I have no doubt you'll make an excellent addition to my consilium.'

He left the room and Geta strolled slowly across to the couches. Taking the last of the pastries he bit into it, once more savouring the aroma of blood, and once more staring sightlessly across the room as his thoughts returned to the moment on a faraway hillside when the man whose fate he had been asked to determine had saved his life.

'So, what are we to do with you, Gaius Julius Civilis, or rather what are we to do with *Kivilaz*, now that you have reverted to your tribal identity? What *are* we to do with you . . .'

Novaesium, Germania Inferior, January AD 70

'The worst of it appears to be over, Legatus.'

Legion commander Dillius Vocula turned from his introspective contemplation of his sword's mirror-bright blade to find his first spear standing in the doorway of his command tent. He was dressed in his muscled bronze cuirass and magnificently plumed helmet, as he had been all night, waiting for the mutiny whose violence he had escaped by the narrowest of margins the previous evening only by the ruse of posing as his senior centurion's slave, to either wash over his headquarters or come to an exhausted end, as the mutinous army's alcohol-fuelled rage dissipated in the dawn's cold light.

'Thank you, Antonius. Our legionaries have all finally returned to their barracks?'

His senior centurion nodded, his face shadowed with exhaustion from a day and a night spent bringing the mass insubordination of two legions under control.

'Now that the drink has worn off, and they've squandered every last sestertius of the donative that Flaccus awarded them, yes, they've given it up and gone to their beds. I've given orders for this morning's parade to be cancelled, not that I had very much choice in the matter.'

'I see.' Vocula put the weapon down on his desk and rubbed a hand across his similarly fatigued features. 'What's the damage?'

The senior centurion took a tablet from his belt pouch.

'Thirty-three dead that we know about. To which we can probably add another ten or fifteen we haven't found yet. Disturbances on this scale are usually an opportunity for the settling of old scores.'

'So half a century of casualties and what, another hundred or so in the infirmary?'

'More like half that again. The chief medicus tells me that most of them will live, but their injuries span the whole range from cuts and bruises to severely broken limbs. More score settling.'

Vocula nodded.

'And then there's Hordeonius Flaccus himself. Has his body been recovered?'

'Yes, Legatus . . .'

The first spear paused for an instant too long.

'But?'

The first spear sighed.

'Legatus Augusti Flaccus's body has been mutilated beyond recognition. His own family wouldn't know him other than by his stature.'

Vocula stared at him numbly.

'Nothing can surprise me, Antonius, not where these men are concerned. The men of the First Germanica and Sixteenth Gallica have a reckoning coming their way when the war against the Germans is over and done with.'

Antonius put the tablet back in his pouch.

'Are you sure that you want to pursue such a path, Legatus? After all . . .'

'After all what, Antonius? Should we excuse their crime? Forgive them for murdering a Roman senator on the grounds that they were provoked by the belief that he had been collaborating with the enemy by colluding in the defeats that resulted in the Germans laying siege to the Old Camp? Or because they held him responsible for abandoning the Fifth and Fifteenth Legions to their fate in that fortress, rescued from their siege by our advance north and then told to stay put in that death trap, and allow the noose to close around their necks again?' He laughed bitterly. 'Which is ironic given it was my decision and not his!'

The other man nodded, his face an imperturbable mask.

'That's almost certainly the reason why the soldiers we drafted from the Fifth and Fifteenth Legions joined the mutiny. The guilt of men that have survived, expressing their anger for their comrades' likely fate the only way they know how.'

Vocula shook his head.

'That only explains their actions, First Spear. It doesn't *excuse* them. I will have justice for Hordeonius Flaccus, and for the rampage that those bastards have visited upon the camp. If it hadn't been for your men then I suspect we would have shared his fate, and that they would have run wild in the streets of Novaesium to boot.'

'I can't disagree with you, Legatus. We're fortunate to have had the time to build a legion worthy of the name before this all started. The Twenty-second has proven loyal, for the most part, and those few men who managed to join the mutiny are being put straight by their officers even as we speak. I—'

A centurion opened the tent's flap and looked in apologetically with another man evidently hovering close by.

'Your pardon, Legatus, First Spear. I wouldn't have disturbed you except that the messenger insisted on it.'

The other man pushed forward, a young tribune Vocula dimly remembered from his time in the Winter Camp, far to the south.

'I have urgent news from the Fourth Legion, Legatus.'

Vocula held out a hand for the message container, the tribune's evident exhaustion as much of a clue to the news contained within it as his tone.

'And I presume it's not good?'

The younger man shook his head.

'No, sir. The Chatti, Usipii and Mattiaci have crossed the river in strength and are pillaging the land around the fortress. The Treveri are holding them on the borders of their own lands for the most part, but our own forces are too weak to do anything more constructive than hold the fortress. The camp prefect told me to assure you that he can hold until their food supplies run out, but that he's powerless to intervene with only three cohorts.'

The legatus turned back to Antonius with a grim expression.

'Perhaps a good long march is just what these mutinous bastards need to take their minds off the gold they'll never see, now that Vespasianus and not Vitellius has the throne. And with Julius Classicus's Nervian cavalry wing and infantry cohorts to join us, we will at least have the strength we need to deal with the problem, even if they bring complications of their own.'

They shared a moment of mutual understanding as Vocula nodded slowly.

'It'll have to be all three legions, of course. If we leave either the First or the Sixteenth here alone they'll mutiny again before we're halfway to the Winter Camp. Have my fellow legates summoned to a command meeting in one hour, enough time for me to consider our best approach to dealing with the invasion.

And have the men of your first cohort ready to defend us, you and me, and the other legates too. If what we're being told about their real intentions by our man in the Batavian camp is true, then with the Nervians back in the fold the risk to us may have increased, not lessened.'

Military encampment near Bonna, Germania Inferior, January AD 70

'Julius Kivilaz. You're clearly not a man who's shy of risk, to travel so far into Roman territory to meet with us?' Julius Classicus, prince of the Nervii tribe and prefect of the First Nervian cavalry cohort, stepped forward from the ranks of his fellow nobles and extended a hand in welcome. 'Greetings, brother, and our welcome is extended to your noble cousin.'

The Batavi prince took his hand, inclining his head in acceptance of the greeting, casting his one-eyed gaze around the fire-lit grove at the men gathered to meet him.

'Nor are you a man to shrink from opportunity, no matter how uncertain it might be, Julius Classicus, and nor is any man here, if I am any judge of men. Evidently your appetite for danger surpasses my own, and your disdain for the risks you also run is clear, risks which, as you say, I know only too well. Risks my people have flouted in our struggle against the tyranny of Rome, bringing us to the verge of triumph – a triumph I invite you to share! Our mutual enemy's grip on its territory north of the mountains is tenuous at best, with a scattering of desperately undermanned legions, most of whose men are disaffected by the defeat of their chosen emperor, Vitellius.'

His cousin Bairaz had accompanied him to the meeting with the Nervii nobleman and his kindred in his honoured position as the commander of his guard cohort, men of the tribe dismissed from their service as the emperor's personal bodyguard the year before. Fully equipped in the parade armour of a guard decurion, he stood alongside Classicus's cousin Montanus with the alert expression of a man who knew when to speak, and when to listen. Kivilaz continued, smiling as he looked around the tribal royalty gathered to meet him.

'And I, of course, am already a wanted man. As Gaius Julius Civilis I was accused of treason twice and escaped execution by the thinnest of margins, and so now I am simply Rome's enemy Kivilaz, my service to the empire at an end and my undying enmity declared in blood. And my tribe's war with the empire has put a price on my head, a reward so high that a man could live in the most luxurious fashion possible for the rest of his life, were he to collect on it. Whereas you men of the Nervii tribe are yet to raise your blades against Rome, and are, in the empire's eyes, the most valuable of allies in counterbalancing our threat from the north. Where I am considered a long-haired barbarian, who has returned to his tribe's former bloodthirsty and ignorant ways, you are all still considered as gentlemen, albeit of a certain class.'

Classicus nodded, raising a hand to gesture at the Batavi prince's face.

'Nobody could deny that you have a . . . warlike appearance, Prince Kivilaz?'

'That's a fact!' Kivilaz laughed, putting a hand to his dark red beard. 'There are few enough men of the Batavi whose hair is this colour, given that the dye is our traditional mark of a man who has yet to kill for the tribe, so I chose to honour that tradition for a second time in my life, to remind my men of the Batavi people's ancient customs. Once the Old Camp has fallen to our siege I will cut away this reminder of my vow to smash Rome's rule over our land once and for all, and I will parade its two legions' eagles for the tribes to see and take heart from.' He looked around at them with his one good eye bright. 'And with the Old Camp's presence erased from our soil, I will unleash my armies to do the same to Novaesium, and Bonna, and Colonia Agrippina. When we're done with them, there won't be a legion any further north than the Winter Camp, a fortress that I trust is a part of *your* thinking?'

Classicus nodded, beckoning the prince to take a seat in the circle.

'Our plan is well advanced. The three legions you chased away from the Old Camp after its brief period of liberation have taken refuge in the camp at Novaesium, and we men of the auxiliary forces who serve alongside them are left in no doubt that they are both demoralised by their recent experiences and utterly dissatisfied with the service of Rome. Two of those three legions have mutinied in the last few days, and their legatus augusti has learned the hard way not to underestimate the danger posed by angry men who feel they have nothing to lose. They butchered him, it seems, and left his mutilated corpse for the dogs.'

'This news has reached us too.' Kivilaz shrugged. 'In truth I have to say that I liked Flaccus. He was an easy man to deal with, alert to the realities of his position. But he was undeniably also a fool to have been so openly in favour of Vespasianus when his legions so obviously wanted the man they put on the throne to remain emperor, and deliver on his promises to make them rich. So who commands their remnants of legions now that he's dead?'

'Gaius Dillius Vocula.' Classicus shook his head in apparent sadness. 'A man more deserving of pity than enmity. Flaccus relinquished his command to him late last year, when it became apparent that the legions weren't going to stand for taking orders from a man they were very sure was Vespasianus's creature. Since then Vocula has kept that army marching and fighting, mainly by the force of his will, executing would-be mutineers and flogging any man that showed any sign of recalcitrance, but it seems their willingness to be beaten into line eventually ran out. The mutiny's over, it seems, and order restored, but those legionaries are ready to change sides, I can tell you that for a fact.'

'How?'

'Our tribes, Nervii, Treveri, Ubii and Lingones, all have infantry and cavalry cohorts serving alongside them. Our men mix with theirs freely, in the taverns and around the campfires, and they report that the First Germanica and Sixteenth Gallica are highly receptive to the idea that they might become part of the army of a different empire. We know the key men, soldiers and centurions, and our discussions with them are very well advanced. At the right time, when we call upon them, with promises of the rewards to be had by their joining with us, we will peel them away from the empire just as easily as pulling a perfectly ripe apple from the bough.'

Kivilaz inclined his head again.

'That would indeed be a blow for Rome. But what of Vocula's Third Legion?'

Classicus waved a dismissive hand.

'The men of the Twenty-second Primigenia are not so easily persuadable, it seems. Their first spear is a man called Antonius, and he has his men in an iron grip. I doubt that they will come over to us with quite the same ease, at least not while he holds their collars. But then no man is immortal.'

Later, making their way back to the waiting cohorts through the darkened countryside, Bairaz leaned close to his cousin and asked the question that had been on his mind from the moment that Classicus had implied the potential for First Spear Antonius to be removed as an impediment to his legion's subversion to the Gallic cause.

'Do you believe they would go so far as to kill a senior Roman officer in such a dishonourable manner?'

Kivilaz grinned back at him, his teeth a white slash in the moonlight.

'Do I think Classicus would have this first spear Antonius killed if he could? Of course.' He laughed at Bairaz's bemusement. 'Why do you think I take you and a century of your guardsmen with me whenever I go to meet our new allies? It isn't just for the pleasure of your company!'

'You think that—'

'Cousin, the Romans would have me killed, if they knew the place and time where they might find me. Of course they would. And I'd do the same to this Gaius Dillius Vocula, if I knew I could get an assassin into his tent at the right moment, not least to have my revenge for the men who died on his legions' spears. And I daresay that Classicus will be looking for any chance to kill the last man capable of providing their army with leadership. Putting a knife between the ribs of his trusted first spear wouldn't achieve quite the same result, but I doubt the men gathered around that fire back there would hesitate for even a moment in having this man Antonius murdered. And unless he keeps a bodyguard of men he can trust around him at all times, they surely will.'

He paused for a moment, looking up at the blaze of stars above them.

'And there's another reason I'd have Vocula killed, if I could get a blade close to him. There's someone in the tribe passing him information.'

Bairaz looked him in astonishment.

'A traitor? But anyone with anything worth telling the Romans would have to be on the council.'

Kivilaz nodded.

'Either that or close enough to the council to effectively be a member. Like yourself . . .' He raised a hand to forestall his cousin's indignant protest. 'I'm not implying it's you, Bairaz, I'm pointing out that finding whoever it is that's sending the enemy information isn't going to be easy.'

'But . . .' the decurion shook his head. 'You're sure? You know for a fact that we're being betrayed?'

The prince shrugged.

'Nobody likes the idea that someone within the tribe might be passing our plans on to the enemy, but it's beyond doubt that the Romans knew we were coming, when we made what was supposed to be a surprise attack at Gelduba. I know the Vascones arriving in your rear at precisely the moment of your victory over Vocula's legions was an utter coincidence, but if they hadn't been given enough warning to get most of their strength out of the camp before you attacked then they would have been trapped and helpless, and the fight would have been over before the Vascones arrived. That act of treachery cost the tribe half its fighting men, and there's hardly a family on the Island that hasn't lost a son, a brother or a father. So when I catch the bastard I'm going to crucify him in front of the great hall. And I'll make very sure that he dies as slowly as possible, no beating, no flogging to help him on his way, just a hammer, three long nails and a very slow and painful death.'

Bairaz looked out into the darkness.

'You sound very sure we'll catch him.'

Kivilaz nodded grimly.

'I have Draco looking for him. If anyone's going to sniff out a traitor it's our Father of the Tribe. Depend on it.'

Germania Inferior, January AD 70

'You think Kiv knows what he's doing this time?'

Egilhard gave his father a despairing look in the fire's dull red light.

'You can't say that. Not in front of me. I'm a watch officer and my position requires me to come down on that sort of statement like a falling oak.'

Lataz shook his head in disgust.

'My own son, coming the—'

'No, *Lataz*.' The younger man overrode him with an ease that surprised them both, raising a finger to forestall any further comment. 'I think the question you were asking your watch officer was whether he *thinks* that *Prince* Kivilaz will be a bit luckier this time round?'

Egilhard's father shook his head again and his older brother Frijaz smirked at his only apparent discomfiture, his eyes vanishing into a nest of crows' feet.

'Don't let him fool you, boy, he's loving every minute of you being an officer. Although he's got a point. Kiv did lead you lads into a right goat fuck that night in December, didn't he? And he doesn't mind being called Kiv either, he came to see us old bastards and children off when we was marching to join you heroes, and he told us—'

'I'm not a child!'

All three men turned to look at the youngest member of the family present, but it was the tent party's leader Lanzo who was first to voice a flat contradiction of Sigu's indignant statement.

'Yes, you are, actually. The age of fifteen doesn't make you a man, and now you're a warrior you have to have killed for the tribe to be considered a man, no matter how—'

'But I— Ah!' Sigu shot his father a hard look, rubbing the back of his head where Lataz had knuckled him. 'What was that for?'

'To teach you to show a bit more respect for your elders and betters! Your brother is a watch officer now, which means that you have to go where he tells you, do what he tells you and don't, under any circumstances, give him any lip. An experienced soldier like one of these ugly specimens might get away with the occasional piss-take, but you, young Sigu, you don't speak unless you've been spoken to, and even then only to say "yes" or "no" depending on what the question was. Not if you don't want the centurion to give you a taste of his vine stick!'

'Who's going to taste my vine stick?'

The tent party's eight men jumped to attention, but Alcaeus waved a hand, having walked up to their fire unseen while their attention was directed inwards. Bareheaded, taking the chance of enjoying the cold night air on his thick head of grey-streaked hair, he had left his helmet and its wolf's head cover, which indicated his status as the cohort's chief priest, lying on his pack.

'At ease, soldiers. And he's right, Soldier Sigu, until you've taken the life of an enemy in battle you're not a man, not in the only way that really matters to us. That's why your hair is dyed red, as a badge that you're yet to shed blood for the tribe. Of course those who never serve will call themselves men, and not one of us will ever look to shatter their illusions, but you ask any man that ever marched with the cohorts and he'll tell you the same. And on top of that, you're not even a trained soldier yet, so don't let me catch you abusing your watch officer, eh? He might not want to punish you, but I'll be left without much choice. Won't I?'

Egilhard flashed his brother a look, but Sigu had been well coached by his father and uncle.

'Yes, sir, Centurion Alcaeus, sir!'

All three of his family members breathed silent sighs of relief, and Alcaeus looked at them with a soft chuckle.

'Good. Now get some sleep. Tomorrow morning is going to be *busy*.'

Walking across the darkened camp he listened to the voices of men talking in the dark, most of them incapable of sleep with the prospect of battle the next day. Where the Batavi tribe's eight cohorts of warriors would previously have been abuzz with the thought of a fight, the snippets of conversation he heard as he passed their fires were quiet, introspective for the most part. Finding the headquarters tent, he squatted down by the fire and spread his hands to warm them.

'And what did you learn in doing your rounds, Priest?'

He looked up at his prefect, the man in command of the tribe's military strength, keeping his face carefully composed. The big man was regarding him with the hard, closed expression that Alcaeus had become used to, his evident disapproval barely masked by the vestiges of military professionalism that had been drummed into them both by long years of service to Rome.

'What did I learn? That our men are tired but that will hardly surprise you. They're quiet, Hramn. They're talking about the men we lost at Gelduba the last time we attacked, when those Vascones came out of the night behind us and trapped us against the legion's shields.'

'And they're wondering whether I'm going to lead them into another disaster by attacking that same camp again? Even though the scouts tell us that it's deserted, as we expected.'

Alcaeus nodded, pursing his lips.

'Yes. How could they not be? They wonder if our gods have turned their faces away from our fight for freedom for Rome.'

'They wonder if their leader is cursed.'

The priest conceded the point.

'That too, perhaps, even though none of them voice such a

sentiment. Show me a soldier who doesn't believe he could do better than the men who lead him, with the luxury of making decisions after the battle is done with.'

Hramn regarded him levelly across the fire.

'And you, Priest? Do you believe that you could have done any better?'

Alcaeus raised an eyebrow.

'Are you sure you want to explore in that direction, Prefect? You know me well enough to know that I will never speak ill of any decision made by the prefect of these cohorts.'

'I do. And I know you well enough to know that your smooth face conceals the thoughts of a man who killed not one, but seven wolves, alone in the forest, for his initiation in the priesthood. You have the blood of heroes in you, Alcaeus, for all of your sermons to the recruits not to seek glory at the expense of their own lives, and I sense a hero's disdain for failure in every word you speak, no matter how carefully you place your words. So tell me, truly.'

'Could I have done any better at Gelduba?' The centurion stared levelly at his superior, Kivilaz's nephew and former commander of the imperial bodyguard, appointed to command the cohorts on the death of his predecessor Scar. 'I couldn't have led a better approach march, or attacked with any greater aggression.'

'And . . . ?'

Alcaeus shrugged.

'What do you *want* from me, Hramn? Recognition that our attack was betrayed to the Romans by somebody within the tribe? Acknowledgement that the Vascones arriving on the battlefield at that precise moment, given that they had marched all the way from Hispania, was the grossest piece of ill-fortune? Both are probably true. And it is assuredly true that without that betrayal we would have caught the legions in their tents ready to be slaughtered, rather than drawn up before their camp in a defence that held us just long enough for the Vascones to tear into us from out of the night, turning victory into disaster in a single moment.'

'And yet?'

The centurion shook his head in bemusement.

'And *yet*? You insist on the naked truth? Very well. We attacked without a rearguard and we paid a steep price for that gamble. If it was a gamble, and not simply the lust for revenge of a man slighted by Rome in his dismissal from the emperor's service. No.' He raised a hand in the face of his superior's rising ire. 'You asked the question, Prefect, now stomach the reply. In all his time as the prefect of these cohorts, Scar never committed all eight of the cohorts to a fight at one time. He always kept one or two in reserve to watch our backs, or to intervene when the battle was at its most difficult. I broke that rule in an instant the only time I ever led these men, after his death at Bonna, taking them into the Romans like mad dogs wild for blood to have my revenge on them, but then I am not a cool-headed calculator of the odds like Scar was.'

'And neither am I?'

The question was bitter in tone, and Alcaeus smiled gently at his superior.

'Perhaps not.' He shook his head. 'Hramn, the one thing the Romans gave us, when they adopted us to be their favourite sons, delighting in our bloodthirsty love of rampage and slaughter, was discipline. Oh yes, they gave us all this iron to fight with, so much iron that the tribes across the river still marvel at our wealth, but their principal gift was the ability to calculate the odds rather than just to laugh at them. The self-control to fight in formation as one man, to make eighty men the match of three times their number of warriors fighting the old-fashioned way. Scar knew that, and he respected their teachings above everything else, as did his predecessors before him. But you, Prefect, abandoned that long-ingrained restraint in search of a chance to rip out three legions' throats.'

The other man sat in silence, staring at his deputy.

'I did. And I'd do it again, given such a prize.'

'I know.' Alcaeus nodded slowly. 'And while there's a part of me that exults in the same urge to spill our enemies' blood, there's another part that's terrified of the disaster that might result.'

'A disaster, Centurion? Let's hope not, for the sake of the tribe.'

Both men turned at the sound of an unexpected voice, finding the leader of their tribe's elders standing in the shadow of the command tent.

'Draco? What are you doing here?'

The older man stepped into the light, leaning, as he always did, on a sturdy wooden staff, limping from the wound that had invalided him out of his role commanding the Batavi cohorts a quarter of a century before.

'You march in the morning, with orders to burn out the Roman fortress at Gelduba before they can re-occupy it, do you not?'

Hramn nodded.

'We do. But no assistance is required from the council of elders. And where we're going there's every chance of our bumping into a legion or two. It'll be no place for—'

'A cripple?' Draco smiled lopsidedly. 'Say it as you see it, Hramn, and so will I. And as to there being no assistance required, I'm afraid that's not entirely true. Your uncle agreed with the council's decision that it would be useful for a veteran officer to accompany the cohorts south this time, to provide you with any insights that come to mind in the event of there being a need to fight. You may recall that my limp was the result of wounds I incurred at the battle of the Medui river in Britannia? I believe that you were nine years of age at the time.'

The prefect stared at him for a moment in silence, and Alcaeus tensed with the expectation of an explosion, but when he spoke his tone was one of reason rather than conflict.

'And how could I refuse such valuable advice when you put it that way? You're very welcome to ride along with us, Draco.'

'Excellent. I'll sleep here tonight, wrapped in my cloak just like I did in Britannia, so that I don't miss the early morning start. Mind you, I'm not just here to provide you with the benefit of my experience. I'm also keen to have a look at the Roman camp before you set fire to it. Who knows what might have been left behind in their haste to evacuate the place, eh?'

*

The Old Camp, Germania Inferior, January AD 70

'It's as if I've imagined the whole thing.'

Marius looked out over the ground beyond the fortress's walls, earth pockmarked by bootprints and mantraps frozen hard by the bitter cold that had fallen over the battlefield that surrounded the Old Camp, shaking his head in disbelief. Men of his Fifth Legion were standing guard along the wall's length, combat veterans to a man who, only months before, had been inexperienced new recruits for the greater part, but who were now hard-eyed and pitiless soldiers who knew that they were fighting for their very lives. More than a few of them now bore the marks of bitter combat fought to the death along the walls from which they now stared out over the Batavi siegeworks, and Marius himself had been fortunate not to lose an eye in the desperate fight that had left his right eye socket bisected by a scar from temple to cheek.

'Three months of siege. The battles to keep the Germans from overrunning us. The men we sacrificed to get the news of our position to Legatus Augusti Flaccus and persuade him to attack and relieve us. All so much straw on the wind. Because there they are again, camped around us as if they'd never been driven away.'

His colleague Aquillius, senior centurion of what was left of the Fifteenth Legion after its systematic weakening by casualties, desertions and detachments sent south to fight in the civil war, shrugged, pulling his thick woollen cloak tighter about a heavily muscled body which he kept taut and ready for battle by means of a punishing daily routine of exercise.

'We held them off for three months before we were relieved. We've been resupplied with food and bolt-thrower ammunition. So what's to stop us holding them off for another three?'

Marius turned and looked at him with the expression of a man who had long since become accustomed to his colleague's blunt statements, no matter what the men around him believed, exasperation and a kind of fondness combined in his quizzical stare.

'Three more months? With half the strength we had at the start of this siege three months ago?'

He shook his head at the memory of the near panic-stricken flight of those men who could no longer stand the grinding mental pressure of being trapped in the fortress by such implacable enemies, hundreds of them having attached themselves to the two cohorts of the defenders' legionaries who had, in a master stroke of irony, been conscripted into the army that had been supposed to rescue the Old Camp's garrison at the end of the previous year.

'Legatus Vocula might well have had logic on his side in leaving us here, and in taking a thousand of our best men with him when he marched south, but what logic it was that made you allow all those cowards to piss off with them and leave the rest of us to it still eludes me.'

He turned and stared at his fellow senior centurion, but the big man shook his head dismissively,

'I allowed a gang of ration thieves to leave the fortress, men whose contribution in a fight would have been little better than useless and whose departure will enable us to hold on for weeks longer. Besides, look out there and tell me what you see?'

Marius shook his head.

'I don't need to look. I'd see a double line of fortification all the way round this fortress, dug out by the Batavians to keep us in and a relieving force out, and I'd see the smoke from the fires of the ten thousand men of the German tribes who've joined their leader Civilis in the hopes of razing this place to the ground.'

The other man grinned.

'There's that. But I see something different. Look . . .' He pointed at the ground beneath the twenty-foot-high walls. 'Look down there and tell me what you see.'

Marius raised a weary eyebrow and turned to do as he was bidden. The battered and pitted expanse of turf around the fortress was rimed with frost, but among the silver-edged blades of grass were glimpses of unnatural shapes, their lines and curves discoloured by rust and dried blood, weapons and shields that had belonged to men who had died in the fruitless attempts to overcome the Old Camp's defences.

'I see their discarded weapons rusting in the grass.'

'Exactly. Weapons dropped by dead men. We must have killed five thousand of them, or close to it. There won't be a single family in half a dozen tribes that hasn't lost a man, that hasn't dragged his rotting corpse from that ground for burning if they were lucky, or just never seen him again. They've tried three times to break us, and every time they tried we made them pay dearly for the effort. They won't come at us again.'

'You sound very sure about that.'

Aquillius nodded.

'I am. They'll look to starve us out. After all, Vocula's taken his legions back south and left us here to hold a symbol of Roman power he knew he couldn't simply abandon to its destruction, so they can afford to take their time with us, like cats toying with a mouse. And let's face it, they know that we'll have to come out of our hole eventually, when we're reduced to eating boot leather and grass.'

'Vocula will come back for us. He promised Legatus Lupercus that much before he marched for Novaesium.'

'Perhaps. But good intentions aren't the same as the deed already being done. Here's the legatus, you can ask him what he thinks.'

Munius Lupercus was walking down the wall towards them, wearing the pre-occupied look of a man carrying the responsibility of commanding two legions trapped deep in enemy territory. His hair, which three months before had been dusted with grey at the temples, was now mostly shot through with silver, and his face was thinner and more deeply lined than before, the war wound carved into his left cheek when he was a young man more prominent against his sallow skin. Both men saluted as he reached them, and the legatus returned the gesture with a wry smile and a glance over the wall at the ruined and detritus-studded ground under the Old Camp's walls.

'Gentlemen. I presume you're discussing how long we can hope to hold off the Germans now that we've been abandoned to our own devices once again?'

Marius nodded.

'My colleague is of the opinion that we can expect the enemy to be content with starving us out, whereas it's my expectation that they'll come at these walls again soon enough, when boredom gets the better of them.'

Lupercus looked out across the encircling siegeworks that had been dug out and fortified by the Batavian regular troops who were the core of the rebel army.

'My opinion tends towards that of your colleague, First Spear. But not because I believe that the Germans are capable of restraining themselves for long enough that we'll run out of food and surrender as a stark alternative to starvation.'

Marius frowned.

'I don't understand? If they haven't got the patience to wait us out, what's to stop them making another attempt at breaking in?'

The legatus shrugged.

'I'm no expert in matters of strategy, First Spear, I'm simply reflecting on something that my colleague Vocula said to me before he took his legions south along with those reinforcements he took from us, and the broken men who couldn't restrain themselves from attaching themselves to his army without orders.' He leaned on the wall, staring out to the fortress's south. 'We have a spy in the Batavian camp, gentlemen, someone so highly placed that he only risks sending us messages when the news involved is of the greatest importance. His last message to Legatus Augusti Flaccus, the news that there was an attack on their camp at Gelduba imminent, was a warning that gave Vocula just enough time to form a line outside his camp, and to hold their cohorts off until his reinforcements from Hispania made such a timely appearance in the enemy rear. But it was accompanied by another piece of information that was equally revealing. Perhaps more so.'

The two centurions waited patiently while he thought for a moment.

'The spy's other revelation was that Civilis's focus has changed. This is no longer simply a tribal revolt, gentlemen, a simple matter of the Batavians rebelling against Rome and needing to be put back in their place. Nor is it even just the wider German uprising, to which we represent the last flimsy resistance north of Novaesium. What's at stake now is more than just Germania, gentlemen, because it seems that Gaul is dry tinder waiting for a spark. And Civilis plans to put a flame to that tinder, and summon a blaze that might result in our losing every scrap of territory we have north of the Alps. Don't forget that it was a Gaulish revolt led by another tribal prince that resulted in Nero's suicide, and which started the civil war that ended up with Vespasianus on the throne and four other emperors dead inside eighteen months.'

'The Gauls? But surely . . . ?'

Marius fell silent at the look on his superior's face.

'Surely they're too pacified to even consider rising up? I very much doubt it, First Spear, much as I wish for our sakes it was true, because if, or rather *when* it comes to pass, it will leave us far more isolated than we already are now.' He smiled tiredly. 'As the diligent pupil of a set of very thorough teachers, I read my history assiduously, and I was left in no doubt that it took a military genius like the Divine Julius to subjugate them, a man driven by dreams of glory and empire and gifted with abilities given to one man in every generation. The Gauls may have been softened by a century of imperial peace, but their royal families are still intact, just like the Batavians', and, just like Civilis did in the days before his rebellion, those men dream of their former glories. If he's successful in arguing for a Gallic uprising in support of his war, which is what our spy in the enemy camp tell us is his aim, then my colleague Vocula might find himself with more on his plate than the need to relieve this siege. So whilst our position here might result in an outcome so ugly that none of us wish to consider its implications, I don't envy my colleague's position, because if Gaul does rise against us he'll find himself caught between two equally implacable enemies. His only hope, and ours too, is that Vespasianus can get half the empire's legions marching north quickly enough to reach us before the inevitable happens. If he doesn't we're going to end up facing the stark choice of either taking the honourable way out of this life or surrendering to those barbarians suffering the wrath they bear for us. Speaking of which, First Spear Aquillius . . .'

'Legatus.'

The big man's face was impassive, but Marius smiled at his back, knowing what was coming.

'I hear that you've been hunting the Germans at night. They come out to search the battlefield for the lost possessions of the men we killed by the thousand when they attacked us, and you, it seems, have taken to climbing down a rope to join them. The rumour is that you've taken to carving an aquila into the foreheads of some of the men you catch, and then releasing them to bear that disfigurement for the rest of their lives.'

Aquillius turned to look at Marius with a questioning expression, but his colleague shook his head dismissively, and Lupercus's voice hardened.

'Your colleague was appropriately tight-lipped on the subject, First Spear, but you can hardly expect such acts to remain unknown to me when your preferred means of calling for the rope to be thrown down to you when you've done with tormenting the locals is to bellow for it at the top of your voice, can you?'

'No, Legatus.'

'No indeed. And under the circumstances I'd be grateful if you could just control that urge to make every man for fifty miles terrified of you just a *little* better? Some time very soon we may find ourselves having to entrust our lives to those barbarians, and I'm fairly sure that the more of them you mutilate then the more of them are going to be baying for us to be handed to the worst of their priests. Do you take my point?'

Aquillius nodded dourly.

'Yes, Legatus.'

'Perfect. Carry on, gentlemen.'

Military camp outside Rome, January AD 70

'Good morning, First Spear. Please do come in and take a seat.'

Legatus Tiberius Pontius Longus waited behind his desk as his legion's senior centurion marched briskly into his office, stamping to attention and saluting with a vigour bordering on violence.

'First Spear Pugno. Please take a seat. Will you join me in a cup of wine?'

The centurion sat stiffly facing his new senior officer and accepted the drink from the legatus's servant, remaining silent until the slave had withdrawn from the office.

'Thank you, Legatus.' He sipped politely at the cup, the expression on his face immobile. 'Very nice, thank you, sir.'

The legatus played an appraising stare over him for a moment before speaking.

'You have an interesting name, First Spear. You're the first man I've ever met by the name of Pugno.'

'Indeed, Legatus. It's a Twenty-first Legion tradition for the new recruits to choose a name that they believe sums up their personality. The choice is theirs but whatever they choose they have to live up to. We use it as a means of encouragement in training, and we threaten to re-name men who fail to live up to their own expectations. When I joined the legion I asked what the Latin was for "fist". And when they told me, I replied that that was the name I would fight under for Rome. My first centurion told me that I was arrogant, and that I'd soon regret taking a name that made such a target for every would-be hard man in the cohort. I proved him wrong quickly enough.'

Longus smiled faintly.

'I can just imagine. Well it's good to meet you, Pugno. As an experienced legion commander I'm only too aware that while the duty of command is mine – and mine *alone* – the ways in which my legion will go about making my decisions into reality is very much dependent upon yourself. We are the two most important men in this legion, First Spear, and our working relationship will be of critical importance to our success in the coming war with the Batavians.'

The centurion nodded dourly.

'Indeed, Legatus. My relationship with your predecessor was a happy one, all in all. I was sorry to see him leave.'

The senior officer nodded.

'I enjoyed a similar cordiality with the senior centurion of my last command. I was legatus of the Third Gallica in Syria for three years.'

Pugno inclined his head.

'A good legion, Legatus, although the eastern legions are quite different from those raised north of the Alps. And very different to the Twenty-first.'

The legatus smiled, leaning back in his chair.

'I totally agree, there's hardly a comparison to be made between them.' He paused for a moment, allowing the man in front of him a small smile of superiority before delivering the throwaway comment's punchline. 'After all, the Third has never lost its eagle in battle, or surrendered to any enemy for that matter, indeed it was instrumental in our victory at the second battle of Cremona. Whereas the Twenty-first Rapax . . .'

Pugno's eyes narrowed as his superior's barb sank deeply into a sense of pride that had already taken a beating in the previous weeks.

'Our commander chose the wrong side, Legatus. It's as simple as that.'

Longus shrugged.

'You'll forgive me if I'm forced to inform you that that's *not* the way things are being portrayed in Rome, First Spear? I tell you this in order that you have a clear understanding of the way this legion, and all the other legions from the German frontier, are being talked about elsewhere. The officers of the German legions, it is being said, put Vitellius on a throne of their own making – given the empire already had a perfectly serviceable emperor in the form of Galba, a man of unimpaired honour – purely in the hope of earning generous donatives from their own emperor in the not unlikely event that their seven legions, and the three from Britannia, were to triumph over Galba's army. And when it all came to a head at the first battle of Cremona, after Otho had murdered Galba and taken his throne, gifting your rebellion at least a fig leaf of legitimacy, the Twenty-first Rapax, the legion with the proudest and the most bloodthirsty reputation on that battlefield was taught a salutary lesson by the newest legion in the entire empire.'

He leaned back again with a faint smile, waiting for the other man to respond.

'That's hardly—'

'Fair, First Spear? Were you *at* the first battle of Cremona? As I've heard it, recounted to me by a man who observed the matter at close quarters and whom you will meet soon enough, the Twenty-first lost its eagle to the First Classica, a legion composed entirely of marines from the fleet at Misenum, recruited by Nero for his abortive attempt to expand the empire's boundaries in the east. They offered you a trap into which you obligingly put your head, they cut off that head, they stole your standard and, were it not for the Batavians we're now being sent to subjugate, would have kept it long enough to plunge you all into the deepest possible shame.' Pugno stared back at him in silence. 'I know. It still hurts. It hurts worse than the second battle of Cremona, despite the fact that you were on the losing side there too, because at least there you didn't have to deal with the ignominy of having your eagle handed back to you by headstrong barbarian mercenaries like the Batavians. Perhaps putting them down will help to assuage your wounded pride. Perhaps participating in a successful campaign in Germania will help to put this legion back on the pedestal it occupied until not very long ago, that of the proudest, the most blood thirsty and positively the deadliest of the emperor's legions, ferocious in battle to the point of savagery. And I'm sure that *you* can be a pivotal force in restoring that lost pride. So tell me, First Spear, is my legion ready to fight? Ready to fight and *win*, that is?'

Pugno visibly swallowed his anger.

'It is, Legatus. The Twenty-first musters three thousand, seven hundred and ninety-eight men, all of whom are ready to march at your command and fight for the legion, the emperor and our gods whenever, wherever and however you direct.'

'Good. We've been directed to join an army group under the emperor's son-in-law Quintus Petillius Cerialis, with orders to clear the lower reaches of the Rhenus, a force initially consisting only of this legion and a legion's strength of auxiliaries, but to be joined in due course by the Second Classica, Sixth Victrix and Tenth Gemina from Hispania and the Fourteenth Gemina from Britannia. Otho's former general Gallus has been offered a chance to redeem himself by restoring order to the upper reaches of the river with four other legions, but we'll have the bulk of the fighting to do from the look of things. Legatus Augusti Cerialis's orders are to crush this rebellion so completely that no Batavian will ever consider raising a sword against Rome for a thousand years to come.'

Still simmering at the mention of the legion that had shamed his men at Cremona, Pugno nodded at the news.

'Four legions ought to have the measure of that barbarian scum. And doubtless my men will be delighted to share a camp with the First Classica's sister legion.'

The legatus smiled.

'I'm sure they will, given those marines will be equally delighted to have the chance to remind you what their brothers of the First Legion did to you last year. And you can point out to your fellow centurions that any man caught provoking trouble with any other legion will have the skin flogged off his back in front of the entire Twenty-first, without exceptions, excuses or any hope of clemency. Let's save all that pent-up fury for the battlefield, shall we?'

He looked meaningfully at the door, and, taking the hint, Pugno stood, drained his cup, saluted with the same exuberance and left the office. Nodding at the punctilious salutes of the legionaries he passed as he walked out into the camp, he made his way to the centurions' mess, where the men who commanded the Twenty-first's other nine cohorts were waiting for him.

'Give me a beaker of wine.'

He raised the large cup, muttering their ritual toast.

'Blood and glory.'

Sinking half the contents in a single swallow, Pugno looked round at their expectant faces.

'The new legatus? He's just like every other senior officer I ever met. He served me a drink in a cup so small that I couldn't get one of my balls into it. Not even one of your balls, Quintus.'

The recipient of the tried and tested insult raised a jaundiced eyebrow but refrained from comment, knowing from their long service together that this was not a moment to hand his superior a return dose of the rough humour he was dishing out.

'So he's careful with the wine. What about the man himself?'

'He's an arrogant bastard. He took pleasure in reminding me about losing our eagle at Cremona, and effectively told me that since we were shamed by a collection of nautical arse-pokers, we'd better fucking well find a way to get our pride back or we'll be biting the mattress for the rest of our careers. He also told me that we'll be marching alongside the Second Classica and two other legions at some point in the next few months when we go north to teach those uppity Batavian cunts a lesson, and that he'll have the back off any man caught fighting with their men, no matter what the provocation.'

Another of his officers grinned widely.

'He sounds like a right bastard.' He looked around the circle of men gathered around their senior centurion. 'So he's a perfect fit for the Twenty-first, right?'

Pugno nodded, swallowing the rest of his wine and holding the beaker out for a refill.

'Totally.'

Marsaci tribal land, January AD 70

'You animal!'

The voice speaking to Claudius Labeo was weak, its tone quavering, but when he turned to see who was speaking he found the old man's eyes were alive with hatred. Disdaining to notice the spears whose shafts were preventing him from approaching the younger man any closer, his slightly stooped figure was stiff with anger.

'If I were thirty years younger then these two fools would already be cooling corpses, and you'd be face down in a puddle of your own blood, you piece of shit!'

Labeo looked the old man up and down, nodding his understanding.

'And if our desires all came true then the poorest of men would ride horses, but the sad fact is that the world is as it is. Take him away.'

'No! You can listen to me for a moment, Claudius Labeo!'

Labeo nodded at his men.

'I suppose he has the right to speak his mind, given what we're doing to his village. So you know who I am?'

Pushing the spears away the old man stepped forward, eyes blazing with anger, ignoring the fact that both of Labeo's bodyguards had lowered the points of their weapons to within inches of his back.

'Yes, I know who you are. Claudius Labeo, once the prefect of the First Batavi Horse, now condemned as a traitor to your tribe. And apparently determined to prove that accusation true, but not by attacking your own people. Instead of confronting the Batavi, and facing the ire of men trained to fight, you take your revenge upon the Cananefates and we of the Marsaci, who lack the strength to stand up to your band of renegades and traitors. Stories of your bloody progress across the land have been reaching us for weeks, of farms and villages burned out, food pillaged and families left starving, forced to depend on the charity of those of their neighbours who escaped your attentions. I hoped not to see this day but when the smoke rose in the south this morning I knew it would only be a short time before your boots defiled our fields.'

'And so you sent your people away with the bulk of your grain?' The elder stared at Labeo in silence. 'And you'll keep the secret of whatever little hidey-hole they've run to no matter what we do to you, won't you?' He shrugged. 'I'm not interested in persecuting the people of your tribe, old man. This isn't about vengeance on the Batavi or on your tribe for supporting them in this war with Rome. This is *war*, old man, and in a war a man finds a way to encumber and impede his enemy, any way he can. *Any* way. I was falsely accused of harbouring ambitions to be king of my tribe, an accusation made ridiculous by the fact that the man making it has already effectively taken that power onto himself, and made that accusation as a means of having a potential restriction on his power removed. Kivilaz exiled me to live among the Frisii people, but they were no keener to keep me prisoner than I was to be held by them, and we reached an accommodation soon enough. They fear an independent Batavi, you see, and view my people as a potential threat to the freedom they won from Rome in the time of the emperor Tiberius. They look at the Cananefates, and the Marsaci, and they see vassals to the Batavi. They imagine how the men who lead my tribe could see them as another potential client state, contributing their strength to that of the Batavi. And so they freed me. I rode east, a single unremarkable man on horseback, keeping to the quiet ways and travelling at night when possible, and I found my way to a legion camp where I was faced with the very men I had betrayed while pretending to serve as a loyal ally of Rome. Roman generals, men swift to take revenge for the empire. And yet I did not find myself choking out my last breaths on a cross.'

The old man snorted derisively.

'A pity. But when you do find yourself nailed up, look for me in the front row of spectators.'

Labeo laughed softly.

'That won't happen. Rome may be swift to take her vengeance, but she's nothing if not pragmatic. You see, I might have changed sides on the battlefield, and led my men to attack an auxiliary cohort, but unlike my former brother-in-arms Kivilaz, I never raised a spear against Rome herself. No legionaries died as a result of my actions. No defiance was offered to any Roman.

And no Roman fortress was insulted. And when I pointed these facts out to Legatus Vocula, commander of the legions facing the Batavi, and told him what it was that I might do for Rome, he was swift to see my point. He freed me, and appointed me to command the frustrated men of the Batavi, the Cananefates, the Tungri, and yes, of your own tribe too, with the instruction to cause as much disruption to the Batavi's ability to wage war upon Rome as possible.'

'Traitors!'

The old man spat on the ground at Labeo's feet, but the rebel leader only smiled back at him.

'You do realise what will happen, don't you? Rome will march legions north from all over their empire to confront this piss-pot of a rebellion. Yes, Kivilaz has managed to besiege two half-strength legions in the Old Camp, although from what I hear he's lost thousands of men knocking fruitlessly at their door, and yes, he has another three equally weakened and dispirited legions on the defensive further south, but all that matters not one little bit. The new emperor will gather every man that can be spared, forty or fifty thousand of them at a guess, and he will send that army north to deal with the Batavi in as brutal and efficient a manner as possible, under a commander who will have little fellow feeling for your tribes and a reputation to enhance. So if you think my few hundred men represent the worst that Rome can do to your people, think again. Ten legions will take a lot of feeding, and unlike my men, the legionaries who will subjugate your people will not observe my strict orders for no woman or child to be misused. And no hiding place will safeguard your people, not with thousands of eager men who haven't seen a woman for months flooding your land.'

The old man stood in silence, digesting Labeo's words.

'But enough of that. Perhaps Kivilaz will see sense, and surrender on terms that leave the peoples of our tribes in peace. After all, he's a rational man. Or rather he was, before all this enmity between my people and Rome came about. Perhaps we can go back to the old relationship, if matters haven't gone too far. But in the meanwhile I'll go on doing whatever I can to make the point to you all, you who live far from Batavodurum, and who see the war with Rome as a distant matter, of no interest other than in that your menfolk form the point of the Batavi spear, that this war is real. And that it will come to you in all its terrible majesty sooner than you think. Spread the word.'

2

Germania Inferior, January AD 70

'That's no way for a man to die.'

Levonhard pointed grimly at the carrion-picked corpse of what had evidently been a well-built man before his death.

'Dead for a week, and he still looks better than you do.'

The strikingly ugly soldier shook his head at his comrade Adalwin, his grimace displaying a disturbing assortment of teeth set in a face that had been known to repulse even the most eager of prostitutes at close quarters.

'Not funny, Beaky, not seeing what they did to him. Put yourself in that poor bastard's boots and then try to make it amusing.'

Tied naked to a tree, his arms had been pulled around the trunk behind him to their furthest extent before his hands had been nailed to the living wood at the wrist, the barely protruding iron nail heads evidence that whoever had punished him had intended for him to die in that position. A dozen such grisly remnants lined the road south, barely a mile from the deserted Roman fortress at Gelduba, every one of them picked clean to the bone by carrion birds and animals. Egilhard shook his head in disbelief as he imagined the horror of their last hours.

'That's why.'

He gestured to a daubed warning that had been painted onto the tree's trunk above the last corpse in the line.

'Latrones?'

'It's Latin for "robber".' Alcaeus was marching alongside Draco's horse, and he waved his vine stick at the surrounding countryside to emphasise his point. 'The Romans burned out every farm across a ten-mile front as they came north to relieve the Old Camp, which meant that anyone with money fled to the nearest settlements while their slaves were left to fend for themselves. Some of them fled too, and the remainder are living in the ruins of their farms, eating whatever they can salvage from the wreckage or steal from their neighbours. There's a war of sorts being played out here, a dirty little war in the fields and hedgerows with only a few men on either side, and it'll be the cleverest of them who will come out on top. I'd imagine this lot never even saw the men who nailed them up here coming for so many of them to have been taken alive. Captured while they slept, perhaps.'

'We used to see the same thing in Britannia, during the conquest.' Draco spoke without taking his eyes off their objective, the wooden walls of the empty fortress rising high over the flat farmland that surrounded it on all sides. 'As the Britons retreated they burned whatever of their crops they couldn't harvest and take with them, rather than let us have them, not realising that we had a constant supply of grain from across the sea. Every mile we advanced was just as bloody as that . . .' he gestured back over his shoulder at the human remains arrayed along the roadside, 'men accused of collaborating with us, or of theft from communal stores, or simply the settling of old scores when the opportunity presented itself. We'll see worse, before this war's done.'

When the column reached the fortress he climbed down from the horse, pulling his staff from its straps and leaning on it to take the weight off his weaker leg.

'Keep your men out here, Hramn, I want to see the place as they left it, not with hundreds of soldiers climbing over it and getting in my way.' The prefect nodded silent understanding and Draco turned to Alcaeus. 'Centurion, perhaps you could send a few men in with me, just in case there are looters hiding in there?' He pointed to Egilhard. 'This fine young man here and a few of his men would be perfect. No more than a dozen spears though, I don't need the distraction.'

'What is it you're looking for?'

The veteran looked at Hramn and shook his head.

'I don't know. Anything that will provide us with intelligence as to what the Romans will do next would be welcome, or perhaps give us some clue as to how they were warned that you were about to attack? I will simply follow my instincts and see what I can find.'

Alcaeus nodded to Egilhard.

'Take your old tent party and make sure that Prefect Draco isn't interrupted by unfriendly men while he's searching for clues.'

The young watch officer turned to Lanzo.

'Bring your men and follow me, and be ready to use your spears.'

He led them forward through the fortress gates, following Draco's instructions to advance straight up the central street to the imposing praetorium at the heart of the camp. The soldiers formed a line across the street and advanced with the caution of men who had seen action, and who understood that the blow that killed a man wasn't always one he saw coming.

'These men of yours, Watch Officer, some of them seem to bear a striking resemblance to you.'

Egilhard looked back at the older man, seeing a spark of amusement on the veteran's face.

'My father, uncle and brother, Prefect.'

The older man inclined his head in evident respect.

'Your family makes a great contribution. It is to be hoped that this war with Rome can be resolved before we suffer any more disasters like the one that happened here.'

Egilhard turned away to resume his overseeing of the tent party's careful advance, but to his horror his uncle spoke without taking his eyes off the barrack blocks to his right.

'I remember you, Prefect. I wasn't much more than a lad at the battle of the Medui, but I'll never forget the way that you and the prince led us up the hill into those Britons.'

The veteran officer nodded.

'And I remember *you*, Soldier Frijaz. A good officer knows every man under his command, their strengths and their weaknesses.

Even then you were known for your fondness for drinking and gambling, and I presume nothing's changed in that respect? Not that you're alone in that urge to take risks, of course, it was Kivilaz who led us into the Britons in that bloody dawn, not me. He was always the bold one, the most likely to slip his collar and rampage forward in a blood rage if there was an enemy to hand, wasn't he?'

Shaking his head he muttered a terse comment to himself, the words so quiet that even Egilhard, standing alongside him, was uncertain as to what he'd heard, then looked at Frijaz, his face hard with certainty.

'I've heard men saying that this war he started can only end one way, in disaster and defeat, and that may be true, if we lack the iron in our backs to keep them at bay, but we can never doubt that he took us to war to avert the threat of a Rome that was ever more overbearing and dictatorial. Question his methods all you like, Soldier Frijaz, but never his reasons.'

He pointed at the looming bulk of the praetorium.

'And here we are. If there are secrets to be found anywhere in this place then this is the place they'll be waiting for us. I'll go in first, and you men can stay out here, all except for you, Watch Officer. Let's go and see if we can find anything of interest.'

Inside the building the rooms were sunk in darkness, their window shutters closed, but Draco strode confidently away into the gloom, limping slightly from the decades-old wound that had ended his military career, his staff tapping at the floorboards.

'Always the same layout. They're creatures of habit, the Romans, always following their manuals to the last letter. Get those shutters open and let's have a little light to show us what they left behind, eh?'

Unfastening the shutters, and throwing them wide to admit the daylight, Egilhard could hear the elder's staff tapping away into the gloom of the building's inner sanctum. The noise stopped abruptly, and Draco called out in urgent tones that put the soldier's hand on the hilt of his sword without his even registering the reaction.

'Come in here, Watch Officer!' Hurrying into the next room he found the veteran officer staring at something in one corner. 'Let's have some light in here, shall we? Open that door as wide as you can.'

Standing in the half-light, he pointed to one corner of the room, where a small, flat wooden box bound in tarnished silver lay on the floor.

'You'll be my witness that we found whatever that is in here. This is the office that would usually be used by the legion's legatus, if I remember correctly. And that, from the look of it, is a writing tablet.'

Rome, January AD 70

'Gentlemen . . .'

The consul's lictors swept into the audience chamber twelve strong, taking up their positions on either side of the magnificently decorated doors with the easy precision of long practice, and the assembled legati and their senior centurions responded with equal formality and precision, snapping to attention as the head lictor announced the arrival of the august personage they had been waiting for. The officers were dressed in formal togas, while their first spears had been advised to wear their very smartest off-duty uniforms, and so it was that, freshly bathed and groomed, five men who would have been far more at home wearing forty pounds of iron and silver found themselves feeling strangely out of place in their dress tunics, their discomfort at being unarmed only partially assuaged by the gleam of their belts and boots and the comforting presence of their vine sticks, the closest thing to a weapon any of them had been allowed to bring onto the Palatine Hill despite their exalted status in their own military worlds.

'Gentlemen! Consul Gaius Licinius Mucianus!'

The great man paused in the doorway and looked at the assembled officers in an apparently frank appraisal. After a moment his expression softened, and he nodded pleasantly at them in a manner that caused more than one man's heart to lighten just a little, inclining his head fractionally to the two men who would be commanding the campaign to choke off the most widespread and dangerous tribal revolt in recent memory.

'Thank you, gentlemen.' He nodded to the two army commanders in turn, then opened his arms to encompass the wider gathering behind them. 'Appius Annius Gallus, Quintus Petillius Cerialis, gentlemen legati, honoured members of the imperial centurionate, welcome to the Palatine Hill. And please, there's no need to stand on ceremony. I, just like you all, am no more than a loyal servant of the emperor. We men who hold the empire's fate in our hands on his behalf have no need of such barriers, especially on the eve of your commencement of yet another campaign in eighteen months which has already seen very little other than marching, fighting, mourning our losses and then marching once again.'

Standing towards the rear of the group, in the company of the other legion first spears who had quickly recognised that their place was as far out of sight as possible, Pugno fought the urge not to smile at the patrician senator's words. The stories he had heard in the weeks following the defeat at Cremona, as victors and vanquished alike had worked hard to reintegrate the defeated Vitellian legions into Vespasianus's army, had made it very clear that Mucianus was far from being any sort of simple servant of the emperor, even if his loyalty to Vespasianus was evidently iron-hard. His new legatus had breezily confirmed the opinion of his colleagues from the other legions when asked.

'Mucianus? We can all be very grateful to him in my opinion. He and Vespasianus used to be at daggers drawn, when Mucianus was governor of Syria and Vespasianus was sent to take command in Judea, mainly because Mucianus had failed to put the Jews back in their place and Vespasianus was sent to do the job properly. But they reconciled their differences soon enough when it became clear that poor old Galba had been murdered. After all, who wants a man like Otho or Vitellius on the throne? And don't mistake his affected senatorial gentility for anything other than a very clever disguise for an absolutely razor-sharp intellect combined with a ruthlessness to match the best of them.' He caught the fleeting look of disbelief that had crossed Pugno's face. 'What, you want proof? Look at Legatus Augusti Antonius Primus. The proudest, most headstrong commander I've ever met, and all the way to Rome completely determined to ignore his very clear instructions to wait for Mucianus. He was fixated on being the first man into the city, and we all knew that his plan was to play with the senate for a week or two, and try the throne for size without actually having his centurions insist on his becoming emperor immediately. After all, Vespasianus is still far away in Egypt, and who knows what a man in command of several legions might achieve given a few weeks with the free run of the capital? But Mucianus was wise to his game, so he force-marched his own legions south and arrived in the city the day after Antonius. And that, my dear Pugno, was *that*. Antonius has been slid quietly aside and will doubtless find himself, in the fullness of time, quietly retired to his estates and forced to read accounts of the campaign that make it very clear where the fault lies for the extreme barbarity that his legions visited on the town of Cremona. If not for Mucianus there would probably still be two emperors, instead of which we have the luxury of something approaching normality once again. And we can thank the gods for that, Pugno, because it means that we can get back to something more like soldiering.'

Mucianus turned to the two armies' commanders, beckoning them forward.

'I have called you all here simply to offer you my very best wishes for your campaigns on the Rhenus. Your legions, and those that will join you as you march north from elsewhere in the empire, have been given responsibility for the swift and pitiless return of the empire north of the Alps to normality. The tribes from the wild country across the great river are to be chased back to their dung heaps. Our legions remaining in the theatre of war are to be rescued from their plight, put back on their feet and enabled to take their places in the defence of the empire's frontiers. And taxes are to start flowing once more.' He looked around them with a knowing smile. 'After all, your men consume food at a prodigious rate, and someone has to pay for all that bread and pork. Which means, gentlemen, that your march north must be brisk, your performance on the battlefield must be effective, and your men's behaviour towards the Batavians when they inevitably succumb to the strength of your legions must be not that of conquerors, but rather of disciplined soldiers charged with the difficult task of bringing back errant allies. And the reason I invited you here, all you senior centurions skulking at the back of the room . . .' he smiled to show that his words were intended warmly, 'is because nobody else can influence the behaviour of your legions like you. If you and your brother officers set an expectation of leniency and good behaviour, punishable in its absence by the most severe of sentences, then I expect that, by and large, that expectation will be delivered. And be under no illusions, gentlemen, the emperor expects his wishes in this matter to be respected. You must act vigorously to put down this rebellion, but in victory you must be magnanimous and sympathetic. The emperor wants the Batavians back in the fold, so to speak, and reincorporated to the body of the army as quickly as possible, and what the emperor wants is of the utmost importance to us all, *if* we value our places in this newly reformed army.'

He looked around at them all, and Pugno felt the force of his personality in their brief exchange of glances before the consul started speaking again.

'Speaking of our august emperor, I should probably share with you what he has recently communicated to me, revealing his innermost thoughts on the subject of the rebellion that you're ordered to suppress. Thoughts that might help to explain the instructions I've just issued you on his behalf.' He looked around at them again, his gaze level. 'The emperor finds himself more than a little troubled by this revolt of our dearest allies. For a century we have regarded them as our most effective auxiliaries, savage, fearless and terrifyingly efficient on the field of battle. You will all be aware, no doubt, that he fought alongside them in Britannia, an experience that left him in no doubt that they were an ally beyond compare with any other. And yet, he muses, here we are at war with them. And no longer deniably so. This rebellion is long past the point of our being able to quietly draw a veil over skirmishes and insults that can be ignored. Their prince, Gaius Julius Civilis, a man who has given a lifetime of service to the empire, has become so disaffected with our rule that he has taken up arms, and gone so far as to place a legion fortress under siege. And for this, the emperor is absolutely clear, we have only ourselves to blame. Only a fool like Vitellius, he tells me, would have arrested Civilis on a charge of treason, the second such accusation to be levelled at the man, and then allowed him his freedom for reasons of the most nakedly obvious pragmatism, freeing him to go and make mischief in the sure knowledge that the charge would be renewed when the circumstances were more auspicious. In his idiocy Vitellius left Civilis with absolutely nothing to lose, and free to rouse a tribe already smarting from Galba's mistaken decisions to dismiss the emperor's German Bodyguard, a source of much pride to them. And he compounded that idiocy by ordering conscription from among them, something totally forbidden under the terms of the treaty agreed with them a hundred years ago by the divine Julius.'

He looked around the room, shaking his head and raising his hands in an invitation for them all to join in his evident incredulity.

'Which means that it was effectively *us* that caused this revolt, gentlemen, let's be under no doubt as to that fact. Yes, perhaps Civilis was already plotting an uprising, but without those errors of judgement the emperor very much doubts that his people would have been sufficiently aggrieved to humour his demands for war. Which is why he is determined to tread softly around them, within the limits of good sense, once they are defeated. Recognising the sound common sense of this approach, I have appointed a man known to the Batavian cohorts to be the emperor's emissary to the tribe, once they have been dissuaded from any further violence. Alfenius Varus?'

A toga-clad senator who had been standing on the edge of the room stepped forward and bowed.

'Consul.'

Mucianus gestured to him.

'This is Aulus Alfenius Varus, former commander of the Praetorian Guard under Vitellius but, rather more to the point, also the man who commanded the Batavian cohorts at the first battle of Cremona. This, gentlemen, is the man whose cohorts turned the battle, and who rescued a legion's eagle from the hands of men who might otherwise have carried it away and brought shame upon the legion in question.' He shot Pugno a glance so swift that the senior centurion was more than half-convinced that it had been pure coincidence that he had picked that moment to look in his direction, and yet knew in his bones that it had been no accident. 'He knows the Batavians as well as any man among us, and it is to be hoped that his rapport with their senior officers will make it easier for us all to learn to rub along once the fighting is done. Time, I suppose, will tell. And so, before we take wine and talk more about the situation as we understand it to be in Germania as we know it, does anyone have any questions? You, First Spear, I suspect there is at least one thing you'd like to ask me?'

Pugno was momentarily taken aback at being addressed by the emperor's right-hand man, but, feeling the eyes of his peers upon him and determined not to allow his legion's reputation to be sullied in their eyes by a failure to respond, he snapped to attention and saluted.

'Legatus Augusti! My name is Pugno, First Spear, Legio Twenty-first Rapax!'

Mucianus smiled.

'I know it is, First Spear. And your question, from the heart of the legion famed as the most brutal and bloodthirsty body of men in the army?'

'Legatus Augusti, I am curious as to how far the emperor's mercy towards the Batavians extends? Are we to spare their military commanders if we capture them?'

The senator nodded.

'Straight to the heart of it as ever, eh, First Spear? Your answer is this: if, in the course of the campaign to retake the Batavian homeland, acts are committed that render the enemy guilty of a charge of brutality, the murder of prisoners, for example, then their leaders can consider their lives forfeit. Messages to that effect will be sent to the enemy, to ensure that there can be no doubt in the matter.'

'Thank you, Legatus Augusti. And this man Civilis?'

Mucianus smiled more broadly.

'Civilis? At this point in time the emperor's thoughts on his eventual treatment are . . . shall we say, as yet unsettled? Yes, he has led his people in an act of war against Rome, for which the usual punishment would be death, whether prompt or delayed by his transport to Rome for the purposes of the act's visibility. On the other hand, he has twenty-five years of service to the empire, service which cost him an eye in the final battle with the Iceni people in Britannia. And his revolt, as I have intimated, was at least partially rooted in our own actions. Vespasianus has called a former colleague to his side, a man who shared battlefield dangers with him during the conquest of Britannia, and who will, he expects, provide him with a suitable ability to reflect and decide upon the most appropriate penalty for Civilis to pay. And so the answer to your question, First Spear Pugno, is that I literally have no idea whether the emperor will order the man to be crucified as an example to others, or retired to Rome with a comfortable pension, to serve as an example of the new man on the throne's ability to show mercy when appropriate. Doubtless you'll have orders on the matter before the time comes, borne to us by the fastest message ship in the whole of Our Sea. And doubtless you'll follow those orders through to the letter. After all, we are just instruments of the emperor's will, are we not?'

Germania Inferior, January AD 70

'Two months for them to build it, and a day for us to reduce it to ashes.' Egilhard followed his father's stare at the remnants of the Gelduba fortress, the timbers that had formed its walls still glowing with a heat both men could feel on their faces at two hundred paces. 'Seems a bit like our relationship with them, doesn't it?'

The two men were standing guard on the cohort's marching camp, freshly built from turves, Lataz having drawn the lot to stand the second watch and Egilhard having swapped guard duty with his taciturn tent mate Wigbrand to keep his father company, much to the older man's relief at not having to endure a watch spent in the big soldier's brooding silence.

'What do you mean?'

Lataz was silent for a moment.

'Do you remember your uncle Wulfa?'

Egilhard started at the mention of his father's younger brother, long dead and hardly ever mentioned by his father or uncle, his loss still raw for both men even after so many years.

'Not very well. He was gone before I was old enough to know him.'

The older man nodded, sunk in thought for so long that Egilhard was on the verge of speaking again.

'He was a wild one, was Wulfa. Our mother's despair and our father's pride and joy. Old Frijaz now, he was the gambler, always looking for a way to get his hands on a drink, or a woman, but he was never a warrior, not in the way you are. And neither was I, for that matter. I was the quiet one, the sensible one, always having to pull my stupid older brother's chestnuts out of the fire. Don't get me wrong, we were decent fighters alright, we stood in the line and killed our share, but we were neither of us gifted, not like you. And not like him. He was . . .' he paused, smiling at the memory, 'he was magnificent. Faster than any man in the cohort. I see all three of us in you, boy. A good-sized portion of me, a little bit of Frijaz, may the gods help you, but mostly I see Wulfa. Every time you draw Lightning he's there in your eyes. Every time you look at me over a shield's rim on the practice ground, there he is. My younger brother didn't give a fuck about the risks, he just loved to dance with his iron and see the other man's face as his spear's blade took the poor bastard's life. It killed him in the end, of course. I've told you often enough that all heroes fall to the curse that makes them famous, and he was no different.'

He fell silent again, and Egilhard knew his father well enough to let him think.

'He danced into the Iceni at the battle that settled things for them, and that was the last time I saw him alive. He probably killed a dozen of them before they put him down, he was that good, but he had the curse of the hero on him alright. We found him after the battle, while the rest of them were busy hunting down what was left of the Britons and enslaving their women. There were wounds all over him, boy. All over him, his arms, his legs, his neck – someone had hit him with a spear hard enough to put it right through his mail, front and back – but there were dead men all round him. He'd still have been serving now, if he'd not had that restless spirit whispering blood and glory in his ear. Which is why I've told you not to be a hero so many times, not that you've ever listened. We burned his corpse that night, and doubtless we'll have to do the same for you one day . . .'

His son stood in silence, knowing that no response to his father's musings was needed, and Lataz sighed deeply.

'You're wondering why I brought him up. It's because seeing that fortress burn reminds me of something he said when he came back from Rome.'

It was a well-established family story that the youngest of the three brothers, having earned the singular honour after barely five years of service of having been selected to join the Corporis Custodes, the imperial bodyguard whose members had been the emperor's protectors since the days of Augustus, had needed no longer than a month to decide that the routines and tedium of standing guard on the most powerful man in the world were not for him.

'He strolled back up to his old tent party one day, almost a year after he'd left to go south to Rome mind you, told the man who'd replaced him to be on his way, then sat down by the fire like he'd just been down to the latrines for a piss rather than away for ten months, across the sea and over the mountains and all the way back again. I had no idea he was coming back, of course, so when I laid eyes on him I was speechless with amazement, although Frijaz called him all the names you can imagine for being such a fool. We sat him down for a beer or two and tried to understand how a man could be so stupid as to walk away from the Bodyguard, but all it came down to was that he was bored, and Wulfa didn't handle boredom all that well, so that was that. But one thing he did say . . .'

Silence fell again, as the older man smiled at the memory.

'He said that the only reason to stay would have been for the city itself. Not the taverns, not the whores, and you can imagine the names Frijaz started calling him when he said that, but rather the buildings. He told us that Rome was like a forest of stone, a city five hundred years in the building that would last forever. He loved walking the streets when he was off-duty, he said, staring up at the temples and arenas in wonder, but in the end his need to dance with his iron in the company of men overcame even that delight. That and his disdain for the men serving in Rome. He said that the men of the Bodyguard had grown fat and idle compared to us men of the cohorts, as if Rome got under their skin and made them soft as the men of the city. And one night, after Frijaz had got tired of abusing him and gone to bed, he shared his private thoughts with me, just once, serious as you like. Of course, he was the same old Wulfa the next day, but for a short time he showed me the man I knew was in him, beneath all that urge to fight.'

'And?'

Lataz smiled at his son.

'As you grew into manhood I saw that same man in you. Thoughtful and clever. Cleverer than Frijaz and me put together, I suspect. It was the only time he ever really opened his mind to me, may the gods grant his spirit peace, and he was dead inside the year, which meant I never got the chance to see that thinker again. He told me that Rome and the Batavi had what he called a relationship of opposites.'

'What did he mean by that?'

'I asked him the same question. And he told me that from what he'd seen of the Romans, the senators and equestrians who run the empire, he took them to be civilised men, men who think, and build, and create, but men who loved to play the barbarian when the opportunity presented itself, and who idolised the barbarian because he is everything that they are not, but would have secretly liked to be have been. Whereas we, he told me, are everything the Romans can never be. Where they create, we destroy. Where they are a disciplined people, we wear our discipline like a cloak we have chosen to put on for as long as it suits us, and cast it off when the chance for glory presents itself. We are little different from the tribes over the great river, but we chose to ally ourselves with Rome for the iron they gave us, and the glory we enjoyed as their hunting dogs. And for a long time, it seems, that was enough for both Rome and the Batavi.'

'Until now.'

'Yes. But now that friendship is at an end all we have left is our urge to destroy.' Lataz gestured to the glowing remnants of the fortress. 'They build, we burn.'

'They build, we burn? I didn't know you were a philosopher, Soldier Lataz?' Both men snapped to attention as Alcaeus strolled out through the opening in the marching camp's wall behind them. 'At ease, I'm only taking the night air to put me back in the mood for sleep. I was woken by a dream.'

Egilhard and Lataz exchanged glances, the wolf-priest's ability to see what was yet to happen in his dreams an article of faith among the soldiers of his century, who knew only too well the blow that had shaken him to the core when his presentiments of disaster had become reality in the battle they had fought close by the previous year. The bloody defeat at Gelduba that had resulted in the death of his friend and chosen man Banon, and caused Egilhard's promotion to watch officer, seemed to have both strengthened his faith in the gift he had been granted by the gods and challenged his faith that those same gods viewed the Batavi with favour.

'Off to your bed, Soldier Lataz, your son and I will serve the rest of this watch.'

Lataz saluted, nodded to Egilhard and disappeared into the camp, leaving centurion and watch officer standing in silence.

'Your uncle Wulfa was right, of course. We were Rome's hunting dogs, their bravest and best, but when a dog bites his master he can expect to pay the price, one way or another.' The centurion looked at the fortress's burning remnants for a moment before speaking again. 'So, what was it that Draco found in there, before we put fire to timber?'

'A writing tablet, Centurion. Bound in silver.'

'A rich man's possession. Did he open his find?'

Egilhard shook his head.

'No. He looked over the rest of the building and then took his leave.'

'And did he say anything to give any clue as to what it was that he thought he'd found?'

'No sir. Although he did say something interesting before we entered the praetorium.'

Alcaeus regarded him levelly for a moment.

'Lataz is right. There's more of his younger brother in you than meets the eye. So tell me, Watch Officer, what was it that the tribe's foremost elder had to say that caught your attention so much you feel the need to relate it to me?'

Egilhard thought for a moment, recalling the exact words Draco had used.

'We were discussing Prince Kivilaz, Centurion. My uncle had told Prefect Draco that he remembered the Prefect leading the cohorts into battle at the Medui, and the Prefect replied that it had been Kivilaz who took our men up the hill.'

Alcaeus nodded.

'That's as I've heard the story told as well. Something possessed the prince that day, and he was invincible, driving the Britons back wherever he went, and Draco was at his side until he took the spear to the thigh that ended his career, and couldn't fight any longer. It was Kivilaz, they say, who led the Batavi to rout the Britons, not Draco. But that's old history.'

'The prefect said something else as well. I only half heard it, as if he was speaking to himself, but it sounded like "and now he's got us into a fight that we can never win". He told Frijaz that he could question the prince's methods but not his reasons for going to war, but it sounded to me like he was questioning both a moment before.'

'I see. Well, Watch Officer, as you rise higher in the ranks of our army you will discover that what our leaders profess to believe is not always going to be what's in their hearts. And the older you get, the more you will come to understand the reasons why they are not always as honest with us as we might like. In Prefect Draco's case, I believe that he finds himself horrified at the losses we have taken, whilst of course remaining totally supportive of his prince, which is only right. And we must be the same, you and I, and give both men everything we have. So let this be between you and me, yes?'

Egilhard snapped to attention.

'Of course, Centurion.'

The wolf-priest smiled, patting him on his mail-clad shoulder.

'Good lad. Shall we take a turn down the rampart and back again?'

The Winter Camp, Germania Superior, January AD 70

'Legatus, you and the men of our legions are a very welcome sight!'

Vocula accepted the camp prefect's welcome with a tired smile, watching as his Twenty-second Legion marched past them and in through the Winter Camp fortress's main gate.

'I wish we could have arrived sooner. The countryside seems to have suffered badly at the hands of the barbarians.'

The other man nodded, tight-lipped.

'More than you might think, I'm afraid. They crossed the river in strength, more than ten thousand of them, and while they were careful not to come inside the range of our bolt throwers, they burned out every farm and township for miles. They clearly knew we were too weak to come out and challenge them, and I doubt they had much interest in this fortress when there were women and gold to be had elsewhere.'

The grim evidence of the tribes' rampage had confronted the three legions as they had marched south along the river, in company with the Nervian auxiliaries commanded by their prince, Julius Classicus. The farms they passed had been reduced to blackened skeletons littered with the corpses of their occupants, while the stink of death from the settlement at Bingium, twelve miles distant from the impotent men inside the Winter Camp, powerless to intervene while it had been sacked, had turned stomachs in the column of legionaries before they had even got within sight of its ravaged buildings.

'So we saw. And, sad to say, that's all we saw. We snapped up a few dozen of them, men less wary than might have been wise, and crucified them by the roadside, but for the most part they seem to have melted away back over the river rather than face us, which is probably just as well given that our three legions don't have very many more men than would be following a single eagle at full strength. And, to make things even worse, given their apparent state of mind.'

The older man nodded, casting a glance at the legionaries trudging in through the gate to occupy fortress barracks designed to accommodate the ten thousand men of two full-strength legions.

'I knew the First and Sixteenth Legions had sent men south to fight for Vitellius, but I had no idea they were both so . . .'

Vocula's lips twisted in a wry smile.

'Disheartened? Demoralised?'

'Well . . . yes. I'm sorry, Legatus, I meant no insult.'

'None taken. The First was given a sound beating by the Batavians on their march north to rejoin their own people, and I don't think they ever truly recovered from the experience. And the Sixteenth are little better. Weak leadership, the removal of too many of their best officers, coming so close to defeat in battle that only the intervention of some Hispanic auxiliaries saved them, it's all added up to despair, I'm afraid. They're beaten men, more or less, and it's only my own Twenty-second Legion that's kept the army intact all this time.'

The camp prefect nodded knowingly.

'That'll partly be down to your First Spear, I imagine. He was never showy in the days when I commanded him, but everything I ever asked of him always got done quickly, efficiently and with the minimum of shouting. Now you know why it was I recommended he replace me in command of the legion. So . . .' he looked along the length of the column marching slowly through the fortress gates, 'what now?'

The legion legates and their senior centurions gathered in the fortress headquarters that evening, once their men were settled into barracks and enjoying an evening without the tedious and tiring task of digging out a marching camp.

'At least the local shopkeepers will get a small fillip from having three legions in camp, even if the legions in question are shadows of their former strength. What's left of the local shopkeepers, that is. The whores have an uncanny ability to make themselves scarce when iron is bared, and then to pop up again the moment silver replaces it in men's hands.'

Vocula nodded absent-mindedly at his colleague Gallus's opinion, still finding it difficult to meet the eye of a man who had so comprehensively lost control of his First Legion.

'True. Not that we'll be able to stay here for long. Now that the Germans have retreated across the river our duty lies to the north again. I left the Old Camp's garrison to continue resisting the Batavian siege when I should really have withdrawn them as soon as we had temporarily lifted that siege back in December. I felt it necessary to keep a foothold close to the enemy homeland, and to deny Civilis the prestige of having destroyed a legion fortress, and I promised Munius Lupercus that I would relieve him permanently as soon as I felt able to do so. Now I need to make good on my promise not to leave those good men to their fate.'

The camp prefect raised a hand to speak, but the Nervian prince Julius Classicus got to his feet and strode into the middle of the room in a preemptory manner that had every man staring at him. Unabashed, he addressed Vocula directly.

'*My* duty, Legatus, is not simply to the empire, but to my own people as well, and those of the other allied tribes. And the news from our neighbours the Treveri is not as happy as I might have wished. Their warriors, those men not sworn to the service of Rome, armed themselves to resist the German tribes' attempts to push west onto their land, in search of yet more wealth to loot and defenceless people to despoil. The fighting that resulted was bloody on both sides, and while they managed to repel their attempts to pillage their land, a good many of their men gave their lives to make that victory possible. I understand that you must take your legions back to rejoin the fight against the traitor Civilis, but I cannot abandon the peoples of Gaul to the fate that must be theirs if the German tribes are allowed to cross the river again. If I am to accompany you in this mission to retake the Old Camp once again, then I must insist that the garrison of this fortress be reinforced, and the enemy across the river deterred from making any further attempt to spread their destruction into the homelands of your loyal allies.'

Vocula looked up at him.

'It seems that you're in luck, Prefect Classicus. While I would have been minded to refuse your request, given that it will yet further weaken my army at a time when more strength, rather than less, is what I need to bolster legions so weakened by loss of men and adversity that I can barely keep them operational, my orders state otherwise.'

He held up a message scroll.

'From Rome, dispatched a week ago by the new emperor's ruling council. I am ordered to detach the Twenty-second Legion from my army and use it to reinforce the defence of the Winter Camp and, thereby, both provide a more effective defence of our Gallic allies and safeguard the integrity of Germania Superior. Or, reading between the lines, Rome realises that Germania Inferior is lost and is determined not to allow Germania Superior to be jeopardised. What we have, we hold, it seems, at least until such time as an army can be mustered to cross the Alps and put down this rebellion. It seems that Vitellius's original decision to send me north with the Twenty-second is being viewed as too much of a risk to our grasp of the land north of the mountains, and that the empire now intends to minimise that risk and make sure that we don't lose this fortress as well.'

Classicus stared at him for a moment.

'I see. And your own orders, Legatus?'

'I am allowed the tactical freedom to do whatever I feel appropriate with my remaining force, Prefect Classicus. And I feel it appropriate to march north at my remaining legions' best speed, relieve the Old Camp for a second time and bring my colleague Munius Lupercus and his men to safety. We will consolidate our combined strength at whichever of the fortresses along the Rhenus feels appropriate and then decide whether to stand and fight or withdraw back here and await the inevitable flood of reinforcements, now that the civil war is ended and Vespasianus has a firm grip on Rome.'

The Nervian officer smiled slowly.

'And I, Legatus, applaud your commitment to your fellow officer and his men. My soldiers will march north alongside yours and assist you in the task of liberating the Old Camp's legions from their siege.'

Vocula stared at him for a moment before replying.

'Thank you, Prefect. We'll start planning and preparing for the march north in the morning, with the intention of leaving here in two days. The legions need a little time to replace their worn-out hobnails and for their feet to recover from the march south, and I will use the time to put my affairs in order before putting my head back into the lion's mouth. That will be all.'

He waited for them to leave the room, signalling to Antonius to remain behind.

'This is, of course, perfect for Classicus and his allies. If our spy among the Batavians is right in his belief that they are in league with the Nervians, Ubians, Trevirans and Lingones, then the removal of my only effective legion will leave the remainder of my army incapable of resisting them. And so I have a favour to ask of you – a century or two of your men to act as my bodyguard.'

The first spear raised his hand.

'You have no need to ask, Legatus. I've already spoken with the Fourth Macedonica's first spear and told him that he'll be taking command of the Twenty-second as well as his own men. It'll give him the best part of a legion in total, less my first cohort.'

'You mean . . . ?'

'I mean, Legatus, that I plan to march north alongside you, and to bring my most loyal men with me.'

Vocula stared at him for a moment in silence.

'I'm humbled, Antonius. You're sure about this? You know as well as I do that if the Gauls revolt we'll be a few hundred men in a sea of enemies with only the disaffected at our backs?'

Antonius shrugged.

'Having come to know you, Legatus, I do not believe that I could look myself in the face were I to allow you to embark upon such a dangerous course of action without having at least one friend at your side.'

The legatus nodded slowly, his lips tightly compressed.

'And I may well never be able to thank you properly. But nevertheless, you have my thanks, for what they're worth. Your presence will be of more value to me than you might suspect, given the sheer loneliness of my position. At least while Flaccus was alive I had someone to blame for this terrible mess. Mind you . . .' he smiled ruefully, 'if I think this is tough, I'd imagine the position of our spy in the Batavian camp is every bit as nerve-wracking.'

Tigernum, Gallia Belgica, January AD 70

'And I, Claudius Labeo, have had enough of burning out innocent men's farms.'

The big Tungrian centurion loomed over Labeo, who remained where he was, sprawled in a chair that in happier times would have been occupied by the master of the villa that had become his ragtag force's temporary encampment. The smell of cooking was wafting into the room through its open shutters, as the small army's men busied themselves cooking freshly butchered meat, their horseplay audible through the farm's windows as they enjoyed the unaccustomed luxury of a river to bathe in and anticipated the hot food that would soon be filling their bellies. The Batavi nobleman shrugged at his officer with an unconcerned expression.

'And you have a better idea, do you? Even with the cohorts so badly reduced in strength I doubt that we could match them on a battlefield, not without some quirk of the landscape to help us. What would you have me do, march my men east and seek them out?'

The Tungrian shook his head brusquely, putting a hand to the scabbard at his side and tapping it meaningfully.

'Of course not. But there is a way that we could end this war in a single bold act, and bring honour back to our blades.'

Labeo shook his head, spreading his hands in question.

'Have we not discussed this before? How many times will you chew on this bone before you realise that what you propose is certain suicide?'

The big man turned away with a headshake, his voice acid with frustration.

'So *you* say. But then you, Claudius Labeo, are hardly the most aggressively minded of your people, if indeed you are a true son of the Batavi. Perhaps some Roman crept into your mother's bed while your father was serving in a distant land, and gave her a Roman son.' He looked back at Labeo with a tight smile, shaking his head again at the other man's apparent indifference to the grave insult. 'See? Even when I question your parentage you simply look back at me with nothing more in your face than calculation of what it is that I want. Were Kivilaz in that chair I would be looking down the length of his sword, whereas you . . .'

Labeo threw his head back and laughed.

'I'm supposed to air my iron because you seek to provoke me on a whim? I have better things to occupy my mind than responding to your predictable and stale jibes. Men have been accusing me of being too careful in my thinking to be a real son of my tribe for so long that I've long since learned to ignore them and spend my time on bigger and better matters. Such as how we can lure Kivilaz onto favourable ground for an ambush, or where we should attack next to do the maximum possible damage to his ability to wage war – not on the wild schemes that you keep pushing me to support. You would have me throw my army at Kivilaz's camp in the hope of catching him unawares, and by ending his life, end the war in a day, where in reality we could not hope to approach within ten miles without being detected by his scouts. Your plan, as I have told you a hundred times, is doomed to fail, and I will not throw my men away to satisfy your urge to do something, even if that act of defiance would almost certainly end both our struggle and our lives.'

The Tungrian stared at him for a moment.

'*Your* army? I still struggle to see how it is that you feel entitled to claim the command of men from half a dozen tribes. Perhaps they might prefer to make their own decision as to the best way to fight this war?'

Labeo got slowly to his feet, his gaze locked on the Tungrian.

'Rome, Centurion. That's who gave me this command and restored me to the rank of *prefect*. Dillius Vocula recognised a leader in me, when I told him what I might achieve for him. He saw a man he knew could unite the soldiers of the allied tribes who had flocked to Rome's eagles in disdain for their tribes' rebellion against the greatest power in the world.' He walked slowly forward, his pace deliberate, until he was toe to toe with the taller man. 'Clearly he saw something in me that was lacking from any other man in this army of disaffection. Lacking, it has to be said, in you, Centurion.' He raised a hand to forestall the big man's outburst. 'I know, that's verging on an insult that will have your iron leaping from its scabbard. But think. If you kill me, as you probably could, you will be hunted down like a dog once Rome has control of this land once more, hunted down and executed out of hand for the crime of murdering your superior officer. Rome hates insubordination, but it reserves a special punishment for men who raise their hands in mutiny. And besides, I have a better use for that indignation.'

The Tungrian looked down at him.

'What better use?'

'You seem fixated on trying to kill Kivilaz. You hope to catch him unawares, and be the man who ends this war in a heartbeat, seeking glory and honour for your people and yourself. And why not? Perhaps your wild scheme might work. The odds are certainly not so long that a few men might be wagered to make such an attempt.'

The big man gaped at him.

'But . . .'

'But I have refused every request you have made for such an act of desperation?' Labeo shrugged. 'I have. But what I have refused, in point of fact, is your desire for the army to seek such a knock-out punch, for fear that it will be our chin that takes the punch. When it comes to you personally I have no such qualms. So yes, why not? Take any of your own century who wish to accompany you in this wild cast of the dice and ride east. Find the enemy camp and use whatever ruse or stratagem you think appropriate to worm your way close to my old colleague Kivilaz, then strike with all your venom. If you kill him then you will indeed put your sword into the Batavi's heart, and make a hero of yourself for all time, whereas if you fail . . .' he shrugged, 'you will at least die with some measure of honour.'

The Tungrian's eyes narrowed.

'You want to rid yourself of my threat to your leadership.'

Labeo laughed in his face.

'Your threat to my leadership? You keep on thinking that way.

Use that certainty as to your own superiority to fire your determination to prove me wrong. And for me, sending a small force of trained killers led by a wild animal like you after my old adversary Kiv represents a gamble that might just work. After all, Centurion, and unlike you, I am not a man to rest on his pride. If you think you can kill the man who leads the tribe then you go ahead and give it your best effort, and I'll sacrifice to Magusanus himself for you to succeed. And if you *do* succeed, I'll happily say what a great man you were in your funeral oration. Or does the realisation that seeking Kiv's head is likely to cost you your own dull the shine on your blade?'

Batavodurum, January AD 70

'Well now, let's see who we have before us.'

Draco eased himself into his accustomed chair in the Batavi council's chamber, gesturing to the two men standing on the other side of the table.

'Relax, brothers, you have been invited to a discussion of a problem the tribe faces, not hauled before the council for judgement.'

Both men stared back at him with the offended air of men who felt themselves traduced by the very fact of their having been asked to attend the meeting, glancing nervously at the men standing to either side of them with blank expressions.

'So . . .' He paused for a long moment. 'You know, I imagine, what it is that I wish to discuss with you all?'

'Yes.'

The wealthier of the two men nodded, hard-faced. A successful merchant, who specialised in trade with Britannia and Rome, buying tribal jewellery from the land beyond the imperial frontier and selling on to Roman gentlemen at enormous mark-ups, he had been accompanied to the chamber by a pair of bodyguards, but the militiamen guarding the room had turned them away with blank faces, admitting only their master.

'You believe there is a spy in the city and you have been entrusted by Kivilaz with the job of finding him.'

'Indeed I do, and yes, I have been entrusted with the critical task of uncovering this treachery.'

Having responded, Draco waited in silence, staring unblinkingly at him. When the pause had stretched beyond the point of discomfort it was the other man who broke it.

'And you seriously believe that this spy could be *me*, of all people?'

The older man shrugged.

'It's possible. Why else would I have asked you to come here and discuss the matter?'

'But that's *ludicrous*! I realise that you have to be thorough, Draco, but I have two sons with the cohorts! Why in Hercules's name would I betray them to the enemy?'

Draco shook his head.

'They weren't serving with the cohorts when whoever it was that betrayed our battle plans to the Romans inflicted the grievous loss of half their strength in a single night on the tribe, were they? They were too young to be serving, and they only joined the army after that disaster, when we were forced to ask for volunteers from those too old and too young to serve in the usual course of matters. So at the time that whoever it was sold our plans to the enemy, the defence you've raised simply wasn't the case. And we don't worship Hercules now that we're free of Rome's control, we serve Magusanus.'

He stared at the trader for a moment.

'Whoever it was that betrayed the tribe is likely to have a strong interest in Roman victory over us. An interest in the renewal of the status quo. An interest in the resumption of trading between the Batavi and Rome, and with the Britons for that matter. As do you. And whoever it was that betrayed the tribe would appear to have lost a slave. We know that because our spies in their camp reported that the message warning Legatus Vocula, telling him that they were about to be attacked unexpectedly and out of the night, was delivered by a man who appeared to be a freed slave.'

The other man stared back at him in bemusement.

'How could they know *that*?'

'Deduction. For a start he was dressed like a slave, a simple tunic, rough boots and a cloak that had seen many better days. And for another thing, his purse was heavy, holding enough coin to enable him to start a new life, perhaps, as the reward for his delivering the traitor's message to his Roman friends. It looks to me as if the traitor in question decided to take the loss of a valuable asset in order to get a warning to the Romans that they were about to be attacked, as the price of saving them from almost certain defeat. And was therefore someone clearly not short of money.'

The merchant shook his head in bafflement.

'The way I've heard it, our men lost because they were attacked unexpectedly as a result of the very worst luck possible.'

Draco nodded.

'True. But if the legions had not been warned they would have been cooped up in their camp when our men attacked. It would have been a fight that ended before it really began. Instead of which they had time to come out and form a line, and had sufficient warning to put up enough of a fight that the most appalling mischance had the time to come to pass. Tell me, you've lost a slave recently, haven't you?'

'Yes, but he simply vanished one night! I have no idea—'

'Thank you. I just wanted to confirm the facts. You have indeed lost a slave in the last few weeks. As have you . . .' he switched the focus of his attention to the other man, an ex-magistrate who had stared at him with barely disguised disgust all the while he had been questioning the merchant. 'Have you lost a man recently as well?'

The ex-official stared back at him with evident anger.

'You have the nerve to accuse me, a magistrate of the tribe—'

'Ex-magistrate.'

'What?'

'You *were* a magistrate. An official whose primary duty was not to the tribe, in reality, but to Rome. You were voted into your position by the men of the Batavi, sure enough, but you owed your loyalty to the empire, not to us.'

The other man shook his head in angry bafflement.

'You know as well as I do, Draco, that I am a faithful servant of the Julian families. The same families with whom you have made common cause in your service of Prince Kivilaz. As magistrate I did the bidding of the oldest and most influ—'

'Prefect.'

'What?'

'My rank, both former and current, is that of *prefect.* I have been asked to fulfil the role of safeguarding Batavodurum both from open attack by some renegade like Claudius Labeo and his fellow scum *and* from subversion from within. Which is what I'm investigating at the moment. And so I will repeat my question. Have you *lost* a man recently?'

The other man stared back in sullen silence for a moment before answering.

'No. None of my men has gone missing.'

'Thank you. And that wasn't so hard, was it? Just a statement of the facts. To which I could add that your friend here's man went missing around the time of the defeat at Gelduba, which is the reason for this investigation. Didn't he?'

He turned back to the merchant, who held his hands wide in mystification.

'Yes. Although how you would be aware of such a small matter is beyond me. *Prefect.*'

The two men stared at each other in silence for a moment in a battle of wills.

'These things tend to be noticed. Especially when they're not reported at the time they happen.'

The merchant bridled.

'What about you, Prefect? Hasn't a slave left your household recently?'

Draco smiled at the challenge with such apparent good humour that the ex-magistrate's face creased into an involuntary frown.

'Why yes, now you mention it, that's completely true. I did free one of my men before Yule, and what's more I gave him a purse with which to buy the woman he loves from her mistress. The last that we heard of them they were crossing the river to go back to the tribe from which his father was enslaved as a boy. At least a dozen of his comrades will vouch for that, whereas nobody seems to know where the man you lost went. So now that you've tried to paint me with the same tar that's plastered all over the pair of you, we'll continue. Do neither of you have anything to say?'

The trader was the first to answer, spitting out the words.

'I have nothing more to say to you, Draco. This is a transparent attempt to make me look like the guilty party in a matter of which I have no knowledge!'

The veteran prefect shrugged dispassionately.

'The tribe must have justice for the men you betrayed.'

'The men I betrayed? I haven't betrayed . . .'

His protests died away as Draco raised an item for him to look at, a wooden writing tablet, a presentiment of doom furrowing his brow.

'Why are you showing me one of my writing tablets?'

Draco stared at him questioningly.

'So you agree that this is yours?'

'One of mine, of course. My name is engraved on the outside, and those hinges are silver. I'd know it anywhere.'

He stared in bemusement as the veteran opened the case to reveal that the shallow wooden boxes that usually held the wax were empty.

'It's an old trick. The message is written on the tablet's frame and then covered in wax on which an innocuous message is scribed. When I found this the wax had already been removed.' He raised the tablet and read aloud. *'To the legatus augusti commanding Roman forces at Gelduba. The army of the Batavi tribe is approaching your camp and will attack without warning before dawn. The army is composed of eight cohorts of part-mounted infantry and one cohort of guard cavalry. In providing you with this warning I have discharged my debt to Rome in full.'*

He looked at the other man while the magistrate stared at his fellow accused in horror.

'Your debt to Rome, eh?'

'But that isn't mine!'

Draco raised an amused eyebrow.

'And yet a moment ago it was. How very strange.'

'It's a fake, planted to make me appear guilty!'

'I see. Well whoever planted it must have been *very* keen to make you seem guilty because I found it in the wreckage of the Roman camp when I rode south with the cohorts the *second* time they attacked Gelduba, with a witness of impeccable honour to vouch for the discovery. Before they put the Roman encampment to the torch I had a good root through the buildings, sifting through what remained after they had left the camp to march north and relieve the siege of the Old Camp. And I found this discarded in their headquarters. The Romans may well have considered your debt paid, but it doesn't seem as if they had very much concern for your safety, does it?'

'But I didn't—'

'Write this? I think you did. Take a closer look.'

He held out the tablet for the merchant to see.

'I have compared it with your writing from official tax documentation. The same hand clearly wrote both, the similarities are striking even if you have tried to disguise your style. No, I'm afraid it's somewhat too obvious even to a simple soldier for me to come to any other conclusion than that you've been playing a quiet and clever game all these years. What was the debt that you were repaying to our would-be masters, I wonder? Some kind of blackmail? Did they know things about you that you'd rather not be known among the men of the tribe? Perhaps someone with close links to Rome recruited you to their cause in just such a way . . .' He turned to look at the magistrate. 'Someone in a position of power, with the ability and the resources to pry open matters you might prefer to have left closed?'

The former official jabbed a finger at him, his face white with fear and anger.

'I have no knowledge of any of this, Draco! My duty was always to the tribe first and to Rome second, and for as long as I served I always kept it that way! You can ask Prince Kivilaz, he'll tell you—'

'The prince and I have discussed your doings at length, and reluctantly come to the conclusion that while you *seemed* to recognise that your duty was to the Batavi, there were several occasions on which it also seemed that you were in fact a dutiful servant of Rome. Cases that went against Batavi claimants, in the interests of justice being served, of course. Compensation for damage caused by the Roman military, which were a fraction of the actual costs. You revealed your true sympathies in a host of ways, now that we understand better, thanks to this.'

He raised the tablet again, but the former official's vehement denials cut him off before he could speak again.

'But those decisions were always agreed with Kivilaz's father! Damages claimed by Claudian families, those most recently granted citizenship, were always played down, at his order, in favour of the ruling Julian families! And as to the legal cases . . .' his brow furrowed as his thought process caught up with Draco's words. 'What? Thanks to . . . what?'

'This tablet. I didn't quite finish reading the inscription made by your fellow conspirator here.'

'I am not his conspir—'

The merchant grunted as one of Draco's men sank a fist into his fleshy gut at the prefect's signal, doubling over and whooping for air to replace that driven out of him by the blow.

'The time for you to protest is done with, I'm afraid. You stand condemned by your own hand, and the only question now is not whether you're guilty or not, but how to most appropriately punish that guilt. Now, where was I? Ah yes, the tablet.' He reopened the wooden case and resumed reading from the point where he had stopped. *'I have discharged my debt to Rome in full. Your man in Batavodurum assures me that he will continue to report via the usual route by means of his frequent visits to the capital of the Tungri.* You have visited the Tungrian city of Atuataca several times in the last year, Magistrate, have you not?'

'Yes. But it is well known that I have a daughter married into the Tungri tribe, wife to a former member of the emperor's bodyguard. She has children, and my wife and I—'

'Use them as a pretext to visit the city, and there to pass on intelligence as to the state of the Batavi now that war has come, and before that doubtless our readiness to fight, our sentiment towards Rome and a dozen other different subjects pertaining to the potential for war to break out. Don't bother to lie to me, the last time you journeyed to the city you were followed from your daughter's husband's house to the office of the governor, where you spent the morning deep in conversation, it seems.'

The former magistrate looked at him aghast, then nodded slowly.

'Very well. I was indeed asked to provide Rome with some assessment of our readiness for war, and to be a quiet go-between in the event that the tribe openly opposed the empire, a channel of communication for a time when rationality might otherwise be completely absent. But I never, *never* stooped to spying for the empire! And as for this fool being some sort of co-conspirator?' He waved a hand at the hapless merchant. 'Don't you find the idea ludicrous? He would be no more likely to spy for Rome than to give his fortune away on the street! The man's totally self-interested, with no regard to anyone else!'

Draco nodded slowly.

'I see what you're trying to say. You, a simple man of letters and the law, are selflessly willing to risk censure in the noble interests of peace. And your co-conspirator here, as you just termed him, with the perfect mask of greed and venality, is far too bound up in making a profit to care about such matters.'

The merchant nodded eagerly at the description, but his face fell as Draco stared at them both with a quizzical expression.

'Indeed, it's the perfect cover. As the less likely of the two of you he can afford to be the more daring, and was willing to gamble his life on Rome's behalf, whereas you are the more subtle, playing the long game for your Roman masters. I salute you both, gentlemen, your performances were almost perfect. Almost. If not for this tablet we would never have known how deeply committed to Roman rule you both were. All that remains now, I suppose, is to decide upon the date and manner of your punishment.'

Both men stared at him in horror.

'You can't . . .'

Draco shook his head at the terrified merchant.

'I can, it seems. And I must, I'm afraid. Were I to show you leniency then when it got out that you were in league, conspiring against the tribe with the Romans, almost as great an outcry would be levelled at myself for sparing you as at you for your crimes. Face the facts, gentlemen, you both know that you have to die.'

'But that tablet is a fake!'

Draco shrugged.

'It's possible that the Romans planted it in the wreckage of Gelduba, hoping to implicate an innocent and take the heat off someone else, but I doubt they're that clever. And besides, what were the odds it would come to light? It's too subtle for them, and the handwriting alone is enough evidence to see you both dead. You're guilty. Accept that.' He paused, and watched the last vestige of hope leave the merchant's face. 'Good. And perhaps not all is lost. I'm empowered by Kivilaz himself to offer you a quiet death, one that won't drag your respective families into the matter and leave them publicly living with your shame for the rest of their lives. You will simply disappear, and nobody will be any the wiser. Your sons will continue to serve with the cohorts as if nothing had ever happened.' His gaze slid from the merchant to the magistrate. 'Your daughter will never know that her father betrayed his people for an ideal. Or we can do it the other way, if you both wish to continue denying the facts of your treason? A trial, public exposition of the evidence, shame and vilification of your loved ones – is that what you'd choose as an epitaph?'

Both men shook their heads. 'I thought not. Which is why I have statements ready for you to approve as being truthful and accurate. The work of moments, after which you can compose yourselves and then go to meet your ancestors cleanly, without blood or even very much pain. I trust you'll both agree with me that this is by far the better approach to this difficult matter?'

3

Near Novaesium, Germania Inferior, January AD 70

'I'm afraid I don't quite understand what it is that you're trying to tell me, Prefect Montanus. You'll have to spell it out a little more clearly.'

The Nervian officer stared at Vocula for a moment before replying, a look of slight exasperation creeping onto his face as he considered just how much more he could clarify a message that from his perspective was already perfectly clear. He had been escorted into the legatus's campaign tent by several of Antonius's men, chosen by the first spear for their size and brooding demeanour, and was evidently feeling the pressure of their close scrutiny.

'Well, Legatus . . .'

'Yes?'

'The cohorts provided to your army by the people of Gaul have decided that it is no longer in our interest—'

'To continue to serve Rome. Yes. You've made that quite evident.' Vocula leaned forward in his chair and turned his head slightly, as if he were afflicted with a hearing difficulty, a slight smile creasing his face, and Antonius realised with a start that despite the massive risk that the Gallic cohorts' defection from the army presented to his life, his legatus was actually enjoying the situation in his own way. 'Perhaps it was *I* that failed to make myself clear. My problem, Prefect, isn't with your very sparsely worded message, it is with the meaning behind it.' He held up a hand to forestall Montanus from replying. 'And no, I can't see any value in your simply repeating it yet again. Instead, allow me to help you by speculating as to what it might be that you're trying to tell me on behalf of your superiors.'

He sat back in the chair with a thoughtful expression, shooting his first spear an amused glance.

'Perhaps, Prefect, what your message means is that the men who aspire to rule Gaul have decided that Rome is a spent force north of the Alps? After all, we have two legions besieged in the Old Camp by the Batavians, and these two legions I intend – *intended* marching north to rescue them, before this unexpected decision, are evidently barely fit for purpose in terms of both their physical strength and their resolve. Am I right?' Montanus nodded fractionally, unsure as to what game the Roman was playing with him. 'Of course I am. And your leaders can see that, they're no fools. The temple of Jupiter in Rome has been burned to the ground in the fighting to control the capital, they tell each other, and Roman power is crumbling as Jove himself turns his back on eight hundred years of majestic progress.'

He smiled at the Nervian, who was clearly becoming unnerved by his apparent bonhomie in the face of disaster.

'Have no fear, Prefect, I'm not the vindictive type. But indulge me a little longer, if you will? You see, I'm still baffled at such an unexpected turn of events.' Antonius fought to keep a smile from his face at the Nervian officer's evident discomfort, as Vocula continued in his conversational interrogation. 'Yes, we've heard rumours, of course, of Gallic unrest at the threat from your neighbours to the north and east, fuelled by the way you were forced to defend yourselves from the depredations of Julius Civilis's German allies when they crossed the Rhenus to invade your lands. We're also very well aware of your collective dealings with Julius Civilis, or Kivilaz as you doubtless call him, and that you Gauls feel forced to offer him an alliance in order to protect yourselves from the threat of a dozen German tribes surging south at his back once the Old Camp falls. But still, what on earth could possibly persuade you to such a foolish . . .' He fell silent for a moment, apparently pondering some new thought, then barked out a brief laugh. 'I have it! I know what it is that's brought about this betrayal of your treaties with Rome! You think . . .' He mastered another guffaw with evident difficulty, shaking his head and theatrically wiping away an imaginary tear. 'You think that with Rome on her back, and no longer able to maintain order in Gaul and Germania, you have the chance to establish an empire of your own! A *Gallic* empire!'

Shaking his head in amusement, he waved a dismissive hand.

'An empire of the Gauls, Prefect? Is that the intention behind this treachery?' His face hardened abruptly. 'Have you people taken leave of your *senses*? Rome's empire was built on her irresistible urge to rule, a destiny willed to the people of Rome by the gods themselves which has enabled us to subjugate everyone and everything to the city's will. I would tell you of the omens that foretold the city's rise to empire, if only I thought you had the education to understand them.'

He sighed, shaking his head sadly.

'You've no more chance of building an empire out of your patchwork of tribes than I have of persuading my legions to grow a collective pair of balls and start acting like soldiers! Your people have grown soft after a hundred years of our influence, become used to being protected by our legions on the Rhenus. Your cohorts are fit for little more than turning tail at the first sign of a real army, you've proven that by never once standing up to the Batavians! So what are you going to do when a dozen legions cross the mountains and come for your heads? What will you do when the Twenty-first Rapax is facing you across a field with every intention of painting themselves red with your blood in their time-honoured manner? Yes, you can probably suborn my legions, but tell me truthfully, can you really see them resisting the battle-hardened men that Vespasianus is going to send at you? They'll melt away like butter in sunshine, Prefect, and you'll be forced to rely on your own men. Your own worthless cohorts, incapable of any manoeuvre other than running away in the face of a determined enemy. You fools.'

He fell silent for a moment, staring up at the tent's ceiling and shaking his head.

'Very well. The die is very clearly and irrevocably cast. Your cohorts have separated from my army and declared yourselves no longer under my command. But you can still spare yourselves the horrific indignities that will be visited upon you all, if you limit your rebellion to that extent. Allow my legions to withdraw to Novaesium unhindered, and Vespasianus may see the sense in retaining your forces when this has all been set to rights, rather than having you all summarily executed as felons in the worst possible manner.' He waved a hand in dismissal. 'Take that message back to your masters, Prefect. To rebel is one thing, forgivable under certain circumstances as a short-term expedient intended only to protect your people from the real threat from the Batavians. But to raise a hand against Rome? You'll pay for that pleasure in blood. It is your choice. I suggest you choose wisely.'

He gestured to Antonius, who escorted the nonplussed Montanus from the tent and returned to find the legatus deep in thought.

'So, Legatus . . .'

'What now? We need to get away from those Gauls, Antonius, as far away as possible. While they're camped within bow shot of our own men, what's left of the legions is at severe risk of being tempted to mutiny again. We'll march them back to Novaesium and see if we can avoid another uprising, once news of this defection gets around.'

'We can march at dawn tomorrow, Legatus. But I very much doubt that doing so will decrease the potential for further disloyalty. The Gauls have been free to come and go within the camp for weeks now, so if our own men plan to betray the empire alongside them then the deed is probably already planned.'

Vocula nodded.

'I know. But as long as I have command over these two legions I must do everything I can to keep them from defecting to this so-called "Gallic empire".'

'Legatus . . .' Antonius struggled for the right words momentarily before abandoning any attempt to speak diplomatically. 'I appreciate that men of your class are raised to consider the risk of death in the service of Rome as . . .'

Vocula nodded briskly.

'No more than the purest expression of our duty to city and empire? True enough, First Spear.'

'But surely you can see that this latest betrayal is certain to encourage the legions to mutiny again? And we won't get away with trying to spirit you out of the camp again, not once their blood's boiling. You should leave now, find a pretext for my cohort to march away from here, a scouting mission to the north even, and the Gauls will let you leave happily enough if it eases their takeover of the First and Sixteenth and removes the problem of having a legatus's blood on their hands. They'll be forced to kill you, if you stay, if the legions don't do it for them first.'

Vocula shook his head.

'I can't. My duty is to Rome, and Rome needs these legions to stay loyal.'

'And if they kill you for doing your duty?'

'As you said a moment ago, the risk of dying in the service of the empire is simply what's expected of my class. Running from that duty would require me to die a thousand deaths of shame, First Spear, whereas my actual death, if it is required of me, can only happen once, and will reflect great honour onto my family.'

Antonius nodded slowly.

'You're set on this?'

'I am. But I'm also set upon one other thing, and that's for you and your men not to be caught up in whatever it is that's going to happen to me, now that the Gauls have decided to join the Germans in their revolt. Yes, we'll march back to Novaesium tomorrow morning, but when we get there you're going to leave the army and take your cohort with you. You can provide me with security one last time, while I tell these bastards what I think of them, and then you're going to preserve the lives of five hundred good men by doing as you're ordered.'

Batavodurum, January AD 70

'The Council recognises Kivilaz, honoured prince of the tribe and former prefect of the cohorts, war leader of the Batavi people.'

The prince walked slowly out in front of the gathered elders of the tribe, his face set in solemn lines and the man himself apparently bowed under the weight of his responsibilities. Standing before the semi-circle of their chairs he looked slowly around the council's members, meeting each man's gaze in turn.

'Honoured elders of the tribe, I bring news from the south, and I seek guidance with regard to a matter of the Batavi people's honour.'

Draco leaned forward in his chair, fixing him with a stare which, given his newly reinforced reputation for ruthlessness, would have cowed most men, but the one-eyed war leader met his scrutiny with evident confidence.

'This is to do with the siege of the Old Camp, I presume?'

Kivilaz inclined his head in recognition of the point.

'In part, Father of the Tribe. And partly to relate news to the council with regard to the situation elsewhere.'

The elder leaned back in his chair.

'Tell us your news first, Kivilaz. This is to do with your latest meeting with the Nervian prince Julius Classicus?'

'Yes. I have recently met with the leaders of the Gauls, and I am now convinced that what we have suspected ever since the defeat of Vitellius is finally coming to pass. A Gallic empire will be declared within days, and the Roman legions under the command of Dillius Vocula will switch their loyalty to that of the Gauls rather than Rome. The Gallic auxiliary cohorts have already separated their camp from that of Vocula's legions and declared that they will no longer fight for Rome. Their messengers have the freedom to roam the legion camp at will, and the men who follow both eagles have proven easy prey for their promises of the gold that they expected Vitellius to donate to them, had he survived as emperor.'

Draco shook his head in a mixture of amusement and disdain.

'Scum. If their loyalty is that easily bought the Gauls would be better off putting them to the sword. And a "Gallic empire"? I'd laugh if I didn't feel such disgust. The Gauls? The people whose war bands roamed freely on both sides of the mountains for hundreds of years, and whose ancestors once sacked Rome? The tribes that used to terrify the Romans now wish to emulate them, and establish an *empire,* seduced by wine and baths? What will they defend this empire with, I wonder? Their soldiers have run from us at the first sign of iron being aired in every battle we've fought against their masters in this war, and now they hope to hold off an enraged Rome with two pitifully under-strength legions whose ranks are filled with the disaffected and incapable? What will they do when the legions come over those mountains with the scent of blood in their nostrils, I wonder?'

The prince smiled.

'I'm forced to agree, but not only could I not have dissuaded them from their insanity, it's undeniable that their revolt moves Rome's frontier north of the mountains to the feet of the mountains themselves. And it also strips them of their last legions, other than those few men clinging on to the Winter Camp. And even they must surrender when the whole of Gaul rises against them. Rome might well decide to write off Gaul and Germania.'

Draco nodded.

'I see your argument, and there is potential for such a decision to leave us all well alone, at least for a while until the empire regains its strength, but any emperor who started his reign by meekly accepting the loss of so many provinces could expect to be dead inside the year. And Vespasianus, as you well know, is no man's fool. He will attack with every man he can spare, and any such Gallic *empire* will melt away like spring snow when the full heat of Rome's wrath is turned upon it!'

He stared at Kivilaz for a moment, his expression thoughtful.

'And now, more to the point, what of the Old Camp? Are the Romans ready to surrender? No other news will find a welcome here.' Kivilaz bowed his head in recognition of the sentiment, and the watching wolf-priest standing at his back alongside Hramn, studied Draco's face surreptitiously as the elder spoke again. 'The Batavi and our allies have suffered enough loss at the hands of these men. Enough men have been killed, enough men wounded, enough men maimed and dishonoured by this man our allies have taken to calling the *Banô,* who takes men in the darkness and kills or disfigures them for his own amusement. So tell us, Kivilaz, what is this guidance you seek?'

'It is our estimation, honoured elders, that the Romans can have little more than a week's supply of food remaining, two at the most. We know to the last sack of grain what they had in store when the siege started, and we can estimate the amount of food they managed to ship in during the short time that Vocula managed to lift the siege. They must be within days of starvation.'

Draco shrugged.

'So they will either surrender or die. Either eventuality will be greeted with the greatest of pleasure by the members of this council, Prince Kivilaz. We stand at your backs with a grim resolve that is the match of your own, and that of our sons and brothers of the tribe's cohorts, and *nothing* other than Rome's abject surrender will satisfy us.'

'Quite so, Father of the Tribe. There remains one question to be answered, however, a matter of the greatest possible importance to our allies from across the great river.'

The elder tipped his head to one side, his eyes narrowing in question.

'What question? What possible relevance can the men of the . . .' He stopped speaking, then slowly nodded his understanding as the meaning of the prince's words dawned on him. 'Ah. I see. The Roman legions that surrender to the Gauls at Novaesium will be sworn to the service of their "empire" and their lives spared.'

'Exactly. But where the legions at Novaesium will surrender tamely, without having killed a single one of our allies' men, the legionaries in the Old Camp have resisted us for six months, and their defence has claimed the lives of thousands of men of a dozen tribes. Our allies are . . .' he weighed the word for a moment, '*obdurate* in their insistence that their warriors be allowed to take their full revenge on whatever is left of the garrison when they surrender.'

Draco nodded with a hard smile.

'Obdurate? I'm sure they are!'

Alcaeus kept his face carefully composed but his memory of the gathering of tribal war leaders two days before was still fresh in his mind. Led by the Batavi ally Brinno, King of the Cananefates, princes and kings of a dozen tribes from both sides of the great river had united to demand the lives of any captives as their natural right.

'It is *our* lives that have been spent to take this fortress, Kivilaz of the Batavi, *our* men who have fought, and bled, and died in such numbers that no village in all *our* lands has been spared the wail and sob of mourning.'

Kivilaz had looked across the table at Brinno, his voice less strident than his ally's but no less firm.

'The Batavi have hardly been spared in that respect. Close on half of our cohorts will never march home to their families again.'

Brinno had shrugged.

'Every man you lost has been avenged, if I am to believe the stories your man tells of the battle at Gelduba. Rome's legions were grievously bled in that battle, and only saved from destruction by the purest of good fortune. Whereas our men, as well you know, have seen little blood in return for their suffering under the lash of the Romans' arrow machines, and their cowardly use of falling stone and boiling water to defend their walls. But now they are running out of food, and the day of their reckoning is upon them. *Our* reckoning, not yours! There can be no quiet ending to this matter, not after they have so grievously insulted us with their cowards' way of making war. We will not be gainsaid in this matter, not unless the Batavi wish to kindle the flames of hatred under the foundations of our alliance.'

Kivilaz looked around the council chamber, his face hard with certainty.

'The tribal leaders will not be denied their revenge. And they will take that revenge whether we seek to prevent them from doing so or not. Too much water has passed under that bridge, Father of the Tribe, for any thought of allowing the Romans to surrender to be realistic.'

Draco nodded, looking to the men on either side as he replied. 'I – *we* understand, Prince Kivilaz. So tell me, what is it that you propose?'

Novaesium, Germania Inferior, January AD 70

'Soldiers of the imperial First Legion Germanica and the imperial Sixteenth Legion Gallica! I am going to speak to you today on a matter of the greatest importance to the empire, and therefore to yourselves!'

Vocula stared bleakly out across the ranks of legionaries paraded before him, seeing in their faces the disinterest and hostility he had been warned to expect by Antonius. His trusted first spear had spent most of the previous day taking quiet soundings of his two remaining legions, and little of what he had related to the legatus the evening before had held any encouragement for the Roman. Taking a mouthful of the wine that Vocula had poured for him, he had shaken his head in bemusement as he'd told the other man what he had discerned in the course of his discussions with his peers.

'I'm afraid it's this far and no more, Legatus. Both legions are pretty much united in the matter. The soldiers are refusing to march any further and at least half of their officers are in full agreement with them. They're tired, demoralised and utterly susceptible to persuasion that the time for them to give unquestioning service to Rome is at its end. And, as you suspected, messengers are moving between the Gallic cohorts and our own men with complete freedom, with a purpose that's not hard to work out. Both the First and the Sixteenth's first spears are at their wits' end, and neither of them seems to have any answer to the question as to how they might get their men to march north again. I told them that they've lost control of their legions and neither of them could deny the accusation. They're passengers, Legatus, and they're taking the path of least resistance to avoid having their men turn on them like the masterless dogs they are.'

The legatus had nodded slowly.

'And we know what's going to happen next. Mutiny, encouraged by that treacherous animal Classicus. I will either be murdered or imprisoned, more likely the former than the latter if I'm any judge of a situation. The legions will go over to the Gallic cause and our shame will almost be complete. All that'll be left is for those poor bastards in the Old Camp to realise that there's no relief force to rescue them, and that they have the simple choice between surrender and starvation. But I won't live to see that sorry day. Which means that I have nothing to lose from telling that leaderless rabble exactly what I think of them.'

He played a disgusted glare across the two legions' ranks, allowing the silence to stretch out, then barked out a derisive laugh.

'Not that many of you men care about the fate of the empire, do you? Like those Gallic dogs who have followed us south, sending their spies into my army's camp to suborn you to their rebellious cause, you believe that Rome's empire is at an end!' He paused again, looking across the ranks of men. 'You *fools*! There is enough military strength marching north from Italy to crush their "Gallic empire" into the dust of next summer like an overripe plum stamped on by a hobnailed boot! *You* see Batavians to the north, Germans to the east and Gauls to the west and the south, and you believe that neither Gaul nor Germania will ever again be ruled from Rome! I see the same enemies as you, but all I can see are armies of dead men waiting for their time to enter the Underworld. Fresh legions will march over the Alps very shortly, and they will crush the Gauls, and anyone foolish enough to align with them! They will bury the Batavians in the mud of their Island and chase the German tribes back across the Rhenus, then choose the time and place at which to exact Rome's revenge on them in their turn! But that revenge *will* be taken, you can be sure of that, whether a year or decades from now. And it will most assuredly be taken upon you too, if you're foolish enough to succumb to the blandishments of men who wish to establish their own piss-pot of an *empire*!'

He fell silent again, waiting for any man to challenge his assertion, but both legions stood in perfect silence.

'I also understand that not only does our military position appear to be precarious, but that many of you are dissatisfied politically as well, if self-interest and concern for the contents of your purses can be dignified with the description of "politics"! You thought you'd chosen an emperor in Vitellius who would consider your interests as his first priority!' Antonius smiled grimly at the legatus's euphemistic turn of phrase in describing the soldiers' greed in placing their general on the throne. 'But now your emperor is Vespasianus, and not the man you wanted! You see the likelihood of you all becoming "rich soldiers" as small, as you believe he will look to reward his loyal legions first! And you're *right*! A year-long civil war will have left the imperial treasury bare, without the gold required to pay donatives, so you'll have to be content with your lot! But that's not what the Gauls are telling you, is it?'

He shook his head angrily.

'I *know* what their spies and agitators are telling you! "Join us, and we will rule the land north of the Alps together! Join us, and share the riches of a new empire! Join us, and kill your officers!"' Antonius smiled again at the looks of horror on the other legates' faces, as they realised their predicament. '"Join us and rule everything north of the mountains!"' Vocula's voice softened from its previously hectoring tone. 'And you fools are going to do it, aren't you? You're going to rise up and murder your commanders, in the name of a Gallic empire that will be crumbling even as you help the Gauls to found it! I give it six months, no more, and you'll all be facing the dissolution of your legions and being sentenced to spend the rest of your pitiful lives as unpaid labour in some dark corner of the empire, those of you that aren't immediately executed for treason!' He grinned at them, openly contemptuous. 'Who knows? Perhaps the commanding general will have you all crucified, as an example to others, one every fifty paces along the course of the Rhenus! I would!'

The soldiers stared back at him in amazement, and he raised his voice to bark defiantly at them.

'Yes! I'd have you all executed now, if I could! I despise you all! You were Roman soldiers at one time, but all you are now is honourless traitors getting ready to turn intention into deed and put a knife into the empire's back! I see you all staring back at me with murder in your hearts, and do you know, I couldn't care less! Kill me or spare me, it no longer matters! I'm sick to my stomach at the sight of you! Indeed I'm more troubled by your singular lack of courage than I am with the prospect of my own death! I was raised on stories of Roman bravery and steadfastness, legions fighting to the last man, if the need arose, rather than abandon their position, men who defied the odds and the enemy, even at the cost of their lives! And now what do we have? *You!* Weak-hearted cowards, ready to march behind Germans or Gauls, against Rome itself if so ordered! Not that you'll ever get anywhere near Rome! Will you take orders from a Batavian? Will you mount guard duty for the Nervians? Of *course* you will! You have fortresses close at hand to fight from, plentiful grain to eat, and enough men to hold Novaesium's walls until the relieving force arrives, but instead you cowards intend to abandon five hundred years of proud tradition, and spit on Rome for having "let you down", don't you? Well I'm done with you all! This is my last speech to you as your legatus augusti, so if you have the courage to fight on then choose some other leader who will offend you less! Do what you think right! And if you're set upon my death, I'll be in my tent . . .' he paused and looked across the ranks with silent contempt, '*if* any man here has the courage to face me with a sword in his hand, knowing that the revenge Rome will surely exact for my murder will be slow, painful and humiliating! You *fools*!'

He turned and walked away, the legions behind him erupting

into a hubbub of voices raised against his words as he offered Antonius his hand.

'Go now, while they're working out what to do. They won't try to stop you, not with a full cohort behind you. March south and join the relieving legions, head for Vindonissa and meet up with the Twenty-first Rapax, they'll see you right. And take these with you . . .'

He unbuckled his belt, handing his sword and dagger to the dismayed first spear.

'I'd be grateful if you could deliver them to my wife, Helvia Procula. They're an heirloom, handed down from the days of my grandfather, so I'd die happier knowing they'll serve the next generation of my family.'

The centurion looked at him imploringly.

'I'll ask you one last time. Come with us, Legatus. You're too good a man to sacrifice yourself—'

'To sacrifice myself for Rome?'

'Yes.' Antonius's tone was suddenly emphatic. '*Yes*. You've given this command everything you have, you've been undermined and frustrated by Rome and this damned civil war, and you can leave these . . . *cunts* to stew in their own juice with a clear conscience. Surely that has to be better than allowing them to murder you, alone and unregarded?'

Vocula stared back at him for a moment before replying, and when he spoke his tone was soft.

'Except I won't die alone, First Spear. The eyes of Rome will be upon me, and my example will spur Rome's legions to vengeance on this scum. I know my people.'

'Perhaps you do, Legatus. And I know Rome too, perhaps better than I'd like, after the events of the last few months, and I consider your example to be wasted on your people. But I'll assure you of one thing, Gaius Dillius Vocula,' he leaned close to the Roman, lowering his voice to make his words private between the two of them, 'if any of these men takes a blade to you, as you seem to expect, their name won't stay secret for long. And that man will need to bury himself very, very deeply if he wants to escape my vengeance.' He raised the weapons the legatus had entrusted to his safekeeping. 'And when I find him it'll be your iron that takes his life, I promise you that.'

He stepped back and saluted crisply, nodded respectfully at the man he had come to consider a friend, then turned and walked away without looking back.

A mile down the road to the south Antonius stepped off the cobbled surface and shouted the order for his cohort's short column to halt, waving for his deputy to join him at its head and looked back at the distant turf walls while he waited for the centurion to reach him. Their exit from the camp had been peaceful enough, the naked threat of their uncovered spearheads enough to reduce any potential hostility to a few barbed taunts flung by men who had been careful to remain anonymous in the watching crowd, but the fact that they were in effect running for their lives had nagged at him with every step of the march.

'You *just* can't walk away, can you?'

The grim-faced first spear shook his head.

'No. I can't. I know he's told me to leave him to it, and that he's happy to die here, but . . .'

'You like him too much. So we're going back for him?'

'No. *We're* not going back. *I'm* going back.'

The other man stared at him, realisation dawning as Antonius pulled off his helmet and handed it to his chosen man.

'No. You can't . . .'

His superior's mirthless smile cut off his comrade's protest.

'Can't I? Who's going to stop me? Not you, not if you know right from wrong. Here, give me your helmet, Chosen.'

His men goggled at him as he settled the other man's helmet on his head, handing over his own heavily decorated headgear.

'But they'll kill you alongside him!'

Antonius laughed.

'What? That lot back there? Did you see anyone standing guard on the gate as we marched out?' He turned back to the chosen man, reaching out a hand to take his brass-bound staff. 'Give me your *hastile* and swap cloaks with me. You can hold my vine stick while I'm gone.'

'And if you don't come back do I get to keep it?'

The other centurion turned and looked him incredulously.

'He's about to walk back into a camp full of men who are more than ready to tear him to pieces, and you're doing the "can I have your spare boots if you die" joke?'

Antonius shrugged, pulling the borrowed cloak over his shoulders and fastening it with the brooch the chosen man passed him, then took the heavy brass-bound staff that was his chosen man's badge of office and weapon of choice when it came to imposing discipline on his men.

'It'll make no odds to me, will it? Right, can you see my *squamata*?'

His fellow centurion looked him up and down, looking for any sign of his distinctive armour under the cloak.

'No, there's not a single scale to be seen, but—'

'Good. So with a bit of luck they won't realise who I am. Stay here, but don't hang around if I don't come back.'

He turned and strode back towards the legions' camp, his men staring in disbelief at the sight of their first spear in a subordinate's uniform.

'How long do we need to wait for you?'

Antonius called the answer back over his shoulder without stopping, his eyes fixed on the distant earth walls.

'That's your decision! Your first duty now is to the cohort!'

Covering the distance back to the camp's walls at a swift pace, he prepared a story with which to talk himself past any gate guards, but, as had been the case when they marched out, no sentry was to be seen. A growling rumble of voices drew him towards the centre of the camp's rectangular layout, the ground around the legatus's headquarters tent now thronged with men who were evidently arguing amongst themselves. Elbowing his way through the scrum of men, some in full armour while others wore only their boots, tunics and belts, he ignored curses and complaints as the men he had shouldered aside took in his crested helmet and the fixed scowl of features rendered brutally anonymous by the helmet's closely fitting cheek pieces, and decided that, on the whole, it would probably be best to let a pissed-off chosen man go on his way than risk a swift and brutal beating. Reaching the front of the crowd gathered around the tent he glanced keenly to either side, waiting to see who was in effective command of the mob.

'I say we do him now!'

A wiry-looking legionary raised his dagger and pointed it at the tent's closed flap, but not only did he not take a step forward but neither did any of the men he was exhorting to murder their legatus augusti. Another man extended his arm in a theatrical gesture.

'You go right ahead then, if you want to be the man who killed an army commander. I'm a bit too fond of my life to risk ending it nailed up as an example to others!'

Antonius looked around himself, seeing men whose resolve was wavering in the face of the enormity of what they were considering.

'We killed Fatty Flaccus!'

A man standing close to him raised the challenge, and the centurion realised that Vocula would be hearing every word inside his tent, readying himself to die with the dignity expected of him.

'Yeah, but that was different, wasn't it? Flaccus was a traitor to Vitellius, but Vocula's been straight up and down with us. And whoever puts the knife in can be sure his name will be known in Rome soon enough. And I don't want to be that man because Rome will find a way to have its revenge on him.'

A chorus of agreement greeted the gloomy prediction, and Antonius flicked a glance to the tent's rear, wondering whether, against all expectations, he might still manage to spirit his friend away to safety. If the mob dispersed for even a short period he could cut his way in through the back wall and try one last time to persuade Vocula to accompany him out of the camp. Perhaps, he mused, if the threat of death receded and the legatus came to see himself as no more than a prisoner he would be more inclined to consider flight.

'I'll do it.'

A soldier had stepped out of the crowd while his attention had been elsewhere, and was standing in the open space in front of the command tent with a drawn sword in his hand.

'Longinus? But you . . .'

'Deserted? Yes I fucking well did, once that cunt in there started beheading men for the crime of speaking their minds and telling the truth!' He looked around at the men surrounding the tent with an expression of naked glee, and Antonius realised that with his arrival any faint hope of saving the legatus's life was gone. 'I ended up with the Gauls, and they've sent me to put some backbone into you pussies! So, if nobody else has the guts for the job . . . ?'

Silence greeted his challenge, and the newcomer strode forward to within two paces of the tent's closed door flap.

'Legatus Vocula! Come out and make recompense for the good men you killed!'

After a moment the leather was pulled back to reveal the legatus, white-faced but evidently resolved to face his would-be murderers. He stared at the deserter for a long moment and then stepped forward quickly, reaching down to lift the waiting sword blade, placing its point against his sternum.

'If you're going to kill me, have the decency to make it qui—'

The soldier lunged forwards, ramming the gladius into the Roman's chest with such force that the blade burst from his back, then stepped backwards, wrenching the sword free and leaving the legatus tottering, bloody-lipped as he coughed gore in a crimson spray.

'*You men . . . will . . . regret . . .*'

He staggered, consciousness fading, then slumped to the ground and lay motionless. The gathered soldiers stared down at his body for a moment before the murderer's voice broke the silence.

'Regret killing you? I don't think so, Roman! Your time has come and gone, and now I serve a new empire!'

'But will you men of the First and Sixteenth Legions join with us?' The crowd of men turned to find a single man behind them, tall and patrician, dressed in the polished bronze armour of a Roman general with a scarlet cloak draped over one arm in the classical style, exuding the authority of a man born to power with one hand resting nonchalantly on the pommel of his sword. 'You have taken a step towards your destiny that can never be reversed! And now the moment of an even greater decision is upon you! Now that you have freed yourselves from the dead hand of Rome's failing hold on power, will you choose to serve the Gallic empire, or will you be content to remain leaderless, loyal to no man and a threat to all? After all, two of Rome's mighty legions are a formidable prospect in these difficult days! Will you accept the offer of the safety and prosperity that service to a new empire will afford you, or should I regard you as masterless and make my exit? After all, you may consider that you have no need of allies.'

The deserter raised his bloody sword, shouting a challenge at his former comrades.

'I say we swear to serve the new empire! Rome is finished! The Gallic empire will rule north of the mountains from now on! Will you join me?'

The men around him erupted in cheers, shouting their affirmation, and Antonius watched in disgust as the deserter and the Gallic general exchanged knowing, triumphant glances.

'Very well!' The Gaul nodded imperiously, raising his free hand and turning on the spot to encompass them all before administering his verdict. 'I, Julius Classicus, prince of the Nervians and general of the empire of the Gauls, accept you into that empire's service! The oath will be sworn at the right time and with the right solemnity, but from this moment on you can be proud to consider yourselves Gauls, each and every one of you! You will be paid at the same rate as under Rome, and when the time is right you will all receive the donatives that Vitellius promised you as a mark of the Gallic empire's high regard for your service! You will have the gold you are owed!'

More cheers erupted, louder than before at the unexpected but welcome promise of what every legionary hoped for. When they had died away Classicus spoke again, pointing to the deserter.

'Aemelius Longinus is promoted to the rank of centurion as a reward for his courage in ending Rome's hold over you! Let him be awarded his phalerae for this act, and take his place among your proud centurionate! Now dismiss, and equip yourselves for the march. At dawn tomorrow you will swear your allegiance to the Gallic empire, and then we will march north to demonstrate to the men holding out in the Old Camp just how futile their resistance really is! Find your other officers, Herennius Gallus and Numisius Rufus, and make them secure, without any harm being done to them, in recognition that the time for violence is past! They will have a key part to play in demonstrating to the Old Camp's commander that the time to give up his doomed struggle has arrived. And remove that poor man's body – we should at least accord him some respect in death!'

The Nervian turned and walked away, and Antonius paced slowly through the dispersing crowd of soldiers to stand over his friend's corpse, unconcerned as to whether his disguise was still effective as the men around him turned their back on the scene, laughing and joking at the prospect of being paid a donative that they had long since decided was destined never to be honoured. Waiting until the ground around the legatus's tent was deserted, with only Vocula's remains for company, he knelt by the legatus's body, pushing a silver denarius between his lips and into his mouth.

'Farewell, Gaius Dillius Vocula. I failed to save your life but I promised to avenge its loss. And at the right time I will. Your murderer will spend the time from this moment to that looking over his shoulder, whereas you are in Elysium with your ancestors. Among whom you have no need of shame.'

He nodded down at the corpse and turned back to the camp's southern gate, adopting the persona and gait of an evil-tempered chosen man in a hurry, one hand on the handle of Vocula's dagger, muttering to himself as he strode back through the camp's rows of leather tents.

'And I promise you one more thing. When the time comes, your murderer will depart this life a good deal more slowly than you did.'

Outside Batavodurum, January AD 70

'Make sure you walk the guard posts properly once it gets cold. This lot will be sneaking away for a warm by the closest fires if they think you won't be along to keep them honest.'

Egilhard nodded, tying his helmet's cheek pieces tightly together and reflexively putting his hands to the hilts of his sword and dagger, and the century's chosen man Hludovig shook his head at the younger man.

'Always with the blades, eh? The sharpest thing you'll need tonight is your tongue, Watch Officer. Lash one or two men with it and the rest of them will soon enough come to respect you. You show them any softness, they will take advantage like the bastards they are.'

Looking over his superior's shoulder Egilhard fought to keep his face straight as Frijaz pulled a face at the chosen man's back, eyes crossed and tongue protruding, the other men of his old tent party wearing various expressions of boredom and indifference at Hludovig's words. Since his promotion to chosen man he had carried on with his generally reviled approach to his responsibilities as if nothing had changed, bringing his own particular brand of irascibility and casual violence to the role in stark contrast to his predecessor's more easy-going approach to discipline. Certain in his own mind which approach he would be better emulating, Egilhard was nevertheless more than intelligent enough to say and do what was expected of him when under the older man's hard-eyed scrutiny.

'Yes, Chosen Man!'

Nodding his satisfaction, Hludovig turned away, leaving his deputy to the pleasures of keeping several tent parties of soldiers alert through the depths of the night.

'I'm away for a beer. You see anything to worry you . . . *anything* . . . you send for me and let the grown-ups sort it out, right boy?'

Egilhard watched him stalk off into the sea of tents that constituted the cohorts' camp, Hramn having refused to countenance any attempt to make it more permanent or comfortable for the men of the cohorts despite their proximity to their own city, on the grounds that they could be commanded to march at any moment. Once the older man was out of earshot he turned back to his soldiers with a sigh of relief.

'Very well, you heard the man. You "bastards" can all consider yourselves well and truly shouted at, and once you've recovered from it you can get the watch fire burning properly and start cooking. And make sure there's plenty in the pot, nobody on my watch goes hungry.'

Leaving his father and uncle bickering over the best way to encourage the fire's dull embers back to life, he walked off along the camp's four-foot-high turf wall, stopping at every guard post to exchange a few words with the tent parties manning the defences. Respected for his almost supernatural abilities with a sword, he knew the soldiers he had counted as comrades only months before well enough to wear his authority lightly, encouraging rather than cajoling, his growing confidence evident in both his relaxed approach to the groups of soldiers and their respectful responses. Walking back along the wall to the camp's eastern entrance, which was his main point of responsibility, he found the fire burning properly under Lataz's expert gaze, while Frijaz offered helpful suggestions to the tent party's other men as they chopped meat and vegetables into the large pot that would then be suspended over its heat.

'All good?'

Lataz nodded, grinning affectionately at his son in the fire's soft light.

'Once I persuaded your uncle to bugger off and leave me to it, yes. And not a bad night for it either.'

Egilhard looked up, taking a moment to consider the cloud-free evening sky, fading from dark blue to black in the east as night fell properly. Something on the western horizon caught his eye, and he raised a hand to point at the sparkling flecks of light, dancing golden specks against the indigo backdrop.

'Do you see that?'

Lataz stared out into the dusk for a moment before responding.

'Torches. Moving fast too, so they're probably horsemen. Best you call out Hludovig.'

The chosen man answered the runner's summons quickly enough, joining the tent party as they watched the approaching riders, the cooking pot forgotten.

'Whoever it is, they're bold enough to be riding out after dark. Only a handful of them though, so it's not likely to be anything more exciting than a messenger.'

'Shall I call out the rest of the century?'

Hludovig shook his head.

'For half a dozen men? We'd be the laughing stock of the camp. No, just have your lads form up and look fierce, and let's find out what this lot want.'

The leading rider dismounted, a blazing torch in his right hand, nodding to the chosen man as he stalked forward.

'I have a message for Prince Kivilaz from Atuataca. The men of my tribe have decided to join the Batavi in your war with Rome. So if you'll take me to the prince's tent I'll—'

'Not a chance.' Hludovig raised a hand, shaking his head. 'Nobody sees Kiv without being approved by our prefect, and definitely not a Tungrian. You cowardly bastards have taken Rome's side, which makes you . . .'

He fell silent as the centurion raised his hands in meek surrender.

'No problem, Chosen.' He looked to the men behind him, some unspoken signal passing between them. 'We understand. And besides, you just told me all I need to know.'

'What do you m—'

The bemused chosen man grunted in surprise and pain as the Tungrian's dagger punched into the side of his neck and before his men could react, the newcomers were on the attack, flinging their torches into the camp and flashing out their swords. The centurion himself seized his opportunity, hurling his brand at Egilhard and diving into the camp's rows of tents while the watch officer was distracted by having to dodge its flaming arc.

'He's after Kiv! We'll deal with these!'

Realising that Lataz was right, Egilhard turned and ran for the centre of the camp still carrying his shield, knowing that the Tungrian would be doing the same, using his long familiarity with the camp layout that the Batavi habitually used, as the result of long association with legions who were in turn accustomed to following the dictates of their instruction manuals to the letter. Hurdling campfires and dodging between tents, he would be intent on reaching the command tents before the alarm could be raised, gambling on finding the Batavi leader in his quarters. Breathing hard, the young watch officer ran to a halt in front of the largest of the tents, its door flap guarded by a pair of Bairaz's guardsmen who stared uncomprehendingly at the young soldier. One of them stepped forward, raising a hand to deny the young soldier access.

'Nobody enters without—'

Knowing that he only had seconds to act, Egilhard stepped forward, bending his knees to lower his centre of gravity, then lunged upwards with his shield, hammering the closer of the two away with its iron boss, then quickly stepping back off his leading foot to put his shoulder into the other man's chest with enough force to send him sprawling. Striding into the tent's living space, ignoring the shouts of alarm from the momentarily discomfited guardsmen, he came face-to-face with the Tungrian in the act of climbing through a long slit he had hacked in the tent's back wall. The intruder snarled a challenge, leaping forward with his sword extended, intent on gutting the only man standing between him and his target, only to find his blade pushed harmlessly aside by the Batavi's shield and the point of his attacker's sword raised to strike.

'Alive!'

Nodding grimly at the shouted instruction from behind him, the young soldier stepped forward and butted his opponent between the eyes with the brow guard of his helmet, smashing his shield's iron rim into the reeling Tungrian's sword arm to disarm him. Turning to leap through the hole in the tent's wall, the would-be assassin doubled up in agony as Egilhard sank his blade's point into his calf, dropping him to the ground, then shouted in pain and indignation as the Batavi warrior stamped down on the scrabbling fingers of his left hand with the nailed sole of his boot to stop him drawing his pugio. The first of the guardsmen came through the tent's doorway with a murderous expression only to come up short as Kivilaz raised a hand to forestall any attempt at revenge for his humiliation, having emerged from the tent's inner quarters.

'Restrain this man, and fetch a bandage carrier to bind his wound, I want him alive for long enough that we can understand what, or rather *who*, is behind this attempt on my life. And as for you, soldier, it seems that I owe you a life.'

Hramn and Alcaeus arrived moments later and pushed their way through the knot of guardsmen gathered around the tent, the wolf-priest raising a knowing eyebrow at the sight of Egilhard standing in one corner of the prince's tent while a pair of guardsmen stood over the captive as his leg was bandaged. Kivilaz gestured to the fallen centurion with a flick of contempt.

'He had a message from Tungria, or at least that's what he told the men at the gate before killing their chosen man and making this attempt to put me at the end of his sword. In truth, however, I suspect that he will sing a different song with a little encouragement from fire and iron, a song that includes the name Labeo. This suicide mission bears the stamp of my former colleague's plotting, and it has set me to thinking that perhaps I have ignored his flea bite incursions onto our lands for too long. Added to which, I am forced to conclude that this attempt to decapitate the tribe's war leadership might well have been successful if not for this soldier. After all, Labeo only has to get lucky once. Which makes me wonder if the time has come to deal with Claudius Labeo once and forever, after the matter of the Old Camp has been satisfactorily concluded.'

Alcaeus nodded at Egilhard.

'Hludovig?'

The younger man straightened.

'The chosen man is dead, Centurion. This man struck him with his dagger without warning.'

Hramn snorted derisively, kicking the supine Tungrian in the side.

'Another act of cowardice to add to the long list perpetrated by Claudius Labeo and his followers.' The Tungrian ignored him, sunk in his own misery, and the prefect spat on him with a growl of disgust. 'We'll make an example of you that won't be forgotten by your people for a long time, the next time we see each other across a battlefield.' He shot Alcaeus a knowing glance. 'It seems that the position of chosen man in your century is a perilous one, Centurion, almost as if the gods have decided to single your deputies out for some reason. Do you have any thoughts as to who should replace this latest casualty and be the next man to risk their displeasure with you?'

The wolf-priest stared at him for a moment, a look of murderous calculation in his eyes, then slowly relaxed as he regained control over his fury at the jibe. He gestured to Egilhard, who stared back at him in amazement.

'I have a man in mind, Prefect. If there's anyone in my century equipped to survive the risks the position seems to present, I'd say he does.'

The Old Camp, Germania Inferior, January AD 70

'I didn't think I could be any more downcast than I already am, Herennius Gallus, but here you are to help my spirits sink to a new low.'

The former legion legatus nodded dejectedly at his senatorial colleague's bitter disappointment on discovering the defection of what had remained of Vocula's army. The arrival of a cohort from each of the two traitor legions along with their captive legati had initially caused excitement within the Old Camp's walls, a state of near-delirium at the prospect of rescue, which had swiftly been dispelled when it became clear that the newcomers, far from being the vanguard of a relieving force, were in fact firmly under the control of the Batavi and their Gallic allies.

'You might try being in my position, Munius Lupercus, if you want to know what being abject feels like. You're not the one under sentence of death. You don't go everywhere in the company of half a dozen of men who used to obey every order issued to them and now want nothing more than to kill me. They watch me all the time, Munius Lupercus, they watch me eat, they watch me sleep, they even watch me defecate.'

Lupercus shrugged.

'You had your chance to make a dignified exit. If you'd drawn your sword when they came for Dillius Vocula, and stood alongside him like the Roman you're supposed to be, you wouldn't be suffering this humiliation. Would you?'

Gallus shook his head disconsolately.

'No.'

In the silence that followed, Marius considered the news that the former legatus had brought with him to the Old Camp, knowing from the look of concentration on Aquillius's face that he was doing the same thing.

'So, let's be sure I've understood these depressing tidings, shall we?' Lupercus fixed a hard stare on his colleague. 'Vocula marched his army north from the Winter Camp with the sole purpose of relieving this siege and getting us out of this death trap?'

'Yes. He said that a promise had been made, and that he wasn't going to be the man to abandon two legions to their fate.'

'Although he already knew that the Gauls were planning a revolt?'

Gallus nodded again, laughing bitterly.

'Yes. As conspirators they lack a certain finesse. There's not one of them would last a day in Rome. Spies were sent into our camp at night when we were camped alongside the auxiliaries, and it didn't take long for the more loyal among our officers to report the approaches they were making to our men.'

'Join with us, murder your senior officers and participate in the glory of the Gallic empire?'

'Yes. And given the enmity the men were feeling towards us, it was an easy sell for them.'

'Because they felt betrayed by your support for Vespasianus.'

Gallus nodded with an expression of misery.

'I didn't realise how bad it was until the mutiny at Novaesium. You will have heard that they dragged Hordeonius Flaccus from his residence and tore him to pieces like wild beasts?'

His fellow legatus nodded grimly.

'The Germans made very sure that we knew of his murder. You saw it?'

'Vocula's man Antonius smuggled us away dressed as slaves, but I saw them mobbing Flaccus in the moment that we passed the gates of his residence. Animals . . .'

Lupercus shrugged and Gallus flinched at his flint-hard look of disdain.

'I know, you think I'm a coward.'

'You can find your own label. But you're not fit to be called Roman. And Hordeonius Flaccus was the agent of his own destruction, so you can save your pity at his violent end for your own likely fate, when your usefulness to the Gauls is at an end.' He shot a hard-eyed glance at Gallus, who recoiled fractionally at the hatred in his gaze. 'Continue.'

His former colleague swallowed.

'We marched north again, but without the Twenty-second Legion that had been the only thing standing between us and the threat of another mutiny. Vocula had orders from Rome to leave them behind to reinforce the Winter Camp.'

Lupercus shrugged.

'And Rome was right. If the Winter Camp falls then who knows how long it'll take to re-conquer Germania with all the major fortresses in rebel hands? And without the Twenty-second Legion to stand between you and another mutiny, the Gauls finally revealed their intentions.'

'Yes. The legions refused to advance past Gelduba and Julius Classicus gave up any pretence of loyalty, so we gave up all hope of relieving you and headed south. But the Gauls followed us, and when we got to Novaesium they must have issued some sort of command to their men within the legions, because that was that. The First and the Sixteenth both turned their faces against us, refusing to listen to our orders. Vocula addressed them that morning, and for a moment I thought his words might work the same magic as they had half a dozen other times, but this time it was different, as if the animals he'd cowed by the force of his personality were no longer afraid of his threat. He sent Antonius and his men away, and then went back into the camp to face them. He knew he'd be killed, of course, it was common enough knowledge that the Gallic leaders wanted him dead as a demonstration of their power, but no one would face him. Not one man was willing to take the final step and kill him, so he retired to his tent to await his fate. In the end it was a deserter from my legion who came for him, sent by the Gauls to do what the legions wouldn't. He cut Vocula down, slaughtered him like a dog in the street, and then the rest of them came for us.'

'They didn't kill you though.'

Gallus shrugged.

'They will. When the time requires it, when the Gauls give the order, I'll be used as a public spectacle of the new empire's ascendancy over Rome.'

'And until then you'll spend your time waiting for the blow to fall.' Lupercus turned dismissively away. 'Go back to your shadow-life, Herennius Gallus, and leave those of us who still defy this revolt to defending Rome's tattered reputation.'

'But what about the message? Surely—'

'No.' The legatus turned back with real anger. 'I won't even deign to answer the offer that you were sent to make. Surrender? To what end? Why would I offer my enemy possession of something I've shed so much blood to keep? The Old Camp will not be surrendered, not while we have food to eat.'

Gallus shook his head in amazement.

'But the legions from Italy will be months getting here, even if they can fight their way through the Gauls and Germans. And I know how much food you have, I was part of the planning for the convoys that restocked your granaries before Saturnalia. You can't have much more than—'

'None of it matters, Herennius Gallus!' Lupercus rounded on his former colleague with sudden ferocity, shaking his head in angry denial. 'It doesn't matter that we're trapped in here with the nearest formed legions so far away that they might as well not exist! It doesn't matter that we're on half-rations, and starting to wonder what the few pack animals we have left are going to taste like! And it doesn't matter that the men gathered around this camp get more and more frustrated every day, making it ever more likely that they'll fall on us like wild dogs when they eventually get inside these walls, which, as we both know, unless some miracle happens they eventually will! All of these indisputable facts are of no interest to me whatsoever!'

Gallus looked at the two senior centurions standing behind their legatus and found their faces set equally hard.

'You feel no fear as to what must result?'

Lupercus laughed aloud.

'Well of course I do! How could a man not fear the death that awaits him under these circumstances? There is one man who doesn't feel that dull blade probing his guts when he wakes in the morning, and remembers where he is . . .' he gestured to the taller of the two centurions, 'but then First Spear Aquillius is one of a kind, and perhaps not quite as sane as the rest of us. And the rest of us, I can assure you, are all shitting ourselves at the thought of what awaits at the end of this siege. But I fear the dishonour of surrendering before my command is incapable of resistance more than the pain of death itself. You've chosen the former, colleague, and in consequence you die a little every day in anticipation of your actual end. Whereas I will hold my head high until the moment that I'm relieved of my burden. So go and tell whoever it is that sent you in to share the news of your craven capitulation that the Fifth and Fifteenth Legions will not be surrendering today, and not anytime soon either.' He turned away in dismissal, his voice that of a tired man seeking rest. 'Now get out.'

Gallus turned to leave the office, stopping as the bigger of the two senior centurions spoke for the first time, his words as harsh as his stare.

'Legatus Gallus, there is a way that you could regain that honour you threw away.' The scrape of iron on iron as his gladius rasped against its scabbard's throat tightened the other man's features in an involuntary flinch. 'Take my sword and kill yourself, while you have the chance to do so. It is a chance you will not have again.'

The disgraced legatus stared at him for a moment before shaking his head and looking at his own feet, no longer able to meet the centurion's stare.

'I . . . can't.'

Lifting his gaze he looked at all three of them in turn.

'I envy you more than you can imagine. The simplicity of your refusal to betray Rome, and your acceptance that your deaths will result, both baffle me and leave me in awe. If I could find it in me, nothing could make me happier than to fall on that blade and end it here. But I can't. It isn't in me.'

Aquillius nodded, re-sheathing his sword.

'I understand. And perhaps your ancestors will understand, when you join them to explain how it was that your family's honour came to so small an end. Do you have children?'

Gallus nodded.

'Three boys.'

The big man nodded.

'Then it is to be hoped that they can find it in themselves to make amends for you. Go well, Herennius Gallus. And pray that your end is as swift and merciful as the one you have refused.'

Graian Alps, February AD 70

'What a glorious landscape, wouldn't you agree, First Spear Pugno? To see the view from the top of the world like this makes all our hardships of the last week worthwhile, don't you think?'

The senior centurion looked up at his legatus from his place marching at the head of the Twenty-first. Pontius Longus was riding alongside Legatus Augusti Cerialis, both men wrapped in double thickness cloaks and comfortable in the saddles of their horses. He gestured out across the sea of mountain peaks that marched away from them to the north in a gentle downward slope towards the distant valley of the Rhenus, still far beyond the distant horizon.

'It is indeed most impressive, Legatus. Although I daresay my men will be a good deal more interested in exchanging all this ice and snow for grass and some warmer air.'

The legion's long column was stretched out along the road that descended from the pass's highest point, the legionaries eager to put some miles behind them and descend to the gentler conditions of the lower valleys, having spent a bitterly cold night camped at the fort beneath the summit, wrapped in their cloaks and blankets and huddled together for warmth. Cerialis smiled down at him from his horse.

'Come now, Pugno, surely your men are more than capable of living with a little cold weather!'

While Pugno was groping for a suitably diplomatic answer that still managed to point out that the senior officer had spent the night in the warmth and comfort of the mansio at the pass's highest point, while his men had cursed and shivered around their campfires through a night cold enough to freeze water solid, the man marching alongside him interjected.

'Indeed they are, Petillius Cerialis, but perhaps we can be grateful that the Twenty-first has already crossed these mountains through this very pass, and at much the same time of year, because I suspect that without the precautions that First Spear Pugno and his officers took, we might well have lost more than a few men to the cold. After all, we hardly shared their hardships last night, did we?'

The legatus augusti nodded graciously in appreciation of the point the former praetorian prefect was making. Alfenius Varus had elected to march on foot early in the long journey from Italy, and had shown no sign of regretting the decision despite suffering all of the usual discomforts that were suffered by soldiers as their feet adapted to the brutal pounding of day after day on the road.

'True enough, colleague, true enough. Although I did feel some hint of their privations while I was sacrificing at the mansio's altar to Jupiter this morning. Hopefully his goodwill will keep the weather this fair, and grant us somewhere to sleep with a little more sophistication in both board and bed, eh?'

Varus and Pugno exchanged knowing glances, Cerialis's sexual appetite having already become very evident in the course of their march from Rome, his aides discreetly but routinely procuring a woman from among the prostitutes that were to be found at every overnight halt, even one so distant from civilisation. The sky above them was a bowl of blue, the low sun's meagre warmth just discernible through the layers of clothing that Pugno had insisted the men of his legion be equipped with before they had set out from their camp in northern Italy. With every legionary wearing three tunics and two pairs of socks, and wrapped in thick woollen cloaks whose bright red dye had been the legatus's choice once he realised that gold was going to have to be spent to get his legion across the mountains intact, most of Pugno's men had thus far avoided frostbite, and the legion medicus had only been forced to amputate toes from a handful of the less wary who had been foolish enough to sell their socks to wiser men in order to whore and drink prior to the climb to the freezing pass.

'So tell us, Alfenius Varus, since you have been sent with us to treat with the Batavians, what do you make of them?'

'I found them unruly, headstrong, self-interested and vain.' Cerialis nodded, and was about to comment when Varus continued. 'I also found them brimming with martial prowess, skilled with spear, sword and shield to a degree that I have rarely seen in any other body of men, and possessed of such remarkable courage that they appeared unbreakable by any normal standard of assessment. You saw them in action, First Spear, what did you think?'

Pugno nodded agreement.

'The Twenty-first is the emperor's foremost legion when it comes to ferocity in battle, and the reason for that is simple – my centurions and their leading men foster the iron truth of our invincibility with every new man that enlists to serve under our eagle, telling them that they are lucky to have been given the opportunity to join such a bloody-handed legion and encouraging them to match the tales of heroism and sacrifice that are told around the campfires. No man in my legion is under any illusion as to what is expected of him. And yet I would say that these Germans are every bit as dangerous as the Twenty-first. They yearn for battle, and the chance to cover themselves in glory with which to challenge their sons and grandsons to even greater feats.'

'All true. They swear on their swords at the start of every parade, promising to do the blades carried by their fathers and grandfathers before them great honour, and never to step back in battle.'

'I see.' Cerialis looked back down the marching column. 'So while the Twenty-first is the most martially-minded of the emperor's legions . . .'

He glanced at Pugno, who nodded firmly.

'You can count on it, Legatus Augusti. My officers and I will give you victory on any battlefield you care to put us on.'

'Thank you, Pugno, I'll be counting on that. And yet the Batavians have long been the fiercest and most dangerous of Rome's allies. And here we are, one solitary legion marching north to meet them in open battle now that my colleague Annius Gallus has taken the route through the western Alps to secure Gallia Lugdunensis. And, for all we know, by the time we reach the Rhenus, the legions besieged in the Old Camp may have been forced to surrender. And if these latest tidings of a Gallic revolt are true, the army of the Rhenus itself may be under such threat that we are indeed the only surviving legion on the river, until the reinforcements from Hispania and Britannia arrive. Can we face them across a battlefield and hope to win, even with the support of the auxiliary cohorts we've been promised?'

Varus answered, his voice and expression sober at the prospect of battle with the men he had formerly and briefly commanded.

'Having commanded them in battle, I would be the first man to praise their exploits at the first battle of Cremona, and not simply because those deeds brought me to the attention of Vitellius.' He laughed bitterly. 'Indeed that was attention that I could well have done without, given the way in which it exposed me to the serpentine behaviour of that man's closest supporters. But they were irresistible on that day, breaking the First Classica in less time than it took them to sing the whole of their paean, although it would be fair of course to note that the marines from Misenum had already taken a mighty beating from this very legion prior to that brief and one-sided fight.'

'And the praetorians they put to flight thereafter had already been bludgeoned to bloody tatters by the First Italica, had they not?'

The former praetorian prefect nodded at Cerialis's question.

'It's true, they did little more than threaten their most hated enemies before the guard took to their heels, but trust me when I tell you this: even if they had been properly formed and unblooded, the praetorians would still have broken and fled in little more time than was the case when they were at the end of their rope, and ripe for defeat. Those Germans were nothing short of elemental in their fury at seeing the men who had contrived their proud imperial bodyguard's dismissal from Rome in such disgrace. And so if you ask me who would win, the legion at our backs or the Germans waiting for us at the far end of the Rhenus . . .'

He thought for a moment.

'I cannot in all honesty make such a prediction. Perhaps the ground on which the fight occurs will be the deciding factor, perhaps the losses that the Batavians have already taken, if the stories of their being surprised and savaged by the Vascones at Gelduba are true. But I'll make you a prediction that I'd happily wager my entire fortune on.'

Cerialis and Longus stared at him expectantly, and Pugno raised a questioning eyebrow.

'Which is?'

Varus smiled bleakly.

'Whenever, wherever and however we come to face the Batavi, as they call themselves, we'll need every bit of that ferocity your legion's reputation is based on. Because they'll fight like wild dogs, and doubly so if they're defending their homeland. Mucianus has sent me with you to help broker a peace agreement, if such a thing is possible in this disaster of a situation, and it might be better for the empire if the Batavians were restored to their former position of pre-eminence within our armies, with previous sins forgiven and forgotten. Because the alternative seems to be for both of us to bleed ourselves white bringing this war to a conclusion, and that can only result in everyone losing.'

4

The Old Camp, Germania Inferior, March AD 70

'Priest. Gather the men of the cohorts and have them ready to fight. Not that fighting will be required of them today.'

Alcaeus looked up from his sword's blade, tinged blue with the gritty paste that each pass of his sharpening stone deposited on its surface even as it honed the iron to a deadly edge. Reaching for the waiting cleaning rag he passed it down both sides of the weapon's length with the speed of long practice, stood and slid the sword into its scabbard.

'I was not warned of any attack, or I would have—'

Hramn smiled, a rarity in itself, but the warm tone of his voice was enough to set the wolf-priest's instincts twitching.

'There is no attack planned. Nor have you failed in your duty on this occasion. This call to arms is unexpected, and all the more welcome for that. Today will be that rarest of things, a bloodless victory.'

Alcaeus looked at Hramn in surprise, realising exactly why it was that his superior was in such unexpectedly good spirits.

'The siege is over. The Old Camp legions have surrendered?'

'As good as. They've sent a message out to Kiv asking for terms. Seems they've run out of food at last, and now they want us to take pity on them. And it also appears as if Kiv's inclined to show them that pity. The Gauls are collecting legions, it seems, so he's minded to send them south as a gesture of goodwill to his new best friend Julius Classicus and their shiny new emperor.'

The wolf-priest shook his head in unfeigned surprise.

'But what about the ten thousand men who've been camped around that fortress like cats waiting for the mice to come out for the last three months? Surely they're not going to just watch those legions march away unscathed?'

The prefect shrugged, scratching at his beard.

'That's Kiv's problem. But, for all that it's none of our business, I asked him what he thought their reaction would be if he spared the Romans, and he told me that he's come to an agreement with the tribal chiefs that they'll have to be satisfied with him sending their legatus to the Bructeri priestess Veleda. Can you imagine the shame that will be heaped on Rome when they discover that one of their senators has been made a slave of the woman who predicted their defeat and gave the German tribes the push they needed to join with us?'

'What about their senior centurions? One of them has disfigured well over a score of men while we've been waiting them out—'

'And he'll die for that. Kiv's promised the tribal kings that he has a special revenge planned for the *Banô*.'

'And the other . . . Marius, isn't it?'

'Is under my protection.'

Alcaeus turned a disbelieving stare on his superior.

'Your *protection*?'

The prefect stared at him flatly.

'He is known to me, Alcaeus. I've fought him on the harpastum field and I've sweated and drunk with him after a close game, so he's under my protection. Understood?'

The wolf-priest nodded, evidently still not quite believing what he was hearing.

'Understood. You want all three of them keeping from any harm, one to go and be a slave for a Bructeri priestess, one to make some sort of bloody recompense for making the tribes look foolish, and one because he's an old friend you've traded punches with. Right?'

Hramn looked back at him with the same dead-eyed expression to which Alcaeus had become well-accustomed, his momentary good-humour abruptly dispelled by the disbelief in his deputy's voice.

'Follow your orders, Priest.'

'Your request to surrender has been considered by both the leaders of the German tribes and the men who command the armies of the Gallic empire, Munius Lupercus.' Kivilaz stared up at the painfully thin man standing above him on the walls of the Old Camp. 'There are many among our peoples who would happily sit and wait while you starve to death, but we remain civilised men, despite the grievous losses that this siege has inflicted upon us. And so we have decided to permit you to leave this place, and to demonstrate that we remain capable of showing mercy even when our first instinct is to revenge. We will feed you sufficiently well to allow you to regain your strength before you go to serve your new masters. Although there are conditions.'

Lupercus nodded impassively.

'Name them.'

The Batavi grinned up at him.

'You will all swear allegiance to the Gallic empire, and you will do so today. My allies have some use for your men, it seems, in their preparations to resist any attempt by Rome to return them to imperial control. You yourself, Munius Lupercus, will become the property of the Batavi, to be disposed of as we see fit. I have it in my mind to offer you to the Bructeri priestess Veleda, as the living proof that her predictions of Batavi victory were well founded. Doubtless she can find some use for you.'

Lupercus remained stony-faced.

'What else?'

Kivilaz smiled up at him with the smugness of a man who knew he had the whip hand.

'As stoic as ever, I see. Very well. Your legionaries will parade outside these walls, with their swords and shields but leaving their spears behind them, and they will swear to fight for the Gauls. Any man resisting that oath in any way whatsoever will forfeit his life immediately. And all heavy military equipment will be relinquished to the Batavi, intact and undamaged. Those bolt throwers will make a useful addition to our strength. Do you accept these conditions?'

'I will consult with my officers.'

'Very well. But be swift about it. My offer will not last forever.'

The legatus turned to Marius and Aquillius, lowering his voice so as not to be overheard by the waiting Germans.

'There it is, gentlemen, we have to choose between accepting abject surrender, dishonour and quite possibly our murder, or staying inside these walls until starvation has weakened us to the point that we're no longer strong enough to man them. Which will probably be a matter of days at best, at which point the enemy will come over them unopposed and put us all to the sword. I can save the lives of thousands of men by agreeing, at least for today. And once terms are agreed I'll fall on my sword, and go to meet my ancestors with some share of honour and dignity. As might you both, if you so choose.'

The two centurions nodded, and Marius spoke for them both.

'It would be our greatest honour to die with you, Legatus, and share in the legend that will be born in doing so.'

Lupercus turned back to look down at Kivilaz.

'Your conditions are accepted, Julius Civilis.'

The Batavi grinned up at him knowingly.

'I thought of one more, while you were debating the rights and wrongs of surrender to German barbarians. You may surrender, and the safe passage of your men from this place is guaranteed, if, and only if, you and your first spears surrender alongside them. If we discover that you've taken the easy way out in order to escape the shame of capture then your men's lives will be forfeit. Do you understand?'

Lupercus stared at him in silence for a long moment before answering.

'You would deny me a dignified and honourable death?'

Kivilaz nodded, his face creased in a knowing smile.

'Your life, Munius Lupercus, has long been mine to command. I've owned it since that morning in Britannia when you would have fallen to a better swordsman had I not saved you from his blade, and now I'm calling you to account. As for your twin war-dogs, one at least is eagerly awaited down here by my German allies. I expect that there will be an audience of men who bear the disfigurements inflicted by his hands when he makes his slow and tortured exit from this life, eager for every scream they can tear from him. Those are my terms, Legatus. Do you accept them?'

'We accept. But anyone expecting to hear my voice express pain will be sadly disappointed.'

Lupercus looked round at Aquillius, who had stepped forward to stare flatly down at Kivilaz. The Batavi prince laughed out loud.

'The legendary *Banô* himself. Do you know what the name my allies have given you means? No? It means that you are their bane. A particularly appropriate name, given that you have caused so much death and distress among them with your brutal exploits on this field of bones. They have sworn to make you pay a hundredfold for those crimes against their sons and brothers, both for those left scarred and humiliated and those unable to deal with their mutilation who chose to end their lives in a dishonourable manner. So I look forward to seeing your vow to stay silent under their very close attention tested to its very limits.' His gaze shifted back to Lupercus. 'Very well. Assuming that the centurion speaks for you all, you will open the fortress gates and march out, ready to disown your empire and swear loyalty to another. No man is to bring any personal possessions other than his sword and shield, and any man found in possession of any form of wealth will be killed immediately. Be about it, Legatus, before I change my mind and leave you all to die of hunger.'

The legatus turned to his officers.

'It seems we're to be denied even the simple dignity of taking our own lives. No matter, we'll take whatever fate has chosen to throw in our path and treat it with the disdain of men who know they are in the right. Whatever happens from now, it's been my greatest privilege to have served with you both. Now muster your men and bring them to the South gate, we'll perform this one last action in a manner fitting for men of Rome. I'm damned if I'll give Kivilaz the pleasure of seeing me cowed.'

Egilhard and his men watched as the legions marched slowly out of the fortress they had held for so long, Frijaz shaking his head at the sight of so many men brought so low by hunger. The legionaries were parading out of the western gate, after a fashion, the weaker among them supported by their more robust comrades, barely able to stand themselves under the weight of their equipment.

'This is the might of Rome? I've had harder shits.'

His nephew shook his head, standing close behind the century with Hludovig's brass-bound *hastile* held in both hands.

'They've killed their own number and more, defending this place. Their bolt throwers killed my leading man, if you remember, and they felled so many Germans that the pyres burned for days each time we attacked.'

The older man grunted disparagement.

'From behind twenty-foot-high walls. With bolt throwers and stones. They wouldn't have lasted an hour in open battle. And now we're expected to keep the tribes off their backs, so that they can go and play at soldiers for the Gauls?'

'Now we're expected to obey orders, brother.' Lataz's gaze had remained fixed on the Romans as he spoke. 'So let's do as we're asked without expending any more of that hot air you're so good at showering us with.'

Frijaz sneered back at him, but was cut off before he could reply by a voice from behind him.

'I always wondered if you'd missed your place in life, Soldier Lataz. You could have been a leading man, if you'd not been so intent on remaining a soldier and keeping the respect of your mates.' The tent party came to attention, but Alcaeus waved a distracted hand to return them to their previous state of relaxation. 'Although Frijaz, and may Magusanus forgive me for my surprise in the matter, is, just this once, in the right. They wouldn't have lasted an hour against us in battle, and, given the state they're in now, they wouldn't last a dozen heartbeats. And yes, we've been sent here to provide them with an escort to the camp where they'll be fed and strengthened up for the march south. If the tribes were allowed to get among them then there'd be a slaughter that would have the road gutters ankle-deep in blood.'

He pointed out a trio of men standing to one side of the legions as they struggled onto the Old Camp's parade ground.

'I need a tent party of good men to guard those three in particular. That's their legatus in the middle, with the bronze armour, and he's promised to Veleda as a gift from the tribe. If anything happens to him then Kivilaz is going to be very unhappy with Hramn, who'll be equally displeased with me, and in that event I'll make sure that my resulting sense of disappointment rolls all the way downhill and expresses itself upon *you,* and in the most uncompromising fashion. Is that clear, Achilles?'

Egilhard nodded briskly.

'The legatus is promised to a priestess and must be protected against any attempt to get at him. What about the other two, Centurion?'

'The other two, Chosen Man Egilhard, are every bit as important. The one on the left of the legatus is Marius, and Prefect Hramn wants him to be protected from any attempts at revenge. Apparently they've played harpastum together . . .' he paused, shaking his head in disbelief, 'and Hramn respects him in some manly fashion that's common to the sport. I expect he'll be spared to accompany his superior across the river and end his days as a slave to the priestess alongside him, which isn't a fate I'd wish on a warrior but which, I suppose, is better than being peeled by one of those mad bastards the tribes call *priests*. And the other, somewhat more importantly, is Aquillius.' He watched their faces. 'Yes. Exactly. The *Banô*. The man who's been hunting our allies in the night, either gutting them and leaving them to die or cutting an eagle into their foreheads and then melting back into the darkness. There are a lot of men who'd very much like some time alone with him, and Kiv's got something special planned for him but I've neither any idea what it is nor any desire to find out. All

I know is that he's to be kept alive for long enough that whatever's planned for him isn't spoiled by some revenge-crazed warrior with a knife getting to him first. So when I call you forward I want you and your men to guard those three as if your lives depended on it.'

Drawing themselves up in their sadly depleted cohorts, the two legions stood under the watchful eyes of the Germans who thronged the parade ground's edge, held back by lines of Batavi soldiers, their snarling curses and gestures making it very clear what revenge they would have been taking if not for the protective cordon of their allies. Lupercus and his senior centurions stood to one side, knowing that their fate was likely to be different to that of their men but determined not to demonstrate any fear. At length, with the Romans paraded and their fortress emptied out, Alcaeus approached them and saluted Lupercus without any sign of irony.

'Greetings, Legatus, my name is Alcaeus, wolf-priest to the Batavi cohorts. My orders are to administer a sacred oath of loyalty to the Gallic empire and then to march you away to the site of your new camp. When we get there you will be fed, and have the chance to rest before the new commander takes your men away to serve against Rome, and the three of you to your own fates.'

Lupercus nodded tiredly.

'I see. And what exactly are our fates?'

The Batavi looked at him in frank appraisal.

'You are a fortunate man, Legatus. Your colleague Vocula was murdered by one of your own, a man in the pay of the Gauls, but you have surrendered to the Batavi, and my people have more honour than to use another man to do our killing. You and Centurion Marius, a man known to us from the harpastum field, will be sent on a journey that may enlighten you when you reach its end, for you are to meet the priestess Veleda. I'm almost jealous of such an opportunity, although I realise the shame of such servitude. You may be assured that she is a civilised woman, and that you will be treated fairly while you perform whatever labours are demanded of you in her service.'

'And me?'

Alcaeus turned to look at Aquillius.

'You, Centurion, have no such happy fate awaiting you. You have incurred the deep enmity of the tribes by your actions, and you will be called to account for those actions in a manner that will undoubtedly result in your death.'

The big man shrugged.

'As expected. Tell your Germans that they'd best make it quick, because I'll be fighting them until the moment they stop my wind, and nothing will warm my departed spirit better than to take a few of them with me.'

The wolf-priest smiled sadly.

'You should have been born Batavi, Aquillius, your spirit burns too brightly to be happy in the company of these sad remnants. Call your men to attention, and I'll administer the oath.'

At the two senior centurions' bellowed commands the tattered remnants of the two legions came to attention, standing still as Alcaeus strode out before them and raised his voice to be heard along the length of their weary formation.

'You will repeat the oath of allegiance to the Gallic empire after me! And if you want to be fed today you'd best make sure I can hear you! Repeat after me . . .'

He gave the legionaries a moment to compose themselves before starting the oath.

'We swear before Jupiter, Best and Greatest, to serve in the army of the Gallic empire . . .' He waited while the soldiers echoed his words, shaking his head in disappointment at the jumble of weak, confused responses. 'We can stay here and do this for as long as it takes for me to be convinced that you're sincere! So let's try again! We swear before Jupiter, Best and Greatest, to serve the army of the Gallic empire!'

The responses were louder, and more coherent, as the hapless legionaries realised that they had no choice but to do as they were bidden.

'We swear to sacrifice our lives in the service of Julius Sabinus, emperor of the Gauls!'

Stumbling over the unfamiliar name, the legions promised their fealty to yet another emperor with a dispirited ease that spoke volumes for the number of times they had already been asked to swear loyalty to a bewildering succession of emperors.

'And we promise to fight all enemies of the Gallic empire with the righteous fury demanded of us, and to the death! And may Jupiter, Best and Greatest, cause us to die in shame and agony if we break this holy oath!'

'They've just signed their own death warrants, more or less.'

Lupercus nodded at Marius's words.

'Possibly so. If these Germans and Gauls lose the war against Rome then every man here will be at risk of execution. But then in the last year they've sworn allegiance to four men, first Galba, then Vitellius, after him Vespasianus, and now this man Sabinus, whoever he is. I do find myself wondering how much difference one more emperor can make to such a long list?'

Alcaeus turned to the officers, gesturing to the road that led away to the west.

'My orders are to take you and your men away from here, to a camp that has been prepared for you in the privacy of the forest, where you will be fed and given the time required for your strength to return. Order your legions to march, and my men will escort you and ensure that none of the tribesmen whose people you have slaughtered in defence of this fortress decide to take matters into their own hands.'

Aquillius stared at him dourly.

'And to prevent me from escaping?'

The wolf-priest nodded solemnly.

'I have a special guard for you.' He gestured to a waiting tent party led by a chosen man, whose soldiers approached at his command and arrayed themselves around the officers. 'These soldiers are among the best we have, led by a man whose prowess with a blade is beyond mine by the same margin by which mine is beyond that of a raw recruit. If you make any attempt to flee, or to fight your way out of the trap that holds you, he has orders to hamstring you like a mad dog, but to keep you intact for the revenge that is planned for you.'

The exhausted legionaries trudged away from the parade ground and onto the road to the west, Batavi soldiers marching ahead of and behind them in cohort strength. Lupercus watched as the column headed down the track, turning to Alcaeus with a look of concern.

'How far is this camp, Centurion? You can see how little stamina my men have.'

Alcaeus shook his head.

'I've not seen it, Legatus, so I can't tell you exactly. My instructions were that we'll be met on the road and guided to the right place.'

'And you believe that?'

The Batavi turned to look at Aquillius, who was marching steadily and without any sign of distress despite the gauntness that hunger had etched into him.

'What do you mean?'

The Roman laughed softly.

'You are a priest, Centurion. Your role is to support the established order of the world, calling on the gods in support of your pronouncements. And so you believe the things you are told, even when they lack logic. You believe that your prince Kivilaz will allow another two legions to be gifted to the Gauls, to join the two they already have, despite the fact that your own cohorts have been grievously weakened. A Gallic empire with four legions would surely represent some sort of threat to your people, would it not?'

Alcaeus shrugged.

'I'm a soldier first and a priest second. My role is to ensure that these men are ready to fight the tribe's enemies, nothing more and nothing less. The workings of strategy are beyond me, and so I do not trouble myself with them.'

'My officer is right though.' Lupercus looked out across the open farmland on either side of the road. 'Not that the problem is mine any longer, but I too am curious as to why the Batavi would be happy to concentrate so much power in the hands of a potential rival.'

The wolf-priest shook his head.

'Such matters are not for me, although I expect that all will become clear soon enough. One thing I can say about Kivilaz is that he very rarely makes any decision without knowing exactly what it is that he wants to happen as a result.'

The column marched on for another two miles, following the road in its slow climb into the forest. Just as the malnourished legionaries were starting to flag to the point of breakdown, a familiar figure stepped out onto the cobbles, pointing down a rough track that had been hacked into the trees and undergrowth. Alcaeus called for the column to halt, walking forward and saluting his superior.

'Prefect.'

Hramn grinned at the sight of the exhausted Romans.

'These are the legions of Rome? Woe to the defeated indeed.' He gestured to the track. 'Their camp has been cut out of the forest down there, so point them in the right direction and tell our men to stop here, there's no need for them to accompany the prisoners.'

The wolf-priest frowned.

'But what's to stop them escaping into the forest?'

His superior laughed tersely.

'Look at the state of them! Tell them there's food a mile down that track and they'll totter off down it without a second thought. And where could they run to? Back to their fortress? Into the woods? There's not a man among them with the energy to try any such thing.'

Alcaeus nodded, calling orders for his men to step back from the road, then pointing down the forest track with his vine stick.

'There is food and shelter down that road! March!'

The exhausted legionaries obeyed without thought, turning off the cobbled road and trudging away into the trees four abreast, weaving to avoid the stumps of trees that had been left protruding from the track's surface as they followed the wolf-priest's directions. As the last of them made the turn and headed away into the gloom, Hramn grinned savagely, and, turning to Alcaeus, gestured to their waiting men.

'Get half of the cohort across the road in battle order, Priest, and warn them that they'll be killing Romans soon enough. The other half can set up stop lines in the forest to either side, to catch those among the poor bastards who have the brains not to use the track. And have the prisoners moved back up the slope, away from the road, I wouldn't want to lose any of them to a stray blade.'

Alcaeus stared at him uncomprehendingly for a moment before he realised what it was that the prefect was telling him.

'Surely not . . .'

Hramn shrugged, untroubled by his subordinate's evident disgust.

'And what was it that you were expecting, exactly? That our allies would happily sit back and watch the men who've killed their kith and kin just walk away, free of any consequence? At least this way they'll die quickly, with the chance to defend themselves, which is more than anyone showered with boiling water underneath their walls got. You'd better get your men in place quickly though, I doubt the Germans will be showing much patience today. While you carry out my orders, I'll have the men guarding the officers ready their weapons. I'd imagine they're not going to be very happy when they realise that they've been sold a dog in a bag rather than the pig they were promised.'

Alcaeus nodded and walked away, barking orders to block the track's end and picket the forest to either side, then stalking back to where Hramn stood waiting close to the Roman officers who were standing, clearly furious, under the raised spears of Egilhard's tent party. The Batavi prefect grinned into Lupercus's evident disgust, listening with his head tipped ostentatiously on one side.

'Any moment now, I'd imagine. Picture it, Legatus. The first of your men is staggering into the clearing that our Germans cut out of the forest, hoping that there will be tents, and fires, and food, but all he's going to find waiting for him are more tree stumps. And as more of your legionaries join him they'll be looking about themselves in confusion, praying that there's been some sort of mistake because the alternative is just too awful to even consider. Of course, some fool among the men waiting for them will give the game away too early, laughing out loud or just charging into them while they're still trying to work it out, before the realisation hits them that they're not going to be spared after all, but all the same—'

A distant scream reached them, an unearthly wail from deep in the trees and then, after a moment's pause, another. For a moment the silence descended again and then, as if the door to a room full of lunatics had been thrown open, a distant hubbub of anger and surprise rolled up the rough track.

'And there it is. The harsh intrusion of reality.' Hramn grinned again, nodding as the sounds of horror and confusion grew louder. Looking over the heads of the ranks of men set to close off the track, he pointed at the first signs of what was happening in the forest's depths. 'Look, there they are!'

Legionaries were in sight, running as best they could under the twin burdens of their armour's weight and their own exhaustion, lumbering back up the track's incline with their swords drawn, heads turning in search of a way to escape but finding only the merciless stares of the Batavi soldiers waiting on either side of the path. With a shouted command, the centurion leading the ranks of men blocking the path ordered them to ready their spears, raising a line of shields to absorb the Romans' frantic, straggling charge.

'This will be a slaughter.'

Hramn nodded in happy agreement with Alcaeus's dull-voiced opinion.

'It will be as Kiv agreed with the tribal kings, and as approved by Draco and the tribe's elders. Two legions will be destroyed, and our allies will have enough revenge to satisfy the hardest of hearts.'

Exhausted, terrified and desperate, the leading legionaries

collided with the waiting wall of shields hard enough to push the soldiers behind them back a pace or two despite the enervating hunger that had eaten into their strength so badly. The Batavi held them at bay for a moment, waiting while more of the fleeing Romans blundered into their comrades' backs, and then, at a single shouted order, began the grisly task of slaughtering their hapless enemies. Spears licked out, reaping a rich harvest of blood as throats and faces were opened by the viciously sharp blades, then the men wielding them stamped forward into the line of stricken legionaries, punching hard with their shields to throw their victims back into the men behind them. Stabbing down the evil spikes at their weapons' opposite ends to finish men who had fallen but still remained alive, they punched forward again, leaning into their shields and pushing upwards to force the men facing them off their feet and into the confused and milling crowd behind them.

'Again!'

The spear blades flashed out again, and more blood sprayed across the raised shields as more legionaries died, their swords and daggers beating raggedly against the Batavi shields in a desperate attempt to fight back against the inexorable advance of the men who were taking their lives with apparent impunity from any counter. Once more the soldiers' line stepped forward in one movement, more of the fallen dying under their butt spikes, another heaving push further destabilising the mass of men railing at their shields. Legionaries were still fleeing up the track behind their embattled comrades, but finding the way blocked by the mass of men bottled up by the Batavi shields, had begun to spill out to either side, to where more ranks of grim-faced soldiers were waiting for them. A faint chanting could now be heard, and Hramn nodded, putting an ostentatious hand to his ear.

'Hear that? That's the Germans, singing as they tear into your men and sending them to meet their gods!'

Aquillius's eyes narrowed but as his body tensed to spring forward and attack the Batavi prefect, he felt the prickle of a spear blade against the back of his neck, while another dimpled the skin of his thigh. The voice from behind him was cheerful but the Roman knew enough about men to recognise the deadly threat implicit in its tone.

'I wouldn't advise it, Centurion. I might be a bit slower than I used to be but my brother still has enough in him to put that spear clean through your leg. And even if you could take both of us, my boy would carve you to ribbons without breaking a sweat. They don't call him Achilles for nothing.'

The two senior centurions exchanged sideways glances, Aquillius realising that Marius was similarly under threat of death if he attempted either to run or to intervene in the murder that was being committed before them. Hramn grinned at him for a moment and then turned back to the slaughter, drawing his sword and calling back over his shoulder as he stepped off down the verge's slope.

'I see no reason not to join the fun. Watch them, Alcaeus, keep them safe for what's to come.'

He hurried away, climbing the opposite verge and disappearing into the trees, and the Romans turned their attention back to the slaughter playing out before them. The trapped legionaries were barely fighting back, their scant energy seemingly exhausted from the initial flight back up the track and the shock of being confronted by the waiting Batavi warriors, but were instead huddling behind their own shields, those men who had not already thrown away the weighty boards, more like penned sheep than soldiers, as the blood-slathered advance of the German tribesmen compressed their remaining number into a slowly shrinking amount of space. The watching centurions could see the Germans now, their swords and spears flickering palely in the forest's green-tinged gloom as they pressed up the track into the embattled legionaries, a cacophony of grunts, shouts, agonised bellows and the screams of dying men punctuating their onslaught. Looking across the slopes to either side of the roughly hewn track, Marius could see more legionaries fleeing for the safety of the open forest, realising with a small glow of satisfaction that their sheer numbers were in some places overwhelming the lines of Batavi soldiers set to cut them down, individual men bursting through the porous cordon and streaming away into the gloom in ones and twos, but even as his heart lifted his hope was cast down again by Alcaeus's softly spoken words.

'They might have been better to stand and take the death stroke they were offered. At least my men have the discipline to finish a man cleanly, once he is down and can no longer fight. The men who run into the trees will find themselves alone, for the most part, or as good as alone, and hunted by tribesmen who are as happy in the forest as a goat on a mountainside.'

The soldiers to either side of the track were moving, closing the net around the remaining legionaries, while the Germans pressed in from their rear, the survivors milling in the centre of the swords and spears that surrounded them like fish caught in a net, looking to all sides for an escape route but finding nothing in any direction except the sharp iron and hard faces of their enemies. As the centurions watched in sickened fascination, unable to tear themselves from the horrific sight of their legions being destroyed, the Germans pressed the trap tighter still, their blades darting in and out of the heaving mass of men, each stabbing thrust slaughtering another of the helplessly penned Romans.

'You'll die for this! All of you!' Alcaeus turned to look at Aquillius, seeing the tension tightening every muscle and cord in the big man's body as he spat out his murderous rage. 'There won't be anywhere you can hide from Rome's revenge! There won't be anywhere far enough from here where Rome won't find you and tear you limb from limb! If not me, then men like me will see you beaten and crucified, all of you, your guts pulled out for the crows to feast on while you watch, your—'

He went down on one knee with the force of Frijaz's blow, a powerful punch to the back of his neck that would have felled most men, turning his head to stare up at the Batavi soldier with unfocused eyes.

'I'll—'

The veteran punched down again with all the force in his body, twisting his torso with the effort of putting his fist squarely into the spot below and in front of the big man's ear, stepping back with a grimace and shaking his hand as the Roman slumped onto the forest floor, nodding to Alcaeus almost apologetically.

'Better he saves all that piss and vinegar for the tribes, I'd say.'

The wolf-priest nodded tiredly, turning back to watch as the doomed legionaries milled and fought to little avail, fewer and fewer of them remaining standing with every moment of hopelessly one-sided combat.

'Yes. Although I can't deny the truth of his words. His people will come after us like ravening wolves when these events become known to them, and any hope of lenient treatment for an ally driven to revolt by Rome's betrayal of our former amity is a forlorn hope after this . . . *this* . . .'

'Sad day?'

The priest looked at Marius, nodding slowly.

'Yes. The day that Rome and the Batavi finally lose any fellow feeling. After this there is nothing left for your emperor but to grind my people to dust. And nothing left for my people but to die with honour, and take as many of you to the Underworld as they can. It is indeed a sad day for both of us.'

'Leave them where they lie, *Banô*! If you try to pick them up before you're told to do so then bad things will happen to you very quickly! You won't die, but you'll wish you had.'

Aquillius looked at the sword and dagger that had been dropped onto the stone slabs before him with the hunger of an alcoholic scenting wine, his fingers twitching with the desire to wrap themselves around the weapons' hilts. A half-dozen men surrounded him, their spear points unwaveringly aimed at his body, which had been stripped of its armour while he had been unconscious to leave him with nothing more than his tunic and boots, a length of twine serving as a belt. Above his head he could hear the restive rumbling of a crowd, their voices rendered indistinct and distant by the walls and ceiling of the cell in which he had awoken, but unmistakably the sound of a mob of men whose blood was up. He had regained consciousness in the cell's gloom moments before, groggily stumbling to his feet and regaining his wits under the spears' blades, realising from the unmistakable stench that his tunic was cold and wet with his captors' urine.

'Where—'

'Silence!'

A spear blade floated in front of his face, so close that he could have snatched the weapon's wooden shaft and taken it from its wielder, but for the knowledge that to do so would be to invite something worse than a quick death. The men around him were not the Batavi soldiers who had escorted the Old Camp's surrendering legions to their doom, with none of the cohorts' crisp discipline, but rather German tribesmen, clearly fresh from the massacre of the two legions to judge from their aggressive demeanour and the blood crusted under their nails and in the joints of the pillaged legion armour they all wore. The man before him leaned forward behind the blade, someone more than a simple warrior to judge from his clothing and ornamentation, his face so close that it was all the big man could do to restrain himself from snapping out a hand to pinch his windpipe shut.

'You will speak when you are spoken to, Aquillius the *Banô*!'

He shrugged, looking around at the men encircling him with a tired grin, then shaking his head in morbid amusement at the way each man tensed as his eye alighted on them. Their leader sneered at him, his face twisted with hatred.

'Laugh now! You will not laugh soon, when we take you out there to die! I am Brinno, king of the Cananefates, and I have promised my warriors revenge upon you. A long, hard death awaits you out there!'

The German pointed a hand behind him at the cell's heavy wooden door, and in Aquillius's head a piece of the puzzle as to where he was dropped into place. Reaching into a bag, Brinno dropped a leather flask on the ground before him, followed a moment later by a half loaf of bread.

'Drink water and feed yourself. Make yourself ready, for you will be tested to your limits by what is to come.'

Aquillius ate the bread and drank sparingly of the water,

knowing the danger of allowing himself to be too bloated if what he expected to happen next came to pass, and the German watched with a smirk.

'This is your last meal, *Banô*. Enjoy it!'

With the bread consumed and enough water taken to rehydrate his parched mouth, but not so much as to slow him down, he stood and gestured to the weapons with a questioning expression. The German shook his head.

'Not yet. But soon enough.'

The roars of the crowd above were louder now, clearly in response to something at which he could only guess. Silence fell over them with an unexpected suddenness that confirmed Aquillius's suspicions, a long silence broken momentarily by a collective roar of approval, after which the sound died away to the thin buzz of a mob momentarily sated of their blood lust. Brinno kicked Aquillius's foot, gesturing for him to rise.

'Now. Take the weapons. But keep the blades pointed at the ground. My people won't care if you walk out before them or are dragged out with a spear in your thigh, as long as they get to see you suffer.'

Bending to pick up the sword and dagger, he turned to face the wooden door with eyes already hardened against whatever he might see on the other side. At a signal from the king it was opened, and a push in his back propelled the big man through it, blinking in the light as he stepped out onto the sand. Jeers and abuse broke out on all sides, and, ignoring the spittle that showered down as the tribesmen realised who he was, the Roman looked around him to confirm his expectation as to where he was. The arena was circular, and in the days of peace before the siege had been surrounded by wooden seating rising to a height of thirty feet to ensure that every man in the stadium would have an uninterrupted view, but the seats had long since been torn out for wood to be used in the Old Camp's defences, leaving an encircling earth bank thronged with Germans, every one of them barking and baying for the blood of the man standing before them. The Old Camp's walls were visible over their heads, the fortress apparently having not yet been put to the flame. Brinno led him out into the centre of the sandy expanse, the arena floor already marked by half a dozen bloodstains where, he presumed, men had already fought and died for the tribesmen's entertainment. Brinno raised his hands for silence, and when the crowd's roar had died away to a loud hum he shouted at them in their own language.

'My brothers! I bring you our most hated enemy!' Turning a slow circle, he raised his hands in recognition of the warriors' drunken shouts and bellows. 'Aquillius the *Banô*!'

A fresh chorus of abuse showered down onto the Roman, his lips twitching in a faint smile as the reason why he had been spared became clear.

'Bring out your killers then.'

Brinno turned to smile at him knowingly, raising his voice to be heard over the roar of the mob baying for Aquillius's head.

'You'd like that, wouldn't you, *Banô*? A chance to kill yet more of us? An honourable death in combat? You will have *none* of these!' He spat in Aquillius's face, stepping back and raising his hands again as the crowd of drunken Germans went wild with roared approval. 'My people *hate* you, Roman! They *despise* you for disfiguring the men you captured and leaving them with the choice of a dishonourable suicide or living among their fellow men with the mark of their enemy cut into their faces! And now you will pay for those crimes!'

He turned to the men waiting on the arena's far side, gesturing for them to open the wooden door opposite to the one that the centurion had been driven into the arena. After a moment's pause a man staggered through the dark opening out onto the sand to be showered with spittle by the incensed Germans, emerging into the arena to stand blinking in the sunlight, identical weapons to those Aquillius was carrying hanging at his sides. Dressed in a legion-issue tunic and boots, his cropped hair immediately identified him as a soldier, and the big man strode towards him with his weapons held at his sides until he was close enough to be heard over the mob's howling, ignoring the men at his back.

'Who are you?'

The soldier looked up, any hope left in him crumpling at the sight of the one man in the Old Camp's two legions who was both universally respected and feared.

'Petrus, Centurion. Chosen Man, Second Century, Ninth Cohort, Fifth Legion.'

'Petrus? What kind of name is that?'

The other man shrugged, the question clearly a familiar one.

'My mother was part-easterner, daughter of a slave. You know how it is.'

Aquillius nodded.

'You know me?'

The other man smiled wryly, and Aquillius found himself taking strength from such fortitude in the face of certain death.

'I know you, First Spear Aquillius.'

'You know what these bastards expect of us?'

Petrus nodded, lifting his head to stare into the big man's eyes.

'They expect you to kill me. And you will.'

Aquillius nodded soberly.

'You must fight me as best you can. But yes, I will kill you.'

The chosen man shrugged.

'At least this way it'll be quick. You, I suspect, will be a long time dying, Centurion. And be warned, there are two dozen of us back th—'

A spear point indented the back of Aquillius's neck, Brinno stepping between the two men and gesturing to the arena's centre.

'Enough! Move!'

Aquillius paced backwards at his command, feeling the spear's cold iron point hard against his skin, watching his fellow soldier with the concentration of a man who knew that one of them would have to die if the other was to survive.

'It would be better for you to die now, Centurion, you do realise that?'

Aquillius twisted his feet to roughen the soles of his boots against the sand, hefting his weapons to feel their weight and balance.

'Clearly. But I am no more capable of surrendering to your

blade than of throwing myself on my own. Life is for those with life in them, Chosen Man Petrus. And I am not ready to die yet.'

The soldier nodded, crouching into a fighting stance. Brinno gestured to his warriors to back away from the two Romans, then bellowed an order at them.

'Fight! Fight *now*!'

Rather than throwing himself forward at his opponent, Aquillius walked slowly around to his right, pacing in a circle around the other man, ignoring the jeers of the Germans, eager for blood.

'Do you have a woman, Chosen? Family?'

The other man nodded, turning on the spot to keep the big man in front of him.

'Mother and father, if they still live. And a woman who gave me a son. She lives with them.'

'Where?'

'Colonia Agrippina.'

Aquillius stopped pacing, facing the other man with his weapons raised. Petrus's sword point was less than an arm's length from his own, the blade trembling slightly.

'I'll make this quick and clean. And I'll tell your parents, and your woman, and your son, that you died with honour.'

'Thank—'

The attack was instantaneous, the big man raging forwards with sword and dagger, his short blade deflecting the chosen man's wavering sword, a powerful thrust of his gladius punching its lethal length of shining iron through his torso with clinical precision, blood spraying across his already sodden tunic. The two soldiers were eye to eye for a moment, Petrus's hissed whisper the last breath to leave his body as his heart stopped.

'Thank . . . you.'

Aquillius stepped back, pulling the sword free as the soldier's corpse slumped to the sand. The Germans surrounding him jeered and booed their disapproval, and Brinno walked forward with his escort to address them once more, calling for silence.

'The *Banô* has survived this time, but you all know that he will never leave this arena alive! And with every fight that he wins, he will become more tired, more likely to make the mistake that will cost him his life! And . . .' he paused to allow the unabated buzz of hatred and abuse to quieten, 'with every fight that he wins, he has no choice but to be the man who sends more of his comrades to the Underworld before him, damning his spirit to their torment once he has given up this unwinnable struggle. My brothers, this is one day of bloodshed that will live in our history forever! The day we avenged ourselves on a hated enemy *and* turned his bloody hands on his own people! Bring out the next men to face him!'

A pair of soldiers were herded into the arena at spearpoint through the same door that the dead chosen man had used moments before, one armed, the other cautiously crabbing forward to pick up the weapons that Petrus had dropped in his death throes. They stared at the big centurion in undisguised horror, only the spears of the Germans behind them preventing them from shrinking away from the blood-spattered first spear. Aquillius walked forward to meet them, calling out the same question he had asked moments before.

'Tell me your names and where you're from. And make peace with yourselves.'

'I can't do it!'

Kivilaz rose from his wooden throne, beckoning his son to him and waiting until the boy was standing in front of him before addressing his frustration.

'You're twelve, my son. At your age I was just the same, strong enough to throw a spear but insufficiently skilled to make it hit the spot I chose. The secret, as you well know, is to practice, time and time again until the act of throwing the spear is to know that it will fly to the target without any conscious thought. And part of that practice is to learn to follow the spear with your arm and eyes after you've thrown it, as I'm sure your trainers have told you on more than one occasion. Watch me.'

The prince picked a spear from the rack that had been set up alongside his throne, walking out onto the parade ground's wide open space and raising it to his shoulder, staring down the weapon's length at the three men lashed to heavy wooden posts twenty paces from where he stood, the spears cast in his son's previous attempts to hit them protruding from the ground before them. The prisoners' faces and naked bodies were painted in flickering orange by the Old Camp's burning walls, the fortress having been torched as darkness had fallen. Tribesmen who had spent the afternoon baying for the blood of the legionaries who had been forced to fight each other in the arena had flocked back to the symbol of the two defeated legions' long defiance, eager to see it burn, and the Batavi prince had been happy to indulge them. Steadying himself, breathing deeply several times, he stepped forward with two quick paces and hurled the spear with the easy expertise of long practice, his throwing arm outstretched as he watched the missile arc briefly upwards before arrowing down to strike his chosen target in the abdomen. The legionary grunted in agony, his body pierced clean through by the pilum's needle-pointed iron head, staring glassily at the Batavi noble as he strolled across the gap between them, beckoning his son to join him.

'You see? If you follow the spear with your arm, and watch it all the way to the target, you can almost will it to hit the spot you choose. And this, my son, is what a Roman spear does to a man.'

The men on either side of their dying comrade could only watch in terror from the corners of their eyes, their heads tied to the posts to prevent them from looking away from their impending deaths. The prince reached out and grasped the spear's shaft, the weapon's movement inside his body making the wounded soldier groan in fresh agony.

'Do you see how efficient the Romans make their weapons? This long iron shaft puts all the weight of the spear behind that tiny sharp point, not like the fighting spears we use with their leaf blades for killing in close combat, and that means that it can punch through a shield and the armour behind it. This is a weapon made to be thrown and forgotten, and even if it only pierces a man's shield the shaft will most likely bend and be impossible to remove. Which means he has to discard his shield. And look at this . . .'

He led the boy around to the dying legionary's other side, tapping the blood-streaked spearhead where it protruded from the soldier's trembling back.

'It is barbed, do you see? Almost impossible to remove without killing the man. The only way to get this out without pulling half his guts out with it would be to cut the shaft with a saw, while he screams and thrashes about with the pain. A man pierced through in this way will be the last to be treated by their doctors, because they know that it is the least likely wound to be survived. They are nothing if not pragmatic . . .' he grinned at the boy, '. . . a new word for you, I expect. It means that they always do what is most logical even if the cost to the individual concerned is his death. So let us practice what they preach, shall we? Let's leave this man here, with my spear through him, and see how long it takes him to die. And now you can try again, and see if you can master this difficult art. I will be watching, I promise.'

He turned and walked back to his throne to find Hramn and Alcaeus waiting for him, the former standing in a relaxed posture while the wolf-priest was holding himself erect in the presence of his prince.

'Greetings, sister's-son.' He embraced Hramn, then inclined his head to Alcaeus, who bowed deeply in return. 'It is done then. The long siege of the Old Camp is at an end, and this symbol of Rome's power over us will burn to the ground before the sun rises again.'

Hramn grinned at his uncle through a grimy mask of ingrained blood, which he was yet to wash out of his skin's pores, his armour sprayed and spattered black with the dried gore of the massacre in the forest that morning.

'You have triumphed, and led your tribe to a victory that will echo down the centuries when the histories of this time are written. And cut your hair, I see.'

Kivilaz grinned ferociously, stroking his freshly trimmed beard, previously long enough to touch his chest and dyed a dull red in accordance with his oath to retain the colour, traditionally that of an unblooded warrior, until the fortress fell.

'I put the blade to my beard even as you were marching those Roman fools to their deaths.' The boy let out a grunt as he hurled a spear at the captive legionaries, the weapon's point bouncing off the parade ground's sandy surface a foot short of his target's feet. 'Good throw! Just a little more distance and you would have hit him!' He turned back to the officers. 'These few we retained for sport are the last of them, I presume?'

Hramn shrugged.

'A small number will have escaped into the forest, it's inevitable, but their liberty will be short-lived. Other than these three, there were another twenty-two taken to their arena, including the *Banô*.'

'He's dead, I presume?'

Hramn shook his head with a wry grin.

'Not yet. It seems the man has a charmed life. We matched him with over a dozen of his men, two and even three at a time, but every time he managed to leave them all face down and walk back to centre of the arena as if the whole thing were no more than a training session. I would not wish to face him alone.'

Kivilaz nodded slowly.

'Perhaps you've toyed with him enough. Our allies must see him dead, if their anguish at the horrors he has carried out is to be calmed, and I am wary of creating a symbol of further Roman resistance.'

'You wish him to die tonight? I can bring him here to be made an example of.'

The prince shook his head.

'That would deny the tribes their moment of revenge. But tomorrow, once the arena is full, release *all* the remaining prisoners onto the sand. Tell them that they can have their freedom if they take him down and make him die slowly. Use your imagination as to how they do that, but make sure his howls of pain and desperation are heard by every man within a mile of the spot. And if they refuse then I'm sure Brinno will find sufficient men who lust after revenge to do the job.' A muffled shriek of agony interrupted him, and he turned to look at the tethered prisoners, one of whom had a spear through his right thigh, the boy turning to his father with a delighted smile. 'Very well done! You see, you are becoming a warrior fit to fight alongside Hramn and his wolf-priest! Now sit and listen as we discuss what is to be done with our captives.'

Hramn waited respectfully until the boy was seated alongside his father's throne before speaking again.

'And after Aquillius is dead? What would you have me do with them?'

Kivilaz shrugged.

'Free them, of course. We need survivors, a few men to spread the word of the horrors the men who defied the will of the Batavi have endured. I want Rome to know what's waiting for any legion they send north, and I want the Gauls to be under no illusions as to which of our two kingdoms is the more vindictive in victory. And the more likely to achieve that victory, for that matter, despite their captured legions.'

Hramn nodded.

'Very well, my prince.'

Kivilaz turned his gaze to the wolf-priest, whose eyes were fixed upon the captive legionaries.

'You disapprove, Alcaeus.'

'I do, my prince.'

The older man smiled, his eyes hard, as the centurion turned his grey-eyed gaze to stare levelly at his ruler.

'As straightforward as ever, forthright without fear for any consequence. I like that in a man, and more so in a priest. So tell me, do you believe that these men fought with honour?'

'No, my prince.' Alcaeus shook his head firmly. 'Far from it. I believe they hid behind their walls for half a year and used deceit and trickery to keep us at bay, forcing us to spend our men in vain attempts to break into their fortress.'

'You lost comrades?'

'I lost *friends*, my prince. As one always does in battle. But men lost in such a way do not die with glory, in the heart of the enemy's line with their swords and bodies painted red, deaths to be celebrated in stories and songs. They are killed by men they will never see, and without any opportunity to sell their lives dearly. My friends died with arrows in their throats, or crushed by rocks thrown from the walls. One was burned alive, pinned to the wooden shell of our testudo by a bolt. For these deaths, and many more, I despise these men for the cowards they are.'

Kivilaz raised a questioning eyebrow.

'But for all that, you still disapprove of this?'

'I do not believe the slaughter of hapless men at the end of their endurance brings any cause for pride to our tribe. Our warriors' deeds are watched by Herakles, and he must surely have turned his face from what we did today.'

Kivilaz nodded, smiling faintly.

'Herakles. Clever of you, Priest, to use the Greeks' name for our god rather than what the Romans prefer. But why not simply call him Magusanus?'

Alcaeus inclined his head in respect.

'Magusanus is a tribal god, my prince, a god of hunting, and raiding, and feasting. Whereas Herakles is a soldier's god.'

The two men stared at him for a moment, Hramn's gaze stony while his uncle's was kinder.

'I understand. Your upbringing and training have invested you with certain beliefs that are hard to abandon. So tell me, what would Herakles do to restore our honour, if he were here now?'

The wolf-priest thought briefly, then gestured to the rack of spears.

'I will show you, if I may?'

Kivilaz extended a hand.

'Be my guest. Perhaps you can provide my son with an example to follow.'

Alcaeus selected three spears, weighing them in his throwing hand in turn and rejecting one, nodding satisfaction with its replacement. Walking to a spot twenty paces from the tethered prisoners, he turned to face them, muttering a few brief words of prayer before stamping forward and slinging the first weapon in a low arc, the spear thudding into the left-hand man's chest. The Roman tensed, fought the iron shaft's agonising intrusion for a moment, then slumped, his chin sinking onto his collarbone. Taking the second spear from his left hand, the centurion repeated the prayer and then threw again, putting the weapon's evil iron head through the right-hand man's breastbone and killing him instantly. The last man, barely alive with the prince's spear still transfixing him, raised exhausted eyes to stare at him for a moment, nodded fractionally against the rope's grasp, then slumped down again, held up only by his restraints. Alcaeus prayed swiftly, then hurled the last spear with all his strength, sending the missile in a flat trajectory to pierce the last legionary's chest, killing him as surely as he had done with his comrades. Stepping back from the dead captives, he turned to Kivilaz and bowed deeply.

'Thank you, my prince. I will pray to Herakles, and ask for his continued favour in granting us good fortune in the battles to come.'

Kivilaz inclined his head with equal respect.

'You have indeed provided an excellent example of martial prowess, Alcaeus. Now leave us and ensure that the prisoner Aquillius is secure in his captivity. I have much to discuss with my nephew.'

The centurion bowed again and turned away, leaving the two men staring after him.

'You indulged the man, Uncle, and in return he went too far.'

Kivilaz shrugged.

'Too far? Really? Not everyone is as much of a hothead as you, Hramn. Alcaeus is the expression of a warrior religion that our family have always encouraged, bringing the favour of the gods through their sacrifice and bravery, and inspiring our young men to feats that might otherwise remain out of the reach of their courage. What would you have me do with him, for his crime of pointing out that the ways in which we are indulging our tribal allies' need for fire and blood run counter to the beliefs of that religion? You need men like Alcaeus and his fellow priests to keep your cohorts fighting, otherwise your men might start to despair, given the loss of half your strength at Gelduba. Do you not?'

Hramn nodded fractionally, his lips pursed in silence at what he knew, for all the mildness with which it was phrased, was a rebuke, and after a moment the prince continued.

'We agree then. You have your differences, that's obvious, but I know you can find a way to work together rather than pulling in different directions. For your own sake, for my sake . . .' he pointed at the boy squatting alongside his throne, 'and for *his* sake, I suggest you do so.'

Aquillius sat cross-legged in the darkness of the arena cell into which Brinno's spearmen had herded him after the day's final bout, resting his back against the room's wooden wall with his bound legs stretched out in front of him, his lips moving as he recited the list of fourteen names and towns to himself, only ceasing the exercise when he was sure he had all of their details perfectly memorised. The tribesmen who had gathered to watch him die had stared down at him in awed silence as he left the fighting surface, their hatred rendered impotent by astonishment at the sheer ferocity with which he had torn through the legionaries sent to kill him. His body was bone tired, exhausted beyond fatigue by the succession of combats that had demanded every ounce of his prowess and speed with a blade, and half a dozen minor wounds bore evidence to the narrowness of some of his victories, cuts and abrasions that he knew would slow his reactions and sap his strength in the morning. Their combined effect would probably result in a fatal loss of speed and power, when combined with the lack of any food or water since the scanty meal he had consumed on recovering from the blow that had stunned him that morning. His tunic was stiff with blood from the dead men's wounds, his legs streaked with the gore that had puddled across the arena's surface as the afternoon had worn on, and his nostrils were filled with the rich aroma of the blood spray that had dried on his face. His hands and feet were numb from the harsh bite of the ropes that had been used to bind his wrists and ankles, trussing him so effectively that the hourly check by the tribesmen set to watch him presented no opportunity for escape whatsoever. Whoever's turn it was to leave their fire and open the cell's door to check that he was still there made a cursory and contemptuous inspection of their prisoner before heading back to drink more beer and crow at the Old Camp's blazing ruin.

This time, the door's bolts were drawn back but without the usual drunken gusto and in a manner better suited to stealth than had hitherto been the case, a shadowy figure slipping into the cell and closing the door behind him, almost invisible in the darkness.

'Centurion Aquillius.'

Straining to see the indistinct figure, Aquillius nodded.

'Yes. You're no German though. You speak Latin as well as I do.'

'Speak quietly, if you'd prefer not to toss away this last chance for freedom.'

Puzzled, the Roman squinted at the newcomer for a moment before realising who it was.

'I remember your voice. You're the Batavian centurion who was sent to negotiate with us, the wolf's head, the man who showed such disgust at the slaughter of my legionaries. But how can *you* be my last chance for freedom?'

Alcaeus moved closer, dropping a fragment of iron the length of his finger on the floor at the captive's feet.

'Yes, I am Alcaeus, and the answer to your question is simple: I can give you what you need to make your escape.'

The Roman frowned up at the Batavi priest.

'Why would you betray your own people?'

Alcaeus smiled down at him, his teeth a pale gleam.

'I dream, Aquillius.'

'You dream. And what of it? We all dream. I dream of battle and the most efficient ways to defeat an enemy so completely that no man remains standing to offer me his surrender.'

'My dreams are somewhat different to yours. So listen to me, if you wish to live?'

Aquillius nodded.

'I am, you will have noticed, unlikely to have any more pressing engagement. Speak as you wish, priest.'

'We have met on several occasions, Aquillius the *Banô*, and every time I have seen your face I have been struck by the sensation that I know you from another time and place.'

Aquillius stared back at his dark silhouette.

'I can assure you that we never met before the day your cohorts marched past this fortress last year.'

'I know. And yet even that first time that I laid eyes upon you it was as if I already knew you, and knew the kind of person you are. And over time, as I have spoken with you in our negotiations, that feeling of familiarity has grown until I am completely sure. I have seen you fight, Aquillius, in my dreams.'

Aquillius shook his head incredulously.

'In your *dreams*.'

'Scoff all you like, Roman, but be assured of one thing. I do see the future. Sometimes I see the most inconsequential of things, sometimes I am witness to events that are to come to pass, matters of the greatest import. I dreamed about the battle at Gelduba.'

'The battle in which the arrival of the Vascones turned the fight against you?'

'Yes. In my dream I was leading my century forward, just as was the case that night, driving the legions back over their walls, forcing them into the camp that was to be the scene of their deaths, but all the time I knew that something terrible was behind me, something the dream had never revealed to me.'

'And it came to pass.'

'It did. In the instant before those auxiliaries tore into our rear and started the disaster that cost us half our strength, I relived the last moments of the dream, knowing that when I turned it would be to witness horror.'

'And?'

'The first thing I saw was my chosen man dying on their spears. A lifelong friend whose life I might have saved, had I just discerned what it was that the gods were trying to tell me.'

Aquillius shrugged.

'You cannot be responsible for what you do *not* see in these dreams.'

'No? Perhaps it is a punishment from the gods, revealing enough of what is to come that I see its possibilities without giving me enough to avert such a disaster.' He sighed. 'Perhaps it is the price I must pay for my chosen path in this life. But I have other dreams, *Banô,* and in one of them, as I have said, you have made more than one appearance. I have watched you fight, Aquillius, alongside a man I judge to be the greatest swordsman in our tribe.'

The Roman stared up at his indistinct silhouette.

'And you believe that if you free me, this dream will come to pass.'

The priest shook his head.

'I do not simply believe it. I *know* it. And when the time comes I will call on you to fight, and you *will* answer that call. Because you will swear to do so. And I guarantee that doing so will not put your oath of loyalty to Rome at risk.'

Aquillius nodded slowly.

'And this dream, will you tell me what it holds?'

Alcaeus shook his head slowly.

'If I do then I may jeopardise its coming to pass. Whereas if I free you, I trust that Hercules will ensure that the path you follow will bring you to the right place at the right time. I can say no more.'

The Roman stared up at him questioningly.

'And what is to stop me from promising to do as you wish and then disappearing into the countryside, never to be seen again. You know I'm capable of doing just that.'

'I'd guessed as much. But there are two reasons why that won't happen. The first is that you are a man of honour above all else, from the little I know of you. If you promise on that honour to answer my call then I know in my heart that when the time comes you will act exactly as I have dreamed it.'

'And the second?'

'Is simpler by far. Whether you are Aquillius or the *Banô,* you can no more run from your fate than any of us can. What I have dreamed will come to pass, be assured of that. In freeing you now I make certain that you will be to hand when you are most needed.'

'So why do you need my promise, if I have no choice in the matter?'

The Batavi centurion smiled tightly.

'Because when I call on you to fight the odds will be heavily stacked against you. A rational man would decline the combat.'

'Do I die, in your dream?'

'I cannot say. I have not seen the end of the fight, but what I have seen is savage and glorious. A man could be proud to die in such a moment of utmost achievement, if that is the price the gods demand for a such a pivotal role in these matters.'

Aquillius looked up at him for a moment and then shrugged.

'It seems I have little choice, if I wish to live beyond tomorrow's dawn. Very well priest, free me. In return I swear on my honour that I will do as you wish when the time comes for this dream to become reality. Let us hope that neither of us comes to regret this bargain.'

5

Vindonissa, Germania Superior, April AD 70

'At last. It's about time we got some more support.'

Legatus Longus nodded, assessing the long column of auxiliary infantry marching onto the Vindonissa parade ground with an experienced eye. The Twenty-first Legion had reached their home fortress a week before, and the legion's relief at the completion of their long journey across the Alps from Northern Italy had quickly changed to eagerness to march on the enemy, albeit tempered by an acute awareness that they were still only one legion potentially facing ten times their own strength if the Batavi, the Germans and the Gauls were to combine.

'What do you think, First Spear? Do they look sufficiently warlike to you?'

Pugno nodded slowly.

'Eight cohorts of auxiliary infantry are very welcome, Legatus. Will they come under your command?'

'No, they will not.' Both men turned to find Petillius Cerialis behind them, Pugno snapping to attention while his legatus inclined his head in respect for the legatus augusti's rank despite their social equality. 'Gaius Sextilius Felix is not the average auxiliary commander, gentlemen, and I expect he'll make that very clear as soon as he gets the opportunity. He was awarded the rank of legatus, and put in command of these eight cohorts, pretty much every auxiliary soldier in Noricum, on the orders of Antonius Primus as a mark of the loyalty he has shown to Vespasianus. And he was given very specific orders, to watch the procurator of Raetia like a hungry dog, ready for any sign that

Porcius Septimius was sufficiently loyal to Vitellius to send his own cohorts to war. Given that Septimius didn't manage to find the courage of his apparent convictions and join the fight, Legatus Felix's men have been sitting on their arses for the best part of six months, and you can take it from me that he'll have been the most frustrated man in that camp. Now that he's been called forward to join the war against the Gauls and Germans, I expect he'll be straining at his rope to be unleashed on the first enemy we find. Shall we save him the trouble of coming to us?'

The three men walked across the open space to where the cohorts were arraying themselves, centurions and their chosen men making swift work of chivvying their men into tidy formations, the ranks of mail-clad soldiers swiftly falling silent as their officers, spying Cerialis's approach, bellowed for them to come to attention. A bronze-armoured officer strode forward and saluted crisply, waiting in silence for Cerialis to respond, the cavalry officer behind him echoing the gesture of respect an instant later. The legatus augusti nodded, looking up and down the paraded cohorts before speaking.

'Welcome, Sextilius Felix, and you are very welcome indeed! Your men are well turned out and well disciplined, they do you great credit and they will make an excellent addition to my army, which is doubtless what Licinius Mucianus had in mind when he directed you to join us. Allow me to introduce Legatus Tiberius Pontius Longus and First Spear Pugno of the Twenty-first Rapax. And who's this fellow you've brought along with you? He has the look of a German.'

The words were spoken with a smile, but the challenge implicit in them was unmistakable. Pugno, guessing from his superior's jocular tone that Cerialis knew exactly who the cavalry wing's leader was, maintained his expressionless mask as he waited to see how the other man would respond. Stepping forward, the big man saluted again, his confident gaze fixed on the Roman general.

'I am Julius Briganticus, Legatus Augusti, appointed commander of the Ala Singularium by order of Aulus Vitellius after his victory over the usurper Otho, and more recently confirmed in that position by order of Consul Mucianus. I received orders from Rome to join Legatus Felix's command, and to march with his cohorts and report to you here. I am to operate under your command in ridding Germania of any and all enemies, whether from inside the empire or from outside its borders. My cavalry wing is formed of picked men from half a dozen other wings and was originally intended to form a bodyguard to Vitellius. When his advisors decided against such a thing it was agreed that rather than returning them to their various units they would be retained as a formed unit, in order to demonstrate the excellence of the empire's cavalry. My only regret is that we did not participate in the battles that ended the civil war.'

Longus nodded slowly, looking the cavalryman up and down.

'You seem very familiar to me, Prefect. You have the look of a man that I used to see on the Palatine Hill, the commander of the imperial bodyguard, in the days before Nero killed himself and Galba sent the Germans home at the behest of his praetorians, the fool.'

'You speak of Hramn, Legatus, a nobleman of the Batavi tribe. My cousin. I have not spoken to him for two years, not since it became clear to both of us he did not share my belief that Roman rule is the most beneficial way for our people to prosper, a belief that swiftly led to my family turning against me. I volunteered for service elsewhere in the empire as a means of avoiding the mutual hostility that would have resulted had I remained within our cohorts.'

Pugno looked at the German with fresh interest. Even Felix seemed momentarily taken aback.

'I was aware that you were of the Batavi tribe, Briganticus, but the fact that you are so closely related to their prince Civilis was not communicated to me. He's your uncle, if I'm right?'

'He is, Legatus. Although I have sworn scared oaths to Hercules, Mars and Jupiter that if I meet him in battle only one of us will leave the field. I will spare myself and my men no hardship in the pursuit of victory over this rebellion.'

'Why?'

The German's gaze flicked from Longus to Pugno, his momentary surprise at being addressed by the senior centurion betrayed by a narrowing of his eyes, and the legatus smiled, raising a hand to defuse the tension.

'Forgive my first spear his apparent abruptness, Prefect. My new legion raises its officers in a rather less formal tradition than you might have become used to.'

Briganticus nodded impassively.

'I am Batavi, Legatus. My people treasure "abruptness" as a sign of manliness no less than the Twenty-first Legion. And so to answer your question, First Spear Pugno, my path diverged from that followed by my uncle when he determined on fomenting revolt against the empire among the men of my tribe. His encouragement to Vindex when that fool led the Lingones in their doomed rebellion against Nero was not the first sign I had seen of his true intentions, but when the result was his brother's execution I knew that I could no longer tolerate him. I—'

'Your father was Civilis's brother, Claudius Paulus?'

Briganticus turned to Cerialis with a shake of his head.

'No, Legatus Augusti, but he might as well have been. My father was killed in Britannia during the revolt of the Iceni, and as my mother's older brother, Paulus assumed responsibility for my training as a warrior, and took my father's place in explaining the ways of the tribe to me. He was a prince of the tribe, but not yet a citizen of the empire, and Kivilaz must have known that this would make him vulnerable to Rome's need to be seen to exert its authority, once Vindex was inevitably defeated, but still he took my adopted father with him on his mission with the avowed intent of counselling the Lingones against confronting Rome.' He shook his head disgustedly. 'Which was, of course, nothing but a pretext for meeting Vindex and determining his readiness to start a full-blooded war with Rome, a war the Batavi might take a side in. And, since the governor of Lower Germania had to be seen to be acting decisively, his brother, a non-citizen, was a quick and easy target for reprisal when Vindex's revolt had been brought to its inevitable brutal end. He was executed, as I'm sure you know, and my uncle sent to Rome where Galba pardoned him.'

'This man Claudius Paulus was executed for his older brother's crimes?'

Briganticus nodded at Pugno, his face stone-like.

'My adopted father was always in thrall to his older brother. Kivilaz was the hero of the family, always at the point of the tribe's spear. At the Medui river, at the defeat of the Iceni, at any major battle the Batavi fought in twenty-five years, he was always there, and my adopted father forever lived in his shadow, aspiring to the greatness that seemed effortless to Kivilaz. It killed him in the end, that need to stand alongside a brother whose first thought was always for himself, and on the day that he was executed I swore a blood oath to tell Kivilaz the depth of my hatred for him at the moment I take revenge for that betrayal of family duty. I will spit the words into his face as I put my iron into his guts, or as he kills me. You can depend on one or the other.'

The Old Camp, Germania Inferior, April AD 70

'Well now, Munius Lupercus, here you are, ready to travel west to meet your new mistress. I wonder what use Veleda will decide to put you to?'

The Roman looked down from his horse at Kivilaz, his face wan from a week of captivity during which he had seen daylight for no more than a few minutes at a time, his features still drawn from the privations of the siege's last weeks. He was seated on a horse in the middle of the half-dozen men of the Batavi Guard who had been detailed to escort him safely to the priestess Veleda's tower in the heart of the Bructeri tribe's land to the east of the river Rhenus, Marius mounted alongside him. The burned-out remains of the fortress loomed over them, the heads of hundreds of dead legionaries and their officers staring blankly at them from the stakes on which they had been crudely impaled as a warning to others.

'Julius Civilis. I see you've cut away your red hair, now that you've finally managed to starve my men into submission. Does it irk you that in six months you never managed to get so much as a single man inside my camp, other than those we threw down from the walls to have their throats cut by the legionaries waiting below? The deaths of your men used to trouble me, at first, although in the end you threw them at us in such numbers that their slaughter lost all meaning for me. I thought I understood the depths of your barbarism when I saw you send them forward to risk the most horrific of fates.'

The Batavi leader grinned up at him.

'Surely the moment our "barbarism" became fully clear was when you marched your men into the forest expecting us to feed and shelter them, only to discover that wasn't our intention?' The Roman stared down at him in silence. 'What, you've got nothing to say? No curse to spit down at me? No threats of Rome's revenge?'

Lupercus shook his head wearily.

'I never was a man who conducted warfare with his mouth, I usually left that to men whose verbosity outweighed their martial prowess.'

The German smiled again.

'In another man I'd mark that down as an attempt to provoke me to kill you, and spare you the shame of being enslaved to a barbarian woman, but in your case I think it's just weariness with the world around you that makes you so dangerously frank. I shall have to warn your guards not to rise to what they will consider provocation.' He turned to look at Marius, who was sitting in gloomy silence beside his legatus. 'And you, First Spear, do you have nothing to say? No gratitude for my nephew here for having spared you the indignity of dying in the massacre that took so many of your men?'

The Roman looked down at him expressionlessly.

'I would rather have died with a sword in my hand than found myself likely to live out the remainder of my days in the service of a servant of barbarian gods. Your nephew has doomed me to shame and a memory sullied by a lifetime of captivity, where I might simply have taken my leave of this life with dignity.'

Hramn laughed curtly.

'With dignity? There was no *dignified* death planned for you, friend Marius. You would have gone to the arena with your colleague the *Banô,* and been doomed to kill your own men until one of them managed to kill you.'

Marius shrugged.

'Then that would have been a quick and easy death, because I would never raise a blade against my own men.'

'Unlike your friend. He took fourteen of your legionaries apart that first afternoon.'

Lupercus nodded knowingly, a faint smile creasing his lips.

'Something at which neither the first spear nor I are in the slightest surprised. But tell me . . .' he waved a hand at the sea of heads arrayed in front of the burned-out camp, 'if our colleague Aquillius is dead, as you say, then where is his head in this sea of grisly trophies, if you sent him to the arena to meet his death at the hands of his own men? If you hated him so much, why is he not here in the best position to be seen and gloated over? After all, it's clear enough that you despised him to a man.'

'He's *dead*.' Kivilaz had spoken before Hramn had the chance to reply. 'And his head has been preserved in oil to serve as a reminder of the ill that you Romans do when you are allowed to establish dominion over the German tribes.'

'And of course it is by now far from here, which means there's no chance of our wishing him farewell.'

Kivilaz looked at Lupercus for a moment before replying.

'How perceptive of you.'

The legatus shrugged.

'Well, wherever he is now he can't be of assistance to us, so I suggest you get us on the road to this barbarian priestess of yours.'

The Batavi prince nodded, gesturing to the man in command of the small group of guardsmen.

'On your way, Bairaz, and make sure that you get these two precious specimens to the lady Veleda undamaged. Promises have been made, and the Batavi keep our promises!' He bowed mockingly to the legatus, unable to keep a hard grin from his face. 'Farewell, Munius Lupercus! Think of me from time to time, while you live the rest of your life far from your home and family, unknown and largely unlamented! I'll be sure to make it known that you surrendered the Old Camp to me, just in case any shred of honour still clings to your name among your people!'

Lupercus nodded tautly.

'Be quick spreading that news. Someday soon the only people you'll have to talk to will be the legions who will come north with your death in their hearts.'

His horse turned to follow that of the guardsman holding its bridle, and he rode away without a backward glance. Marius nodded soberly to Hramn and followed, leaving the two Batavi noblemen watching as the small party trotted towards the road that would take them to the river, where a boat awaited to carry them over the Rhenus and into tribal territory.

'Have your men worked out how it was that the *Banô* came to make his escape yet?'

Hramn watched the riders for a moment longer before replying.

'His ropes had been cut, but not cleanly. Whatever it was that did the cutting was small, and ragged, from the look of the ropes. The closest we can get to knowing what happened is to surmise that he managed to palm a fragment of a broken sword blade, and use it to saw at his ropes while he was waiting for the dawn to come. The rest you already know.'

'What about your deputy. What did Alcaeus have to say?'

'Just what you'd expect. He found the prisoner unrepentant, when informed that he was to die in the morning, and so he left the bastard to cook in his own juices, and reflect upon his coming death. He also said that if he'd known what it was that the man was planning to do to his guards he'd have cut his throat on the spot.'

Kivilaz nodded, his lips a tight line of white flesh. The men set to guarding the hated Roman centurion had been found the next morning, one of them dead in the captive's cell with a broken neck while the other three had been set about with his knife, their corpses left sprawled in the stink of their blood and faeces with Aquillius's trademark eagle carved into each of their foreheads.

'What sort of man would do that?' Kivilaz shook his head in bafflement. 'I don't mean the disfiguring of our dead, we know why he feels the urge to leave his mark on them well enough from our own attitude to our enemy's fallen. But what is it that makes a man waste precious time in which he could be putting distance between himself and our revenge?'

Hramn shrugged.

'Perhaps he believes that he is a man with a reputation to uphold. Or perhaps it was simply the urge to show us that his spirit is unbroken. Either way he's going to die slowly and in great pain when we recapture him. After all, the fool can hardly expect to avoid discovery from here all the way to the Winter Camp, can he?' His mouth twitched in amusement. 'And when we do recapture him I'll grant my priest the pleasure of being the man who ends his life. Not only will the *Banô* be dead, but Alcaeus will have taken his chance to convince me that he remains committed to the tribe's cause.'

'You continue to doubt the man who led the massacre of the First Legion at Bonna?'

The prefect nodded.

'I do. Whatever else I may or may not be, I am a fair judge of men. And something about this priest troubles me. Both he and Scar always struck me as a little bit too smooth. They seemed too close to the Romans in some ways, too . . .'

Kivilaz raised an eyebrow.

'Too professional for your taste?'

Hramn's face hardened, but he ignored the implied jibe.

'Too *Roman*, Uncle. Draco served for the best part of twenty-five years and yet he has never been anything less than a faithful member of the tribe. And Alcaeus has an air of detachment from our cause that cannot help but communicate itself to our men. He considers the cohorts to be men apart from the army you have raised from the tribes, and so in turn do they. I wonder how well he and his men will fight when the battle I choose for them does not conform with his views as to what is appropriate for the tribe's sons to shed blood over.'

Kivilaz pursed his lips, nodding in understanding at the frustration in his nephew's words.

'If there's even a hint of truth in your concerns then we'd be best knowing the depth of his commitment to our cause sooner rather than later. And he'll have plenty of chances to prove himself as the true Batavi we need them all to be soon enough. The elders have agreed with my opinion that it's time Claudius Labeo and his Tungrian allies were removed from the field of play, to borrow an image from your favourite pastime. Which means marching west, cohorts and tribesmen alike, and running him to earth wherever he can be made to stand and fight. You'll soon enough have the chance to see how well your priest performs when he's pointed at the Gauls, won't you?'

Mosa Ford, April AD 70

'That's close enough, I'd say.'

Alcaeus peered through the leaves of the few trees between the three men and the forest's edge, kneeling in the shadow of a massive oak to survey the scene playing out two hundred paces to their left with Egilhard and Lanzo on either side as his newly promoted chosen man and watch officer. The fortified village of Mosa Ford huddled on the opposite bank of the river, stout wooden walls having long since been erected to defend such an important river crossing, a one-hundred-pace-long bridge carrying the road from Germania Inferior into the Tungrian heartland, built to allow easy passage of grain to feed the armies safeguarding the frontier. On the eastern bank the Batavi cohorts were arrayed ready for battle with the Batavi Guard stood behind them in reserve, while the walls of the small fort that acted as both defence and customs post were lined with equally well-armed fighters seemingly ready to repel any attempt at seizing the crossing.

'Looks like they'll fight.'

Alcaeus nodded his agreement with Lanzo's musing.

'They'll fight. Labeo knows that if he doesn't stop us here there are no defendable barriers for another hundred miles. If we get across the Mosa then his only alternative to a quick death is to run as far and as fast as he can, while we tear the rest of his band of deserters to shreds and then visit our anger on their capital. Ah, there's the prince.'

A single figure was striding out onto the bridge, apparently heedless of the risk posed by the Tungrians' spears and bows, coming to rest a dozen paces from the heavy wooden gate that barred his way.

'And now he's telling them that their resistance will be pointless.' The centurion shook his head in amusement. 'You have to admire the man's balls. There are probably a hundred men on those walls within spear throw of him and he strides out in front of them without so much as a pair of men to hold up shields. He's telling them that they've made their point, burned out a few farms and made a nuisance of themselves alright, but that the time for playing games is at an end. Rome's rule north of the mountains is at an end whether they like it or not, which means that they're on their own. He's willing to accept their surrender if they throw down their weapons and join with us now, and he'll even spare their homes the fate they've dealt out to the Marsaci and Cananefates. He doesn't mean it, of course.'

Egilhard nodded, the innocent recruit of a year before replaced by a battle-hardened soldier who had already watched as their leader had casually broken his word and condemned thousands of defeated Roman legionaries to a brutal death at the hands of his German allies.

'The allied tribes won't allow him to let the Tungri off the hook that easily.'

Alcaeus shrugged.

'How can they? It's their farms and villages that Labeo's been preying on. Their women his soldiers will have been raping, given half a chance. If I were one of his men I would already have either made my peace with my gods or made a quiet exit one dark night, because there's no way this ends with a renewed brotherhood between us and the Tungri, not the way I see it. No, this is just Kiv rolling the dice to see if he can persuade Labeo's men to turn him over to us without bloodshed. *Our* blood, that is.'

They watched as their leader stood before the fort's walls with his arms raised in an apparent appeal for sanity to prevail, then lowered them and stood in silence.

'And now Labeo's telling his men that they can't trust his former ally. He's recounting the story of how Kiv turned on him, once he'd played the part they'd agreed, and how the Romans who surrendered to him at the Old Camp were massacred.' Alcaeus waited for a moment, the sound of the enemy leader's voice reaching them in snatches as the wind gusted through the trees surrounding them. 'And now he's telling them that their position is impregnable, with only the bridge for us to fight from unless we try to swim the river, which of course we won't dare because they could rush two or three hundred men to any landing site before we could cross the Mosa and meet us head on as we come out of the water. He'd have them believe that this is a stalemate, and that we'll get tired of the whole thing and march away soon enough.'

As if on cue, the Batavi leader turned on his heel and retraced his steps, the jeers and curses of the men defending the bridge ringing in his ears as they gave vent to their hatred for everything he represented.

'It's a fight then.'

'Yes, but not until Kiv's provided Labeo's men with an example of what's awaiting them.'

Kivilaz stalked back down the bridge, the men on the Batavi's side of the river waiting until he was out of sight before bringing forward a heavy wooden punishment frame with a man's body spreadeagled wide across it. Half a dozen soldiers advanced in front of it to the bridge's eastern end, their shields raised to prevent Labeo's archers from putting their former comrade out of the misery to which he was about to be subjected, while the captive looked about him in evident terror, the bombast of the early hours of his captivity eroded away to nothing by his evident realisation of what was about to happen to him.

'Distraction.' Alcaeus stared at the scene unfolding before them unblinkingly, as if committing it to his memory. 'He'll keep their attention riveted on that poor soul while the real battle is fought elsewhere. It's clever. And it will work, most likely. But it is not fitting for the Batavi.'

The pair of long-haired tribesmen who had accompanied the cohorts west as Kivilaz's honoured guests stepped forward, the unmistakable glint of knives in their hands loosening the captive's tongue and bowels in simultaneous emissions of terror, his horrified wails increasing in their intensity as they approached the frame on which he was spread helplessly.

Alcaeus nodded at Egilhard.

'I don't think we need to see any more of this unnecessary bestiality. While Kivilaz's German priest hold the defenders' attention, we'd best be getting on with playing our part.'

He led the other two men away to the north along the foliage-lined riverbank, emerging from the trees to find the three-hundred-odd men of his first cohort standing ready alongside their horses.

'What a pleasure, eh gentlemen?' The centurion raised his voice to be heard by every man. 'A river to cross, and every last horse that survived the disaster at Gelduba!' He rubbed his hands in satisfaction at the chance to fight in the way that had been the tribe's most feared weapon throughout the years of their service to Rome. 'This is going to be just like the good old days! Chosen Man, go forward and make the signal!'

Beckoning Lanzo to join him, Egilhard moved quickly and quietly to the riverbank, staying in the cover of its trailing, chaotic vegetation as they stared out across the water at the far bank. He nodded to his comrade, who put his hands to his mouth and blew, imitating the high-pitched call of a coot three times in brief succession, then twice more. Both men stared intently at the opposite bank for several moments, the bushes and long grass at the river's margin seemingly undisturbed until, with a sudden flurry of movement, the men for whom the signal had been intended struck. After a moment, Egilhard's nervous expression was split by a grin, as Frijaz appeared through the greenery with a man's decapitated head held aloft by its hair. He waved, and his uncle vanished from sight to carry out the next part of the plan that had been agreed the previous night, before Frijaz, his brother and nephew had slipped into the river's ink-black water and crossed with the slow, stealthy strokes of men who had practiced swimming without disturbing the water for most of their lives. Lanzo nudged him.

'Best go and get the cohort, hadn't you? I'll watch here.' Egilhard nodded and turned to go back through the trees, only to stop as his friend put a hand on his arm. 'And Egilhard, the things that Alcaeus says about Kiv . . .'

The younger man frowned.

'Yes?'

'Take my advice.' The older man leaned closer, lowering his voice in a subconscious signal of his fear of being overheard. 'Listen to him by all means, he's our centurion, and we both know that he holds the traditions of the cohorts dear. But don't ever repeat what he says. Not even to Lataz. Don't ask me why, it'd take too long to explain, but take my advice in this one thing and you'll lighten my mind.'

The chosen man stared at him for a moment and then nodded.

'You've never given me bad advice. But sometime soon I need you to tell me what you're afraid of.'

He turned and vanished into the thin veil of trees flanking the Mosa. Finding Alcaeus waiting at the cohort's head, he saluted briskly.

'The men watching the other bank have been dealt with, Centurion. Nobody got away.'

His superior grinned fiercely.

'Good. Knobby and Stumpy haven't lost their touch yet then. Are they ready?'

'They will be.'

'Good.' The wolf-priest turned to face the waiting soldiers. *'First cohort! Follow! Me!'*

Advancing in a column four horses and eight soldiers wide, he led them through the vegetation to the narrow beach on the river's bank, the spot where the scouts had entered the water the previous evening, taking a firm grip of the leather handle sewn into the saddle of the horse beside him as its rider expertly walked it into the river without allowing the beast to break stride. Holding onto the handle on the saddle's other side, pushing his body away from the animal as it began to swim with swift, urgent kicks of its hoofs, Egilhard cast his mind back to a cold Italian dawn a year before. The river Po's water had been bitterly cold on that spring day, numbing his entire body in the time it had taken for the horse that had been his transport to cross fifty paces of swift-flowing snow-melt, rendering the young soldier so cold that he had staggered onto the far bank incapable of fighting, and yet less than half an hour later had killed his first man in a vicious skirmish with enemy troops taken by surprise by the raid's audacity. Alcaeus raised his head to grin at his deputy over the horse's back.

'This might . . . be the last time . . . we get . . . to do this! Enjoy it . . . while it lasts!'

Egilhard smiled at his centurion's levity, panting for breath as he fought to keep his armour's dead-weight from dragging him under the water, straining muscles protesting as his feet found the shelving riverbed and thrashed in the mud for purchase. The horse staggered to its feet and advanced up the bank alongside its fellow beasts while the men who had been dragged across fought their way out of the river's dark, sticky mud and staggered past the waiting scouts. Lataz took a grip of his son's armour and pulled him from the river with a grin.

'That trick just never gets old, does it lad? Where's the centurion?'

'I'm here. Your report?'

Suddenly the veteran was all business, and Egilhard realised that his father had always been more than competent enough to have achieved something better than a simple soldier's life, if he had allowed himself to escape the seductive trap in which a blunt refusal to accept responsibility had ensnared him.

'There were three sentries, Centurion, changed every eight hours or so from the look of it. We watched them until my lad there gave the signal, then took them by surprise and killed them all.'

'Well done. Any casualties?'

Lataz shook his head with a grin.

'Only my youngest boy's virginity. He took one down himself, once the bastard had given him something to match that.' He pointed to the scar on Egilhard's chin. 'I had to wait until he had his plait cut off before he'd let me dress the cut.'

Alcaeus grinned ferally.

'Good for him. In that case let's get the rest of the cohort ashore and join the party.'

While the remaining horsemen and the soldiers hanging from their saddles were crossing the Mosa, he skirted carefully down the riverbank to the south with Egilhard and a pair of soldiers for an escort, waving them into cover as they came within sight of the bridge, then beckoning his chosen man forward. The Batavi cohorts and their Cananefates allies were still waiting patiently around the crossing's eastern end while the torturers wrung scream after weary, despairing scream from the hapless Tungrian who was paying a heavy price for his attempted assassination of their leader.

'Depressing though it is, it looks as if Kivilaz's scheme is working, and he has their full attention. I suspect that our arrival in their rear will come as a complete and very nasty surprise. Come on.'

Rejoining the waiting cohort, he took his place alongside the horse that had carried him across the river, shouting a command that was repeated by each of his centurions.

'We will advance at the trot to the rear of the enemy defences! If we encounter any opposition we don't stop, just hit and move on! When I give the command, be ready to deploy into battle line!'

He waited until the orders had reached the column's end before speaking again.

'We'll win this fight in minutes, once they see their rear has been captured and there's nowhere to run! If they surrender then just remember who you are, and leave any vengeance to the tribes! But if they choose to fight?'

The response was immediate.

'We kill them all!'

The column advanced swiftly in a wide arc designed to take them from their landing point to the bridge, their drumming hoofbeats sending coveys of wildfowl to squawking and flapping frantically into the morning air, swiftly drawing the attention of the men watching the Tungrian position's flanks, but the sentries were able to do nothing more than point at the oncoming horsemen and shout warnings that were too late for the defenders to do anything but stare in hollow-eyed disbelief at their doom as the Batavi column closed off their escape route and sealed their fate. Halting his men just outside of bow-shot from the small settlement's western edge, Alcaeus waited patiently until the cohort was deployed into line of battle before strolling forward alone into the space between his men and the bridge fort.

'Now let's see how defiant Claudius Labeo feels, shall we?'

The rebel leader came out to meet them, shaking his head in disgust at the ease with which his defence had been turned.

'It seems you have me, Centurion. Alcaeus, isn't it? I don't suppose I can presume on your fellow feeling for a brother of the tribe to allow me to escape the rather obvious fate that my former ally Kivilaz will doubtless have in mind for me? I imagine it will be rather similar to that being dealt out to my former centurion.'

The wolf-priest shook his head.

'I think my life would be worth little more than yours, were I to accept your surrender and then allow you to escape. Do you think your men will fight?'

Labeo shook his head doubtfully.

'I'd be surprised. Kivilaz will come up with a reassuring lie or two about how they'll all be spared, they'll throw down their weapons and then we'll see if he can hold Brinno and his tribesmen back from our throats. Myself, of course, he'll have other plans for. Something involving a cross and nails, I suspect.'

Alcaeus shook his head.

'Too Roman a punishment by far. I'd have thought that he'd hand you over to the Cananefates and let them see how long you can live without your skin. But I will make you a bargain, of sorts.'

Labeo cocked his head to one side.

'What bargain?'

'An oath sworn to Hercules by you, in return for the little I can do to help you escape. And with your life forfeit to me if you choose to break your word, as seems to have become your habit.'

'And your terms?'

'You know that I am a priest. What you do not know is that I am blessed, and cursed, with the ability to see small slices of the days that are yet to be. I see these things in my dreams. And I have seen you, Claudius Labeo, in one such dream. Far from here, but on ground familiar to us both. The dream will come to reality, I know that in my bones, but for that to happen the men I have seen in it so many times must be to hand. And you, Claudius Labeo, are one such man.'

'And the others?'

'Are outside of my control, for the most part, Romans and our own people, great men and common soldiers like myself. But they will be drawn to take part without knowing it, whereas you must seek out your place if you are to complete the picture I dream every night.'

'I see. And what must I do to make this happen?'

'Do you swear to play your part as I instruct?'

Labeo shrugged with a grim expression.

'It seems that I have very little choice in the matter, does it not? To stay here is, as you say, to invite a slow and painful death.'

'Swear it.'

The rebel commander shook his head in amusement, then squared his shoulders and looked Alcaeus straight in the eye.

'I swear to Hercules—'

'And to Magusanus.'

'I swear to Hercules and to Magusanus, beloved god of our tribe, that I will follow whatever instruction you give me, if I manage to escape the vengeance of Kivilaz and Brinno. And if I break my oath then you, as Hercules's and Magusanus's chosen priest, may do with me as you wish.'

The priest nodded.

'Time is short, so listen and then act without thought. You must first escape. The ground to the south of here is open, free of any of our people, which means that a man on a fast horse – if that man can detach himself from followers who are likely to see him as a means of bargaining for their own lives – could easily evade capture. And you must *not* be taken. If your capture seems inevitable then you must fall on your sword, for once Kivilaz's priests have you it seems certain I will die alongside you, condemned by your ravings under their knives.'

Labeo nodded, grim-faced.

'Suicide before capture. That seems . . . preferable. And what if I manage to get away?'

'Rejoin the armies of Rome. Make yourself indispensable to their general, so that you will be at his side when the time comes for events to play out as I expect.' He smiled wryly. 'After all, if my dream is correct you wouldn't want to miss what will come to pass, I can assure you of *that*.'

'Tungrian brothers!'

The words were distant, but audible, bellowed at the top of the speaker's voice. Labeo turned back to the bridge, both men realising that the screams of the captive's torment had died away as they had talked, replaced by an almost total silence in which Kivilaz's unmistakable voice rang out sonorously.

'My Tungrian brothers! You know we have you in a trap from which there can be no escape other than death! But we men of the Batavi did not start this war with Rome with any intention of making ourselves masters over any other tribe! The very thought of such arrogance goes against all that we believe and hold dear! Accept an

alliance with us and be at peace!' He paused momentarily, then shouted a final challenge. *'See? My sword is sheathed! And I am coming to join you, whether you want me for your leader or as a simple common soldier!'*

'He's good. You have to admit that much.'

Labeo smiled wanly at the centurion's wry comment.

'Good? When it comes to swaying the minds of men there's nobody more convincing.'

Voices were shouting from behind the defences, strong and clear, men among Labeo's rebel force urging their comrades to sheathe their weapons and surrender.

'That's Companus . . .' Labeo tilted his head to listen. 'And there's Juvenalis. If they've both given up then their men's weapons will already be back in their scabbards.'

He looked at Alcaeus.

'The south?'

'Yes. And quickly! And remember, death before capture!'

Germania, April AD 70

'And so we leave the empire. Never to return.'

Marius looked out over the ship's rail at the turbulent waters, churned by the meeting of the Rhenus and its tributary the Lupia for a moment before replying, his face every bit as bleak as his legatus's.

'Never is a big word, Legatus.'

Lupercus's mouth twitched in an attempt to make equally light of their predicament.

'But appropriate. Put any thought of rescue from your mind, Marius, because Rome isn't going to be in any position to attempt it for a good while yet.'

Bairaz leaned forward from the bench seat behind them to speak in both men's ears.

'Rome won't be in any position to rescue you in your lifetime, Munius Lupercus. We're taking you so far up the river Lupia into

Bructeri territory that you'll never be heard of again, other than whatever news Veleda chooses to share with your people. Ten legions were required to take revenge upon the tribes after Arminius triumphed over Varus, and your strength north of the mountains will never again be sufficient for anything more than holding what you have. As far as Rome is concerned, you are lost forever along with that surrendered territory. You are now no more than a name, to be consigned to the sad histories of these times.'

He sat back and left the Romans to their contemplation of the river, as the ship that was carrying them away into captivity slowly gathered speed against the river's flow.

'He's right. We'll never be heard of again other than as a distant rumour, a story for the men of my class to tell each other when they swear to take their own lives rather than submit to a coward's fate.'

Marius bristled.

'A coward's fate? No man could have done more for the empire than you in the last year! You were betrayed by Vocula when he left us to rot in the Old Camp!'

Lupercus shook his head with a soft smile.

'Dillius Vocula did exactly what I suspect I would have done, given the same circumstances. To have abandoned the Old Camp would have been to relinquish the empire's last foothold in what had become enemy territory, and I know for a fact that it was his intention to gather more strength and come back to finish the job. If only his legions had been steadfast . . .' He sighed. 'But they weren't. We bled them of their strength to fight a pointless civil war on behalf of an undeserving, incompetent opportunist, and then we diluted it further by recruiting the dregs of the local population to make up our numbers, and in the end we got exactly what we deserved for such rank idiocy. I may have had no part in the decisions that have resulted in you and I finding ourselves in such shameful captivity, but as the representative of my class, the men whose decisions resulted in this disaster, I find it hard to argue with the outcome. And it would have come months earlier if not for you and Aquillius.' He raised his voice to call a question back to Bairaz. 'There's still no sign of Aquillius, is there Decurion?'

'The *Banô* is dead.'

The Roman shook his head.

'I don't think so. I think that he was in the wind from the moment you let your collective guard down and gave him the one tiny opportunity he needed to make good his escape. You don't get a second chance with a man like that, because he can vanish into the seams of the land like a louse diving into a straw mattress. If either of us were to gain our freedom we could no more live off the land around us than I suspect you could, but Aquillius is a man apart. He made a point of learning to hunt and fish years ago, with just such an eventuality in mind, and I doubt you'll get as much as a glimpse of him until you see him facing you across a battlefield with your death in his eyes.'

'The *Banô* is—'

'Dead. Yes, you've told me that a dozen times since the first time your cousin Civilis tried to make the lie work on me, and trust me on this, Decurion, he's ten times the liar you'll ever be. Take that as a compliment if you like, because I suppose it is given the disgust I feel for the man, but be very clear that I know you're lying. Aquillius is out there, somewhere, steadily working his way south, taking no risks of being caught. You Batavians may have missed your one chance to rid yourselves of the most dangerous man in the army, and if you thought he was bad when there was nothing personal in his way of waging war, just wait and see how bestial he can be now that you've given him a reason to be angry.'

Vindonissa, April AD 70

'Greetings, First Spear Antonius. You have arrived on the eve of our advance to confront the forces of this so-called Gallic empire. Your timing is perfect for my own needs but perhaps somewhat less than perfect from your own perspective. Your cohort will make a welcome addition to my own forces.'

Legatus Augusti Cerialis smiled to indicate that he spoke with some measure of understanding of the blow that this news would represent to Antonius's men given their long march south into the mountains to reach Vindonissa, only to find themselves ordered to march north again the next morning, but the man standing to attention before him shook his head in swift denial of any such emotion.

'Thank you, Legatus Augusti. Our only concern is to avenge the death of your colleague, Legatus Augusti Vocula. If marching back into the war will bring that revenge closer, I and my men will embrace that opportunity with both hands.'

'Ah. Dillius Vocula. Yes . . .' The senior officer's smile vanished abruptly with the blunt reminder of his colleague's fate. 'Tell me, First Spear, you were there when it happened, how did our colleague die?'

Every man in the room hung on Antonius's words, torn between horror at the murder of a respected senator by his own men and the urge to know what had happened to provoke such an act of infamy.

'Yes, Legatus Augusti. I disguised myself as a common soldier and returned to the camp, after the legatus had ordered me to leave and save my men's lives. I hoped to save him from the dogs who had gathered around him. But I failed.'

Cerialis nodded, his expression sympathetic.

'I am aware, First Spear, from Dillius Vocula's dispatch to Rome at the start of the year, that you had already saved him from one mutiny, on the night that Legatus Augusti Flaccus was murdered by his own men, but on this occasion I presume there were simply too many of them?'

'Not really, Legatus Augusti, their numbers were made meaningless by their lack of resolve in the matter. Indeed, for a time I wondered if their diffidence would provide me with an opportunity to rescue him, but the Gauls had recruited a deserter by the name of Aemelius Longinus, and he showed the legatus no mercy.

One man murdered Legatus Vocula, and when this war is over I will hunt him to the ends of the earth, if that's what is required to find him and put him to my sword. I have sworn this.'

Cerialis nodded, exchanging glances with his senior officers.

'And I will provide you with any and all assistance you require to do so, First Spear, when, as you say, the small matter of the Gauls and the Batavians is concluded to my satisfaction. You will march with the Twenty-first Legion under the command of Legatus Longus, and I am sure that his first spear will assist you in ensuring that your men are ready to march in the morning.'

He glanced across the room at Pugno, who stepped forward and saluted with his usual vigour, then extended a hand to the office's door. Antonius saluted wearily and followed him from the room.

'Let me guess, your men need hot food, socks, a dozen or so pack pole replacements for those which broke on your march here, and hobnails, of course? A lot of hobnails.'

Antonius nodded, and the Twenty-first's senior centurion clicked his fingers at his waiting chosen man.

'Get the stores opened up and invite First Spear Antonius's centurions to take whatever they need to get their men back on the road. Tell that slug Lucius to take it up with me if he doesn't like the idea, but warn him that the men in question now serve the Twenty-first, so he'd better have a good reason for even considering asking the question. I'll be with the Blood Drinkers. Oh, and send a runner to the duty cohort commander to join me in the mess.'

Antonius smiled inwardly as the junior officer turned away with an expression every bit as forbidding as that which, he was swiftly coming to realise, was Pugno's customary outlook on the world.

'Let's get something understood.' He turned back to find Pugno standing close to him, his voice lowered for privacy and, he suspected, a hint of menace. 'Like I told my man there, you serve the Twenty-first now, which means you serve *me*. My legatus tells me that your legion saw combat.'

Antonius shrugged.

'Some. Although none of it went all that well except by good fortune.'

The other man nodded, his lips tightly pursed as he grimaced at his own memories of battle.

'As is often the way. I couldn't say that the Twenty-first has been covered in glory in the last year either, and you'd better be clear that I intend to rectify that state of affairs very shortly. You and your men don't belong to Legatus Augusti Cerialis, nor to Legatus Longus – you belong to me. And I am not an easy-going master at the best of times.'

The weary first spear shrugged, unblinkingly returning Pugno's direct stare.

'And these are far from the best of times. I understand, First Spear. And I know that there can only be one first spear in any legion, so from now until the day we part company I'm expecting you to treat me like one of your cohort commanders. And I'll make you two hard promises. We'll be as good as the best of your cohorts, as good on the march, as good in the fight and as good in camp. I guarantee it.'

Pugno nodded.

'I expect nothing less. And?'

'If I ever suspect that you're favouring your own men over mine, in *any* way, I'll be in your face just as fast as you'd be in mine.'

The other man raised an eyebrow, confident in his position and yet intrigued at his new officer's pugnacity.

'Do you think you can live up to that promise?'

Antonius leaned back slightly as if sizing up his new superior, putting both hands on his hips, evidently unconcerned as to whether the man facing him was convinced or not.

'Let's both hope we never have to find out, shall we?'

A slow, lopsided smile creased Pugno's face.

'You'll do.' He turned away, waving a hand to beckon his newest officer to follow him. 'Come on then, let's get you introduced to your brother officers.'

The air in the centurion's mess was thick with the smell of

beer and cooked meat, every officer without duty seemingly intent on eating and drinking as much as possible in the time remaining before their march north, and Pugno acknowledged drunken salutes and the occasional good-natured insult from those men who were sufficiently long in the tooth not to stand on ceremony with him, steering Antonius towards a round table in the room's corner around which eight men were sitting in various states of inebriation. Seeing Pugno approach they stood, raising their cups in greeting, tensing to reply as he barked out a toast.

'Blood Drinkers!'

The response to his challenge was instantaneous.

'Blood and glory!'

They drank to a man, and a steward came forward with a beaker for Pugno, who passed it to Antonius and signalled for another as his officers retook their seats.

'This is the good stuff.'

They drank, and Antonius nodded appreciatively at his first taste of beer for weeks, sinking into the indicated seat as the men around the table eyed him curiously.

'This is our new brother Antonius. From this moment he is one of us, serving the Twenty-first with his cohort.' Pugno paused and looked around them. 'And in case any of you make the mistake of thinking that he's any less of a man than any of us, this is the man who saw off the Batavians at Gelduba, the only senior centurion to have given those barbarian cunts a taste of what they've been dishing up for us since this whole fucking mess started. He's one of us now, so treat him as such or we'll be discussing the matter in private.'

The assembled officers nodded, one or two of them exchanging wry grins at happily distant memories of private discussions with their leader, others nodding at the newcomer and raising their cups in salute.

'Ah, here's Malleus.'

The duty centurion strode through the mess, heavily bearded, dark of face and bigger than any other officer present, slapping his vine stick down on the table and reaching for a beer, which he threw down his throat seemingly without noticing, holding out the beaker for a refill. Pugno waved him into a seat and signalled to the steward who, forewarned, came forward with a tray of small wooden cups, prompting knowing glances among the men at the table. Pugno turned to his newest officer and grinned broadly.

'We men who command the Twenty-first call ourselves the "Blood Drinkers", brother Antonius, and with good reason. This is the most ferocious legion in the empire, always has been and *always* will be. We're not kept here on our own in this outpost in the mountains rather than being tucked up nice and warm in one of the comfortable double legion fortresses on the great river without good reason. We have a reputation for starting fights, and for finishing them, and that sort of reputation doesn't come about by accident. These nine men and me, we guard a sacred tradition of selecting men to command centuries and cohorts who we know can live up to the name "Rapax". Men whose only worry is that they might be judged to have fallen short of what the legion requires of them. We are only one legion, but in a fight we're worth any two others you care to name, because we're faster, harder and nastier than any other two legions put together. Spilling blood for the empire or just fighting among ourselves, we never step back and we never give in, and if we die then we go down fighting to the last breath. Any of the men around this table would give their lives for the legion like *that* . . .' he clicked his fingers and his comrades nodded their agreement. 'And they'd do the same for any of their brothers. In joining the Rapax, you join the Blood Drinkers, and to join the Blood Drinkers . . .' He grinned at Antonius. 'You can probably work it out for yourself.'

The steward placed the tray in the table's centre, and every man leaned forward and took a cup, the burly newcomer passing his to Antonius with a hard-faced nod.

'Brothers . . .' Pugno raised his cup. 'Blood Drinkers!'

'Blood and glory!'

Watched by a suddenly quiet mess, the assembled officers observing their seniors' ritual with ill-disguised envy, every man stood and raised his own cup, saluting one another with hard stares and then drinking. Antonius made to raise his own cup, but Pugno shook his head, looking around the mess in challenge.

'All in good time. Brother officers of the Twenty-first, welcome our new brother Antonius to the legion in the customary manner!'

The chant started immediately, the gathered centurions hammering their empty cups on the tables in a din of perfectly synchronised salute.

'Ra-pax! Ra-pax! Ra-pax!'

Pugno nodded at Antonius, who grinned back at him and tipped his own cup back, swallowing the contents in one gulp, then placed it back on the table and licked his bloody lips appreciatively. Pugno clapped him on the shoulder and raised his left arm as if saluting the victor in a boxing match.

'Our new brother Antonius! He serves the Twenty-first!'

The mess erupted into frenzied cheers, the men around the table slapping their new brother officer on the back and offering their drunken congratulations. Pugno took his hand and stared into his eyes for a moment, then leaned in close.

'You realise there's no way back from this? The Twenty-first owns you now.'

6

Atuatuca Tungrorum, April AD 70

'Their new wall doesn't seem to have done them very much good, does it?'

Alcaeus shook his head in reply to Hramn's gleeful question, as both men watched the tribesmen who had accompanied their cohorts west from Mosa Ford pouring in through the gap they had torn in the Tungrian city's defences. Those Tungrians who had not been put to the sword by the victorious Marsaci and Cananefates at Mosa Ford, once the terrible reality of their surrender to a mob of vengeful tribesmen had sunk in, had been pressed into service to carry a pair of battering rams into the attack on their own capital, and the hastily built defensive wall around Atuataca had been of scant value in obstructing the Germans, eager to inflict plunder and rape on the tribe whose loyalists had proven to be such a thorn in their side. The Batavi cohorts were drawn up in line of battle to the city's east, but their weight had not been added to a brief and one-sided siege that had resulted in the abject collapse of the Tungrian defence, the remaining men of the city quickly working out that any attempt to resist thousands of angry Germans could only result in their deaths.

'Will there be a slaughter?'

The long-haired prefect shook his head.

'Kivilaz has agreed with Brinno and the other leaders that their men will respect life unless resistance is offered, and that no fires will be set in the city. Although I expect that there'll be a fine crop of newborns nine months from now.'

'Perhaps if the men defending the bridge across the Mosa had known that this would be the outcome of their surrender they'd have fought a little longer.'

Hramn turned to look at his deputy through narrow eyes.

'And perhaps, Priest, had you managed to lay hands on our former brother-in-arms Claudius Labeo when you had the opportunity, this lesson would not have been required. Kiv could simply have made an example of him in front of these walls and the city would have opened its gates within the hour, with no need for them to be punished for their resistance.'

The priest raised an eyebrow.

'I doubt that Brinno would have resisted the opportunity to reward his men with a day's sport whether the city had surrendered or not. As for Labeo, he came out to talk under a flag of truce, and chose to run when the prince persuaded his men to surrender.'

'You sound like a Roman. A flag of truce? There is no truce where he's concerned, just hatred. You men of the cohorts may indeed still be the finest warriors the tribe has, but I find myself wondering if a little *less* Roman influence wouldn't serve us better.'

Alcaeus inclined his head in respectful acknowledgement of the point, refusing to take the bait, and the tone of his reply was mild where Hramn's had been harsh and provocative.

'Your question correctly identifies an issue that I have been considering myself, and one that will doubtless require much discussion once we have triumphed and established the independence from Rome that was our stated aim in starting this war. Although our old ways seemed to work well enough in turning Labeo's flank at the river. I doubt Brinno's men could have swum the river and brought about their surrender without our losing a single man.'

If he was too canny to rise to Hramn's challenge, the prefect was more than ready with a terse reply.

'Without losing a man? Is *that* your concern? How unlike the Romans you seem to deify! You know as well as I do that what made Rome the greatest power in the world – back when they had an empire to boast about, that is – was the fact that they greeted any defeat by simply raising a fresh army and attacking again.'

The wolf-priest nodded his acceptance of the point again, carefully walking the line between docile acceptance of his superior's point and needlessly irritating the man.

'But we are not Rome, Prefect. We do not have a never-ending supply of men to be recruited from an empire of millions. And our cohorts have taken decades to reach their current prowess. We could not replace them overnight, even if we did have the men—'

Hramn cut him off with an angry gesture.

'Our cohorts, Alcaeus, have had their day in the sun. They may remain peerless among my uncle's army, but they are no longer the force they were.' The priest kept his mouth shut, biting down on the obvious rejoinder that Hramn's words were only true because of the disaster at Gelduba over which he had presided, but some sense of his frustration must have been evident, and Hramn's thin patience abruptly snapped. 'You and your men no longer seem as committed to our cause as once seemed to be the case. You have become cautious, lacking the lust for glory that once made us the most feared men in the empire. You've lost your edge, and every man in our army can see it.' He stared at the silent centurion for a moment, shaking his head in an affectation of sorrow. 'I know it, Kiv knows it, and I'm quite sure you know it too. Your men no longer have the stomach for this war, and neither do *you*. It was *your* fault that Labeo was able to escape when *you* had him at your mercy, which means that all this . . .' he waved a hand at the city that was being noisily sacked before them, 'is blood on *your* hands. I even find myself wondering if the *Banô*'s escape was in some way your doing, since you were the last man to see him alive.'

Alcaeus stared back at him levelly, holding his gaze unblinkingly.

'If that is your suspicion then you must act accordingly. Prefect.'

'It is my suspicion. But I can't *prove* it. So no such accusation will be made. But I'm watching you, Priest. And from now on the men of the Guard will stand behind your line at every battle, ready to deal with any man who chooses to run rather than fight.'

'The men of the cohorts will never stand for such an ins—'

'The men of the cohorts will accept Kivilaz's decision to provide them with a battlefield reserve in close support. As will you. Because there are worse options, believe me. From now on the men of *my* cohorts are going to be at the point of the spear. They'll be the first into battle and the last out, and if they show any reluctance to do their duty to the tribe then they will find the tribe particularly unforgiving.' He leaned forward, putting his face within inches of Alcaeus's. 'Is that understood, Centurion?'

The other man nodded slowly, not taking his eyes off his superior's.

'Perfectly, Prefect. You make your intentions abundantly clear.'

Germania, April AD 70

'They're getting careless.'

Marius blinked silently in acknowledgement of Lupercus's almost inaudible whisper. The two men were sitting in apparent silence by the fire their escort had constructed on pitching camp for the night, most of the guardsmen already having fallen asleep having consumed their dinner and drunk liberally from the skins of beer that had been supplied to them in the village through which they had passed earlier. It was the evening of the third day of their march north into Bructeri territory, having reached the limit of the Lupia's navigability by the ship that had carried them upriver. A single man had been set to watching them in the still of the evening, and, as the prisoners had watched, the effects of a long day in the saddle and the fire's warmth had combined to set him nodding. The day's ride had been uneventful, although the behaviour of the tribesmen in the settlement that had gifted their guards the beer had been instructive to both men. Approaching the party in something close to a state of awe, the Germans had stared up at Lupercus with the air of men confronted with a rare animal for the first time, and eventually had to be driven away by their Batavi guards as they grew bolder and more curious. The legatus had laughed at the time, telling his subordinate to get used to the idea of being treated like a performing bear, but it had been evident to Marius that the day's events had brought the reality of their captivity home to him more than any other aspect of the journey. Waiting for the sentry's head to nod again, he risked another whisper.

'They think we have nowhere to run.'

Lupercus looked across the fire at the sleeping Germans for a moment before nodding decisively.

'It has to be now.'

Marius shook his head in disbelief, shocked by his superior's sudden decision, but Lupercus stared back at him with equal certainty. The man with the duty of staying awake to watch them stirred uneasily in his doze, waking sufficiently to stare at the two men with unfocused eyes before his head sank back onto his chin.

'Where can we run to?'

The legatus shook his head fractionally.

'I don't intend running far. I just want one of them alone, and to take his sword.'

Marius stared back at him with the certainty of long association, knowing that the other man craved nothing more than a clean and honourable death, the news of which would revive his family's shattered pride.

'But . . .'

'*This could be the only chance.*' Lupercus nodded decisively, his gaze softening momentarily at the sudden anguish in his subordinate's eyes. '*Goodbye, Marius.*'

Without warning he was up and running, and after a momentary pause for the dozing guard to register the flurry of movement, the Batavi was on his feet and roaring a challenge that jerked his comrades awake, as Marius struggled to stand, his legs numb from sitting for so long.

'After him!' Bairaz was clearly furious, spittle flying as he shoved the red-faced guard at Marius. 'You, watch him! If he escapes you'll die here!'

The other five men pounded away into the evening's long shadows after Lupercus, and Marius instinctively knew that the legatus, still weak from the siege's long, slow starvation, was unlikely either to be able to best any of them in a straight fight or escape their pursuit. Turning to find the abashed sentry within arm's reach, his right fist clenched and drawn back with evident purpose, he readied himself for the blow, pulling his head back as the guardsman threw an angry first punch, rage and mortification at his failure clouding his judgement. Shrugging off the glancing blow's effects with a swift shake of his head, the pugilistic instincts of half a lifetime of fighting on the harpastum pitch took him forward into the Batavi's attack rather than seeking any attempt at escape, stepping inside the other man's reach and hugging him close to pinion his arms, then he snapped his head forward in a headbutt that channelled every moment of the last six month's fear and frustration into the attack. The guardsman's nose popped in a spray of blood, his eyes momentarily losing their focus, and before he could react to the unexpected retaliation, Marius had released his grip on the other man's body and positioned himself for the kill, grabbing the hair at the back of his opponent's head and pulling sharply downwards before snapping a half-fisted punch to crush the reeling soldier's throat. As the guardsman tottered away, fighting to breathe, the centurion pulled the sword from the hapless Batavi's belt and punched the blade through his mail, killing the soldier as the sharp iron slid between his ribs and cut his heart in two.

Looking up, he realised that the remaining guardsmen had vanished from sight, having pursued Lupercus into the forest, and that, if he chose to accept it, his own escape beckoned. Dithering between fight and flight, he looked down at the fallen guardsman again, the germ of a plan forming in his mind as the sounds of pursuit intensified, Lupercus's hunters shouting to each other as they closed in on their quarry.

'I hope you're going to appreciate this, once you're happy with your ancestors.'

Pulling the dead man's mailshirt over the corpse's head, Marius struggled into it, shaking the iron rings' weight down to sit comfortably before fastening the Batavi's belt about himself and picking up his discarded helmet from beside the fire. A swing of the sword partially severed the corpse's neck, another blow releasing the Batavi's head to roll away from his body, and, picking it up by the hair, he tossed it away into the undergrowth leaving only a decapitated body clad in a red tunic, the same colour as his own. Voices sounded in the trees behind him, men shouting in angry triumph interspersed with the grunts and shouted imprecations of a beating, as they dragged the recaptured legatus back towards the fire and confirmed his fears for the man's ability to evade their pursuit and that his friend was paying the price for failing to secure the means of the suicide he craved. Two guardsmen dragged Lupercus into view, his legs trailing across the forest floor as he lolled semi-conscious between two of them while Bairaz strode angrily behind them, the other two presumably still out in the darkened forest.

'Get the rope! We'll tie the bastards up at night from now on if this is the thanks we get for our—' The decurion stopped speaking abruptly as he took in the sight of the headless corpse. 'You've killed him? Why the f—'

He gasped as the man he had assumed was his soldier lunged forward and thrust his bloodied swordblade through the throat of the man on Lupercus's left, then pulled the blade free, whipping it up in a high arc to hack into the other soldier, severing his right arm in a spray of blood. Shoulder-charging the maimed warrior backwards into Bairaz, sending both men sprawling, he vaulted the wounded man to attack the reeling decurion, but fell headlong as his booted foot caught the wounded man's raised arm. Rolling to his feet he found Bairaz facing him with his sword drawn, the Batavi leaping forward to attack with a snarl of anger, thrusting the gladius's blade at his leg. Stepping back, the Roman parried the strike imperfectly, gritting his teeth against the pain as his enemy's sword opened a long wound in his thigh and prompted a predatory smile from his opponent.

'All I have to do now is wait for you to lose enough blood to . . .'

His eyes widened as Marius stormed forward, driven to attack by the certain knowledge that he had a fleeting window of opportunity to win the fight before his opponent's prediction became fact. Abandoning any attempt at finesse, he fought in the only way left to him, channelling his rage at what he had been reduced to into a desperate attack, all of his frustration and loathing in the sword's flickering arcs. Caught off balance, Bairaz barely managed to defend the first lunging thrust, raising his sword to block the swinging hack that followed it, but he was unprepared for the violence with which the Roman sprang forward, dropping his gladius and leaping at him with his fists raised. A swift left jab staggered the Batavi back on his heels but the right-handed uppercut that followed it, delivered with all the strength left in Marius's body, was the killer blow, lifting his body off the ground with its concussive impact and sending him headlong into the dust, his body twitching spasmodically as he surrendered his consciousness. Marius stared at him for a moment before retrieving the sword, using it to cut a strip of wool from the tunic of his first victim and binding his own wound, the makeshift bandage swiftly darkening with blood. Walking tiredly over to the maimed soldier, frantically attempting to stem the flow from his severed arm with his remaining hand, he hacked a single deep cut into the back of the man's neck, snapping his spine, then limped over to Bairaz, whose eyes were fluttering as he started to recover his wits, putting the gladius's point to his throat.

The Batavi's eyes opened, fought to focus and then fixed on the weapon's blade, his body freezing into perfect stillness as he realised the gravity of his situation. Marius stared down at him pitilessly for a moment before speaking, his anger evident as he ground out the words.

'I have a message for Kivilaz! You're his cousin, right?'

The Batavi officer's hand moved fractionally towards the hilt of his dagger, but Marius pushed the blade down to dimple the skin of his neck, and he raised both hands in surrender.

'You know you'll never—'

'Escape? I doubt it. But I can still send your snake of a cousin one last message.'

'What mess—'

'This.' Marius stabbed the blade in, staring down into the Batavi's eyes as the man's realisation of his own death hit him. 'Your corpse will be all it takes to tell him that Rome never stops fighting. *Never.*'

He turned back to Lupercus, who was squatting where he had fallen when Marius's unexpected assault had freed him, staring exhaustedly at his subordinate.

'As practical as ever, First Spear. And now, if you'll pass me a weapon, I'll do what I should have done when I was clear we'd have to surrender.' The first spear handed him Bairaz's sword, and Lupercus got slowly to his feet, putting the blade's point to his abdomen. 'Give me the mercy stroke and then run. I could never survive in this green Hades, but you might just have it in you to prove them wrong.' He braced himself to act, then glanced up at his subordinate with a smile. 'It was an honour to serve with you, First Spear.'

Slumping tiredly forward onto the sword, he groaned in agony as the blade pierced his abdomen, heaving convulsively to drive it deeper into his body until the weapon's point burst from his back.

'N . . . now!'

Marius swung his own sword with all the strength he had left, cleaving his mortally wounded friend's head from his body and standing in silence over the twitching corpse, muttering a prayer as Lupercus's spirit left his body.

'Go well, Quintus Munius Lupercus. And raise a cup to me when you dine with your ancestors this evening.'

Wiping the bloody blade on Bairaz's tunic, he sheathed the weapon, then picked up the dead legatus's head by its hair and hurled it away into the forest, where it was lost in the undergrowth, safe from any further indignity. The sounds of the remaining soldiers reached him through the trees, coarse laughter at some joke or other, and he grinned at the thought of their reaction when they discovered the havoc that had been wrought in their absence, and what Kivilaz's reaction was likely to be when they returned to the Island with such inauspicious news.

'This is one more promise the Batavi will just have to break, I suppose.'

He turned and limped away into the trees, vanishing into the evening shadows and leaving the sprawled corpses as mute testament to his bitter rage.

Tungria, April AD 70

'They're over the mountains? *Already?*'

Classicus nodded at his Batavi counterpart's incredulous tone.

'It seems that reports of the empire's demise in this part of the world are a little in advance of the reality, Prince Kivilaz. And yet it also seems to me as if our opponent has somewhat underestimated what it is that they face.'

He had ridden into the cohorts' camp an hour before, and after a swift discussion Kivilaz had decided to summon his senior officers to discuss the Gaul's news from the south.

'You think they're guilty of hubris? It seems to me as if the men of the Treveri and the Lingones are the ones who've been asleep at their posts. Wasn't your colleague Julius Tutor supposed to be guarding the passes through the Alps?'

Classicus nodded grimly.

'It seems that the Treveri have done little other than gather some of the smaller tribes to their banner, most of whom doubtless agreed to join his army for fear of his retribution if they failed to do so. And that fool Sabinus led his Lingones against their neighbours the Sequani, who promptly sent them home with a bloody nose and inspired him to take his own life. Perhaps we ought to have taken a hand ourselves, rather than seeking to settle old scores?'

Kivilaz shook his head in disbelief, either ignoring or simply failing to comprehend Classicus's reference to his attempt to deal with Claudius Labeo.

'How many legions?'

'Five from Italy, our spies report, but they'll send men from the other provinces as well, given enough time. Two from Hispania and another from Britannia, I expect. But there is one piece of good news. The bulk of their army is under the command of Annius Gallus, four legions in strength and ordered to secure the upper reaches of the great river. Only one legion remains to the force that is supposed to be putting us all back in our place, under Petillius Cerialis.'

The Batavi smiled slowly.

'Cerialis? I doubt he'd have been the first choice for such a responsibility were it not for the fact that his wife's father also happens to be the emperor. He's reckless by reputation, still prey to the same reluctance to avoid taking risks that was his downfall in Britannia.' Classicus looked at him uncomprehendingly. 'Ah, I'd forgotten that you didn't arrive in the province until after the revolt of the Iceni was over. Petillius Cerialis led half of the Ninth Hispania head on into a horde of angry Britons and only just got away with the legion cavalry and his life. He always was one for gambling everything on the outcome of a single wager, and I can't imagine he's changed much. And has only one legion to play with? Let me guess, it wouldn't be the Twenty-first, would it?'

'Yes, it is. But how did—'

'It's obvious. They've given the safer of two loyal generals, men who can be relied on not to start the civil war all over again, four legions, and ordered him to make sure that the provinces on the periphery of our revolt can't be infected with this dangerous disease of freedom from their tyranny. So Gallus gets four legions and a frontier to make safe. And the other, the bolder of the two, with a reputation for pushing his luck to its limits, they've given one extremely dangerous legion, perfectly capable of fighting their way out of any trouble Cerialis's bullishness might drop them into. They'll march fast and hit harder than a bolt thrower, if we allow them to dictate the terms of this campaign. They do have auxiliary support, I presume?'

Classicus opened his tablet.

'A legatus by the name of Sextilius Felix with a legion's worth of various infantry cohorts. And something called the Ala Singularium, under the command of your nephew Briganticus.'

'Briganticus.' Kivilaz nodded slowly. 'I ought to have known that he'd manage to crawl between the spectators' legs and involve himself in this fight.'

'There is bad blood between the two of you?'

Hramn strode forward, glowering at the mention of his cousin's name.

'There is bad blood between Julius Briganticus and every other member of my family. He has sworn to kill my uncle for the perceived crime of bringing about the death of his adopted father Paulus, and I have sworn an oath to Magusanus to kill him first, if our paths cross on the field of battle. In appointing him to lead this Ala Singularium, the Romans must hope that his lust for revenge on my uncle will decapitate our tribe and leave us leaderless. The next time I see my cousin I will take the greatest of pleasure in sending him to join my uncle Paulus.'

Classicus nodded his head in respect for the sentiment.

'I have no doubt that you will defend your prince to the death, Prefect Hramn.' He turned back to Kivilaz. 'It seems to me that our respective rebellions against the empire are far from doomed, as long as we act together and bring our combined strength to confront their advance into the Gallic empire.'

The Batavi pursed his lips, thinking for a moment.

'I agree. With only one legion Cerialis will be forced to fight a war of movement, because he will lack the strength to hold any position against our combined strength. And knowing the man as I do, my expectation is that he will try to fight in the manner of a latter-day Julius Caesar, marching hard and striking where he believes his enemy will least expect the blow to land. It is in his perennial need to take risks, to gamble everything on one roll of the dice that we will find his weakness, and when the time comes we will catch him out, pin down his one legion and destroy it as completely as we tore the Old Camp legions to shreds. And my expectation is that he will move upon the Treveri first, to remove their threat to his rear when he advances north.'

He nodded, pointing to a spot on the map that lay unfurled on the table between them.

'You and I, Julius Classicus, must march our forces to the south and east, and join with Tutor's Treveri to form an army of the Germans and the Gauls, which a single legion will never be able to resist, auxiliaries or no auxiliaries. Send word to Tutor to avoid battle with the Romans at any cost. Let the enemy entertain themselves with petty revenge upon the Treveri people, and once we have our strength concentrated into one army we will make them pay for their acts of destruction a hundred times over. I'll have a road of crosses erected all the way to the Alps and put whatever's left of the Twenty-first Legion on them one man at a time. Hramn, have your cohorts ready to march at first light. If Cerialis can be depended upon to act in his usual headstrong manner the Romans may well be about to thrust their heads into the perfect trap.'

The Winter Camp, Germania Superior, May AD 70

'We have news from Sextilius Felix, gentlemen, and unlike his last dispatch it's good news. Tell them your message, Tribune.'

Cerialis looked around the room at his officers with an expression they had come to know all too well in their short time serving under his command, a look that usually presaged his making swift and occasionally slightly reckless decisions. Their legatus augusti, it had soon become evident, was a man who saw what it was he wanted and moved to take it swiftly and without stopping to consider the potential consequences of failure.

'Yes, Legatus Augusti. My report from Legatus Felix is as follows.' The young officer who had been sent back to the army by the vanguard's commander, the redoubtable Sextilius Felix, licked his lips nervously, opening his message tablet to read the dispatch with which he had been entrusted. He had ridden into the Winter Camp fortress an hour before accompanied by Julius Briganticus and a squadron of his Ala Singularium, a clear indication of the Romans' uncertain control of the land west of the fortress, across which hostile Gauls had so recently roamed unchecked by its terrified garrison. 'Quintus Petillius Cerialis, greetings. I send you news of a victory, and an opportunity to deal with our enemy of the Treveri tribe if we act decisively.'

He paused, and Cerialis's officers studied their commander with fleeting glances, nobody wanting to catch the eye of a man so clearly being pushed to go on the offensive by an officer who was, at least in terms of the army's hierarchy, his deputy, but if he was discomforted by the tone of Felix's message he was showing no sign of it.

'Continue, Tribune.'

'Err . . .' Quailing under his superiors' combined and hawklike concentration, the young officer found his place and started reading again. 'The previously reported loss of my advance guard cohort to an ambush, incurred while scouting aggressively in the march north to the Winter Camp has been gloriously and decisively avenged . . .'

'There's that word "decisively" again. He's laying it on with a spade.'

Antonius nodded fractionally in response to Pugno's whisper, drawing a brief stare from their legatus. He had quickly established himself as a leader among the Blood Drinkers, and Pugno had come both to value his no-nonsense attitude and admire his unbending focus on revenge for his legatus's death, and the two men were frequently to be found together, much to Longus's amusement.

'The Treveri leader Tutor sought to block my progress at the river Nava, fortifying the town of Bingium and destroying the bridge across the river, but in his treachery he has in turn found himself betrayed. His allies the Triboci, Vangiones and Caeracates have deserted him, terrified of our revenge, and the traitor legions have sworn allegiance to Vespasianus and withdrawn to the west, awaiting our army's arrival.'

'This is factual, Tribune, and not assumption?'

Briganticus answered Cerialis's question before the tribune could speak.

'Fact, Legatus Augusti. Recognising my cavalry wing's unique composition and ability, Legatus Felix sent me forward to scout the ground to the west and north of Tutor's position, and I found the Fifth and Sixteenth Legions marching along the banks of the Mosella, away from Tutor's army. They are in no mood to fight for the Gauls, now they realise that they have chosen the side that's likely to lose, and while they are still fearful of Rome's punishment, their men could be brought back into your army, I expect.'

Pugno shifted minutely, an expression of discomfort in a man Antonius knew did not suffer the usual tics and fidgeting that affected most soldiers.

'If we could tolerate the treacherous bastards' stink.'

Cerialis nodded thoughtfully.

'I see. And what of this defensive position on the Nava?'

Briganticus waved a dismissive hand, his lip curled in contempt.

'Swept away. We found a ford close by to Bingium and Sextilius Felix's cohorts were across it like a swarm of angry wasps. They broke the Trevirans soon enough, and Tutor ran like the Gallic coward he is.'

'I see.' Cerialis thought for a moment. 'Which explains my colleague's call for decisive action. He and I have already agreed that we are quite unable to advance any further up the Rhenus than the confluence of the Rhenus and the Mosella, not with the Treviran army intact in our rear. Beaten or not, I cannot expose our line of supply in such a foolhardy way while my colleague Gallus and his legions are tied up dealing with the Lingones to the south, and not yet in a position to safeguard our advance north. No gentlemen, the Treviran army must be broken, and their people bent back to the empire's will, before we can deal with the Batavians. And that means conquering their capital.' He pointed to the map. 'Augusta Trevorum must be occupied, and quickly, before Classicus and Civilis can rejoin the fight. Civilis surely won't continue his apparent quest to subjugate the tribes of northern Gaul once he realises that we're over the mountains and coming for him.'

He looked about him with that familiar expression again, and Pugno breathed a barely audible chuckle.

'Here comes the gamble.'

'We must march at once, with all the force at our disposal, cross the Nava at this ford of yours, Julius Briganticus, and then head across country to the Mosella, and the road to Augusta Trevorum. And if the Trevirans want to try stopping us they're more than welcome. Your men of the Twenty-first are eager for some action, I presume, Pontius Longus?'

The legatus nodded confidently.

'They're thirsty for blood, as First Spear Pugno tells me several times a day. All you'll have to do is show them an enemy and stand back.'

'And the other formations in this fortress?'

Antonius closed his eyes, remembering his horror on entering the Winter Camp's gates the previous day. Longus shook his head.

'The men of the Picentina cavalry wing are solid enough, and reputed to have killed the man who murdered Dillius Vocula when they met him on the road a few days afterwards, when they refused to join with the Gauls and marched here instead . . .' Antonius held his face in stone-like immobility under Pugno's scrutiny. 'But the two legions that are supposed to be holding this fortress are in a dreadful state. Indeed, words fail me when I consider their condition . . .' He paused, apparently searching for the right words.

'If I might speak, Legatus?'

Longus stared at Antonius for a moment before inclining his head graciously.

'By all means, Centurion.'

'Thank you, sir.' Ignoring Pugno's hiss of amazement, he stepped forward and saluted. 'Legatus Augusti, I believe there's nobody better qualified than I to pass judgement on the Winter

Camp's legions. I led the majority of their strength north from here under Legatus Augusti Vocula, taking much of the Fourth to reinforce the Twenty-second, and they were the only men with the guts to stand between the Batavians and victory at Gelduba. They held firm when the First and Sixteenth Legions both turned and fled for the camp, and they held the barbarians for long enough that the unexpected reinforcements from Hispania were able to take them from behind. I had hoped to still find the same obstinacy in them when we arrived here.' He shook his head in disgust. 'But instead I found them broken, exhausted and demoralised by recent events.'

'*This* is your former legion?' Pugno had looked on with amused contempt at the men of the Twenty-second Primigenia as they had gone through their drills alongside their fellow legionaries of the Fourth Macedonica on the Winter Camp's parade ground the previous afternoon, then turned back to face Antonius with an incredulous expression. 'They look more ready for butchering than for battle. You said that they were likely to have some fight in them?'

His colleague had watched sadly as the men he had marched and fought with practiced with their spears and shields in a manner barely meriting the term desultory, their raggedness and lack of energy clearly giving their new senior centurion good reason for the irascible shouts and curses that were being rained upon them.

'They did. That's the legion that held the line at Gelduba, when the First and Sixteenth were already running. But now . . .'

The Twenty-first's senior centurion had spat over the fortress's parapet.

'But now they look ready for nothing better than to be broken up for reinforcements.'

Antonius had shrugged, shaking his head at the scene they were looking down on from the fortress's walls.

'I went to find their first spear last night and he told me what their problem is. They were forced to sit and watch while Classicus and his Gauls camped out there and demanded their surrender, threatening them with the same treatment that the Old Camp legions got if they didn't give it up promptly. He had to execute several dozen men to keep them from mutinying and throwing the gates wide open, and even then it was a close thing. And now the Twenty-first has marched in like something out of the history books, spitting fire and pissing vinegar, and we're looking down our noses at them with, just to add the final insult, their first cohort marching under the Twenty-first's eagle.'

Pugno's stare had remained as hard as before, as he looked dispassionately down at the demoralised legion parading below them.

'Perhaps you should give up this idea of having revenge upon the Gauls and content yourself with whipping these poor bastards back into shape? I can release you from your service to the Twenty-first, if that's what you want to do?'

'No.' The response had been as blunt as Pugno had expected, having had time to get to know his colleague on the march north from Vindonissa. 'If I were to abandon the campaign now I'd curse myself for the rest of my life for missing the chance to find the man who killed my legatus and make him pay. Let someone else restore some pride to my former legion, I serve the Twenty-first until the day this war ends and Legatus Augusti Cerialis delivers on his promise to release me in pursuit of Aemelius Longinus. No, there's only one solution to what we see before us.'

He looked Cerialis in the eye, squaring his shoulders.

'The Twenty-second Legion, Legatus Augusti, is a lost cause. It needs to be put under fresh leadership, to have the defeatists in its ranks dismissed in disgrace, to be given a new name, a new eagle and a new camp, somewhere as far from here as possible. There are good men in those ranks, and given the chance I know they'll build a strong new legion for the emperor.'

'But the rot needs to be cut out?'

'Yes, Legatus Augusti. And for my part—'

'That will be all, thank you, Centurion!'

Antonius blinked at Pugno's intervention, then saluted and stepped back into his previous place at his superior's side, keeping his gaze locked on the wall behind Cerialis's head as the first spear hissed furiously in his ear, heedless of the staring officers.

'Shut your fucking mouth and keep it shut!'

Cerialis shook his head in bafflement and then addressed the room afresh, and with an act of willpower Antonius forced himself to focus on the general's words.

'So, we can't expect any reinforcement from the legions already camped here. No matter. They can hold the fortress, I presume?' Longus nodded his agreement. 'Thank the gods for that small gift. Very well, the Twenty-first Legion will march west at the earliest opportunity, will join with Sextilius Felix's vanguard cohorts and will move to find, isolate and defeat the Trevirans as a prelude to occupying their capital. We have the chance to smash away one of the pillars of this so-called "Empire of the Gauls", and I intend to do exactly that, and before any of the other players in their sordid little game can stop playing with whatever it is that has their attention and join forces with this man Tutor. Prepare to march, gentlemen, I want to be on the road for Augusta Trevorum as fast as you can get your men's hobnails replaced.'

Outside the headquarters building Pugno raised a hand, his face set hard, to forestall any argument.

'You were just about to fall on your fucking sword, weren't you? You were going to tell a room full of men who've never seen combat that your former legion has gone to rat shit because of *you*. Weren't you?'

'Yes, but—'

'*Shut* your mouth, Centurion! The only words I want to hear from you are "yes" and "no".' The hard-faced first spear stared at him for a moment. 'That's better. So, you were going to tell Cerialis that it's down to you that the Twenty-second has given up on life, because you abandoned them to stay with your friend Vocula. Weren't you?'

'Yes, but—'

'Yes but nothing, you stupid bastard. That's just self-pitying bullshit as far as I'm concerned.' Antonius stared back at him in silence. 'And the words you're looking for are *"Yes, it is"*, Centurion. You followed what you believed was your duty, and from what I've heard, you kept Vocula alive for longer than he'd have managed without you. And every day he lived as a result of your taking a hand in the matter was another day that he kept his army in the field, preventing the Batavians and their allies from closing the Alpine passes and denying us the chance to get our legions across the mountains. Believe it or not, my legatus has told me that Cerialis believes Vocula was the one man who's given us a fighting chance of recovering Gaul and Germania, and even if he doesn't know it, *we* both know that the thanks for that should be going as much to you keeping him alive for as long as you did as to Vocula's refusal to recognise that he was doomed to lose his life if he stayed and fought. So we'll have no more talk about you having deserted your men, right? You did what you saw as your duty, and by my standards you did it right. You prick. And speaking of pricks . . .' he grinned slyly at Antonius, who was unable to resist a faint smile himself, 'if we want to talk about officers deserting their posts, I don't think we have very far to look for a perfect example, do we? I suspect our beloved leader could hear a woman's linen hitting the floor in a pitched battle, and I don't think he can keep his sword sheathed any better than the horniest legionary in the army. We'll just have to hope that his exploits don't cloud his judgement, eh?'

Gallia Belgica, May AD 70

'He's going to fight? I thought you told the fool to retreat to join us, and to give the legions nothing but empty country on which to vent their wrath?'

Classicus shook his head.

'My messages were more than clear on the subject, but it seems that events have pushed Tutor into a corner. Events and that young fool Valentinus he's allowed to take command of his army.

They've fortified Rigodulum, it seems, and intend fighting the Romans there rather than allowing them to besiege Augusta Trevorum.'

Kivilaz's eyes narrowed, rimmed with red from the exertions of eight days of marching through the deep forest between Atuataca and Augusta Trevorum, in their dash to join up with the threatened Treveri before Cerialis's army could bring them to battle.

'Valentinus? He's barely more than a child! What was his part in this idiocy?'

Classicus poured himself a cup of wine before replying.

'He and Tutor were unwise enough to leave the Treveri ungoverned, Tutor to go recruiting men from the smaller tribes and Valentinus to attend the conference of the Gauls that the elders of the Remi seem to have thought would be a good idea.'

The Batavi prince shook his head in disgust.

'The Remi? I'll settle matters with those cowards when Rome's attempt to put us back in our box has been broken. They've always been nothing better than puppets of the empire!'

Classicus shrugged.

'Persuasive puppets, it seems. Valentinus argued like a man possessed for war with Rome, but found himself isolated when Julius Auspex of the Remi spoke in favour of peace and received the plaudits of every tribe present except for the Treveri, the Lingones and my own people, curse them. Gaul, it seems, is already rolling over for the Romans.'

Kivilaz spat on the ground at his feet.

'They'll think again, once I have the Twenty-first's standard and Cerialis's head to throw onto their conference table. So, this fool Valentinus has decided to fight.'

His co-conspirator nodded.

'He returned to Augusta Trevorum to discover that the legions whose oath of loyalty to the Gallic empire I administered had thought better of the idea, sworn an oath to Vespasianus, folded their tents and stolen away in the night.'

Kivilaz laughed.

'What did the idiot expect? Did he really believe that men who have already sworn loyalty to Nero, to Galba, then to Vitellius and after all that to Vespasianus, were going to stay loyal, now that Vespasianus's legions have their boots in the Treveri's soil?'

'He knows that he's made a fool of himself, which led him to rant and rave at anyone who would listen until he had the Treveri stirred up to fight. It seems he's made an example of the two legati he was holding . . .'

Classicus stopped talking as Kivilaz put his head in his hands.

'He murdered the only prisoners he had of any value? That's his death warrant signed, if the ink wasn't already dry. And now he plans to take on the Twenty-first Legion without waiting for us?'

'He plans to defend Rigodulum, to prevent the Romans laying siege to Augusta Trevorum itself. The hill above the town is being fortified and he has taken every warrior in the tribe with him.'

The Batavi nobleman looked up at him, shaking his head in exasperation.

'The fool's going to fight a defensive battle. Which means that the Romans can disengage if they find themselves losing, whereas if *he* loses their cavalry will leave a trail of dead men all the way back to Augusta Trevorum. Every last man in that army will be killed or captured, and his city will be left defenceless.' Kivilaz nodded, staring up at the trees' canopy over his head as he pondered the situation. 'But they don't know we're here, do they? As far as Cerialis is concerned we're still in the north, enjoying our victory over the Tungrians. So let's assume that the Trevirans can't stand up to the Twenty-first Legion when they come knocking. Their army is defeated and either killed or enslaved, which will leave Augusta Trevorum defenceless. Cerialis will march straight in, accept their surrender and then allow his men the luxury of a few days in which to recover from several days' forced march and a battle. And, if his reputation is to be trusted, he'll go and find a bed to warm, which means that if we time our moment perfectly we can catch his army leaderless and off their guard. Perhaps this can still be the decisive moment of this war.'

Rigodulum, May AD 70

'Are your men ready for this, First Spear?'

Pugno turned ostentatiously, staring across the narrow valley at the crest of the hill in front of which his legion was arrayed in line of battle, then returned his attention to the waiting senior officers. Cerialis had chosen to locate his command post and his colleague Felix's auxiliary cohorts high on the opposite side of the valley, not only for the sake of a good view of the battle but also, Antonius suspected, to ensure a clear line of retreat in the event of the Twenty-first legion not managing to defeat the Treveri warriors awaiting them. The first spear nodded brusquely, his jaw jutting aggressively as he growled his response to the question.

'We've been ready since the day we marched north from Rome, Legatus Augusti.'

'And will you be requiring any assistance from my auxiliaries?'

Antonius smirked inwardly, both at Felix's question and his first spear's response, which did little to hide his obvious impatience with any suggestion that his legion might not succeed.

'Thank you, Legatus Felix, but I'd be more than a little worried that the presence of your men might result in confusion, once we're nose to nose with the enemy. The Trevirans wear mail armour and so do most of your cohorts, and any man wearing mail who doesn't run from us is going to be dead very shortly after we reach the top of that hill.'

Felix nodded, his expression dubious.

'You seem very confident, First Spear? Surely that number of trained soldiers with the advantage of the high ground must represent something of a tactical problem, even to the vaunted Twenty-first? Bearing in mind the mauling your men took at Cremona – both times – I was just wondering if you might not appreciate some assistance?'

Reading Pugno's thin lips and narrowed eyes at the mention of their rough handling in both battles with the skill of a man who had seen his subordinate's temper snap on more than one occasion in his brief period commanding the legion, Longus interposed himself between the two men before the first spear had the chance to say something that all parties might regret.

'I have a strict policy, Sextilius Felix, of deferring to my senior centurions the moment that battle becomes imminent. After all, First Spear Pugno is the man who'll be going up that hill with his legion, so I'm going to trust that his pride in his legion's abilities is matched by his understanding of just how critical this battle is to the emperor. It was on my mind though, First Spear Pugno, given that your men will find it hard to exploit their victory after climbing the slope and then evicting the current occupiers, to suggest that Legatus Felix's cavalry might be well employed hooking around to the left of that hill and cutting off their retreat? After all, if that young fool Valentinus is up there it surely gives us the chance to capture the man who ordered the death of two Roman legati, does it not?'

He raised an eyebrow at Pugno, who had the good grace to recognise his intention, and accept the opportunity with which he was being presented.

'Thank you, Legatus. I believe that those Trevirans will go down the other side of that hill like a falling building once we're among them, but you're right, of course, we should plan to make sure they don't have the chance to run away and regroup for another go.' He turned to Felix, fractionally inclining his head in a gesture of respect. 'And perhaps, Legatus Felix, your bandage carriers could look after those of my legionaries who manage to stop their spears?'

The auxiliary commander raised a questioning eyebrow.

'What will your own bandage carriers be doing, First Spear?'

The response was as uncompromising as Antonius had expected.

'Killing Gauls, Legatus. My legion doesn't stop fighting to look after the wounded, we win the battle first and deal with the consequences once we're sure of the victory.'

Felix nodded slowly, clearly taken aback.

'I see. Well in that case I'll have my medics sent forward to assist your wounded.'

'Good.' Longus beamed at both Pugno and Felix. 'It's for your approval of course, Petillius Cerialis, but given that these two fire-breathers are in agreement, I hardly feel it requires any further debate.'

The army's commander waved a magisterial assent, and Pugno blew out an undisguised sigh of relief.

'If that's decided, I'll go and get this over with, if I may?'

Gesturing to Antonius to follow him, he stalked away, and in the silence that followed as they hurried down the valley's western side and crossed its small stream, the centurion looked up at the hill before them, its crest lined with evidently defiant Treveri soldiers who, having had time to dig a defensive ditch and line the crest with a rough wall of hastily gathered stones, clearly believed themselves to be in an impregnable position.

'Listen to them shouting the odds.' Pugno spat on the turf in disgust. 'Anyone who didn't know better would think they had a chance of holding us off.' He shot a glance at Antonius, who was considering the waiting defenders with a calculating expression. 'Having second thoughts, Centurion?'

'No. I'm just wondering how quickly we can get up that slope and into them, if we're going to reduce our losses to whatever missile weapons they've got up there.'

The first spear shook his head.

'That's not the Twenty-first's way of fighting, and it's certainly not mine. If we arrive at the top with our wind spent we'll give those animals the chance to counter-attack before we're even into them. Better to walk up at a steady pace and endure whatever they have to fling down at us, so as to be fresh when the time comes to take our iron to them.'

They reached the rear of Antonius's cohort, granted the honour of being in the centre of the legion's line, and Pugno called for his cohort commanders. The Blood Drinkers formed a tight circle around him in what was clearly an established pre-battle ritual, their helmeted heads almost touching. Pugno's briefing was swift and to the point.

'Legatus Augusti Cerialis has ordered me to make such a bloody example of these Treveri cunts that the rest of their tribe will spend the next week torn between mourning their dead and shitting themselves that they're next. And I promised him that the Twenty-first would do exactly what he's ordered. Are your cohorts ready?'

Every man nodded silently.

'Trumpeters ready?'

More nods.

'And are you all ready? Ready to walk into whatever blizzard of arrows and slingshot they have waiting for us up there?'

The gathered centurions stared at him steadily as he turned a full circle, each man meeting his eye and nodding one last time.

'Very well. I'll see you at the top. Blood and glory!'

His men dispersed to their cohorts without having to be told to do so, each of them raising a hand to signal his readiness as he reached his men and then pushing through their ranks to reach the front of the line, the legion's ranks responding with wild cheers and chants as the moment to attack drew near. Pugno looked up and down the line with evident satisfaction before turning back to Antonius.

'This is the way the Twenty-first goes to war, Centurion, as a pack of wild dogs led by the wildest bastards among them. But that doesn't mean that we're just going to charge up there in a disordered mob, or that we shouldn't do everything we can to soften up the opposition a bit first.' He turned to his trumpeter. 'Blow!'

The waiting soldier took a deep breath and blew his horn, the single note rasping out above the legion's tumult, instantly joined by dozens more as each cohort and century added their trumpets' blaring squeal to the cacophony, their collective howl the war cry of an angry beast, a visceral challenge to the men waiting on the hill above the legion and an unequivocal statement of murderous intent, raising the hairs on the back of Antonius's neck as his body instinctively responded to the horns' call. Pugno grinned at him with a hand on the hilt of his gladius, recognising the other man's arousal. 'Fucking lovely, isn't it? Sixty horns sounding together like the spirits of the fallen, calling us down to join them in Hades! From this moment every man in the Twenty-first knows to consider himself already dead, and to ask himself the only question that matters – what will his comrades engrave on his memorial altar? No man here will flinch from the fight, but every one of them will strive to be the one revered for his feats of bravery. What others consider extraordinary is commonplace for us!'

The trumpets fell silent, and Antonius realised that the defenders had stopped shouting their defiance down the hill's slope and were instead huddled into their shields, readying themselves to resist the inevitable assault. Pugno strode forward in front of his men, raising his voice in a parade-ground bellow that could be heard from one end of his legion's line to the other.

'Not so fucking noisy now, are they?'

A roar greeted his words, his legionaries, long accustomed to his bombastic leadership, knowing what it was he wanted from them. At the sight of an officer, several of the enemy warriors lining the hill's crest sprang forward and hurled spears down the hill at him, but even with the advantage of their three-hundred-foot elevation all fell short by twenty paces or more, and the veteran centurion turned to roar a challenge at them.

'We'll get to you cunts in good time!' He turned back to his own men with a happy grin. 'Brothers of the Twenty-first Legion! Do you see those poor fools waiting up there?' He paused, turning again to stare up the slope, shaking his head in apparent disgust. 'They have entrusted their defence to this miserable, pathetic dog turd of a hill! I know you were hoping for the chance to take your iron to the traitors of the legions who defected to their cause, but we can only fight what's put in front of us! These Trevirans are men who see battle as something to be endured! Something to be survived! But you and I know differently, don't we?'

He winked at Antonius, his eyes alive with the joy of a fight.

'You and I, my brothers-in-blood, we are proud servants of the best, the bravest and the most savage legion in the whole of the empire, we know better! We know that battle is not a thing to fear, but a pleasure, to be anticipated! To be welcomed! To be savoured! For when battle comes, my brothers, we are all Blood Drinkers!'

The ranks of armoured men erupted into a clamour that surpassed their previous efforts, and Pugno strolled back into the heart of his cohort with a feral grin that Antonius knew was in no way contrived, addressing his colleague conversationally as he looked up at the enemy waiting for them.

'Some legions ask their men if they are ready for war, but not the Twenty-first. My legionaries are *always* ready for war, because they long to prove themselves to each other, to their centurions, and to me. Those poor fools up there have no idea what's about to happen to them. Now, are you with me, or would you rather fight this one from behind your men?' Antonius grinned back at Pugno's smirking challenge, drawing his sword and setting himself ready to step forward. The first spear nodded, pulling the cord on his helmet's cheek guards tight before drawing his own sword and taking a shield from his chosen man. 'Good man. Now we'll get the chance to see what you and your boys are made of. Sound the advance!'

The trumpets brayed again, and every centurion in the line roared the order to move forward at the same instant, leaving Antonius nodding his respect for the precision with which they were drilled. The legion advanced onto the hill's shallow lower slope, Pugno's legionaries advancing at a steady marching pace as they had been instructed, and the first spear stared up at the waiting Treveri with a gleeful grin.

'There'll be men up there pissing themselves already, and others knowing that their shit's already turned to water that will cascade down their legs the second they have to fight and forget to hold it in. So let's give them something more to worry about. Twenty-first Legion! Make! Some! Noise!'

With the final word of the command every man in the line hammered the blades of their drawn swords against the metal rim of their shields, repeating the action with every step forward so that their advance was a rolling peal of human thunder. Somewhere in the ranks a man started singing, and in an instant the entire legion joined his bellowed challenge.

'Twenty-first Rapax, ever victorious,
Drinkers of blood, long notorious,'

'Did you think it was only meant to keep their heads up on the march?' Pugno grinned at his colleague's momentary surprise, raising his voice to shout along tunelessly with his men.

'Fill your minds with fear and dread,
Gut you, kill you, take your head,
Slaughter enemies, rebel and barbarian,
Leave the dead to feed the carrion,
Twenty-first Rapax, ever furious,
The Emperor's finest, bloody and glorious!'

The slope steepened, making the climb more of an effort than before, but to men who had covered sixty miles in the previous three days, having already marched across the roof of the world at the same gruelling pace, and having undergone Pugno's merciless drills and exercises every day they had spent in camp for the last year, the exertion was almost unnoticed.

'They'll be hoping to stop us with their spears! They'll soon know better!'

Even as the first spear spoke, the Treveri line strode to the crest of the hill and hurled a volley of spears down the slope, a lancing rain of sharp iron that fell onto the legion's swiftly raised shields out of the cold sky. Grunts and agonised groans marked those points in the line where a spear blade flew through gaps in the defence and found a target, but for the most part the main loss was that of shields made unusable by the protrusion of a spear's ungainly length.

'Keep moving! Front rank, rotate!'

The command was repeated up and down the legion's cohorts, the leading soldiers dropping their useless shields and pausing to allow the men behind them to take their places, presenting a new unbroken line of wood and iron against the constant pecking of the enemy's archers as they loosed a steady stream of arrows into the advancing Romans, long arrowheads designed to punch through plate armour hammering into wood and metal with pings and tocks. The occasional missile struck flesh and felled its hapless target, only for the victim's place in the line to be instantly filled by the men behind him. The hill's brow was barely fifty paces distant, and Antonius could see the Treviran soldiers glancing to their rear, getting ready to fall back into the shadow of their roughly constructed wall.

'We're nearly at the top! Get ready to fight!'

Another cheer greeted Pugno's command, and as Antonius looked to left and right he realised that for all the toll the enemy's harassment of their climb up the slope had taken, the Twenty-first was still perfectly formed and advancing in a line tidy enough to have graced a parade ground. Returning his attention to his front he realised that the enemy cohorts holding the ridge were pulling back at the run, hurdling their wall and turning to face the oncoming threat.

'Halt!'

The legion stopped at Pugno's command, his officers swiftly ordering their ranks while the Trevirans waited, a line of white faces behind their flat oval shields, mail-clad and clutching short swords that might well have been forged in the same imperial armouries that had equipped the men advancing upon them. Their three-foot-high stone wall presented a formidable obstacle from behind which they clearly hoped to mount a successful defence of the position. But, he realised, in building the defences the Treveri had surrendered the one advantage that might have helped them repulse the legion.

'They've abandoned the crest!'

Pugno grinned manically, and Antonius realised that he was lost to whatever daemon it was that came to him in battle, spittle flying from his lips as he roared another command.

'And now they die! Sing! Tell these fuckers who it is that they face! Twenty-first Rapax, ever victorious! Drinkers of blood, long notorious!'

The legionaries around them started the legion's battle hymn again, and Antonius felt his own control slipping away as the song's harsh, uncompromising sentiment and the implacable, burning hatred behind it filled him with a sudden need to get into the men waiting for them with his iron. *So this is what it feels like*, he mused inwardly, marvelling at the sudden flight of any instinct other than to kill, raising his sword and roaring out the song's bestial words with the men on either side, no longer anything more than a warrior filled with rage and the burning urge to kill.

'Ready! Spears!'

The legionaries on either side of Antonius shook out into a looser formation to front and rear, giving themselves room to throw as they sheathed their swords and transferred their spears to their right hands in readiness for his next command, and after a short pause Pugno bellowed the command they were waiting for.

'Spears . . . throw!'

At such close range the volley was lethal: long, iron-shanked spearheads punching through shields and mail to pierce their targets in a chorus of screams, and the Treviran front rank shivered as dozens of men fell, some of the soldiers behind them having to be pushed forward into the front rank such was their reluctance to face the legion's blood lust. Some men among the defenders were shuffling backwards, the terror in them growing as they realised that they were face-to-face with the deadliest threat possible, suddenly little better than a mob of individuals for all their officers' remonstrations, and the scent of their fear filled the legions' nostrils, giving fresh life to limbs burning from the effort of their climb to the crest. Pugno roared a command that rippled up and down the line, as his cohort commanders and centurions repeated the order that every man had been waiting for.

'Twenty-first Legion! Air! Your! Iron!'

The legionaries drew their swords, getting themselves ready to charge, and Antonius grinned wolfishly as the Treveri line visibly wavered at the sight. The man alongside him was muttering louder now, repeating the words of the battle hymn's first line over and over, his eyes fixed on a man in the enemy front rank and his knuckles white on the hilt of his gladius.

'Twenty-first Legion! On the command to attack! Show! No! Mercy!' Pugno flicked a glance at Antonius. 'Ready?'

Nodding reflexively, his teeth bared in a snarl he wasn't even aware of, the centurion locked his stare on the closest of the enemy officers and set himself ready to charge. Silence fell over the legion's line, the sudden total stillness of perfect discipline as every man strained his ears for the order to go forward. Pugno allowed his men a moment to ready themselves for the onslaught before roaring the last order he would need to issue.

'Twenty-first Legion! Attack!'

The last word was barely formed as he started forward in the rapid, shuffling pace intended to cover the gap between the front ranks as quickly as possible, the men on either side matching him step for step as the legion lurched forward into the assault that every man had been waiting for. The Treveri ranks trembled, sudden chaos erupting along the hill's crest as increasing numbers of men turned and fled, throwing themselves down the hill's far side, unable to face the legionaries stalking towards them. With a sudden and total loss of discipline the enemy formation broke, those men who had stood resolute in the face of the legion's deadly threat realising that they were being abandoned by their comrades.

Screaming something incoherent, Antonius sprinted ahead of his men, leapt onto the wall's unstable parapet and into those enemy soldiers who remained, smashing a sword thrust aside with his own blade before leaping down and hammering the man facing him back from the defence line with a punch of his shield, stepping in and thrusting the point of his gladius into the reeling Treveri's neck, then ripping it free in a spray of blood as the dying man's eyes rolled upwards in their sockets. Legionaries were fighting on either side of him, and rather than give in to the urge to simply run amok with his blade, he took a moment to search for an enemy, as the Twenty-first's soldiers poured over the rough wall with similar intent. A hulking enemy officer battered the first legionary who went at him aside with his shield, leaving the man sprawled and dazed, and killed the second with brutal economy of effort, simply lunging forward on heavily muscled thighs and ramming his sword into the oncoming Roman's mouth with enough force to punch the point of the weapon's heavy blade through the back of his skull, pulling the gladius free with a savage wrench that scattered the dead man's teeth onto the ground. Antonius strode forward and pushed the dying soldier aside, raising his gladius in challenge.

'Surrender! You've already lost!'

His only answer was a lightning-fast attack, the big man's sword catching his would-be victim's helmet and slicing through one of the two leather ties that secured his crest to leave the heavy wooden box of horse hair dangling by the remaining thong. Not allowing the Roman any time to remove the encumbering crest swinging from his head, he struck again, stabbing out at his opponent's face, but Antonius, forewarned of the tactic by the horrifically wounded man shaking in his death throes on the ground to his right, ducked into his shield and then, as his foe's blade scored the painted wooden surface with a bang that shook his arm, thrust forward and upwards with the full weight of his body behind the shield. The enemy centurion staggered backwards, momentarily thrown off balance, and the Roman seized his chance, thrusting the point of his gladius into the other man's thigh so fast that the blade was in and out before the Treveri officer realised what had happened. Crippled, and bleeding profusely from what was likely to prove a fatal wound, he dropped his shield and threw down his sword, spreading his arms wide and staring at Antonius imploringly, his lips moving in an entreaty that the Roman was unable to hear over the battle's roaring, screaming din, but whether it was a plea to mercy or simply for a quick and honourable death was neither clear nor of any consequence. Driven forward by instinct and the blood fury that still possessed him, Antonius drove his gladius into the staggering centurion's chest with such force that it punched clean through both mail and padded subarmalis, grating between the big man's ribs and piercing his heart. Stepping back from the corpse with a savage kick to free his blade, he looked about him to find Pugno watching to one side as the legion's men continued to stream across the shallow wall and run past on either side, eager to throw themselves into the fleeing enemy cohorts that were now little better than a terrified rabble.

'As I expected! You, brother-in-blood, are indeed the man I took you for!'

Antonius nodded, suddenly weary as the inhuman power that had possessed him with the onset of the fight washed away. He gestured down the hill's long western slope, across which the legion's men were hunting their fleeing enemies.

'Should we . . . ?'

The two men followed their men down the slope, Pugno nodding his approval at the litter of corpses and dying men strewn in the wake of his soldiers' rampage through the terrified mob of Treveri soldiers. At first scattered singly across the hillside, their numbers gradually increased as the two men progressed towards the valley floor until the grassy surface was littered with dead and dying men, almost every one of them marked with horrific wounds to the backs of their necks and thighs where the easiest death strokes could be inflicted. Horns were blowing in the trees ahead of them, and the two men hurried down the lower slope to find their men held at bay by a line of dismounted horsemen whose lances were lowered to make a hedge of iron points, behind which the remainder of the Treveri had taken refuge.

'What's the meaning of this?'

A crested officer stepped forward through the line of his men, and Antonius immediately recognised the Batavi prefect, Briganticus.

'I'm obeying my orders, First Spear Pugno. Legatus Augusti Cerialis told me that anyone who surrendered to my cohort was to be spared.'

Pugno shook his head, his face contorted in anger as he stepped forward to stand within inches of the other man.

'These are my prisoners, Prefect!'

The big man shook his head with a slight smile, not withdrawing an inch in the face of the legion man's evident rage.

'The victory is yours, First Spear. The men you've already killed as they ran are dead, but my orders are that once they've stopped running and thrown down their weapons, they are to live. Legatus Augusti Cerialis is looking to restore the empire's relationship with their tribe, and that will not be possible if we murder every man who stood against us here.'

Pugno glared back at him with stone-cold eyes, holding the stare for so long that Antonius was convinced he would fight, but eventually he nodded slowly, raising his voice to be heard by the captives.

'Very well. Every coward cringing behind your men's spears has the reward of the rest of his life in which to question his manhood. But they would be well advised to stay away from my legion from now on. As far as I'm concerned every one of their lives is forfeit to the Twenty-first.' He turned away, gesturing to his officers to follow him. 'Finish off their wounded, and send our bandage carriers to do what they can for our own. This battle is over, and the Twenty-first can once again hold its head up in the company of our sister legions! *Blood and glory!*'

7

Germania, May AD 70

Marius woke with a start from confused dreams, shivering uncontrollably with whatever malaise had entered his body when Bairaz's blade had cut his thigh open. Sitting up, ignoring the growling of his empty stomach, he untied the now filthy strip of wool that had at least stopped the flow of blood for long enough that the wound had scabbed over, grimacing at the yellow tinge to the skin on either side of the ugly gash. His thigh was hot to the touch, and when he staggered to his feet the pain that resulted made him gag loudly before he managed to control the reflex.

'My time to die may be at hand. And if it is then I ask that the Rich Father receives my spirit into the Underworld and guides me to meet my ancestors.' He laughed bitterly, looking about him at the empty forest in which he was hopelessly lost. 'Although I think it more likely that I'll be met by the spirits of all the men I've killed, eager to have their—'

He froze, realising with a start that a man was squatting in the shadow of a birch tree a dozen paces from where he had slept, studying him with alert, intelligent eyes. Dressed in a leather tunic coat that was black with age and ingrained dirt, his boots were sturdy and well made, evidently Roman in origin, and his heavy fur cloak looked to Marius's untrained eye to have been cut in one piece from the body of either a wolf or a bear. Long hair was tied back away from a face that was seamed with the lines of long experience, and to the Roman he seemed a man past his prime and yet evidently still physically capable, scarred knuckles resting on the hilts of a pair of long hunting knives, an unstrung bow and its accompanying quiver of arrows laid on the forest floor at his feet beside a small pack. The Roman looked about him for his sword, only to realise that it was lying at the German's feet. Swaying, he laughed with the black humour of a man who knew he was already dead.

'Been watching me, have you? Having a good laugh at the stupid Roman?'

The German stared back at him in silence, hard blue eyes in an immobile face, and Marius laughed softly, subsiding back onto the ground on which he had slept.

'You don't speak Latin then. I suppose I should be grateful you didn't kill me in my sleep . . .' He shook his head in dark amusement. 'Although you might have been doing me a favour had you done so. I'm fucked, from the look of my leg.'

'Your blood is poison.'

Marius raised an eyebrow.

'So you do speak Latin.'

The older man nodded impassively.

'Speak Latin when sell fur with Roman. Your blood is poison. Perhaps you live. Perhaps you die. I help you.'

The Roman untied his bandage, pointing to the angry wound and the sickened flesh around it.

'You can make this better? How?'

The hunter pointed to the birch tree in whose shadow he was squatting.

'Watchful tree. It clean wound.'

Marius shook his head uncomprehendingly.

'Why? Why would you help a Roman?'

The answer was delivered with the same deadpan expression as before.

'Here in forest is no *Ro*man or *tribe* man. Here in forest is only *man*. You need help, I give you help. If you live, you give me help. My name Beran. Mean bear, in you speak. You name?'

The Roman shrugged, another bout of feverish shivering racking his body.

'My name is Marius, and if you can make this fever go away then I'll give you all the help you ask of me.'

He subsided onto the forest floor, shaking with the fever's renewed onset, staring helplessly up at the hunter as he took off his fur cloak and draped it across the helpless Roman's body.

'You be warm. I build fire.'

He turned away and walked back to the birch tree, putting out a hand to touch its trunk and speaking quietly, stroking the bark as he talked.

'You're talking . . .' Marius shuddered through another spasm of uncontrollable shivering, 'to a *tree*?'

Beran answered him without turning away from the tree.

'Watchful tree sees all. Is living thing, like bear or wolf. I tell tree you good man, ask it spirit help clean wound.'

'You told it . . .' Marius swallowed his amusement at the idea of a man talking to a tree, knowing that the German held the power of life and death over him, 'that I'm a good man? If you knew how many men I've killed in the last year . . .'

Beran shook his head, still stroking the tree's bark.

'You *good* man. I know it. Have watch you since you escape Batavi. Watch you help other Roman die. You hard man, but you good man.'

'You were watching?'

The German laughed.

'This forest my home. Not Roman home. Not Batavi home. Not Bructeri home. *My* home. And no man come my home without I know. Now you be still. I bleed tree to make *luppi* – is drink to make strong. And I cut branch from watchful tree, put in fire, make *kol. Kol* is burn wood, black, yes? I use kol, clean wound.'

'You're going to heal me with charcoal. That'll be something to tell the medic . . .' Marius shuddered again as the fever sank its claws deeper into him. 'The med . . .'

He felt his eyes closing, unable to resist, and surrendered to the sickness that was burning him alive.

*

Augusta Trevorum, May AD 70

'Men of the First and Sixteenth Legions . . .'

Pugno snorted derisively.

'Cunts.'

If Cerialis heard the expletive, which the veteran first spear had made no attempt to disguise, he failed to show even a hint of concern. Antonius sneaked a swift glance over his shoulder at the ranks of men standing behind the Twenty-first's officers, but despite the fact that their first spear's comments were plainly audible to the closest among them, not a single face was anything other than perfectly stoic.

'. . . you have chosen, after a period of time in which to reflect on the error of your ways, to return to your duty in serving the emperor. You have spontaneously taken the sacramentum, swearing fidelity and loyalty to the service of our emperor Vespasianus. And you have absented yourselves from your enforced service to the so-called "empire of the Gauls", presenting yourselves to me here today in order to receive the empire's judgement on your actions, a judgement you have stated you will accept no matter what it may be.'

The Twenty-first's senior centurion shook his head slowly, staring at the tremulous ranks of men facing them and voicing his own verdict in the same unconcerned tone of voice as before.

'*Useless* cunts. And you should all be fucking crucified, here and now.'

Antonius was unable to conceal the smile that pulled at the corners of his mouth. The two sadly depleted legion remnants had marched in from the south the previous evening, and had been ordered to camp alongside the Twenty-first on the flat ground on the western side of the river from the Treveri capital, a location that Cerialis had deliberately chosen to interpose the Mosella between the vengeful legionaries and the terrified inhabitants of the city. Digging themselves a marching camp alongside that which had been constructed the day before by the weary men who had conquered the Treveri army and captured their war leader, the new arrivals had very much kept themselves to themselves, evidently in fear of reprisals from their neighbours. Cerialis was speaking again, his face a mask of disapproval.

'You men of the First Legion, you have a history of doing this sort of thing! Formed by no less a man than the Divine Julius, you were illustrious in the service of Augustus at Philippi and in Sicily and earned the right to bear his name, but later proved so undisciplined that it was stripped from your title. Again, when the Divine Augustus died you were severely criticised for rebellion by no less a man than Germanicus. And here you are again, guilty not only of mutinying against and murdering not one but two legati augusti, but further to that, of voluntarily taking an oath of allegiance to the Gauls, a subject people of the empire you swore to defend! And you men of the Sixteenth Legion are little better, even if this is the first instance of mutiny in your hitherto illustrious history. Your lion emblem was gifted to you by the young Octavian, before he became our Augustus, and for many years you have brought great pride and fame to that badge, but with these acts of infamy you have relinquished your right to that pride and instead assumed a position of shame and opprobrium.'

'Opprobrium? More like treachery.'

Cerialis flicked a glance at the seething centurion, and Legatus Longus raised an eyebrow which, Antonius noted, Pugno completely ignored, continuing to stare daggers at the sullen, nervous legionaries.

'By rights, as First Spear Pugno has rather forcefully pointed out, I would be entirely justified in having every last one of you crucified, as an example to others who might be tempted to follow your lead. But these are challenging times, and such circumstances call for flexibility.'

'Flexible like their fucking loyalty.'

Ignoring the furious Pugno, Cerialis continued in a magisterial tone.

'And indeed, under normal circumstances, it would be my sworn duty as the emperor's legatus to have you all punished to the fullest extent of my powers. Your legions would be disbanded, and you yourselves dismissed from the army in disgrace, without pay, and with your burial club contributions forfeit to the state. I might also have you decimated before discharge, as a reminder to the survivors as to the price that is always paid by deserters, one man in ten beaten to death by his comrades with their bare hands. But these are not ordinary times. Your crime of mutiny I shall punish with a sentence that is for the time being suspended until the end of this war. What that sentence will turn out to be will depend purely on your performance between this day and that. Fight hard, and make your emperor proud, and we may be able to forget all about this unfortunate episode. The First and Sixteenth Legions might yet be allowed to rejoin the army of Germania as equals, their crimes expunged from the records, free to parade their eagles and standards alongside all other legions, and with their heads held high. Fail to impress me, men of the First and Sixteenth Legions, and I may well decide to carry out a sentence that carries every ounce of my authority to punish you. Observe the Twenty-first Legion as they stand before you, bloodied in more battles in the last year than either of your legions has seen in the last fifty. Consider their example! Bloodied but victorious at the first battle of Cremona! On the losing side at the second battle but unbowed to the end! And victorious at Rigodulum despite having to attack up a hill into the teeth of a spirited Treveri defence! Make them your exemplar, men of the First and Sixteenth Legions, and all can still be forgiven!'

'And when he eventually realises what a crock of shit you are, you'll all be disbanded and given a good fucking kicking. I look forward to that day with an anticipation so keen you could carve the ears off a corpse with it.'

Cerialis smiled beneficently at the outburst, and Antonius realised that, if not a pre-agreed act, Pugno's grim comments were at least a useful and chilling counterpoint to the general's offer of potential clemency.

'And now I shall leave you all to work out how you're going to come together to increase the army's strength, and provide the empire with a salutary example of repentance, which I can hopefully reward with a full pardon in due course. First Spear?'

Turning on his heel to face his commander, Pugno saluted punctiliously, then turned back to stare pitilessly at the waiting legionaries, barking a command at his own officers.

'The Twenty-first Legion is dismissed to light duties! The First and Sixteenth Legions will remain paraded while I brief your senior centurions as to my intentions. Twenty-first Legion – dismissed!'

He signalled to Antonius to remain with him, waiting in silence as his own men marched off parade, the legion spontaneously breaking into their battle hymn as a gesture of contempt for the pathetic remnants of two once-proud legions waiting to hear their fate.

'Walk with me, Centurion Antonius.'

Striding forward with Antonius at his shoulder he halted twenty paces from the waiting legions and bellowed an order that was heard up and down their line.

'All officers, to me!'

Waiting until the thirty odd centurions had gathered around him, he looked around at their faces, some anxious, some beaten down, some chin-jutting and defiant.

'We should start with a clear understanding of our relative positions in life. You, all of you, every last one of you, no matter how pissed off you might be with your lot right now, have sunk as low as you can go without actually being nailed up and left to gasp out your last breaths while the crows compete for a chance to peck out your eyes. And if it were left to me you'd already be on those crosses. You swore an oath to serve Galba, and then you broke it.' He raised a hand. 'I know. You're going to say that we all broke it, you, the Fifth and the Fifteenth at the Old Camp, the Fourth and the Twenty-second at the Winter Camp, all of us. And you'd be wrong, so don't waste your fucking breath. The Twenty-first didn't swear to obey Vitellius until after the news that Otho had murdered Galba and made himself emperor. We swore to Vitellius as Galba's avengers, but you swore to him in the hope of a nice, fat donative, didn't you? So you took another oath, this time to serve Vitellius, who whilst he might have been a useless bastard at least wasn't guilty of the crime of murdering an emperor. And then, when it all got a bit too tough for you delicate flowers, you broke that oath as well. And you murdered not just one legatus augusti, but two! Two Roman gentlemen killed like dogs, Flaccus in Novaesium at Saturnalia, and Vocula in camp nearby not much more than a month later!'

He looked around at the men surrounding him again, silently daring any of them to defy him.

'Does not one of you want to argue with me? Tell me that it wasn't you that killed Vocula, but a deserter from your ranks, no longer part of the legion that raised him? No?' He nodded slowly, his face hard. 'Good choice, because any man that tries that particular line of horseshit on me will find out the hard way what it's like to receive thirty lashes with the scourge. I'm authorised to carry out whatever punishment I feel necessary to put you useless bastards back into fighting condition, and trust me, anyone who fails to admit that you all stood around and watched while your own man Longinus took his iron to an army commander will qualify for an immediate scourging that will leave him broken for the rest of his life. Because my colleague Antonius stood among you and watched it happen too, although in his case he's sworn to have revenge on his legatus's killer. So, ladies, here's how it is.'

The two legions' senior officers tensed, preparing themselves to receive his verdict.

'From this moment onward, you will be considered to be under the command of the Twenty-first. You will no longer be treated as legions in your own right, but as over-strength cohorts attached to my legion, under my command and utterly subject to my whim. You first spears are now cohort commanders, and you will follow my orders in battle, form part of my line, and generally do whatever the fuck I tell you. Got that?'

The two men in question nodded silently, aware they were both very much on their last chance.

'Oh, and your men may be wondering about their pay? After

all, you've not seen a hint of coin since the donative that Antonius here tells me triggered the murder of Hordeonius Flaccus, have you? Well I'm happy to tell you that any gold they might be hoping for has been written off the pay books as the penalty for their betrayal of the empire. Your status as of now is purely probationary, which means that all pay and privileges are suspended until such time as you prove yourselves capable of fighting for the empire. You want to get paid, you fight! I'd imagine there'll be a fight along soon enough.'

Treveri territory, May AD 70

'You want to roll the dice now, rather than waiting for the odds to improve?'

Tutor nodded at Kivilaz's question, clearly not comprehending the Batavi's evident disapproval, and turned to his Nervian colleague Classicus, his hands opened in baffled appeal.

'What better time could there be? Every day that we delay brings the threat of yet more legions, from Hispania, from Britannia, from Dacia, from Italy. We need to strike *now*!'

Kivilaz shook his head in irritation at the Treveri leader's apparent obtuseness.

'When the reinforcements from our brothers across the great river have arrived, *that* will be the time to strike. A German army will always terrify the Romans into panic and chaos under the right circumstances, whereas all you Gauls have achieved so far is to provide them with a whetstone on which to sharpen their blade. Let Cerialis luxuriate in his victory over your army, and the occupation of your city as much as he likes, the destruction of his only effective legion will settle this matter once and for all!'

Tutor leaned across the table around which the revolt's three leaders were standing, jabbing his finger down on the scarred wooded surface for emphasis.

'The legions that have been ordered to join Cerialis's army from across the western half of the empire are all veterans, bloodied over decades of warfare, whereas your Germans never obey their orders, but rather do exactly as their whims dictate, and can only be won over by gifts and gold. And the Romans have more gold than we do, infinitely more, so what is to stop them from bribing your Germans to depart without fighting? But if we fight them now, without delay, two of their three legions are the dregs of their army in Germany, and still bound to our service by oath. As for the fact that they routed Valentinus and his undisciplined levy at Rigodulum, that will only make them bolder and more rash. Which means that when they find themselves faced not by a Valentinus, obsessed by words and speeches and fury, but by Kivilaz and Classicus and Tutor, men who understand iron and blood, when that realisation dawns upon them they will recall the many times they have been beaten by us, and fled empty handed. And the Treveri will rise behind the Romans, for they have no more love for Rome and its legions than we do.'

'You cannot—'

Classicus shook his head and raised a hand to interject, and Kivilaz fell silent, waiting to see which way the spinning coin of their decision would land.

'If there's one thing I learned from my years fighting alongside the Romans, taking orders from the best and worst of them, it's that a swift attack with less force than might be ideal often prevails where a more considered move with greater force can all too often fail. Cerialis, it seems, is that sort of general, always pushing on, always looking for a weak spot to exploit. A week ago he was marching his men into the Winter Camp and they were looking forward to the chance to rest for a day or two after double timing it all the way from Vindonissa. Our colleague here . . .' he gestured to Tutor, 'was unfortunate enough to have an otherwise secure position on the Nava turned after the betrayal of a deserter showed the Romans a ford, which forced him to fall back on Augusta Trevorum, but it was typical of Cerialis that he chose to follow up on that victory with everything he had, knowing that he had a chance to break the Treveri's resistance before the rest of our force could consolidate to resist his advance. Show that man an opportunity to strike fast and he'll take it, because he knows that he can do more with a single legion today than he might achieve with half a dozen eagles in the six weeks it will take for his re-inforcements to reach him. And we must do the same.'

The Batavi tipped his head in recognition of his comrade's point.

'Fortune can often favour those of us who know how to take a risk, nobody knows that better than the Batavi. But we also know that Cerialis is bold to the point of being rash. He lost the best part of a legion in Britannia by rushing at Boudicca's rebels without adequate scouting, and found himself facing several times his own strength. He will do the same again, if we give him the illusion that he is free to manoeuvre in these hills.'

Classicus nodded his acknowledgement of the point.

'Yes, he did. And now he has his head and neck in a similar trap, which only needs us to close it.'

'But he's in a defensive position. And now they've woken up enough to dig out a ditch and raise a palisade around their camp. Surely our best strategy is to wait for him to leave the safety of his earthworks and march north, and to be ready to ambush him on the road?'

Classicus pointed at the rough map of Augusta Trevorum and its surrounding countryside which lay across the table between them.

'No. *Now* is the moment when his army is at its most vulner-able. My spies in the city tell me that the Twenty-first Legion is still recovering after three days speed-marching and a pitched battle, and that the two legions that have abandoned us after such a short service are no more effective than they were when I had them swear an oath of loyalty to the Gallic empire. Their scouting is limited to a few mounted patrols watching the road from the north for any sign of us advancing to do battle. Everything I hear tells me that we need to strike now, using stealth to approach their camp and our rage at their presence on our ground to batter their army to pieces.'

Kivilaz shook his head.

'They number close to six thousand legionaries, with a similar strength in auxiliaries to back them up. What can we hope to achieve by attacking them before the army I know is marching south from the German tribes joins us? Would we not be better to confront them in open countryside, where we can overrun them from all sides and catch them without a wall and a ditch to hide behind?'

The Nervii prince pointed to the map again.

'Half the answer lies there, in the map my scouts have drawn.' He pointed to the line of field defences that ran in a semi-circle from a point a quarter of a mile north of the city's bridge to twice that distance to its south. 'In the daytime, with a conventional approach and a battle fought in the usual way, we are indeed likely to fail. If we allow them to play to their strengths. If they fight as an organised body of men, protected behind those defences, then even if we breach their walls those legions will only have to retreat across the river and defend the eastern bank to hold us off. Our presence would be revealed, the advantage of surprise lost and Cerialis will be able to disengage at his leisure, retreat into the Treveri hinterland and come at us from another direction. But I have something a little more subtle in mind. Something which takes advantage of our opponent's biggest weakness.'

'Which is?'

Classicus grinned at his Batavi ally.

'Come now, Kivilaz, you know Cerialis better than any of us. You know his weaknesses. Like so many other men who aspire to power, as we have both seen on more than one occasion, Quintus Petillius Cerialis is a slave to his own appetites. Some men react to achieving power by indulging their stomachs, and become fatter and more indolent as their influence grows. Others are the opposite, choosing the Spartan approach to their lives and glorying in their moderation and fitness. But there is another type of man, who cannot resist the temptations of another form of self-indulgence, unable to see a handsome woman without feeling compelled to possess her and spend his restless seed in her. And this is the appetite to which your former friend Cerialis is just such a slave. He is compelled to have any woman who catches his eye, not matter what her station is, princess or whore, married or not, and he is not above using the powers of a conqueror to achieve his mastery of whoever it is that takes his fancy.'

'You believe that he has fallen victim to some woman's beauty in Augusta Trevorum?'

'I know it for a fact. Trust me, no information passes from man to man with greater speed than a salacious story, especially one founded in truth. When an army's commander chooses to lie with the recently widowed wife of a prominent citizen, making clear by inference that her willing submission is part of the terms under which the city will not be burned out, looted and sacked by the infamous Twenty-first Legion, then word spreads swiftly. Gossip is rife in Augusta Trevorum that our mutual enemy spends more time in the city than might be expected, especially during the hours of darkness, deserting his field headquarters and leaving his men effectively leaderless. And leaderless men tend to be somewhat more relaxed than those who know that their general might appear at any moment to inspect their readiness. And therein, my brother-in-arms, lies our opportunity. We will strike tonight, at the moment of maximum opportunity, with your brave cohorts on the right, the position with the most honour. The Ubii, my Nervii and the men of the Lingones will attack in the middle, straight down from the ridge and at their central gate, and your Bructeri and Tencteri allies can smash in the far left gate and add to the chaos. We will rampage into their camp from all directions and cause such chaos that the legions will be unable to resist our ferocity. And your cohorts will be accorded the mightiest prize, if you will accept the honour.'

Kivilaz nodded slowly, reluctant but knowing that he would not change the Nervii leader's mind.

'Cerialis?'

'Yes.' Classicus pointed at the city on the Mosella's eastern bank. 'Our tribal armies will be ordered to concentrate their anger inside the enemy camp, but your men will force the river bridge and retake Augusta Trevorum. I have allotted them the right-hand gate because it is in that section of the camp where the traitor legions have pitched their tents. When you attack they will flee, and grant you free access to the bridge. And not only can your men be trusted not to succumb to the urge to sack the city, but they must take Cerialis alive, to use in the bargaining with Rome that must follow if we are to persuade Rome that coexistence with the Gallic empire is possible. Vespasianus will be forced to negotiate with us once we have his son-in-law.'

'I accept this honour on the behalf of the Batavi cohorts. Although if you're expecting the capture of a single senator to alter Rome's murderous attitude towards a rebellious people, no matter what his status might be, I fear that you will be sadly disappointed by their response. And for me all that matters now, given that you have decided to strike here, is that we annihilate the Twenty-first Legion. Nothing else will be worth the price we are about to pay in blood.'

Nodding to the other two men, he walked out of the tent with Hramn and his guards at his shoulder.

'You do not agree with Classicus's decision?'

'I have no choice in the matter. If the Gauls attack and I fail to order our men to join them, then a victory will be theirs, but a defeat will be mine and mine alone if I am seen to fail to support them when they needed it most. And besides . . .'

'Who knows what might happen?'

'Exactly.'

'And if we lose?'

The prince shrugged.

'Then we'll disengage without giving the Romans time to recover their wits and bottle us up for slaughter, retreat to the north-east and fall back on our allies the Ubii. They'll hold firm, I'm sure of that. Why else would I have left my wife and son in their hands, if not to show them my trust?' He grinned at his nephew. 'Trust reinforced by the presence of our even more trustworthy allies of the Chauci and Frisii in their midst, mind you. But that's for tomorrow. Tonight we go to battle again!'

Hramn stopped walking and stared at his uncle, his head shaking slightly.

'My mother always said that you were the wildest of all her brothers and sisters. You actually want to do this, don't you?'

Kivilaz shrugged.

'Don't tell me that you're not excited by the thought of a proper, straightforward fight. The chance to rampage through a legion's camp with sword and spear? Our warriors of old would have accepted certain death, if they knew they could take half a dozen of the enemy with them and write a fresh line in the song of glory.'

His nephew nodded.

'I can see it well enough. I'm just wondering how we're going to get inside their camp. While we've been mustering our combined forces into an army, the Romans have woken up to the fact we're out here, and that we're not far from their camp. A four-foot ditch and ten-foot palisade won't be easy to cross.'

'Agreed. But their camp's defences have one flaw that hasn't been corrected yet. And I know just the man to exploit it. If he and his men succeed we'll have an open gate for the cohorts to push through.'

Hramn nodded slowly.

'And if he fails then our concerns with regard to his loyalty will no longer matter. Will they?'

Augusta Trevorum, May AD 70

'First Spear Antonius.'

Antonius snapped to attention, hearing the rap of hobnailed boots as the men behind him copied his gesture of respect, saluting crisply. Their commander strode forward into the overlapping circles of yellow light, illumination cast by torches on either side of the bridge across the Mosella, which the Twenty-first's men were guarding along with the camp's perimeter.

'Legatus Augusti!'

Cerialis waved a hand in amused acknowledgement.

'There's no need to salute, First Spear, we're all fighting men here, not the type of barracks warriors that sort of thing matters to.'

Antonius inclined his head in cautious respect for his superior's sentiment.

'Indeed so, Legatus Augusti. Although it's good for our men to see the proper discipline exercised. I've seen the results of what happens when it breaks down, and trust me, sir, I never want to see it again.'

Cerialis nodded in his own turn.

'Ah. Poor Dillius Vocula's unfortunate demise, not to mention that of his colleague Flaccus before him. A point well made, First Spear. I shall tolerate the salutes of fighting men from now, and take your experienced opinion seriously, I assure you.'

He grinned, evidently still at ease among his men, and Antonius found himself warming to the man.

'Thank you, Legatus Augusti.'

The general looked about him, taking a lungful of the night's crisp air and looking up at the blaze of stars above their heads.

'So tell me, First Spear, are your men enjoying the luxury of a few quiet days before we march out to find and deal with this man Civilis?'

'Time not spent marching is always welcome to any legionary, Legatus Augusti, as you can imagine.'

'Indeed I can. But . . .'

Antonius reflected for a moment before replying, choosing his words carefully.

'The Twenty-first is a legion with a long tradition of finding, fixing and destroying its enemies, Legatus Augusti. The men are eager to come to close quarters with this man Civilis and his Gallic allies, and show them what a real legion can do on the battlefield.'

The older man laughed, clapping a hand to his subordinate's shoulder.

'And you only a month in the Twenty-first's service! I hear

you've been inducted to First Spear Pugno's inner circle, the infamous Blood Drinkers?'

'Yes, Legatus Augusti, I have that honour.'

'And now you too chafe to be away to find Civilis and put him in his place. Don't worry, Antonius, you'll have your chance soon enough. The latest reports from those men sympathetic to our cause in the country to the north are that Civilis and his Batavians are in close attendance upon us, probably hoping to spring an ambush when we march out to take the campaign to their homelands. I doubt that it'll be very long before we're face-to-face with them, and then you'll all have your chance to test your mettle against whatever's left of their once-vaunted cohorts, won't you.'

Antonius dipped his head again.

'So it seems, Legatus Augusti. And I have no doubt that you'll find your army eager to come to grips with these traitors.'

'I'm sure of it.' Cerialis looked across the bridge and winked at the senior centurion. 'And now, if you'll excuse me, First Spear, there are important diplomatic matters to be attended to. There's no peace for the conqueror, I can assure you of that!'

He strode away across the bridge and the men around Antonius relaxed from their stiff stances, soft laughter from somewhere outside the circles of light betraying their amusement at the general's eagerness for whatever it was he was going into the city to do.

'There are important diplomatic matters to attend to?' He turned to find the commander of the century that had been detailed to guard the bridge standing at his shoulder, his face split in a grin. 'Well let's face it, it's not going to suck itself, is it?'

Antonius laughed despite himself.

'No, I don't suppose it is. Very well, since you're in such good spirits you can go and make sure that the guard posts are all awake and paying attention while I stay here and keep an eye on your men.'

'You think the barbarians might have a go at raiding the camp?'

The senior centurion shrugged.

'It wouldn't be the first time. You can take my word on that.'

'I thought they were going to be slack and sleepy? They look sharp enough to me.'

Alcaeus nodded, his teeth bared in a hard smile at Adalwin's disappointment. Lanzo's tent party were staring down into the legion encampment, huddled against the Mosella's western bank, from the vantage point of the ridge that ran parallel with the river's course four hundred paces to the west. The freshly constructed palisade was lit by the glow of a torch every ten paces, armed and armoured legionaries patrolling its exterior in sufficient numbers to make any covert approach likely to end in ignominious failure. As they watched, a centurion strode out through the closest of the camp's three gates into the torchlight, his brisk walk and evident purpose leaving no doubt that this enemy was alert and ready for any attempt to attack.

'You thought that we were going to be able to stroll up to the gates of their camp and saunter in, did you, Beaky? And there was me thinking that you'd got over that first flush of innocence, but clearly you're still new enough to this life to take what your leaders tell you for the truth.' The tight knot of men gathered around him chuckled quietly as their centurion continued. 'It was ever thus, Soldier Adalwin. The men who lead this revolt have decided that the Romans will be relaxed and lazy after their victory over the Treveri, and so they drew up their plans with that expectation in mind. But while our leaders believe that the guard on those walls will be relaxed, we know from our first-hand experience the Twenty-first legion is unlikely ever to let its guard down, not even after a victory. No, we'll have to do this the Batavi way. But before we do this, you're all sure you want to follow me into the jaws of the beast?'

When Hramn had brusquely passed Kivilaz's order down to Alcaeus, Egilhard had been quick to volunteer alongside his centurion, and Lanzo's men had equally swiftly asserted their right to be the men chosen to accompany their centurion into the heart of the enemy camp. Lataz put a hand on his shoulder, a rare moment of familiarity between two fighting men.

'My idiot son has decided to go in there with you, which means that his uncle and I have no choice but to go in and make sure he doesn't go playing at heroes. Which means that we have to take my other son for fear of the sulk we'll all have to endure if we leave him behind.'

Lanzo interjected.

'I have come along to add some spurious impression that I'm still in command of these idiots, which means that we're stuck with Tiny and Beaky. Although at least that means we won't be short of muscles or bad jokes. And if it gets really bad we can just show them Levonhard's face.'

The centurion looked around his men for a moment, nodding slowly at their taut, determined faces.

'I'll put in a word for you all with the Allfather if I get sent to the Underworld before you. May you all receive Magusanus's blessings and come through this ordeal stronger.'

'I'd settle for being alive and still in possession of my cock and both balls.'

Alcaeus snorted a laugh despite the solemnity of the moment.

'And in that wish, Soldier Frijaz, you and I for once are of the same mind. Very well, if you're all set on this, follow me.'

He led them down the ridge's slope, padding silently through the darkness, out across the tail of the flat plain on which the Roman camp had been built and on, down to the river's edge, crouching low to avoid any risk of being seen by the alert legionaries. Raising a hand to gather the tent party back around him, he waited until Lanzo had brought up the party's rear, his men's boots sinking into the soft mud as they followed his example and squatted near to the ground close to the water's edge.

'Once we give the signal that we're on our way, the cohorts will come forward and wait, far enough from their walls as to be invisible, ready to exploit the opening we're going to give them. All we have to do is open the gate closest to the river and keep it open long enough for them to cross the remaining ground between them and the palisade.'

'Is that all? I can't imagine what I was worrying about . . .'

The centurion smiled at Frijaz's sarcasm.

'That's the problem with being the uncle of a famous hero. Everyone starts to think that you might just be cut from the same tree, and that they must have been doing you a disservice in calling you an idle drunkard for all those years.' He raised a hand to his bowed forehead in prayer. 'Mighty Hercules, I entreat you to cast a favourable eye over your faithful subjects as we go about your work. Keep these men safe from harm and make them strong in body and mind to fight and win this night.' Raising his head, he looked around at his men expectantly. 'Are you ready to die for the tribe? For Hercules?' He waited for a moment, allowing his words to sink in, and baring his teeth in a silent snarl as the men around him nodded and muttered their assent. 'Good. Keep that in mind. Be ready to sell your life dearly to bring glory to our father, but fight like animals to live, so that you can give him that glory and serve him for the rest of your lives.' He chuckled softly. 'Any man joining me in the Underworld with less than half a dozen spirits of enemy legionaries following him can expect a fucking good talking to. Lanzo, give the signal.'

Grinning at their quiet laughs, he turned to the river, stalking noiselessly down to the water's edge while the mournful hoot of an owl from Lanzo's cupped hands summoned the cohorts from their hiding place on the ridge. Stepping into the river's flow with deliberate ease, avoiding making any sound as his body eased into the water, the centurion immersed himself until only his helmeted head protruded above the surface. Moving slowly to prevent ripples that would reflect the torches' light as they got closer to the Roman camp, he allowed the current to carry him downstream, nothing more than a dark spot in the river's black water. Following his example, the men of the tent party sank into the river's cold water, gasping quietly as the chill hit them, then allowed their bodies to drift with the current through the shallows close to the Mosella's bank, plunging their hands into the mud beneath them to slow their progress and ensure that they stayed close enough to the shore not to be washed away into the river's powerful flow. Following close enough to Alcaeus to be able to see the individual hobnails on his boots when they broke the surface, Egilhard held his breath as they floated slowly past the end of the camp's palisade, gazing intently up at the silhouette of a legionary in the wall above them as the man stared out into the darkness beyond the light of the torches that lined the legion's defences. Twenty paces further down the bank, Alcaeus turned his head and crawled slowly out of the water, shuffling up the muddy shore on his elbows and stopping with his calves and booted feet still in the Mosella's flow. Egilhard eased his body alongside him, and followed the officer's example as he scooped handfuls of mud from the river's sodden bank and smeared them across his face, throat and hands. Leaning so close to his chosen man that his lips were almost touching Egilhard's ear, he whispered a final instruction.

'Gift me with a little of your god-given talent and watch my back, Achilles. I'd hate to find myself dead with a spear through me wielded by some lucky bastard I never saw coming.'

Rising slowly to a crouch, he led the tent party forward over the bank's lip, revealing the Roman camp in its full terrifying scale, a sea of leather tents studded with torches and the glowing embers of watch fires, sunk in the profound silence of the night with only the occasional cough from a restive sleeper and the voices of the sentries occasionally breaking the spell that seemed to have settled over the weary legion. Pointing at the closest tent, and the spears and shields propped up beside it, he issued a whispered order.

'Arm yourselves.'

Wincing at every tiny sound of wood and iron, they took the sleeping Roman tent party's weapons, hefting the unfamiliar weight of legion spears with their long iron heads and the Romans' curved oblong shields.

Following Alcaeus between a pair of tents, and resisting the urge to giggle at the noise of snoring issuing from one of them,

Egilhard sank gratefully into the shadow of the palisade, allowing a long exhalation of pent-up breath to escape his lungs as his comrades slid noiselessly into cover one at a time, similarly painted black with slimy mud from the riverbank.

'This smells more like shit than dirt.'

Ignoring Frijaz's whispered complaint, the wolf-priest pointed at the gate that was their objective, fifty paces distant and wreathed in the soft light of the torches set high on the palisade above it.

'Slow and quiet until we get too close to avoid being seen, then fast and quiet until the gates are open. After that you can make all the noise you like. And keep your iron sheathed until we strike.'

He started forward, crouching down into the darkest shadows, then froze in his place as a soldier climbed out of the closest tent, no more than ten paces distant. Reaching under his tunic and sighing gratefully as he emptied his bladder onto the hobnail-scarred turf, the unwitting legionary stared up at the stars, evidently enjoying the peace of the moment. Egilhard put a slow, stealthy hand to the handle of his dagger, ready to leap forward and cut the man's throat.

'Steady.'

Alcaeus's command was no more than a soft exhalation, both men watching the sleepy soldier as he shook himself, clearly still half-asleep. For a moment he stared directly at the shadows in which the raiders were concealed, then yawned, scratched his backside sleepily and crawled back into the tent.

'Move.'

Advancing down the palisade's rough wooden wall, the centurion held up a hand to halt his men with thirty paces remaining between them and the pair of legionaries guarding the gate.

'Wait.'

The two men were talking softly, their voices indistinct murmurs, and as the men of the tent party watched, one of them sank to his knees before the other.

'Gods below, he's sucking the—'

Ignoring Frijaz's incredulous statement of the obvious, Alcaeus tapped Egilhard on the shoulder.

'Go!'

The young warrior was away almost before the command was out of his centurion's mouth, darting past the officer and hurrying down the palisade with one hand on the hilt of his sword, exchanging stealth for speed as he dashed for the gate, leaving his sword sheathed to avoid it reflecting the light of the watch fires. The standing legionary looked up as he drew the blade, the rasping hiss of the iron blade on its scabbard's throat furrowing his brow, then died as Egilhard whipped the point up and speared it through the hapless sentry's throat, wrenching the blade free to leave the dying man swaying on his feet, blood bubbling from his mouth and nose with an explosive cough as he choked on it.

'What?'

The other legionary's question became a gasp of shock as his comrade's blood showered down on his upturned face, giving the young warrior all the time he needed, and he swung the sword's long blade back over his shoulder and then whipped it around as the legionary opened his mouth to shout a warning, decapitating him with the force of the blow. In the silence that followed, the tent party gathered around him, staring in awe at the two dead legionaries, but Alcaeus pointed to their objective with an urgent whisper.

'Get the gate open.'

Lifting the thick wooden bar that secured the two halves of the gate, Wigbrand and Lataz dropped it to one side, while the rest of the tent party pulled the heavy wooden doors back to open the camp's entrance. Lataz looked at the gaping hole in the Roman defences for a moment before speaking, voicing the thought that was on every mind.

'So what do we do now?'

Before Alcaeus could answer, the silence was broken by a challenge from above them, a sentry leaning over and unwittingly hailing them in jocular tones.

'Oi, when you pair have finished pulling each other off, what about one of you come and takes a turn up here? I'm bored of . . .'

He fell momentarily silent at the sight of the intruders, his mouth gaping at his dead comrades sprawled in the mud, then filled his lungs to roar a warning.

'Alarm! Enemy warriors at the gate!'

For a brief moment silence reigned again, and then men started shouting on both sides of the palisade as the sentry ran down the wall, repeating his call to arms at the top of his voice. Alcaeus roared an order over the rapidly growing tumult.

'Tent party, face into the camp! Egilhard, lead them!'

Striding out into the open space outside the gate, the centurion set himself, ready for the legionaries running down the palisade's wall in response to their comrade's shout, while Egilhard pushed his way into the heart of his comrades, finding himself between his uncle and his brother. In the camp men were stirring, voices raised to bellow orders that would quickly have the legion struggling to its collective feet, bleary-eyed and still half-asleep, but in no doubt that there was something horribly wrong. A legionary came running down the palisade's internal face from further round its curve, coming to a halt as he saw the tent party's men in his path. Lataz stamped forward and hurled the spear that he had picked up moments before straight at him, the sharp iron point punching clean through his armour, and the Roman, still not quite comprehending what was happening, died on its long iron shank without even raising his shield. Men were pouring out of the nearest tents and reaching for their weapons, centurions and chosen men bellowing at them to get into the fight, but where the men facing them would have expected a prompt charge, the legionaries milling about amid their abandoned tents seemed strangely reluctant to go forward, even at such thin opposition. A furious centurion drove a ragged wave of a dozen of the braver among them towards the gate, men without armour wielding swords snatched up as they had left their tents and, realising that their opponents' nerve was already at breaking point, Egilhard led his comrades forward into them. Facing off to the centurion, he killed the man with a swift and economical spear stroke before the officer ever got inside sword reach, and the brutal melee that followed sent the survivors reeling back, leaving half a dozen men dead or dying behind them. More men were gathering behind them with shields and hastily donned armour, but still there was no sign of the overwhelming attack that Egilhard had expected. Half-tempted to go forward into the tremulous enemy, Egilhard called to his men to reform, clamping down on his urge to rampage into the defenders and stepping back towards the spot where his centurion was guarding the opening in the palisade.

'We defend the gate! Get back in line!'

Glancing over his shoulder as the tent party retreated back to join him, he saw Alcaeus beset by a pair of legionaries and desperately fighting simply to stay alive. As the centurion fended off a vicious swing of one man's sword, opening himself up to the other's hacking stroke, the young soldier turned and threw his spear with instinctive speed, taking no time to consider the cast but simply putting the weapon's needle-sharp point over his centurion's shoulder and into his would-be killer's face. Nodding his gratitude the centurion sprang at his other assailant, who was still reeling with shock at his comrade's horrific death when the wolf-priest put him to the sword. Turning back to the threat confronting them, he flinched as a spear arced out of the torch-lit half-light, blood spattering his face as Wigbrand grunted with the impact, then dropped his sword and shield, staggering back with the weapon's long shaft in both hands and panting with the sudden, agonising pain. Even as the legionaries finally came at them again, emboldened by their gathering numbers and over a hundred strong, Egilhard's ability to control his need to fight was abruptly lost, dispelled by the stink of his comrade's blood. Abruptly gripped by a rage whose ferocity tore away any thought of self-preservation, he charged past his horrified father with a blood-curdling scream and ripped into the men facing them, heedless of the danger as their ranks parted before the incandescent fury of his attack, hacking and stabbing a vengeful path through the enemy soldiers standing in his way.

*

'First Spear!'

Antonius looked up from his seat by the watch fire positioned at the river bridge's eastern end, forcing himself to snap out of the memories that often plagued him when he was tired and then came to full, vivid life in his dreams, as if his mind surrendered its ability to keep the horrors that he had witnessed at bay when the time for sleep approached.

'What is it?'

The guard century's chosen man saluted apologetically.

'The centurion thinks there's something happening in the camp, sir, and he's asking if we should—'

Getting to his feet he raised a hand to silence the soldier, listening carefully. The sound of shouting was clearly if faintly audible, a rumour of combat that was rapidly swelling as, he guessed, more of the legion came to battle against whatever force had had the audacity to attack the Twenty-first in its camp. Hurrying across the bridge he found the guard century's centurion practically hopping from foot to foot with his urge to join the fight.

'First Spear! There are enemies in the camp! We're fully equipped, so we have to—'

'No.'

For a moment the only response was an incredulous stare, but before the centurion could regain his wits, Antonius leaned close to him, his tone loaded with all the grim authority he possessed.

'*No!* You want to abandon your assigned post and rush into a fight you have no way of understanding? That is not going to happen, Centurion, so put it from your mind!'

'But—'

'The fight will come to us quickly enough, trust me. There are only two objectives for those barbarians, one being to destroy or seriously damage the legions camped here, the other being to find the legatus augusti and kill or capture him. Because if they capture Cerialis then they end this campaign in one battle, at least for this year. They'll try to push through the camp, cross this bridge and get into Augusta Trevorum, because, and you can trust me on this point, they *will* know he's there.'

The other man looked at him for a moment before replying, his tone still one of disbelief.

'So what do we do? Just sit *here* and wait for them?'

'Don't be so fucking stupid.' Antonius shook his head, genuinely angered by the centurion's mulish need to rush into the fight. 'If we stay *here* then when they arrive *here* they will shower us with spears from both of our pathetic flanks and kill us all *here*. Get your men three-quarters of the way back across the bridge and into a decent line, ready to hold them off. I'm going to get some archers.' He reached out a hand, putting his index finger into the other man's face. 'One more thing, and I'll put this in terms you might understand. If you disobey this order then I *will* hunt you down though the madness of this battle and I *will* strangle you with your own guts! Is. That. *Clear?*' The centurion nodded, his eyes suddenly wide with the threat's potency. 'Then *get* on with it.'

Striding out into the camp towards the point where the Hamian archers were billeted, he passed hundreds of men struggling into their armour while their officers bellowed at them to do it faster, desperate to throw them into a fight which, from the growing din echoing from the palisade, was swiftly getting larger and deadlier as more and more barbarians rushed into the fray. He found the archers standing in their tent parties, armed and ready to fight, their prefect looking to the embattled perimeter with evident uncertainty as to what he should do with his unarmoured men.

'Ah, First Spear Antonius! What do you think—'

The hard-eyed centurion abandoned any thought of protocol, raising a hand to silence him and then pointing back the way he had come.

'There's no time, Prefect. Gather your men, tell them to bring every arrow they can carry, and follow me to the bridge! Quickly!'

'Lataz, where's Egilhard? I need him to . . .' The leading cohort had poured through the gate just as Egilhard had charged into the Roman line, and in the chaos that had followed Alcaeus had lost sight of his comrades until the last of the Batavi attackers had passed, pushing through the hapless men of the First and Sixteenth Legions towards the bridge. But having found his men, the centurion fell silent as he realised that Frijaz and Lataz were standing over a corpse around which a handful of dead legionaries were scattered.

'He's dead. My son is dead.'

The centurion nodded, seeing the desolation in their eyes.

'It looks as if he made them pay just as dearly for his life as we could have expected. Get him clear and find somewhere to bury him where the dogs won't be able to dig him up, we can look after him properly once this war's finished.' He waved a hand at the camp's ransacked and trampled remains. 'There are plenty of spades lying around. Where's your other son?'

Lataz pointed at the rear of the cohorts pushing on through the legion's encampment towards the bridge, hollow-eyed with the shock of his son's death.

'With them. Wild for revenge.'

Leading the Hamians back towards the river at a run, Antonius looked to his right, gauging from the roar of battle and the streams of legionaries hurrying to join the fight that the Twenty-first was perhaps holding its own against the barbarian tide, but the scene in front of him told a different story. Where the men of the Rapax were eager to get into the fight, the recently returned defectors clearly lacked any heart for battle, dozens of them streaming away from, rather than towards, the battle.

'They're not going to hold, are they?'

He shook his head at the prefect's question.

'No. Any moment now we're going to be arse-deep in angry Germans!'

Running across the bridge he roared a command at the waiting century lined up close to the eastern bank.

'Friendlies coming through! Open your ranks!'

The legionaries responded with their customary crisp discipline, the rear ranks stepping back to allow the archers to slip through their line. Antonius hurried to the left end of their line to stare across the river, his heart soaring momentarily as he realised that a tide of armoured men was washing towards the bridge, then shook his head as his hopes were cruelly dashed by the realisation that the men in question were not legionaries.

'They're Batavians! Stand by to resist attack! Prefect, put a third of your men on either side of the bridge and send the remainder to find some elevation so that they can shoot down into the enemy once they come at us. Tell them not to wait for an order, just kill anyone that sets foot on that wood!'

While the Hamians ran to their positions, and readied themselves to start killing the oncoming enemy, he stalked down the back of the three-deep line, shouting to be heard over the oncoming mob of Batavi warriors as they pounded towards the flimsy defence.

'You yearn to prove yourselves fit to boast that you're Blood Drinkers? Here's your chance! There are thousands of the best men in the enemy army about to come across that bridge, and they'll all be coming at *you*! If you hold them here you'll be famous, the men who saved the legatus augusti and upheld your legion's proud name! And if you die here, you'll have immortal glory!'

The enemy warriors stampeded onto the bridge, charging wild-eyed down its hundred-pace length, individuals among them falling as a growing sleet of arrows whipped into them from both sides, the Hamians nocking and shooting with deliberate care intended to ensure that every arrow found a target, and at a pace that Antonius knew they could sustain until their shafts were exhausted.

'Twenty-first Legion! Stand by to receive the enemy!'

The tightly packed front rank stamped forward with their left legs, crouching into their raised shields so that only their helmeted heads were visible, the men behind them stepping in close to support them, gripping their belts and crouching in their turn to maximise their own protection and get their weight behind the front rankers. With a thunderous hammering clatter of hobnails on wood the enemy were upon them in a pounding rush, seeking to burst through the line and into the open streets behind them, where their superior numbers would make short work of the defenders and allow them free rein to scour the city for Cerialis. They hit the legion line without breaking stride, the leading rank putting their shoulders against their own shields and pushing with all their strength while the men behind them crowded in at their backs and wielded their long spears to stab at the defenders.

'Hold them!'

The century's officers were close behind the line, roaring encouragement at their men as they started to slide slowly but inexorably backwards under the weight of the Batavi charge. The men of the front rank were pushing back with all their strength, holding their shields with both hands against the monstrous pressure relentlessly driving against their wooden wall and ducking away from the enemy's spear thrusts, but as Antonius watched a legionary fell, stabbed in his exposed front foot, dropping to the wooden surface to be finished by punching downward thrusts of the Batavi warriors' butt spikes. The line slid back one pace and then two more, the legionaries' booted feet unable to find purchase on the smooth wooden surface, and, standing close behind them, Antonius could see a look of triumph on the face of the closest of the enemy as he bellowed the first line of their paean.

'Batavi, swim the seas! Worship mighty Hercules!'

The mass of men behind him burst into song, and looking into his exultant eyes the Roman realised the only way that he was going to turn the fight.

'You!' He bellowed at the closest of the archers. *'Here! Now!'* The bowman hurried to his side with an arrow nocked and ready to shoot, looking apprehensively at the senior centurion's determined face. 'Him! See him? The smug bastard leading the singing?' He pushed the Hamian forward until he was almost close enough to the rear of the Twenty-first's line to be stabbed by their probing spears. 'Can you put an arrow in his eye?'

The archer nodded, mystified at the simplicity of the request. 'I could hit him in the eye from—'

'Just do it! And don't hit the men between you!'

Drawing the bow taut the archer loosed, his target realising that he was the mark for the arrow at the very last moment before it whipped across the five-pace gap between them and sank a third of its length in his skull, protruding from his eye socket. The other eye was suddenly dark red, burst by the missile's impact, but the dead man's corpse, held upright by the press of men to front and rear, swayed with each push by either side, its head lolling loosely. Antonius beckoned more of the archers to join the first, who, having realised the nature of what was expected of him and revelling in the deadly simplicity of the task, was busy nocking and loosing shafts between the legionaries' heads, each arrow killing another man to lessen the tide driving the legion line backwards. An enraged warrior hurled a spear at him, its long blade transfixing the Hamian's throat and dropping him thrashing to the bridge's wooden surface, but suddenly there were a dozen more archers behind the Romans, each one alert to any sign of a spear throw and punishing the attackers with their pointed armour-piercing arrows. Shots were also starting to rain down from the buildings behind the bridge, iron-tipped shafts hissing down into the mass of men funnelled helplessly into a mass target that was almost impossible to miss, each shot taking another Batavi warrior out of the fight, while more archers harassed the men on the far bank with shots that were equally unlikely to miss a human target even without being aimed.

'We've got them! Pour it on!'

He watched, still not daring to believe, as the enemy front rank fought and died under the lash of the Hamians' pitiless barrage, their singing silenced as they struggled to push the Roman line backwards. As increasing numbers of men fell to the archers' murderously unrelenting hail of arrows the remainder were increasingly seeking the shelter of their shields, having lost all interest in anything other than staying alive, and the legionaries were comfortably holding their ground. On the verge of issuing a fresh order, the centurion turned in surprise as a voice behind him caught his attention.

'Well, First Spear Antonius, it seems as if your small guard force has saved the day, does it not?'

Cerialis strolled out onto the bridge with his bodyguard walking to either side and in front of him, their shields raised against thrown spears.

'We do seem to have stopped them. In fact . . .' Antonius gestured to the Batavi ranks facing them. 'If you'll allow me?'

'Do go on, First Spear, I'm all for my officers acting on their initiative.'

Antonius turned back to the legion century.

'Century! On the command to withdraw, century will take five paces to the rear . . . Withdraw!'

Stepping smartly back, the legionaries allowed the weight of the dead Batavi front rankers to slide off their shields, depositing dozens of dead and dying men onto the bridge's surface. The Hamians had taken a vicious toll of the warriors who had so eagerly packed onto the bridge in the expectation of a swift victory, and the continuing rain of iron from both sides of the crossing and the houses behind it was continuing to thin their numbers.

'Should we take the offensive, do you think?'

Antonius nodded.

'Exactly my own thought, Legatus Augusti. Century! On the command, the century will advance one pace at a time! Kill anyone that's not dead and make sure of the corpses, just in case any of them are playing dead! Century, one pace . . . Advance!'

Stepping forward, the legionaries lunged with their swords, putting those men not yet dead out of their agony.

'One pace . . . Advance!'

Cerialis walked slowly alongside him as the century paced forward across the bridge, driving the tattered remnants of the enemy attack before them with archers pressing up close behind to punish those men who still stood against their counter-attack.

'How did these barbarians manage to penetrate our camp so deeply?' He raised a hand. 'No, don't spoil it for me, let me guess. They came through the Sixteenth and First Legions' lines, didn't they?'

'I'm afraid it does look that way, Legatus Augusti.'

The senior officer nodded grimly. 'I was afraid that would prove to be the case when I allowed them back into the army. What's happening now?'

The Batavi, having already been forced onto the defensive by the withering rain of iron that was still beating down on them, had abruptly started retreating, pulling away from the bridge in an ordered formation that was marching back through the cowed deserter legions' section of the camp, the men facing their century huddling into their shields as they backed away. Cerialis watched their retreat with a knowing expression.

'We won't be able to stop them. Which means that Civilis will get most of his men away to fight another day and with nothing much worse than a badly bloodied nose. And doubtless the Germans and Gauls will have managed to disengage too, once they realise that their gamble has failed. It really does seem as if you saved the day, First Spear, and probably my skin with it. I owe you a life, it seems.'

8

Treveri territory, May AD 70

'He didn't even see it coming. One moment he was alive, the next he was with your ancestors. Take some consolation from that.'

Lataz was silent for what seemed like an eternity to his officer, wiping a tear from his face before replying to Alcaeus's softly spoken words of comfort.

'Thank you, Centurion.' He sniffed, wiping his nose and gesturing to the small cairn of rocks that his family had built over his son's grave to enable them to find it again if the chance to give him a more fitting funeral came to pass. 'I know he died the way he would have wanted to, with a sword in his hands, but that makes it no easier to bury a son. And when we march home – if we ever march home – I'm the one who'll have to explain to my woman that her boy died with a Roman spear through him because I couldn't prevent him from running wild.' He shook his head, wiping his face again, then straightened his back and looked at the officer with a harder set to his face, pushing his raw grief to a place where he could deal with it in quieter moments. 'The attack failed?'

Alcaeus nodded.

'It did. We blew through the traitor legions as if they weren't there, once the cohorts got inside the fortress, and the leading centuries reached the bridge easily enough, but some clever bastard on the other side had enough archers at his back to shred them as they tried to cross it. We lost over three hundred men, first trying to force the bridge and then fighting our way back out the way we'd come in, and even that was a close thing. Half the Twenty-first

Legion came after us while the rest of them held off the other tribes like they could have done it with a hand tied behind them. So much for the knock-out punch to take the Romans out of the war.' He looked about him. 'Where's your other son?'

Frijaz, standing close to his brother with the stunned look of a man not yet reconciled with the events of the night, pointed out into the forest.

'Out there in the trees somewhere. He blames himself.'

Alcaeus shrugged.

'That's inevitable. I still blame myself for Banon's death at Gelduba, and in reality that was all down to Hramn's lack of any caution. Take your brother to join the cohort, and I will bring his son back. This is a time for harsh truths best not told by a father.'

He walked deeper into the trees, finding the young soldier sitting on the trunk of a fallen oak with his sword across his knees, its blade black with dried blood.

'You need to clean that iron before it starts to rust.'

Egilhard looked up at him wet-eyed.

'Sigu is dead. Because I couldn't control my need to be the hero my brother followed me into a fight he could never win.'

Alcaeus nodded.

'True. Your example was too great for him not to follow, but it was also impossible for him to live up to. A man like you only comes along once or perhaps twice in every generation, and the rest of us must either bask in your reflected glory or, if we seek to meet the same standards, face the risk that in reaching for that height we may fall.' He took a seat beside his chosen man, looking out into the forest's gloom. 'We must march from here quickly, because once the Romans have restored order to their camp they will come after us brimming with the urge to take revenge. Which means that you must do your mourning later, in the quiet moments of the night.'

Egilhard looked round at him.

'I do not know if I can go on.'

The wolf-priest pondered the desolation in his voice for a moment before replying.

'When Banon died I considered withdrawing into myself in the same way you are now. I pondered walking away into a forest like this one, knowing that had I chosen to do so then no one would have seen me. I would simply have vanished from the cohorts without a trace, no longer responsible for the lives of so many men, freed of the burden I willingly took on when I put that wolf's head on my helmet.'

'But you didn't.'

'No. Although that's not my point. I'm not telling you that you should stay and fight because I did. We all make our own decisions in this life, Achilles, and no man could ever accuse you of having lacked courage over the last year. My point is that if I had walked away I know beyond certainty that the feeling of relief at abandoning my burden would all too soon have become a misery of guilt. My burden is mine, and not to be relinquished to any other man in any way other than my death. If I had walked away I am sure that I would have died by my own hand very soon after.'

'And you think I might kill myself?'

The centurion shrugged.

'I cannot say. This is my story, not yours. But abandoning your burden will not bring Sigu back.'

He fell silent, and after a moment Egilhard drew breath to speak, but as he did so Alcaeus raised a hand to forestall him.

'There is something that I have debated sharing with you, Chosen Man, and always resisted until now. But now, I think, it is time for you to understand that your destiny is not yours alone.' He paused for a moment, gathering his thoughts. 'When I sleep, Achilles, I see visions of what will come to pass. I always have, from my earliest memories. At first I saw inconsequential events, things of no import, but they showed me that I had the power, a gift from the gods, to see the future in small slices. They are imperfect visions, as dreams usually are, never clear enough that I have any ability to influence the fate they depict, but the things I see almost invariably come to pass in some form.'

He raised a hand before the soldier could speak.

'I know, it sounds unlikely. And believe me, I would forsake this gift in a heartbeat if given the choice. I saw the events that resulted in my friend Banon's death, and the catastrophe at Gelduba, but without any of the detail necessary to realise what would come about on that bloody battlefield, or to take the steps that would have saved his life and those of so many other good men. I am a seer without purpose, it seems, doomed to recognise my dreams only as their reality rolls over me. I have cursed this gift, and wished it gone from my mind more times than you can imagine. But . . .'

Egilhard waited while the wolf-priest pondered his next words.

'But, and this is my point, this blessing, this curse, is seemingly an even-handed gift. I see both disaster and triumph. I saw that first battle you fought in, by the banks of the Po in Italy, and your first kill for the tribe, in the days before it came about. And of late one particular dream has been unusually vivid, as if the gods themselves are sending me a message that I cannot ignore. It is a dream that seems to combine a moment of total defeat with some measure of hope for the tribe. And I have seen you in this dream time and time again, at first only occasionally, but more and more frequently of late. I cannot tell you what it is that I have seen you do, but I have been shown the same events so many times that I have no choice but to accept that they will come about in time, and at a moment when the Batavi people's fate hangs in the balance. If my dream is true then you are the key to that moment.' He lowered his head to stare at the ground. 'I have said enough, other than to tell you that I know that your story does not end in some desolate forest clearing or on the blade of your own sword. And that you must therefore move on from this place and shoulder your burden for a while longer.'

He fell silent, and after a long moment the younger man nodded slowly.

'I will do as you wish, Centurion. Like you, I know that walking away from my father and uncle would wound them as badly as my brother's death, and I doubt I could carry that guilt. And as to your dream . . . We must wait and see what comes to be. Whatever it is, I will be ready.'

Augusta Trevorum, May AD 70

'So tell me, gentlemen, how did this near-disaster come about?'

The assembled legati and senior centurions stared back at their commander in silence, Legatus Longus fixing Pugno with a stare hard enough to keep him silent before venturing an opinion on behalf of the gathered officers.

'It seems to me, Legatus Augusti, that the barbarians, having managed to group their forces in the hills to the west and north, decided to try for what I believe we term a "decapitation". Killing you, they reckoned, would end this war overnight. So the Batavians infiltrated the camp, probably by swimming a few men down the river past our defences, forced the southern gate and allowed the rest of their treacherous cohorts to attack through it, straight into the First and Sixteenth Legions.'

Cerialis clenched a fist.

'And those cowards melted away! When the time comes for me to parade them and tell them of their fate I'll remind them of their cowardice here!'

Longus nodded.

'We were saved, it seems, by the Twenty-first Legion's obduracy in defence against the other tribes, by the barbarians' own idiocy in starting to loot that part of the camp they had overrun, allowing us time to equip and come at them in ordered ranks, and by the defence of the bridge, which did such damage to the Batavians. But it also seems to me, Legatus Augusti, that we may have erred in allowing the enemy's various factions the time to gather and make common cause of freeing Augusta Trevorum from our occupation.'

Cerialis nodded with pursed lips, clearly not entirely convinced.

'My calculation was that if we had sought to defeat one of the rebel forces we might only have allowed another to strike us from the rear, and in country so close that we would never know of their presence until it was too late. We're not overly blessed with cavalry with which to scout. But . . .' he nodded gracefully to Longus, 'I will allow you that Prefect Briganticus had located the enemy camp. Perhaps we should have struck sooner, and perhaps if I hadn't been somewhat preoccupied with matters of intelligence and information I might well have ordered such an advance.'

Another awkward silence came over the room, men exchanging covert glances and more than one wry twitch of the lips. Longus fastened his gaze on Pugno again, shaking his head fractionally. Cerialis looked about him with a raised eyebrow.

'I see. And do you all think that I deserted my duty by going into the city last night? Surely one of you has the courage to speak freely to his commander? You, Pugno, you've never been one to avoid the hard facts.'

Pugno stared back at Longus, who nodded with evident reluctance, but before the senior centurion could speak Antonius stepped forward.

'If I might venture an opinion, Legatus Augusti?'

Cerialis nodded gracefully.

'How could I refuse the request, First Spear, given that it was your quick thinking that allowed us to capitalise on the Twenty-first Legion's obdurate defence of our camp.'

Pugno shot his subordinate a meaningful glance. He had taken Antonius aside in the aftermath of the battle, once the attackers had fled the scene of their near-triumph, his facial expression unreadable.

'The guard centurion tells me that you threatened to kill him if he disobeyed your order not to join the fight.' Antonius had nodded, equally straight-faced, waiting for the rejoinder to Pugno's statement. 'You know that we train them *always* to join the fight. "March to the sound of the blood-letting" is the first rule for any centurion in this legion.'

'And you do know that if I'd allowed him to do so, Cerialis would be dead?'

The other man had nodded slowly.

'Yes. It's the only reason I don't have you by the throat.'

'That and the fact that the archers I fetched managed to kill so many Batavians that they won't forget this day in a while?'

'Yes. That too.' Pugno stared at him for a moment before speaking again. 'You're a bloody-minded bastard, aren't you?'

Antonius smiled.

'And you're not? Your entire legion lives to fight, and if there's no enemy to hand they're perfectly happy fighting each other. Perhaps we ought to have at each other, here and now, just so that I can really be one of you.'

Pugno had laughed delightedly.

'There it is! That's what made me like you the moment I set eyes on you, that couldn't give a fuck attitude of a man who's seen and done enough not to care what anyone thinks. You're a Blood Drinker alright, and you're lucky to boot.' He had leaned closer, lowering his voice to a whisper. 'Just as long as your luck holds, eh, Centurion?'

He stood in silence and listened as Antonius ventured out onto the thin ice of having an opinion as to his commander's actions of the previous night.

'It seems to me, Legatus Augusti, and to every man in the camp, that you are a man who lives to take risks. In the civil war, it is reputed, you walked out of Rome dressed as a peasant, and with a pair of bodyguards as your only defence, and walked halfway across Italy to join Vespasianus's army. And your march from the Winter Camp to defeat the Treveri at Rigodulum will doubtless be held up as an example of decisive generalship for decades to come.'

'But?'

'It's not so much a "but", Legatus Augusti, more of an "and".'

Cerialis laughed.

'Oh I *see*. Not a *but*, but rather an *and*, is it? And there I was taking you for a . . . what is it that you officers of the Twenty-first call yourselves, Pugno, Blood Drinkers?'

'Yes, Legatus Augusti.'

'Indeed. I had you marked as a man of action, Antonius, but you apparently also harbour political skills! Go on then, what's this *and* that might be a *but*?'

'It simply occurs to me, Legatus Augusti, that this urge to take risks extends beyond your military skills.'

He fell silent, knowing that he had said enough to find himself under severe punishment if Cerialis took offence at his stated opinion, but after a moment the other man laughed again, shaking his head with an amused smile.

'Gods below, man, you *are* a politician! Very well, First Spear Antonius, since you make the accusation in such a delicate way, I'll be the one to speak frankly. Yes, I have indeed struck up a relationship with a woman in the city. An influential woman, widowed recently enough to retain her beauty but not so recently as to make our friendship inappropriate. And let me say what you can't, since the rules of both our society and the army itself forbid a man of no social standing to criticise a man of my exalted class. You, every man here and every man in the camp for that matter, you all believe that my manhood has triumphed over my common sense in delaying the continuation of our offensive, and given the enemy time to regroup and come at us under the cover of darkness. And I can understand that perception. But here's something you *don't* know. Once we've marched out and thrown Civilis and Classicus and their allies back to the north and east again, they will almost certainly choose to fall back on Colonia Agrippina, hoping to muster more support from its inhabitants. After all, Civilis believes that they still support him, so where better to resist our advance into the Batavian homeland? And when he makes that most predictable of moves he's going to find out that he's not the only man with influence in the city of the Ubii.'

Germania, May AD 70

'You awake. Is good.' Marius struggled to open his crusted eyes, feeling strong hands lifting him into a sitting position, his back against the trunk of a tree. 'You rest on watchful tree. Watchful tree save you life.'

A wet piece of wool wiped at his eyes and mouth, and the Roman managed to open first one eye and then the other. It was dusk, and the fire beside which he had slept was burning close enough for him to reach out and touch. Beran lifted his cloak away from the leg that Bairaz had opened with his sword, pointing to the wound.

'Wound clean. Poison gone.' The gash was scabbed over with a thick crust of dried blood, no longer leaking pus and fluid, and the skin around it had reverted to its natural hue. 'I wrap wound with *kol* from burn wood of watchful tree. *Kol* take poison from blood. Beran burn *kol*, destroy poison, heal you body.'

Marius nodded tiredly, exhausted despite his long period of unconsciousness.

'You made charcoal from the birch tree and used it to suck the pus from my wound. Clever.'

Beran shrugged.

'Using wood of watchful tree known my people since old time. I believe watchful tree, watchful tree help me.' He held a cup up to the Roman's mouth. 'Drink.'

Marius sipped, pulling a face at the taste.

'What is it?'

'Is sap of watchful tree. I cut tree, bleed sap, mix with hot water. Make you strong.'

He sipped again as the hunter put the cup against his lips, swallowing the bitter fluid.

'It would benefit from a little honey.'

'Honey. Hah! I leave you, find honey, wolves eat you while I gone. Better bad taste than wolves eat you, yes?'

The Roman nodded ruefully.

'You're right. And thank you.'

Beran smiled, wearing the expression as if it were a rare occurrence.

'I take thanks in *pell*.'

'Pell?'

The German's smile broadened, and he reached out a hand to lift the corner of the animal skin that had covered Marius during the period of his unconsciousness.

'*Pell*. Skin of animal. Pell make Beran Roman gold, Beran use gold buy good Roman iron. And *horon*. Beran like *horon*.'

'Horon?' Beran put a hand to his crotch, winking at the Roman knowingly. 'Ah. Weapons and women.' He smiled wearily back at the hunter. 'It's not all about trees then? I was starting to wonder.'

The German nodded.

'Weapon and woman make Beran happy. When you heal you help Beran take pell from wolf and bear. I teach you . . . what is word?'

'Hunt?'

'Yes. I teach you hunt. You good spirit, make good hunt. You make Beran hunt brother.'

The Roman smiled weakly.

'I doubt I could hunt a mouse at the moment.'

Beran lifted the cup again, the unaccustomed smile creasing his face again.

'You drink blood of watchful tree. I make you strong, hunt brother. Then *you* go find honey.'

Gallia Belgica, May AD 70

'First Spear Pugno, sir! Centurion Julius asks if you could join him at the east gate. There's a man there claiming to be a legion first spear.'

Pugno stared in disbelief at the watch officer who had been entrusted with the untimely message for a moment, then raised an eyebrow at Antonius. The two men had just completed their rounds of the army's latest marching camp, and two bowls of stew were steaming on the table at which they were about to seat themselves.

'Just when I thought I'd finally got a chance to take my boots off for the night. Come on, let's go and see whether this is a fantasist with a death wish or the real thing. You . . .' he pointed to the nearest of his camp slaves, 'keep this food warm for us, we'll be back in as long as it takes to walk to the gate, put this latest fantasist to the sword and walk back again.'

As the army had advanced warily to the east behind a screen of scouts, trailing the rebels whose camp they had overrun only to find it deserted so recently that the ashes of the watch fires had still been warm, they had found the land before them empty except for the occasional farmer too attached to his land to flee from the oncoming legions. Most days had yielded a crop of sheepish deserters returning to face the inevitable justice. The majority of them had done so meekly and in the hope of a return to service encouraged by the traitor legions' apparent pardon, but one man had strolled in clad in the scale armour of a centurion and had received swift and uncompromisingly harsh military justice when his attempted subterfuge had been revealed by the discovery of the name of the armour's real owner engraved letter by letter into the faces of the thumbnail-sized armour plates on his back.

Reaching the marching camp's eastern gate, the two men found themselves confronted by the hulking figure of a man wearing nothing more than military-issue boots and a tunic, standing, apparently unconcerned, under the spears of a pair of legionaries while their centurion waited to one side with a sword held in one hand.

'I took this off him. It's legion issue, nothing special, but it's one of ours alright.'

'That sword is sacred to me. I will use it to take my revenge upon the Batavi.'

All three officers turned to look at the big man, and Antonius realised that he recognised the newcomer.

'This man is what he says he is. You were one of the officers commanding the defence of the Old Camp, weren't you? Aquillius, is it?'

'Yes. I am Aquillius.'

Pugno shook his head in disbelief.

'You're the one who escaped death when the Batavi destroyed our army at the battle by the river? You've been reported as having been killed when the Batavians took your surrender and then massacred your legions. The men they released to bring us news of that disaster say that you were being forced to kill your own men in the fortress's arena when they were turned loose.'

'That's why the sword will be my instrument of vengeance. I was forced to fight in the arena and kill fourteen legionaries with it, and I promised each of them that I would find his family and tell them that their man died well.'

Pugno shrugged, putting a knuckle to his eye.

'Boohoo. Perhaps you shouldn't have surrendered.'

Aquillius turned a stone-like stare on his fellow officer.

'And perhaps you should have made more haste to relieve us, rather than mincing around Italy feeling sorry for yourselves after being defeated at Cremona?' Something in his face froze Pugno where he stood, rather than obeying his instinct to punish the insult. 'When men are reduced to eating grass and boot leather there aren't many alternatives, even for the bravest of us. I wonder how you would have faced that choice? And if you're accusing me of being a coward you might want to consider the fact that I could bite your throat out before these children behind me could move a muscle to stop me.'

Antonius stepped between the two men before Pugno could overcome his momentary disconcertion.

'Given that this man is undoubtedly a legion first spear, I suggest that we postpone that fight until a better time? Let's get him equipped and in front of the legatus augusti. I'm sure Petillius Cerialis will want to hear his story at first hand.'

Cerialis greeted Aquillius with appropriate respect, smiling at the vine stick in the first spear's hand.

'Old habits die hard, it seems, First Spear Aquillius. Does the feeling of twisted wood in your hand comfort you, given what you've been through?'

'It reminds me of who I am, Legatus Augusti. I have spent most of the last two months hiding from the Germans and Gauls, living off the land and working my way south along the folds and seams in the country, always promising myself that I would regain the company of my peers and become a centurion once again.'

The general nodded gravely.

'And here you are, returned from the dead. Not for the first time, I believe. We can only imagine the things you've had to do to survive. Given your loyal service to the emperor I would be happy to grant you your release from service, honourably of course, and—'

Aquillius raised a hand.

'I cannot accept your offer, Legatus Augusti, even though I made a promise to tell every one of their families how they died like men when the time came. Much as I wish to be released to fulfil that oath . . .'

He paused as Cerialis shook his head.

'Is that wise, First Spear? Surely they can only hate you for what you did to their men?'

The big man shrugged.

'That is as may be. I swore an oath, and so I must carry out my promise to those of my comrades I was forced to kill. But before I can do so there is another oath I must fulfil.'

Cerialis raised an eyebrow, evidently amused by the big man's solemnity.

'*Another* oath? You have been busy.'

Ignoring the general's attempt at humour, Aquillius nodded seriously.

'Yes, Legatus Augusti, another oath. On the day of our surrender, after I had been forced to murder those fourteen men in the arena . . .'

He waited in silence as Cerialis turned to his fellow legati.

'I never cease to be amazed at the depths to which this apparently civilised man Civilis has sunk. And to think that he once dined with me in Rome, without ever providing any hint as to the barbarism that lurked in his spirit.' He waved a gracious hand to Aquillius. 'My apologies, First Spear, please do continue.'

'Yes, Legatus Augusti. As I lay, bound hand and foot in a cell, waiting for the dawn and my inevitable death the next day, a Batavian centurion came to me. He was a man I had met before, briefly, a wolf-priest.'

'A . . . *wolf-priest*?'

Antonius stepped forward.

'An order of priests within the Batavian cohorts who also serve as centurions, Legatus Augusti. They wear the pelts of wolves they have killed on their helmets as a mark of their rank. First Spear Aquillius, what did this man say to you?'

'He told me that he is both blessed and cursed by dreams, in which he sees things that are yet to happen. He told me that he witnessed their defeat at Gelduba many times in his sleep before it came to pass, never knowing what it was he was seeing until the moment that disaster struck. And he told me that he has seen me by your side, Legatus Augusti, on the day that will decide the destiny of the Batavian people, when they finally come to surrender to your army. He made me swear to find you, and offer you my service in whatever role you will give me. And he had me promise to answer his call, on that day, and to do whatever it is that he calls upon me for. To which I agreed, once I was sure that he would not seek to make me break the sacramentum of loyalty to the emperor.'

Cerialis stared at him for a moment, clearly nonplussed.

'Very well, let me see if I've understood your story. You were freed by a Batavian officer who predicted his people's surrender from a dream he had?' Aquillius nodded. 'I see. And he freed you on the condition that you would seek me out, in order to be at my side on the day of that surrender? And he expects that when he calls upon you, you will do whatever it is that he commands?'

Aquillius inclined his head.

'Exactly, Legatus Augusti.'

'And you, as a man of honour, having bought your freedom with that oath, intend to honour it completely.'

The senior centurion met his gaze unwaveringly.

'I do. It is the only way that I can free myself to fulfil the oath I made to the men I killed that day in the Old Camp's arena, while those barbarians howled and bayed for my blood.'

The Roman shrugged, his lips twisting in an amused grimace.

'You're very free with your oaths, aren't you?' The big man bowed his head silently. 'Well in that case I suppose you'd better take command of my bodyguard. You can swear an oath to defend my person to the death!' Smirking at his own joke, he nodded at the hulking centurion. 'Yes, I think that's the best way to ensure that you're at my side when the day of the Batavians' surrender comes to pass, and at that moment I shall release you from that oath to go and fulfil the other two. Or at least the first of them.' He shrugged, looking around the room at his officers. 'After all, if this . . . what was he . . . ah yes, if this wolf-priest has predicted our victory over his people in his dreams, then it seems the very least I can do if we're to make that dream of their surrender become a reality, doesn't it?'

Germania Inferior, May AD 70

'Let's have a song.' Adalwin looked at the men marching alongside him with a hopeful look. 'The bull's in the corn, eh?'

He took a deep breath and starting singing.

'The bull's in the field, the bull's in the corn,
The bull's seen the cows and the bull's got the—'

'No.'

The soldier fell silent at Levonhard's blunt statement, shaking his head sadly.

'I'm only trying to cheer us all up. We've been three days on the road marching twenty-five miles a day, and in all that time we've not said more than a dozen words.'

The soldier shrugged.

'What were you expecting, happy smiles and laughter all the way? We lost two men getting that fucking gate open, one of them hardly old enough to serve the tribe. Hundreds of men died trying to force their way through into the city, and all for nothing, just like at Gelduba! It seems to me that we men of the cohorts did all the fighting and dying, trying to deliver a half-arsed plan cooked up by Kiv and his Gaulish friends, rather than doing the sensible thing and waiting for the rest of the army to get to us. And where were the men of the Guard while we were fighting and dying? Just where they are now! Behind us! They're behind us on the march and behind us on the battlefield! The only time they ever get in front of us is when there's rations to be issued!'

The men around him muttered their agreement in a collective rumble of opinion. The army was marching east as fast as their feet could take them, their path cleared by what remained of the cohorts' mounted strength, the depleted cohorts, now barely fifteen hundred strong, in the vanguard, the German and Gallic tribes following on behind them and the elite soldiers of the Batavi Guard in their customary place at the column's rear.

'I'd be careful if I were you, Levonhard.' Lanzo spoke up from his place in the tent party's second rank. 'You might be the ugliest bastard in the century, but even your face wouldn't benefit from getting a visit from Hramn, never mind your back if he decides to make an example of you. You let him hear you saying any of that and he'll have the shit beaten out of you at the very least, just to make sure the rest of us mind our manners.'

'But the centurion—'

'Should fucking well know better. That's all. And if you're stupid enough to go repeating what he says in the privacy of the century then you'll drop him in the shit alongside you.'

Levonhard shook his head angrily.

'We always used to say what we thought, back when Scar was prefect! Why should we abandon the traditions that have served us well since my grandfather's time?'

Lataz spoke without taking his eyes off the road before him.

'Because times change. And *people* change. Back when Frijaz and I were young soldiers, Kivilaz was a good man to be around, full of the joy of being one of us warriors, and even if he was the son of a man who would have been our king if not for the Romans, you'd not have known it to hear him speak. But now . . .'

He fell silent, and his brother spoke, the depth of their mutual loss all too evident in his voice.

'Power changes a man. Some men get stronger, become more than they were. Kiv shrunk under it, and lost what it was that made us love him. And Hramn . . .'

'Hramn always was a bastard.' The men around Adalwin looked

at each other in surprise at his interjection, his voice dull with anger. 'He was my centurion when I first served, and I came to hate him soon enough. Always going out of his way to make life hard for the new lads, never happy with a joke at his expense, not even a gentle one. When he was chosen to go to Rome and join the Bodyguard I hoped I'd never see him again.'

A moment's silence followed his outburst before Lanzo spoke again.

'And that's all very well, but the fact is that they're our officers and that's that. We have no choice but to do what they tell us, do we?' He waited for a moment. 'No, we don't. As much as we might think this whole sorry revolt is fucked we have no option but to follow Kiv, yes, and Hramn too, wherever they take us, and to do whatever they tell us to do. Because to do anything else is mutiny, and no man in the history of our tribe has ever refused to carry out the orders of the men the tribe places over us. So stop this bitching and if you've got nothing good to say then just say nothing. We've come too far together for me to let any of you end up on a punishment frame with your back hanging off, not just because you don't know when to keep your mouths shut.'

Shouting from the column's head caught their attention, the century's men swiftly pulling on their helmets and unslinging shields from their carrying positions without breaking stride or waiting for orders, their preparations the swift and economical movements of men long since past any need for conscious thought when the call to action sounded. A trumpet call halted their march, and a moment later Kivilaz and Hramn rode past them, hurrying to reach the column's head.

'News from the Ubii, I expect.'

'News from Kiv's new favourite boys more likely.'

They turned to find Egilhard behind them, having walked down the century's length to join his friends. Levonhard frowned at him.

'What does that mean?'

The chosen man grimaced, his eyes red-rimmed from the lack of sleep that had troubled him since his brother's death.

'I heard the officers discussing it. Seems that there's a warband from the Chauci and Frisii tribes that he billeted on the Ubii to make sure they hold firm to their oaths to support us. He believes that they're the best warriors he has left, so he's marching us north to join up with them, in readiness to set up a battle with the Romans on some carefully chosen piece of ground.'

'See?' Levonhard spat on the road at his feet. 'Now that he's wasted most of our strength we're no longer the pride of his army, just mouths to feed. I reckon—' He staggered back as Egilhard snapped a punch into the space between his helmet's cheek guards. 'What the f—'

The young chosen man stepped forward with both fists raised.

'Shut your mouth! My brother gave his life for the tribe back there, and I won't have you pissing on his sacrifice just because it's getting tough. If you don't want to fight for the tribe then just walk away!'

The older man spat a mouthful of blood, his eyes blazing as he stepped forward to confront his former tent mate.

'I never said I wouldn't fight!'

'You might not, but I can see it in your eyes! You think this is over! And it might just be! But as long as we have strength to lift our swords then if Kiv tells us to fight, we *fight*!' He shook his head at the other man. 'Because if we don't, then all those men we've lost might as well just have cut their own throats! And I'll tell you another thing. If we're heard talking that way then Alcaeus will pay for it as well, not just us. Do you want to drop the best centurion in all the cohorts in the shit like that? Hramn would reduce him to the ranks in a heartbeat, given the chance.'

Levonhard looked at him for a moment, then nodded reluctantly.

'You're right. We have to fight on. But I'm only doing it for our people, not for Kiv. That bastard lost my respect when he took the news that we'd lost half our strength to his nephew's incompetence with nothing more than a shrug.'

Egilhard would have replied, but his attention was caught by a man hurrying back down the column and he moved to block the messenger's way.

'What's happened?'

The soldier answered without breaking stride as he hurried on.

'The war band Kiv billeted on the Ubii has been slaughtered! The bastards got them all pissed and then set fire to the hall they were billeted in! We're to march on the Old Camp and mount a defence there!'

The tent party looked at each other in silence, and after a moment Levonhard shook his head and turned away.

'You lot can keep telling each other how we can still come out of this on top all you like. I think we're done. And I think we *all* know it.'

Germania Inferior, May AD 70

'Well that seems to have worked well enough, doesn't it, gentlemen?' Cerialis looked around at his officers, gathered in his command tent, with a satisfied smile. The Twenty-first had pounded east in pursuit of their Batavi quarry for days, and the news that their enemy would not be able to fortify Colonia Agrippina was welcome to the weary soldiers. 'If this report is to be believed, my diplomacy in the city of the Treveri has dealt Civilis something of a blow, and not just because he's lost men he was depending on to stiffen his army's resolve. I told you the lady in question wielded sufficient influence to achieve something that would rock Civilis back on his heels, and she seems to have delivered handsomely.'

Legatus Longus inclined his head in a gesture of respect.

'If any man here ever doubted your ability in that respect, Legatus Augusti, this result will have silenced those doubts, of that I have absolutely no doubt.'

The army commander nodded happy agreement.

'Yes, and so much for the idea that the Ubians might have lost their ferocity after a century living on our side of the river, eh?

We should all have known better, of course, but I'll admit that even I wondered if they had it in them to resist the Batavians.'

The news from Colonia Agrippina had been shocking even to men accustomed to the bestial behaviour of the German tribes. Invited to a feast in their honour, the men who had been left to ensure the Ubians' cooperation with the Batavi had been plied with alcohol until they had fallen into a state of insensibility, at which point the doors of the hall in which they were gathered had been locked shut and the building itself set alight. Not a single warrior had escaped the blaze, and the Ubians had sent a messenger to the advancing Roman army with the welcome news that, denied of their support, Civilis had turned north and was headed for the Old Camp's burned-out ruins.

'We have them on the run, gentlemen! And if that isn't sufficient cause for celebration, I also have word from my colleague Fabius Priscus, commander of the Fourteenth Legion. It seems that he has crossed the sea from Britannia with his entire legion, marched south and engaged both the Tungrians and Nervians, forcing both tribes to abandon their pledges of loyalty to Civilis. Not that I'd imagine there was much force required. The sight of a magnificent body of men like the Fourteenth will have been enough to scare the life out of them, I'd have thought. Apparently the Nervians have raised a good-sized force of men to join our army, and intend taking their frustrations out on the Batavians' allies, starting with the Cananefates. This is the time to strike, now, while the enemy are still trying to work out their next step. And if Civilis wants to abandon the initiative by digging himself a defensive position at the Old Camp, then so much the better! We will march north at first light tomorrow, gentlemen, and you can tell your men that we march to give battle to these rebels one final time. We'll crush what's left of his army and then set about teaching his tribe what it means to defy Rome.'

Longus inclined his head in acknowledgement of the order.

'It will be as you command. But what of the Ubians' other news, Legatus Augusti? This offer of theirs might be a very useful negotiating tool, if we ever reach the point of Civilis suing for peace as First Spear Aquillius's priest friend seemed to think likely.'

Longus smiled at Aquillius, who was standing close behind Cerialis with one hand on the hilt of his sword, evidently completely dedicated to his new role as the general's bodyguard, but the big centurion's only recognition of the point was a curt nod.

'What, their offer to send us Civilis's wife and son?'

'Yes, Legatus Augusti. Surely that's too good a chance to be turned down?'

Cerialis shook his head briskly.

'Not in my opinion. We're not here to conduct war against women and children. And besides, were we to take them into custody we'd be handing a moral advantage to our enemy, and not one that he deserves either, not after the various massacres and betrayals he's inflicted upon anyone that's got in the way of his lust for power. No, send word that his relatives are to be returned to the Batavi Island with all due care for their well-being.'

Longus nodded thoughtfully.

'That's very . . . noble of you, Petillius Cerialis.'

The general shrugged.

'It might be seen as such. Indeed I'll make very sure that it reads that way when the histories of this war are written, a demonstration of Rome's humanity towards the defeated. But in truth, Pontius Longus, my thinking isn't entirely philanthropic. I intend to use every and any means of painting our enemy Civilis as the villain of this whole dirty little war, as a means of detaching him from the support of his people. By the time I'm done they'll be sick of him, and see their sacrifices as being exactly that – *theirs.* When it becomes apparent to them that he's not sharing their tribulations I'd imagine that their patience with their prince will soon wear thinner than a beggar's tunic. Once we're done convincing his people that he's the only man benefiting from their struggles, he's going to wish he'd never started this war.'

Germania, May AD 70

'You ready hunt. Ready *to* hunt.'

Beran smiled across the fire at Marius, tipping his head in recognition of the slow but steady expansion of his vocabulary.

'I feel stronger. But whether I'll be able to do anything more than scare the beasts away is yet to be seen.'

The German shrugged.

'Is simple. My father teach me, I teach you. Got no son, but hunt brother enough. You become hunter, hunt forest, I happy.'

The Roman shifted uncomfortably.

'You know my story. I'm a centurion, which means that I have a duty to my legion.'

Beran stared back at him with an expression utterly lacking concern.

'You legion dead. You tell Beran that.'

Marius nodded slowly.

'That's true. But I swore an oath to serve the emperor.'

The other man laughed.

'Which emperor? Even here in forest Beran know that emperor fight war against emperor. Beran think you oath to emperor dead.'

'Perhaps. But once a centurion . . .' He shrugged. 'So, tell me how to be a mighty hunter like you.'

'Is not hard. But need practice. And must know secrets.'

The Roman raised a questioning eyebrow.

'Secrets?'

Beran nodded.

'Some secrets. You not know secrets, you not be hunter. And first secret this.' He paused for a moment to emphasise the portentous nature of what he was about to reveal to the Roman. 'First, you learn see with ears.'

'To see with my ears?'

The German smiled at the note of doubt in his pupil's voice.

'Yes. *To* see with ears. You learn this, I teach. In forest, you seen, you lose beast. So you not be seen. Listen, not look.'

'See with my ears. Very well.'

'Second secret is that when you in forest, you be forest.'

Marius pursed his lips uncomprehendingly.

'Be the forest?'

'You man. You smell like man. Beast know man smell. Beast smell you, he run. So you must smell like forest, not like man. But that easy. That just smell of skit.'

'Shit?'

'Yes, skit.' Marius grimaced, and Beran grinned at his distaste. 'But more than just skit. Is . . .' the German pulled a face as he pondered the right words to use. 'Is be like forest. Not like man.' He shrugged. 'I teach. You learn. You be good hunter, like you good soldier, yes?'

He continued without waiting for the Roman to reply, tapping a third finger.

'Three. When Beran hunt, he hunt slow. Man not need chase beast through forest. If man understand forest spirit, then beast come to man. When Beran hunt he patient like spider, move so slow that he become part of forest. I teach you this.'

The Roman nodded.

'I can see that I have much to learn.'

The German raised his hand.

'One more secret. Most important secret and hardest for you. Hunt slow, but strike fast. Strike like snake.'

Marius nodded confidently.

'I've been slinging spears for most of my life. I doubt that killing animals is very different to killing men.'

To his disquiet, Beran laughed softly.

'Hah! You think? We soon find out.'

The Old Camp, Germania Inferior, May AD 70

'You think this is going to work?'

Kivilaz nodded at Draco with the confident air of a man certain of his own abilities.

'Without any doubt. Come, I'll show you.'

The two men walked out onto the marshy ground in front of the intended battle line that had been drawn to the ruined fortress's south, its carefully chosen positions marked with a series of wooden posts, Draco supporting his weaker leg with the staff he took everywhere and probing the grass in front of him for potential mud pools.

'You see? The line that we'll take up when the Romans approach is the edge of the higher ground. Standing here, where I expect them to try to come at us, we're a good two or three feet below the ground on which we'll be fighting.'

'And it's this much different in height along the entire length of this line you intend to hold?'

The Batavi war chief shrugged.

'Not at all points. Mostly the difference is a foot or so, but deeper areas like this will trap the unwary and make their advance even more hesitant. Whereas our men will know where the deeper sections are, and will skirt around them. Do you remember fighting in knee-deep water, back in the days when that was part of the training we undertook on joining the cohorts, as preparation for having to fight our way ashore if it came to an opposed landing on the far side of a river?'

Draco smiled ruefully.

'Of course. It was ten times harder than it looked, having to push our legs through all that mud.'

'There you are. They'll come at us through the shallows, thinking it will be easy, but they'll already be exhausted by the time they reach us.'

'And we're going to flood this ground how, exactly?'

'I've had the idea of it in my mind since the first time I saw this place.'

He led the limping elder to the riverbank, where they looked out over the toiling men of the cohorts, their tunics black with thick, cloying mud from the turf sections they were carrying from behind the intended battle line to deposit in the river's shallows, their legs caked from walking out onto the slowly lengthening dam to deposit their loads.

'How long do you think will be needed to start diverting water over the river's bank?'

'Half a day, no more.'

'And the scouts say that Cerialis will arrive in two. Time enough for the flooded ground to soften up, I'd have thought. But what's to stop them from simply going round this water obstacle?'

Kivilaz grinned knowingly.

'There's a ridge of higher ground on the right flank, almost high enough to break the surface once it's flooded, but beyond that the height difference is worse for the most part, and extending out over a mile and more. I've had a channel cut in that bar, only a foot deep so as not to drain this area, which means that by the time there's a Roman army facing us here, the ground over which they might have outflanked us will be a lake. Cerialis will either have to go somewhere else and leave us in possession of the Old Camp, or take a gamble and try to push us off our ground. I'm of the expectation that, as usual, he won't be able to refuse the chance for total victory that I appear to be offering him.'

Draco nodded, looking back at the defensive line the tribes would hold in the event of a battle.

'It's clever, Kivilaz, worthy of the tribe. But surely this won't be enough to stop him? He has fresh legions in his army now, including our former parent the Fourteenth, who, I don't need to remind you, hate us with a passion. Can we really hope to defeat them?'

Kivilaz shook his head.

'Can we defeat them? Not at this battle. This will end in a deadlock, I expect, with neither side able to beat the other. They won't be able to get to grips with us and make their superior numbers work, and we won't be able to live with them if we allow them to tempt us into a straight fight. But my objective isn't to win, Draco, it's to bleed them. If I kill and wound one fifth of their force I'll be content as long as we lose half as many men, because my aim isn't to win this fight, or the one that will follow soon enough. My aim is to handle them roughly every time they come at us, making use of our superior knowledge of the ground, and to send each successive attack away with enough casualties to leave ragged holes in their ranks. After three, or four, or five such battles they will start to think better of their determination, and sue for peace. Peace on our terms. I am sure of it.'

The elder looked at him for a moment before speaking.

'You plan to end this war by forcing Cerialis to the negotiating table?'

Kivilaz nodded confidently.

'When the time is right.'

'You believe we cannot win?'

'I do. We *could* have won, of course we could. At Gelduba, when the cohorts were so cruelly punished for a moment of ill-fortune, we might have destroyed three legions and captured their commanders rather than losing so many of our best men, which would have left us in total control of all the land from the sea to the mountains with Gaul at our feet. And again, if we had followed my preferred course of action when the Romans took Augusta Trevorum, and lured them out into the country where we could have tempted them into a carefully laid ambush, with all our force descending on them from all sides at the same moment, we might have utterly destroyed their army before the other legions had time to arrive. But now, against so many legions, and having suffered so many losses? No, I no longer believe that we can win, but neither do I believe we have to lose, or not in the manner that the Romans intend.'

Draco nodded slowly.

'I concur. You've spoken to no other man this way, I presume?'

'Only to you. I owe you my honesty, Father of the Tribe.' He looked out over the water. 'There will be peace, but it must be peace on our terms. No Roman boots on our soil. Our cohorts to remain based on our land, and not banished to some far-away corner of the empire. And the Batavi to be independent of the empire, our tribe an ally rather than a subject. I know the Romans, as do you, and I also know this man Cerialis and his father-in-law Vespasianus. There will be a written set of instructions from the new emperor telling this legatus what to do under varying circumstances, how to negotiate if they have the upper hand, or if the campaign is deadlocked, and what to do if they have lost so much strength as to make conquering our people an impossibility. All I aim to do is to push Cerialis until he's negotiating from the weakest possible circumstances. And to that I have to kill legionaries. A lot of legionaries.'

The elder pondered for a moment.

'And on behalf of the tribal council I agree with both your strategy and your logic in not sharing it with your army. But I do have one suggestion to make.'

Kivilaz dipped his head respectfully.

'Father of the Tribe?'

'Put a ditch in front of the battle line. It'll stop the legions getting to grips with our men and preserve them to fight another day if the enemy do manage to get this far.'

The Old Camp, Germania Inferior, June AD 70

'This can't be all there is to their defence.'

Pugno looked out across the open ground between the rebel battle line and the waiting legions, slitting his eyes against the glare of sunlight reflecting off the standing water that covered much of its expanse.

'You don't think the water is a problem?'

He turned back to look up at Longus, who had sensibly opted to stay in his horse's saddle rather than soak the leather of his immaculately polished boots with filthy water while Cerialis had ridden down the army's line telling each legion that this was to be the day of their victory, his speech to the Twenty-first having done little to improve Pugno's temper due to its brief and somewhat off-hand reference to the Twenty-first's proud history, and rather more to his stated expectation that the battle to come would cement the legion's reputation. It was, the irascible first spear had barked at nobody in particular and without the slightest reduction in his usual strident tone, not *his* legion that needed to burnish its repute any further, his demeanour still one of disgruntled irritation an hour later, with mutterings such as 'cement *his* fucking reputation, more likely' and 'more like semen than cement'. He waved a dismissive hand at the legatus, shaking his head emphatically.

'A bit of water? I very much doubt that it'll cause us too much difficulty, Legatus. Once we get to grips with them, that rabble will wish they'd put a few dozen miles between us rather than waste their time damming the river to make the ground a bit softer. Four legions ought to make swift work of this.'

Longus nodded, looking along the length of the line that Cerialis's army presented now that fresh forces had arrived from elsewhere in the empire as directed by Consul Mucianus.

'I must say that the army does look pretty much unstoppable. The Fighting Fourteenth Legion, named as blessed by Nero himself. The Victorious Sixth, again named by Nero for gallant service. And the Second Rescuers, marines like the men who proved your legion's match at Cremona. Added to our own strength this must surely be a terrifying prospect for the Batavians, don't you think?'

'Of course, Legatus.' Pugno's mouth tightened to a white-lipped line. 'Walk with me, Centurion Antonius?'

The two men strolled along the legion's line, Pugno raising his vine stick in salute as his officers snapped their centuries to attention with brisk commands.

'The Fighting fucking Fourteenth? What have they ever had to do over the last ten years, other than turn up too late to fight at Cremona? It's their fault these uppity German bastards got too big for their boots in the first place! The Victorious Sixth? Named "victorious" by Nero for *what*, I ask you? They've been sat on their backsides in Spain for the last fifty years with nothing better to do than scratch their holes and toss each other off. And the Second Rescuers? Another collection of naval arse-worriers like their brothers of the First, who, I should point out, we gave a total fucking after they'd been lucky enough to capture our eagle. Cunts.'

He paused, raising an interrogatory eyebrow at Antonius's smile. 'What?'

'The legatus only drew attention to their alleged prowess to annoy you. I think it's all a bit of a game to him.'

Pugno shook his head in disgust.

'And that's all very well for him, he'll be off back to Rome faster than a legionary makes for the whorehouses on payday, once we've finished them off, and so will Cerialis, eager to get his nose right up his father-in-law's arse and his cock up every matron, virgin, whore and stray dog that fancies a piece of war hero. Whereas we'll be left here to make sure they don't get any more bright ideas about—' Trumpets sounded from the rear of the Roman line, the signal the legions had been waiting for. 'And there's the order to get on with it. Come on, let's get our feet wet and get this over with.'

Drawing his sword he signalled to his trumpeter to sound the advance, grinning at Antonius as the massed horns of four legions split the air with their raucous blare.

'Twenty-first Legion, at the march . . . follow me! *Blood and glory!*'

The entire Roman line was moving, the legions advancing out across the battlefield's marshy expanse at a walking pace intended to minimise the legionaries' effort as they pushed through water that varied between ankle and knee deep, individual soldiers staggering, and in some cases falling, into the stinking, stagnant pools as they tripped over tussocks of marsh grass beneath the surface. With a sudden wail of iron flight fins carving the air, a volley of artillery bolts flickered across the space between the Batavi line and the advancing legions, the missiles punching holes in the closely packed Roman ranks. The waiting Batavi soldiers cheered at the sudden discomfiting of their opponents while the legionaries trudged on through the marsh, driven forward by their officers, their pace increasing as they sought to get to close-quarters with the waiting enemy rather than tolerate the lash of the artillery that had been taken when the Old Camp fell. Pugno and Antonius both turned their heads at the shouts and splashes as a section of the Sixth Legion's line blundered into a patch of deeper water, iron-clad legionaries suddenly finding themselves floundering perilously close to being out of their depth, a potential death sentence to men carrying forty pounds in armour and weapons.

'Keep moving! Let's get at them!'

Pugno led his men forward, eager to get onto firmer ground and turn his legion's fury on the Batavi line, but as the Twenty-first's soldiers splashed closer to their enemy they found that the submerged ground beneath their feet had been littered with deeper pits, individual soldiers suddenly sinking up to their armpits and having to be pulled out of the water by the men alongside them. As the legion closed to within twenty paces the defenders began to hurl abuse down at them from their vantage point on the higher ground, Pugno's eyes narrowing as he bellowed an order at his men.

'Twenty-first Legion, attack with spears!'

At Pugno's bellowed command, the legion's front rank raised shields made heavier by water soaked into their layered wooden board, readying themselves to advance into spears' reach and take their weapons to the waiting enemy. But as they went forward to engage the Batavi line, their leading ranks blundered into a trench cut in front of the enemy line, unseen beneath the water, having to be pulled back onto firm ground by the men behind them. The legionaries floundered as the Germans took the chance for which they had been waiting and volleyed spears down at them.

'We've walked into a trap, First Spear! We need to pull back!'

Pugno snarled defiance at his legatus, still mounted at the rear of the legion's line despite the fact that he was presenting a perfect target to the enemy bolt throwers.

'Never! The Twenty-first goes forwards, not backwards, and I won't be the . . .'

He fell silent as the crew of a portable scorpion manhandled their bolt thrower out of the Batavi line and pointed it directly at Longus, readying themselves to loose its heavy metal-tipped arrow, knowing all too well that the weapon's missile would punch clean through his superior's bronze armour and take his life in an instant. Just before the hard-faced Germans released their missile, a bolt launched from the legion artillery line two hundred paces behind them smashed into the weapon, splintering its wooden frame and releasing the massive energy its crew had wound into its tightly stretched cord. The heavy string whipped out and carved a bloody line across the face of the man behind it, sending him reeling back with a scream, blood pumping through hands raised to explore the source of his sudden, agonising pain.

The mounted officer stared at the carnage, white-faced at his close escape. He pointed across the battlefield, and Pugno realised that the Germans were mounting attacks along their line, stepping out where the water was shallower and taking advantage of their nimbleness where the legionaries facing them were made slow and cumbersome by the weight of their armour and the water through which they were wading.

'They're killing our men, First Spear! And they would have killed me, if not for the intervention of the gods! This will be a massacre unless we do something! Have your trumpeter sound the retreat!' The astounded centurion stared at him for a moment, and Longus leaned out of his saddle with a flash of uncharacteristic fury. 'You heard me, Pugno! Do it! Or I'll find another man who will!'

After a moment's delay, the two men staring at each other in a direct clash of wills, Pugno turned to his trumpeter and gave the order, having to repeat it such was the man's surprise. As the legion's horns took up the signal, and the Twenty-first's soldiers started to fall back with expressions of grateful disbelief, Antonius realised that the entire army was backing away from the trap into which their commander had thrust them. Men continued to fall to the captured enemy artillery as they struggled backwards through the marsh's filthy water, although to Antonius's trained eye the Germans were suffering equally badly under the lash of four legions' combined bolt throwers, as crews labouring under the lash of their captains' roared orders subjected them to a constant bombardment of bolts and heavy stones. Longus cantered away to find his superior, the two men falling into deep discussion as their horses splashed back through the marsh towards the army's starting point.

'This isn't a defeat!' Pugno stared at his friend in disbelief, his face a picture of misery and frustrated rage, but Antonius simply shook his head, his face set hard against any argument. 'I mean it! If you stand in line in front of four legions' artillery for long enough then you're going to get torn a new one no matter how clever your choice of ground might be!'

The veteran first spear looked back at the enemy line as another flight of bolts whistled over the legionaries' heads and reaped a fresh crop of enemy warriors, shaking his head in rejection of his colleague's attempt to soften the shame of his legion's failure to stand face-to-face with their enemy.

'This *is* a defeat! And it isn't one I'm going to forget . . . or forgive!'

The Old Camp, Germania Inferior, June AD 70

'So what purpose did that serve?'

Lanzo glanced wearily across the fire at Levonhard, shaking his head at the disgusted soldier.

'You won't give it up, will you?'

The older man shrugged angrily.

'And why should I? Why can't I have an opinion on the things we're told to do, and what results?'

'Not if there's any risk of you being overheard!'

Levonhard laughed bitterly.

'Risk of being overheard? The only people who are going to hear me are the other poor bastards who had to stand out under the Roman bolt throwers for half the day. I mean look at where we are, pushed so far to the edge of the camp that we might as well not be part of this army.'

The men of the tent party stared vacantly into the flames for the most part, no one bothering to comment on his statement of what to them seemed obvious. Away to their left the men of the tribes were shouting threats and insults at the Roman camp, less than a mile distant, while in the gaps between their hoarse and drunken imprecations, the sound of singing could be heard, legion battle hymns and marching songs doubtless being sung to restore the spirits of the legionaries.

'We stood waiting for the bastards to come back and attack us for hours, when it was obvious that they weren't going to, all the while with their artillery chipping away at us while we did nothing better than present them with something to shoot at!'

'It was the same for every man in the line. You can't deny that.'

The veteran soldier rounded on his watch officer with an expression of amazement on his flame-lit face.

'No, it fucking well *wasn't*! Have you forgotten that we had the Guard standing behind us all that time? Because we're not to be trusted, of course, and not because those cowardly bastards just wanted to use us as human shields! Can anyone guess how many men of the Guard died today? Anyone? No?' He looked around, knowing that every one of them knew the answer. 'I met an old friend of mine who serves with them when I went to fetch the water, and even he couldn't look me in the eye. Because the answer's *none*. Not one. In fact the only casualty those fuckers have taken since Gelduba is a decurion who only died because he was stupid enough to fall asleep and let his prisoners kill him with his own sword!'

The story of Bairaz's death in the forest had provided the men of the cohorts with a good degree of grim amusement, although they had learned to keep it to themselves after one soldier who ventured an opinion publicly was given a punishment beating for his temerity.

'And what are the odds that we'll have to do all the hard work tomorrow, eh?'

Frijaz came to life.

'What do you mean, tomorrow?'

Adalwin smiled sourly across the fire at him.

'You and your brother were away getting the rations when your lad came round with the happy news that Kiv's planning an attack tomorrow. We were going to let it be a surprise to you, but Ugly seems to have ruined th—'

'An attack? A fucking *attack*? On four legions that we barely scratched today for all of the hard work Kiv had us do to build that dam?' The veteran was suddenly furious, shaking his brother awake. 'You hear that? We're attacking tomorrow! Now that we've really pissed the Romans off, we're going to try and beat them across ground that's been flooded in order to *prevent* an attack!'

Lataz stirred, yawned and stretched, blinking in the fire's glow. 'An attack. Right. Is that stew ready yet?'

'Is the stew ready? Are you *deaf*? I said—'

'I know. What you said. Brother.' Lataz was speaking slowly and with deliberate emphasis. 'I'm not stupid. But since there's fuck all I can do about it, I thought I might as well fill my belly, get some more sleep and see what tomorrow brings when it's tomorrow, rather than worrying about now. I suggest you do the same. After all, if today's brilliant plan was such a disaster then tomorrow's likely disaster might just turn out to be brilliant, eh?'

The Old Camp, Germania Inferior, June AD 70

'Well gentlemen, just because the day didn't turn out the way we planned it doesn't mean we didn't learn a good deal from it.'

The assembled legati and their senior centurions stood in respectful silence while Cerialis took a sip of the wine that he had had served as they gathered to consider the day's events. To Antonius's eye, having grown used to the army commander's methods, it appeared almost as if their leader was challenging his officers to gainsay his sentiments, but no one spoke in the lengthy silence.

'So, if nobody's arguing with me on that point – not even our greatest fire breather . . .' He shot a swift and sympathetic glance at Pugno, who had been uncharacteristically quiet since leading his men away from the death trap that the Germans had laid out for the legions, but if the first spear even noticed the gesture he did not deign to respond. 'Then I'll tell you why I'm less troubled at such an apparent defeat than you might expect.'

He pointed at the map unrolled on the table before them.

'The Old Camp represents the last piece of defendable land between here and the Batavian homeland. Once we have them off this high ground there is little to stop our superior numbers pushing them all the way back to their Island, where Civilis will at least be able to put a river between our two armies. He knows this, and so he set out a trap for us to fall into, an opportunity for me to blunder rashly in, in my *usual* manner . . .' He raised an amused eyebrow at Longus, and Antonius realised what it was that the legatus had been saying to Cerialis during the long, slow trudge back to the battle's starting point as the two men rode side by side. 'In offering me battle on that ground, Civilis was presenting me with a baited hook, a hook that I very nearly took. That we escaped with casualties is probably due to two things. Firstly, the fact that we retreated when we did, and for that we can thank the quick thinking and selfless example of the most martially-minded centurion in the entire army.'

He extended a hand to Pugno.

'By his selfless example in accepting his legatus's suggestion that he should pull the Twenty-first Legion back, despite his every instinct screaming to attack, First Spear Pugno showed the rest of the army what we had to do. We needed to swallow our pride and step away from an unwinnable fight, and thanks to Pugno we did. So thank you, Centurion, you have educated me in a way I could never have expected.' The astonished centurion blinked, then tipped his head in reply, unable to speak so conflicted were his emotions. 'And the second reason we got away with this error of judgement? The enemy, believe it or not, made their position too secure. By digging a ditch in front of their positions, which flooded and prevented us from coming to grips with them, they also denied themselves the chance to punish us as we retreated. Most men die in battle when the time comes for one army or another to turn and run, all the histories tell us that much, and that deep water prevented them from coming after us in sufficient numbers to turn our retreat into a rout. For which we can be grateful.'

'So what now, Legatus Augusti?'

Longus's question was posed in respectful terms, but Antonius could sense its import, and the assembled officers seemed to hold their breath as Cerialis affected to consider the point.

'Now, Pontius Longus? Now I think we'll give these barbarians an opportunity to find out what it feels like when an enemy takes your tactics and wields them against you. We threaten them just by being here, so tomorrow we'll do just that – be here – and let them come to us. We'll put the auxiliary cohorts in the shop window and leave the legions as a battlefield reserve, ready to exploit any opportunity Civilis leaves for us. Tell your men to sing their marching songs as loudly as they can and far into the night. I want these barbarians to be straining at their collars come the morning, eager to come and find out just how tenaciously Rome fights on the defensive. I know Civilis's plan, gentlemen, indeed I believe that a blind man could deduce it. He intends to bleed us of our strength, until our legions are reduced to shells of their former selves like the First and Sixteenth, and I am forced to sue for peace on terms that effectively leave him on the Batavian throne and guarantee them their independence to make trouble and foster rebellion in Germania. And my answer to that is simple . . .' he paused, looking around at his officers determinedly, 'we bleed *them.* We tempt them onto our line and cut them to ribbons in the old-fashioned way. Tomorrow will be a day for grinding meat, gentlemen.'

The Old Camp, Germania Inferior, June AD 70

'We won. And yet . . .'

'And yet we lost, Prefect Draco?'

The elder nodded slowly, looking across the fire around which the tribal leaders had gathered.

'They were in our hands, ready for that pass of the knife that would drain them of their lifeblood, but before we could wield that blade the chance was gone.'

Kivilaz nodded.

'It's true. And their artillery was too strong for us to press any advantage as they backed away.'

Classicus stepped forward.

'The elders of my tribe have followed you here, Kivilaz, bringing those men of our tribe who continue to believe in a Gallic empire. They wish to know what you intend to do tomorrow. They fear that the Romans will simply stand and wait for us to come to them, and that the conditions we have created will act against us if we make that attack. And, listening to the Romans singing their hymns to victory, they fear that the men of the German tribes will be so set on silencing them in the morning that they will blunder onto their line, taking our men with them and forcing us to suffer losses we can ill afford.'

Kivilaz nodded.

'I understand. Of course I do. Your men are far from home, a home that has been invaded and conquered by the Romans, leaving you as the last hope for your people's freedom from their oppression. You worry that I will order you to throw your lives away in some crazed roll of the dice, depending on the favour of the gods to deliver us a victory against four of the best legions in the empire, do you not?'

Classicus dipped his head in acceptance of the point.

'And without wishing to insult your generalship, sometimes a great captain must make sacrifices in a battle to win the war. My tribe's elders fear that we may be that sacrifice.'

Kivilaz smiled.

'You see my intent then?'

'In truth, no. But I can see that if you have a scheme in mind it may require some . . .'

'Some sacrifice, as you say. And yes, I do have a plan. To turn it from an idea to bloody, victorious reality I will need the bulk of the army to behave exactly as the Romans are expecting when the dawn comes. We will need to form for battle, march out onto that marshy plain and fix them in place with the threat of our massed spears. If Cerialis does as I expect, then he will be delighted, because I expect him to eschew boldness tomorrow, and to fight what the Romans call a battle of attrition, looking to reap as many of our men as possible from the dry ground they hold. And when that bloody battle has begun, and we're behaving just as he hopes and expects, then I will spring the surprise I have in mind. My fiercest German allies will strike the enemy from a direction they will never expect, turn their flank and set them running. And they will not stop running until they reach a defendable location. I should imagine that Novaesium will be that fortress, and I'd have thought that will put them far enough from us that we can re-establish our borders, and yours too, without fear of interference. Tomorrow, my brothers, will be the day that we send this man Cerialis and his vaunted legions back south with their reputations in shreds. Count on it.'

9

The Old Camp, Germania Inferior, June AD 70

'Men of the army of Germania, hear me and know that I speak for the emperor! On days to come you will be able to boast that you were here on this day . . .' Cerialis paused for a moment, allowing the tension among his men to build, 'and you can tell your friends that Quintus Petillius Cerialis gave the speech of his life! Unlike, perhaps, the previous day's effort . . .'

A ripple of laughter played along the waiting ranks of legionaries at the wry tone of his voice, and Pugno looked at Antonius with a grin.

'At least he can laugh at himself. And at least he's taking some time to get them stirred up today.'

The general was addressing his men again, his voice raised to reach as many of them as possible.

'Today I shall address each of my legions by name, and tell you exactly what I expect from you! But before I do, I have counsel for each and every one of you, something to remember before this battle begins afresh! You are part of a glorious tradition, every one of you, men of legions whose names and reputations stretch back into the history of our empire, part of the greatest army the world has ever seen! You have already beaten these barbarian dogs, when they assaulted our camp at the city of the Treveri and you sent them running with their tails tucked between their legs! Running all the way from Augusta Trevorum to this place, where their treachery and lies sealed the fate of two legions who thought they were surrendering to enemies who could be trusted to allow them dignity in their defeat! Remember the Fifth and Fifteenth Legions, my brothers-in-arms! Remember their massacre and resolve yourselves to give these barbarians no mercy, as you sweep through their fleeing ranks! And run they will, for they recall that defeat all too well! That is the reason why they refuse to face us on an even battlefield, these men who carry their terror of us in their hearts and the wounds we have inflicted on their backs!'

He waited for the appreciative cheers to die away before speaking again, pointing to the Fourteenth Legion's eagle, shining like gold in the summer sun.

'You men of the Fighting Fourteenth Legion, you conquerors of Britannia, you more than any other men have a score to settle with these boastful animals who were once your brothers, but who have more recently spurned you and claimed the glory for your greatest victories!'

He trotted his horse along the line as the men of the Fourteenth cheered loudly, singling out the legion standing alongside them.

'The Sixth Legion, named "Victorious", glorious in your status as the legion that backed Galba, and thereby brought Nero's blood-soaked rule to a timely end! And you men of the Second Legion, named the "Rescuers" on your founding, formed of the proud marines of the Ravenna fleet, what better day than today to blood yourselves than in the company of these illustrious eagles?'

Trotting his horse on down the line he stood before the First and Sixteenth Legions, shaking his head as he considered the tattered remnant of what had been proud and powerful forces only eighteen months before.

'You have been called "traitor legions" by those men who have not shared your experiences, whose feet have not trodden the same ground yours have, or shared your tribulations at the hands of these barbarians! There is a part of me that feels sympathy for your shame! I have the power to expunge that shame, and spare you the pain and indignity of having your legions disbanded, but if you wish me to use that power then I can only offer you this advice.' He pointed at the Germans waiting for them on the far side of the marsh. 'If you wish to be allowed to follow your eagles with pride then you must go over there with your swords drawn and ready to fight for your lives, giving your lives if necessary, to take back what remains of our fortress! If you can do this, and play your part alongside your brothers, I may yet decide to allow you to retake your places in the empire's proud army despite your poor showing at Augusta Trevorum!'

He turned in his saddle and pointed to the men of the Twenty-first Legion.

'Let First Spear Pugno and his men be your exemplar! These fine soldiers have fought in every major action since the start of the civil war and they still lust to be allowed to run at their enemy. Men of the Twenty-first, will you gift me with one more battle?'

Pugno nodded to the aquilifer standing next to him, and as the big man raised his eagle high into the air above his head the legion behind him uttered a swift angry cheer, repeating the mutual exhortation twice more as the gilded bird bobbed up and down. Cerialis solemnly saluted Pugno, who snapped off a salute of his own and then turned to face his men.

'Twenty-first Legion . . . prepare for battle!'

'Here they come again.'

Alcaeus cast an experienced eye across the Roman formation facing them across the marsh before responding to Levonhard's statement. The Roman artillery had not started shooting yet, the engine captains clearly waiting for their targets to advance out onto the marsh's killing field. On the far side of the watery expanse the Roman legions were drawn up in formations so precise that they might as well have been parading, rather than readying themselves for a battle that might well end in catastrophic defeat. The German tribesmen along the rebel line were chanting their battle songs, each verse ending with a deep booming *hoom* that intended to intimidate their enemy, individuals stepping forward to wave their spears and bellow boastful threats across the marsh, eyes protruding and tongues lolling from their open mouths to emphasise the dreadful nature of their threats.

'I don't think so, soldier. They lost too many men yesterday to try the same old thing today, not unless this man Cerialis lacks the wit to work out that if he does offer us the same battle he'll lose in the same way. And somehow I suspect that isn't the case. Today they will stand and wait for us to cross that marsh, and let their artillery murder us in twos and threes until we reach their line.'

He pointed at Kivilaz, who was walking towards their column with Hramn at his side.

'We're in columns, and not a line. Which means that Kivilaz has an attack in mind for today.'

The Batavi prince stood before his army, raising his arms as if to embrace every man present, then started speaking, his voice loud enough to be heard but low enough that every man strained intently to hear his words.

'Does it worry you to face Roman legions today, my brothers? If it does, then clearly I need to remind you of our recent exploits! You stand here, my brothers, on the bones and ashes of Roman legions! It was you that brought two legions to bay and forced them to surrender and face their fate! When those Romans look across this marsh, so hideously unsuited to their way of waging war, all they can see is disaster, captivity and death! Dire omens confront them at every turn! We may have lost the fight at Augusta Trevorum, believing that we already had the battle won and allowing them time to regroup and come back at us, but everything since then has gone perfectly for us! This marsh has suited us perfectly, and has proved deadly to our enemy! And here, my brothers, with the gods watching over us, we have the chance to end this war in a single blow! Remember your wives, your children, your parents . . .' he turned slowly to encompass the entire host, 'and most of all, my brothers, remember your fatherland! Today we must either surpass the glory of our forefathers or be ridiculed in the eyes of our descendants!'

He strode across to the cohorts, acknowledging Alcaeus's salute with a curt nod.

'And with all that said, I have one last request of my oldest and most experienced warriors. And I expect you, Centurion, to lead them with your usual lack of concern for anything other than winning the day, and defeating this enemy as we have defeated so many others.' He looked up and down their sadly reduced ranks, barely a third of the strength that had joined his rebellion the year before, raising his voice to be heard by every one of the warriors. 'Men of the cohorts! I know that you have been at the point of my spear since the day you marched into Batavodurum last year and even before that happy day! I know you fought at Bonna and routed the First Legion when they were unwise enough to attempt to stop you joining us! I know you fought and bled during the siege of the Old Camp! I know you came within a hair of defeating the Romans at Gelduba, and were defeated only by the most unfavourable of circumstances, and I know how grievously you suffered in that unpredictable reverse! But now I need one last effort from you, one feat worthy of Magusanus himself! My plan of battle today is to draw the Romans' attention to their front while our most powerful force takes them in the flank! And I need you to lead the way, and show our allies of the Bructeri tribe the way to achieve that surprise. Will you do this for me?'

Waiting until the soldiers' cheers had died away, he turned to Hramn and nodded.

'As we agreed it. And wait for my signal, I want the enemy fully committed before we spring the jaws of this trap closed on them.'

As he walked away, the prefect stood, considering Alcaeus with a level stare.

'So priest, do our men have one last battle in them? A day of blood and glory for the tribe?'

'One last battle, Prefect? If it's in your power to guarantee such a thing then yes, without doubt these men behind me would sell their lives dearly, if it were the price of peace for our people. Is that within your power?'

Hramn stared at him in silence for a moment before replying.

'If we win here, Centurion, if we smash those legions off their ground, roll up their line and then surround them, we could inflict a disaster on Rome to equal their greatest defeats. As terrible a reverse as they suffered at the hands of Arminius sixty years ago. They never sought to occupy their province of Magna Germania again, for all their punitive raids, and it can be the same for us. Let their empire end at the Ubii's northern borders, and we will live free like our German brothers. That is the prize that we can win today. Or were you considering defeat?'

'No, Prefect. No son of the tribe can ever consider such an outcome. With the blessing of Hercules we will triumph over our enemy as we have on so many other occasions.'

Hramn nodded tersely.

'Make sure the men under your command share that belief.'

Alcaeus saluted.

'They will fight, Hramn. You have only to show them where, and tell them when.'

The prefect smiled, and Alcaeus's eyes narrowed as he realised that his superior was about to reveal what it was that Kivilaz had in mind for the remaining men of the cohorts.

'My uncle's plan today is a simple one, but it will result in a victory that will be felt like a punch to the gut in Rome. Today we shatter their hold on our land forever!'

'So not only are we waiting for them to come at us but we're letting Felix's auxiliaries form the first line. It seems like an act of sacrilege.'

Antonius nodded at his colleague's complaint.

'I know. But one of the secrets of being an effective general is to know when it's better to tempt your enemy onto your line than to batter yourself bloody against his, and when to allow your allies to take the edge off the enemy general's blade before committing your main force. And besides . . .'

Pugno scowled across the marsh at the oncoming rebel columns, the barbarian warriors chanting their war cries as they hurried forward across the swampy ground, eager to come to close quarters with the Romans.

'Besides what?'

With perfect timing the bolt throwers massed on their left flank spat their missiles across the two-hundred-pace gap in unison, a dozen heavy bolts tearing into the oncoming columns of tribesmen.

'That.'

Pugno shook his head dismissively.

'That? A pinprick. The only way these boys are going to give it up is if we've killed so many of them that they can't get over the wall of their dead. They'll get one more shot off if they're lucky, then scuttle for the cover of our line when that lot are close enough to smell their shit.' He stared hard-faced at the auxiliaries holding the line in front of his legion, then turned to address his trumpeter. 'As soon as they sound the hold fast, you blow it too!'

The auxiliaries' horns sounded, and an instant later Pugno's trumpeter followed their example with a note loud enough to make Antonius wince minutely, much to his friend's grim amusement. An instant later every other trumpeter in the Twenty-first responded, the blare of their horns loud enough to override conscious thought and lift every man in the legion onto the balls of his feet. Pugno stamped out in front of his men with a glowering expression, shaking his head in disgust.

'Calm yourselves! We have to let Legatus Felix's men have their turn first!'

The cohorts arrayed in front of them were readying their spears, their shields raised against the arrows slanting down into their lines from behind the oncoming Germans. The rebels were trotting, splashing though the ankle-deep water with the easy gait of men unencumbered by heavy equipment, and while men were falling to the auxiliary archers shooting at them from behind their comrades, their losses were no more than a momentary hindrance to the warriors behind them who hurdled their wounded comrades and pressed forward with fanatical determination.

'Spears . . . *ready*!'

The waiting soldiers drew back their throwing arms, every man picking a face in the advancing mass of the enemy and waiting for the command to kill the warrior behind the snarling mask.

'Wait for it!'

Pugno nodded approval as the leading enemy warriors passed the point at which they were inside spear-throw.

'Someone's got some balls, I'll give them that.'

The Germans were running now, eager to get at their lifelong enemies, covering the boggy ground fast enough that another five heartbeats would have them toe-to-toe with the legion, and just as Antonius wondered if the man commanding the cohort in front of them had lost his nerve and his voice with it, their first spear roared the order his men were waiting for.

'Throw!'

At such close range, with the leading runners less than five paces from the Roman line, the slaughter was almost instant, hundreds of spears whipping across the narrow gap almost horizontally while those thrown from the rear ranks arced briefly up before falling into the men pressing up behind the warband's rampaging front rank. A chorus of screams and bellows of pain rang in the defenders' ears as they stepped swiftly back into the defensive stance, drawing swords and crouching behind their shields as the men behind them pressed forward to support them against the impending assault. Pressing past and over their dying and wounded comrades, the Germans sprinted across the remaining few paces, hurling themselves onto and in some cases through the Roman front rank, those men whose momentum had enabled them to burst through the gaps between shields being put to the sword by the soldiers waiting for them, then dragged to the rear of the formation where they were swiftly put to death. Pugno waited a moment to make sure that the auxiliaries were going to leave them where they lay and then turned to his second-in-command.

'Do it.'

Despite knowing what was coming, Antonius still stared in amazement as dozens of men ran forward at the chosen man's command, some with their swords drawn and others carrying stout wooden poles whose ends had been sharpened to fire-hardened points. Hacking down with their sword blades, the legionaries lifted heads severed from the enemy corpses to allow their comrades to impale them firmly on the poles and lift them into the air above their heads, more than one man opening his mouth to catch the blood dripping from their trophies as part of the legion's grisly ritual. Stepping up close behind the auxiliary line, they waved the severed heads above the soldiers' helmets so that the dead men's faces could be seen by their comrades. Pugno nodded approvingly, grinning wolfishly at Antonius.

'These goat fuckers usually fight in family groups, collected together by village and town under whatever passes for royalty, so when we show them the head of a man we just killed we're probably scaring the shit out of two or three others, or better yet making them insane with grief.'

Antonius nodded his understanding as the tribesmen threw themselves at the Roman line with fresh anger, eyes wide with rage and lips flecked with spittle from their incensed howls for vengeance, but where the Germans were incandescent with fury, the men facing them, having long been trained as to what to expect, declined to offer them any outlet for that anger other than the faces of their shields, taking their chances to thrust their sword blades into faces and bodies as the opportunities were gifted to them. Pugno walked up to the rear of the cohort in front of them and studied the flailing enemy warriors for a moment before turning back to Antonius with a satisfied nod, raising his voice to be heard over the battle's roaring din.

'They could hold those fuckers all day. But it's not those fuckers that are worrying me.'

Antonius stepped up alongside him, looking out over the battlefield. All along the Roman line auxiliaries and war bands were fighting for superiority, and at no point was there any sign that the defenders were overmatched, while the ground behind the Germans was empty of any other presence except for the few captured bolt throwers that had not already been damaged beyond repair by the legions' massed artillery.

'Where's their reserve?'

Pugno nodded agreement.

'Yes. And more to the point, where are their cohorts? They

stick out like a dog's dick in all that iron they wear, and I don't see them anywhere near. And if they're not here, then where are they?'

'Tell me why we've dumped our armour again?'

Lataz looked askance at his brother, who was looking down at the river's cold water with an expression of disgust. The closest Roman troops were a hundred paces from the riverbank and seemingly intent on resisting the furious attack that was breaking on their shields in a wave of blood-flecked barbarian madness, although the Batavi soldier's practiced eye could see that the officers at the line's furthermost end were watching them intently, as the purpose of their movement out onto the dam became apparent.

'You know why we've dumped our armour. You could no more swim in your mail then you could persuade any woman to get into your bed without the promise of coin.'

Frijaz shook his head angrily, staring back down the makeshift dam's length to where Hramn stood talking to the Bructeri chieftain who had led his men to the river's edge in the wake of the Batavi warriors, pointing at the riverbank facing the waiting warriors who were jostling for position to be first into the water. The tribesmen were lightly equipped, with small shields, spears and hunting knives for the most part, although here and there men sported captured Roman weapons as badges of previous victories.

'They've paired us off with the maddest set of bastards in the army. That lot have been awake all night getting hammered and singing songs about their priestess, and now they look about as good as the last piece of dried horseshit I had to peel off my hobnails.'

Lataz shook his head.

'I keep thinking "I must tell Sigu about that", only a moment later I remember that Sigu gave his life in yet another meaningless battle, and I've got that feeling now. I was going to warn him not to get in their way once we're over there . . .' he nodded at the riverbank fifty paces from their place on the dam, 'because once they're over there they'll do what the Germans always do when there's the chance of a fight.'

'What, charge in like the madmen they are and get themselves butchered one at a time?'

'Yes, that.'

Lanzo spoke up, the urgency in his voice compelling what was left of his tent party to listen.

'This is a suicide mission, that's clear enough. So don't get caught up in whatever it is that Kiv's cooked up with their chief because I'll bet you silver for shit that all he wants from them is a distraction, a wave of mad painted fuckers coming out of the water like demons from the Underworld and tearing into their right flank with all the screaming and shouting that lot usually do. They'll scare the life out of whoever's over on this end of their line, but they'll get slaughtered all the same once the Romans get themselves sorted out, unless the other tribes manage to break them in the chaos. So we let them charge off into the battle, we get formed and we go forward together, right? I want all four of you alive when this is over with.'

Egilhard put a hand on his shoulder, half-turning the leading man and speaking urgently in his ear.

'I thought you told me not to listen to Al—'

His friend shook his head, his face dark with anger.

'I didn't get it from the centurion. I got it from a friend.' He looked at Lataz and Frijaz. 'You two remember Heru, right?'

The older brother nodded.

'Of course. He was a good man, until an Iceni archer put an arrow in his chest and stopped half his wind. He'd have been here with us if we'd allowed him to.'

'His sons were even better, because he trained them to fight, and he trained me too. Kniba took a spear in the back at Gelduba and was never seen again, but Sparr is still alive, and serving with the Guard. He's one of the prince's bodyguards, which means that he hears everything Kiv discusses with our new prefect.' He leaned closer, lowering his voice. 'I saw him in the camp last night, and when he laid eyes on me he looked like a man with something to hide. So of course I asked him straight out what was the matter, one old friend to another. When he told me I wished I hadn't asked. There are some things a man's better not knowing.'

'He told you *what*?'

Lanzo looked up from his contemplation of the ground at his feet.

'He told me that he was part of Kiv's escort after the meeting that made the decision to attack the Roman camp at Augusta Trevorum, which meant that he couldn't help overhearing them talking about it. Apparently Kiv hadn't wanted to attack, he'd been all for waiting for the tribes to come south but he agreed to send us in because he had to look strong. And Hramn persuaded him to send *us* in to open the gates in the hope that the centurion would stop a spear and solve his problem for him.'

Lataz leaned in close, his whisper so vehement that spittle flew from his lips.

'My son died to make Kivilaz look strong and allow that young fucker to settle a score?'

'Yes.'

'I'll . . .'

'No, you won't.'

Egilhard caught his father by the arm and held him for long enough that Frijaz could take the other, muttering in his brother's ear.

'Oh no, you don't. If there's revenge to be taken I'll be there with you, and this isn't the time! But the time will come! Right?'

Before Lataz could reply, a sudden burst of noise caught their attention. The Germans had started chanting, their priests leading them through the ritual with extravagant gestures and blood-curding yells, every tribesman following their lead as they mimed the violence intended for their lifelong enemies with thrusts of their spears, and echoed their song of death and blood as they bellowed the names of their heroes at the sky. The chief priest called for silence, then shouted a single word at his men.

'Veleda!'

The response was instant, a roar of approval and commitment underlaid by the rattling of shields and spears being banged together.

'Veleda!'

The war band's noise redoubled, individual warriors screaming the priestess's name so loudly that their eyes bulged with the effort.

'And if they didn't know we were already coming . . .'

'VELEDA!'

The priest nodded to his chieftain, who turned to Hramn and indicated that his men were ready, and in turn the Batavi prefect looked at Alcaeus, pointing at the river with an unmistakable purpose. The wolf-priest saluted, then turned to the water and shouted an order over his shoulder with the calm certainty that his men would follow him to the gates of the underworld if he ordered them to do so.

'Cohorts! *Follow me!'*

The tent party watched as the wolf-priest stepped off the dam and started swimming, crabbing sideways with the buoyant wood of his shield and spear in one hand, stroking steadily with the other while his legs kicked in time.

'You have to admire the man.'

Frijaz nodded at his brother's softly spoken opinion.

'Admire him? We might just have to *die* for him. Come on.'

They stepped off the hard-packed mud into the water and started swimming, gasping at the cold. Glancing back as he swam, Lataz grinned at the sight of the Bructeri warriors being herded into the water by their priests, those men whose courage failed them despite their wild collective chanting being tossed unceremoniously into the river to sink or swim, and then fended away from the dam at spearpoint.

'Fuck me . . . they've got . . . a different . . . way of . . . getting their boys . . . to go forward!'

Frijaz glanced back at the splashing chaos of the tribesmen behind them.

'They've got . . . the wrong . . . idea. It's not . . . the river . . . that'll kill them!'

The leading Batavi swimmers were staggering to their feet and dragging themselves out of the river's cloying mud, Alcaeus raising his sword in a signal for the cohorts to reform around him in the scant cover of the straggling foliage that lined the bank, and the tent party splashed out of the water and up the thin strip of shore with clods of mud sticking to their boot soles.

'Once there are enough us to mount a decent attack, I'll . . .'

The centurion fell silent, staring in amazement as the first of the Germans waded ashore, waited a moment for the worst of the river's water to pour from his sodden clothing and then raised his spear, bellowed an incoherent war cry and ran up the bank, making straight for the embattled Romans without any apparent concern for his chances against them on his own. His fellow warriors were emerging from the water in ones and twos, their numbers still scant compared to the hundreds of Batavi coming ashore, but they were no more circumspect than he had been, charging forward into the battle without waiting for their comrades. The auxiliaries were starting to respond to the new threat, bending their line around to meet the stream of barbarians seemingly intent on dying on their shields, and Lataz spat in disgust.

'What the fuck do they think they're doing?'

Lanzo shook his head in bemusement at the veteran soldier.

'I told you. Either this was never a serious attack or Kiv miscalculated when he chose those fools. Either way we get screwed.'

Alcaeus stood and saluted as Hramn strode up the riverbank with water streaming from his sodden tunic and his sword drawn.

'Prefect.'

'What the *fuck* are you doing here? Get into the enemy!'

The prefect was clearly furious, pointing with his blade towards the embattled enemy line, and Alcaeus was suddenly calm.

'I'm waiting for the rest of the cohorts to get ashore, Prefect, at which point we'll go forward as a formed line and kill as many Romans as we can before they overwhelm us.'

'Get these cowards into action, Priest, or I'll . . .'

He was interrupted by the noisy chanting of a party of Bructeri warriors bulling their way through the Batavi ranks, their teeth bared with battle rage, and in the comparative silence that fell after they had passed, his eyes narrowed as he realised that the dozens of men surrounding him were staring at him with cold, hard-eyed anger, their silent glares unnerving where open dissent would have been easier to deal with. Alcaeus stepped closer, lowering his voice until it was barely more than a whisper.

'If I were you, Prefect, I'd think very carefully before using that word again.'

Hramn stared at him for a moment, his knuckles white on the hilt of his sword, then nodded slowly.

'Very well. Get your . . . men . . . moving and we'll forget this happened.'

He pushed his way through the soldiers surrounding him, ignoring their open hostility, and walked back to the water's side where the Bructeri chieftains were gathering with their household warriors ready to join the growing attack that was now pressing the Romans back.

'You might forget but we won't!'

The prefect stiffened at the shouted threat but kept his back to the glowering Batavians, and Alcaeus raised his voice to bellow an admonishment.

'The next man to speak will get his entire century flogged! Get yourselves into a line and ready to attack!'

Lanzo shook his head in disgust and turned back to his men.

'You heard the centurion! Get yourselves . . .' He stopped, looking around himself at the tent party's remnants. 'Where's Ugly?'

His men looked around in confusion and Frijaz shook his head in bemusement.

'He was here, next to me. And now he's not. He must have gone with the Germans when they came past. Either he's gone blood crazy like them or . . .'

The leading man raised a hand.

'Don't even say it. If that bastard Hramn gets any reason to come down on Alcaeus he'll have the wolf off his helmet and the skin off his back, so forget Levonhard. If we ever see him again we can deal with what made him run, but the odds are that he'll be dead inside an hour.'

The veteran grinned bleakly.

'Same goes for you and me. So let's go and fight, eh?'

'Your auxiliaries seem to be holding well enough, Sextilius Felix.'

Cerialis's legatus nodded his agreement as he rejoined the group of senior officers watching the battle from the saddles of their horses.

'Indeed, Legatus Augusti, although I doubt they have the beating of these barbarians in them after so long fighting to hold the line. The secret to these matters, as I learned serving under Gnaeus Domitius Corbulo in Armenia, lies in choosing the optimum moment for our fellow officers to send their legions into the battle. You'll understand that better than most, having taken part in the campaign against the rebels in Britannia.'

'Yes, I do.' The senior officer nodded, his face a mask of self-control at the reminder of the disaster that had befallen him outside Camulodunum and resulted in his spending most of the rebellion trapped in an auxiliary fort. 'We must choose carefully when to move from back to front foot and send our meat grinders forward against their tired warriors. What of the right flank?'

They turned to look down to where their line ended at the Rhenus's edge, the concentration of enemy warriors thickened by the presence of a good number of men wearing Roman helmets driving into the auxiliaries struggling to keep the flank intact.

'It's holding, although the enemy seem to have launched some sort of attack across the river with the hope of turning the line and rolling us up. My right flank cohorts are holding them, and I've committed my tactical reserve to stiffen their resistance and lengthen the line as a counter.'

All along the line of Felix's auxiliary cohorts the tribal assault had burned out its first fury and settled down to a lower intensity struggle, individual war bands surging forward to test the men facing them as their chieftains and priests saw fit, hurling scores and hundreds of warriors against single centuries in concentrations of effort and sheer pushing power that the opposing centurions were swift to match with reinforcements from either side of the embattled soldiers. A dozen individual struggles for supremacy were raging along the Roman defences, the line surging backwards and forwards as attacker and defender gained momentary superiority before being pushed back to their starting point by weight of numbers, leaving the inevitable scattering of dead and dying men from both sides sprawled in the thick, foul-smelling mud that their pounding boots had churned, a slurry of blood, urine and faeces, wounded men of both armies crawling or staggering for the safety of their own lines when the combatants drew apart, soldier and tribesmen alike panting from their exertions and eying their wounded comrades with the dispassion of men who knew that their own survival was no more than a temporary state of affairs.

Cerialis nodded, his face creased in thought.

'I deem it too soon to commit the legions. When we move from defence to attack I want the enemy to be sufficiently tired that our foot soldiers can run them down and finish this matter for good. But perhaps our right could benefit from a little stiffening. These Batavians are the most fearsome of enemies, and perhaps a man with experience of their way of fighting would be the best choice to lead a local counter-attack. Centurion Aquillius.'

The big man saluted from the saddle of a horse that had been procured to enable him to remain at his general's side.

'Legatus Augusti.'

'You are temporarily relieved of your duty to protect me from the interruptions of unfriendly men, and directed to ride to the right flank and ensure that the men there are sufficiently well ordered to hold despite this attempt to surprise us from across the river.'

The centurion saluted and turned his beast to trot down the rear of the line, fixing his attention on the seething mass of tribesmen and Batavi warriors railing at the line that had been extending to curl around the right flank. A pair of prefects in bronze armour were studying the fight from the safety of their horses while centurions and their officers roamed the rear of the line bellowing orders, pushing men into their positions and striking out with the flats of their swords if any soldier showed signs of backing away. Saluting the surprised prefects, he dismounted and handed the reins of his horse to a lightly wounded man standing behind the formation waiting to have his cut treated, but as he turned to speak with the cohort commanders a man shouted at him from close by.

'Banô!'

At first glance the speaker was an auxiliary soldier, clad in the same mail and headgear as the soldiers fighting to defend their line, but the presence of a soldier at his rear with a drawn sword identified him as a prisoner. Aquillius was about to turn back to the fight when the man shouted again.

'I know you! You're Aquillius! I saw you when you spoke to our centurion Alcaeus! I can win this battle for you!'

The big centurion nodded, striding across to where the prisoner stood.

'You deserted?'

The Batavi nodded, his face set determinedly, ignoring the contemptuous sneer on Aquillius's face.

'Yes, I deserted! And I can show you how to win this battle and end this war, if you'll allow me to!'

'How?'

The prisoner pointed at the other end of the Roman line.

'There's high ground over there, a bar of it thirty paces wide that goes all the way to the line we defended yesterday, that's what's keeping the water level here high. Take a legion down that and into their rear and they'll have no choice but to turn and run, before you finish the job and bottle them up.'

Aquillius contemplated him for a moment.

'Why? Why do this? How do I know this is not a trap?'

'Why? Because our leader has turned on us, sending us into fights that halve our numbers every time we fight! This war needs to end, and Kivilaz needs to get what's coming to him! That's why!'

The Roman pondered him for a moment, then turned and gestured for the Batavi to follow him.

'Come with me. What is your name?'

'Levonhard, son of Skaken.'

'Come with me, Levonhard son of Skaken. Although I expect men will call you Levonhard the traitor for the rest of your days.'

'It's time we went forward! How much longer is Cerialis going to let these animals hammer at our shields without sending in the men who can put them to flight with a single attack?'

Antonius remained silent, sharing his brother officer's frustration but knowing better than to encourage his ire to fresh intensity. Both armies struggling for dominance twenty-five paces in front of the Twenty-first's line were showing signs of exhaustion, and to his practised eye the moment when the legions should be unleashed to pass through their auxiliary brothers and confront the enemy was at hand, but the senior officers clustered between them at the rear of the line and the doubtless equally impatient Fourteenth Legion showed no sign of any decision to send their fresh troops in to administer the killing stroke. Feeling compelled to placate his irate friend, he started to venture a soothing opinion, only to fall silent as he saw a pair of horsemen detach from the group.

'Isn't that Legatus Longus? And that's Aquillius riding with him. But who's the runner?'

The riders trotted down the rear of the Roman line with an unarmoured man running alongside them, evidently using one of the horse's bridles to pull himself along in a way that reminded Antonius of the stories he had heard of the Batavi way of war. Both men watched as the horsemen approached, recognising Aquillius as he reined his beast in and climbed down from its saddle, saluting Pugno and pushing the tunic-clad man forward.

'Greetings, First Spear Pugno. This man is a Batavian traitor who has agreed to show us a hidden path into the enemy rear.'

Pugno turned to Longus, who nodded.

'It is as the centurion says. Petillius Cerialis has directed us, as the most fearsome of his legions, to follow this man's guidance to wherever it takes us.'

'I see.' The first spear looked the traitor in the eyes for a moment before speaking. 'You have heard of the Twenty-first Legion?'

The Batavi nodded.

'We fought alongside you a year ago and rescued your eagle for you.'

'You retain your people's gift for provocation even in captivity then?'

'I am no captive, I am Levonhard, son of Skaken, and I am here of my own will. I chose to change sides in this war when I discovered that my own prince was happy to see me dead if it will settle a personal score. I will show you where to march your legions, if you wish to catch the tribes in a trap from which there can be no escape, but I do so to end this war and spare my people any further suffering.'

Pugno shrugged.

'Your delusions are of no matter to me, Batavian.' He looked to Longus. 'Your orders, Legatus?'

The senior officer extended a hand towards the Batavi soldier.

'We are to follow this man to wherever this path of his takes us. What we do then will decide on where we find ourselves.'

The senior centurion shrugged at Antonius.

'Every day a fresh surprise, eh Centurion?' Squaring his shoulders he nodded to his trumpeter, who blew the single piercing note to warn the legion that they were about to move. *'Twenty-first Legion . . . Right! Turn!'*

Four thousand men pivoted where they stood as the command rippled down the length of the legion's line, turning line to column of march.

'You, Levonhard son of Shagga or whatever his name was, with me.' Pugno patted his pugio with a meaningful stare. 'Lead us to this hidden path. But be very clear that if it fails to take us somewhere I consider worth the effort, you'll be joining your daddy in the Underworld somewhat sooner than he might have expected.' He glanced over at Aquillius. 'Tell Cerialis that he'll need to send another legion to block their escape to their right because I'm taking my lads to close their back door!'

The Batavi nodded dispassionately and turned away.

'Follow me.'

As they passed the head of the legion's column Pugno roared the command for his men to follow him at the slow march, his eyes locked on the Batavi captive as Levonhard paced forward, his eyes on the ground.

'Walk faster, son of Shagga. If we go any slower we'll be going backwards!'

The prisoner answered without looking back.

'If I miss what I'm looking for you'll put that knife in my back, so I think I'll take my time.'

'If you miss what you're looking for I'll put this knife right up your . . .'

He bellowed the command for the legion to halt as the captive raised a hand, then pointed at the ground, lifting his hand to indicate a path out into the marsh.

'This is it. Drier ground, see?'

The two centurions walked out onto the wide spit of firmer going, strolling out until they were level with the Germans hammering at the line of auxiliary cohorts barely fifty paces distant.

'If this goes all the way to the positions they held yesterday then we have them by the balls. One legion on that high ground could hold them off for the rest of the day while the others encircle them and cut them to pieces.'

Pugno nodded at Antonius's statement.

'If it goes all the way to their position of yesterday. And if they don't see us flanking them and make a run for it. It seems that our traitor has given us the key to end this war, but only *if* . . .'

His friend nodded, gesturing at the ground before them.

'Shall we go and find out?'

Pugno nodded decisively.

'Sound the advance!' He tucked his vine stick into his belt and drew his sword, lifting the blade above his head as the trumpeter blew the signal that would set the Twenty-first into motion, his teeth bared in a grin that Antonius had come to know all too well. *'Follow me!'*

The two men pounded forward, revelling in the feel of dry ground beneath their feet after so long walking on saturated, boggy terrain. Antonius glanced back to see the Twenty-first in full cry behind them, still in their column but determined to chase down their officers. The legion was sweeping past the enemy right flank at speed, and, looking to his right he realised that the closest of the tribal war bands was already in chaos, their auxiliary foes momentarily forgotten as men pointed at the advancing Romans with shouts of alarm. Pugno followed his stare and laughed out loud between panting breaths.

'Look at them . . . they're shitting themselves!'

The two men kept running, their speed dragging the Twenty-first out across the battlefield and exposing the enemy tribesmen to more risk of being encircled with every step the legion advanced. The Germans were already disintegrating, increasing numbers of warriors turning to run for their lives as their predicament became clear to their chieftains. With a sudden collective lurch away from the Roman line, the tipping point was reached and passed, those men who had not yet turned to flee realising that they were increasingly isolated in front of fresh enemy soldiers as a pair of legions advanced forward through the exhausted auxiliaries, singing their battle hymns and clashing spear shafts against shields in a terrifying rhythm. Pugno looked across at the routing Germans, then back at his objective.

'They're running! Faster!'

The entire rebel army was on the move, thousands of men splashing through the marsh on a parallel track with the Twenty-first for the safety of their former defensive position and the open fields beyond in which, unencumbered by the weight of armour and weapons carried by their enemies, they would be able to outpace the pursuing legionaries. The fastest among them were already leaping up the slope they had defended the previous day, and Antonius realised that the bulk of them would escape thanks to their superior speed and agility even across such infirm ground.

'They're going to—'

Pugno nodded.

'I see it!' He changed course, turning to his right to run out into the marsh in a cascade of splashing water from beneath his pounding boots. *'Into them!'*

The Twenty-first followed him, their column reverting to a line as the running soldiers roared their battle cries and poured across the boggy ground at the fleeing Germans in a wave of raging iron. Smashing an isolated runner to the ground with his shield, the first spear stabbed down into the sprawling man's throat with his gladius and then strode forward into the panicking tribesmen like a wolf picking out his prey from a fleeing herd of deer, clinically selecting a man and swinging the sword low to drop his victim to the ground in a tangle of limbs and flying blood before finishing him with another clinical death-stroke. The legion's leading soldiers were suddenly alongside him, men spreading out to either side and tearing into the terrified tribesmen whose only instinct was to run their gauntlet, twisting and dodging their attacks with no thought but to escape.

'Blood Drinkers!'

Pugno's bellowed challenge was taken up across the advancing ranks of legionaries as they scythed their way into the broken mob of Germans, and Antonius found himself echoing the war cry as he picked a runner and expertly slit the hapless warrior's throat with a perfectly timed swing of his blade, feeling a hot tickle on his face as the man's blood fountained from the wound.

'Blood Drinkers!'

Advancing into the fleeing mass of tribesmen, he quickly lost count of the men he had shield checked and killed, only vaguely aware of Pugno beside him fighting and killing with equal ferocity as the two men led the legion out across the marsh. Stopping to get his breath back he realised that the battlefield was suddenly comparatively empty, most of the tribesmen who were going to escape its lethal confines having run the gauntlet of the enraged legion leaving the slow and lame to their fate. The initial mindless slaughter had burned out of the Twenty-first, replaced by something more calculated and brutal as the legionaries toyed mercilessly with the remaining Germans, soldiers raising their shields to block the hapless stragglers' paths and leave them stranded, all hope of getting away from the legion's harsh justice lost. Pugno shook his head, still panting for breath after their rampage through the fleeing tribesmen that had left both men painted with blood.

'Twenty-first Legion! Kill the rest of them and re-form! *Now!*'

He waited while the legionaries obeyed the order, swiftly putting the remaining Germans to death and then returning to the ranks of their formation, looking across the battlefield with a practised eye.

'We killed a thousand or so as they ran, and probably twice that in the fight beforehand. Not enough.'

Antonius shrugged, watching as Briganticus's Ala Singularium thundered past in a shower of spray to take up the pursuit, their long spears held low, eager to catch the running tribesmen and make them pay for their defeat.

'They ran. And they're still running. Those horsemen will kill more of them, but the rest won't stop until it's dark. Half of Civilis's army will melt away back across the river in family groups, and what's left will be in no hurry to take us on again, not unless they can wield the knife at our backs in the dark. We won, Centurion, and that's that. All we have left to look forward to is the occupation of their homeland and whatever resistance he has left. This war is over.'

'I know. But that was our last chance to show those long-haired fuckers what it means to piss Rome off, and we didn't kill enough of them for my liking.'

Antonius shrugged.

'If this war is over then there's only one man I want to see dead now.'

*

'Total victory! Congratulations, gentlemen, you've just thrown the Batavians and their German allies off the last piece of defendable ground between here and the Island! Here's to you!'

The assembled legati and their senior centurions raised their cups in response to their general's toast, and for a brief moment there was silence as they all drank.

'We have to admit that we were lucky, do we not?' Alfenius Varus had a quizzical expression, and after a moment's pause Cerialis smiled at him beatifically.

'Lucky, Alfenius Varus? Of course, we were lucky. If that Batavian deserter hadn't swum ashore at just the right place to be brought to me, rather than just being gutted and left to die at the water's edge, then we'd have been none the wiser as to that high ground that allowed us to get around them. But luck's a funny thing, as I'm sure you can attest from your experiences of the last eighteen months, eh?' Varus inclined his head in respect for the other man's point. 'We make our own luck in this life, and I was doubly fortunate to have placed the Twenty-first Legion on my left flank, where they were best placed to exploit that weakness in Civilis's plan.'

He would have continued, but Julius Briganticus strode into the command tent, his big body spattered with mud from a long afternoon in the saddle pursuing the retreating Germans, the bronze of his armour heavily flecked with dried blood.

'Prefect Briganticus, what do you have to tell us? I presume it's urgent from the fact that you didn't have time to bathe and change your tunic before reporting?'

The Batavi officer ignored his commanding officer's jest and saluted smartly, snapping to attention and scattering yet more flakes of dried mud across the tent's carpeted floor.

'The enemy are still running, Legatus Augusti.'

'Excellent! I presume you've been squabbling with their rear guard, from the state of your armour?'

'We've been killing the wounded as they fell out of the line of march, Legatus Augusti.'

Cerialis nodded knowingly.

'Mercy killings, eh?'

The Batavi stared back at him uncomprehendingly, and the legatus augusti smiled at his confusion before turning to the rest of his officers.

'So, we have them on the run. They're abandoning their wounded and if I have the measure of things they won't stop retreating until they reach their Island. We'll follow up behind them, of course, but I have a task for you that you may find distasteful, Julius Briganticus. I want you to ride out tomorrow morning, get ahead of them and take your cavalry wing all the way to your tribe's homeland. I presume you can swim the river, if they've destroyed the bridge?'

Briganticus nodded.

'You want me to raid across the Island?'

'I want you to *ravage* the Island, Prefect. More specifically, I want every farm burned out by the time your uncle gets his men back across the river, every farm *except,* that is, those belonging to him and the rest of your family. While every man of substance in your tribe will see his property ascend into the sky in a column of smoke, I want your uncle's fortunes to be untroubled. If that doesn't make them think twice about supporting him in this doomed war then perhaps the sight of your horsemen operating on their soil with complete impunity will.'

'Just the farm buildings?'

Cerialis raised an eyebrow.

'What do you take me for, Briganticus? No blood is to be shed unless you encounter resistance, in which case the killing is to be limited to those men who are armed and not running from you. Of course, I only want the buildings burned out, and on no account is fire to be taken to your tribe's ability to feed themselves. If any crop has been brought in then the barns in which it has been stored are to be spared as well. I'm not stupid enough to want to have to feed an enraged population of your countrymen, I just want them to feel Rome's long reach tightening around their collective throat, and to realise that their only hope to end this insanity without a bloody campaign across the Island is for them to surrender now.'

*

'We have to keep moving!' Lanzo looked back at Egilhard worriedly, beckoning him on. 'If we don't keep up we'll be dead before dark because without our armour and spears we've no way to face those bastards!'

What was left of the Batavi cohorts was half running, half forced marching across the open farmland to the north of the Old Camp, the exhausted warriors huddling together for protection against enemy cavalrymen roaming along their flanks and rear, their spears gleaming red in the evening sunlight as they darted in to pick off exhausted stragglers and those of the wounded unable to sustain the brutal ground-covering pace any longer. In the distance horns were blowing, a reminder that the legions that had so decisively routed the rebel army were following close behind, eager to kill more Germans before the sun sank to meet the western horizon.

'He's lost too much blood to go much further!'

Lataz's face was deathly pale beneath the weathered, dirty skin, his features stretched taut with the grinding effort required simply to put one foot in front of the other as his strength ebbed, even with his brother under one arm and his remaining son supporting his other side. He looked down at the bloody stump of his right arm, still leaking blood into the filthy rag of wool that had been all they could find for a makeshift bandage, shaking his head in despair at the sudden loss of such an intrinsic part of his ability to soldier.

'I'm nothing without that. Just leave me.'

'Fuck that!' Frijaz shook his head angrily at his younger brother's words, slapping the back of the wounded man's lolling head. 'If you think you're going to take the easy way out when the rest of us are stuck in this shit, you can give it some more thought!'

Lanzo dropped back to march alongside them, casting uneasy glances at the horsemen tracking their progress less than a hundred paces to their right, their presence clearly intended to put a hedge of spears between the defeated Batavi and the Rhenus, to make sure that none of the retreating warriors tried to escape by throwing themselves into the river.

'Not long now, eh? They'll piss off to make camp soon enough, if they don't want to be spread out all over the countryside for the night. All we have to do is just keep moving for another half-mile or so. Don't tell me you don't have another half-mile in you, you old bastard, you're tougher gristle than that.'

Lataz grinned weakly back at him, nodding wordlessly, and Egilhard took up the harangue that was evidently meant to distract the wounded man from his state of enervation.

'He's right! Hear that?' In the distance the legion signallers were blowing a different call, summoning their legionaries to make camp for the night, and the men of the cohorts cheered raggedly at the sound. 'They'll call those riders off soon, and we can—'

A horn sounded close at hand, but not playing the signal the fleeing Batavi had hoped for.

'They're attacking! Stand to! Form a circle!'

The century reacted instinctively to Alcaeus's bellowed command, dropping the wounded men they were supporting into the middle of a rapidly forming defensive ring and facing outwards with shields and spears ready to fight as the cavalrymen who had dogged their steps for hours abandoned the pursuit and turned to ride in at them with their spears raised in one last attempt to break their enemy's resolve before nightfall. A dozen riders selected the century, whose place at the edge of the pack of exhausted men made it an easier target than the units buried deeper in the cohorts' mass of men, the thunder of their hoofs drumming in the ground beneath the waiting soldiers' feet as they bored in with their spears lowered. Alcaeus was shouting again, bellowing at his men to give them the hope that had been battered out of them by the day's disastrous events.

'One last attack and they'll be gone! Give them nothing!'

Egilhard looked about him, his senses slowing to a trickle with the usual lurch of his stomach at the prospect of combat, his sword held ready to fight, his shield's metal rim rattling against those held by the men on either side of him as they presented an unbroken wall of wood and iron to the oncoming horsemen.

'Stand fast!'

He nodded at Lanzo's barked command even as the riders loomed over their circle, stabbing out with their spears at men whose own javelins were long since lost in the chaos of the fight on the Roman right flank, a fight whose winning had been within their grasp when the rest of the army had taken flight and left them standing alone, with no choice but to follow their fleeing allies' trail with a vengeful enemy close behind. The man alongside him died with a spear blade in his throat, gurgling as his lifeblood flooded into his lungs, and as the dying man's shield slumped to the ground, one rider, braver or more skilful than his comrades, backed his beast into the circle, scattering the defenders with the brutal impact of its hindquarters.

'For Sigu!'

Egilhard stepped forward where most of his comrades were backing away, swinging his sword low to hack at the beast's leg and dropping it kicking to the ground, its rider trapped beneath the flailing animal's dead weight, screaming with the pain. He lifted the blade high as he paced round to where the horseman lay helpless, his helmet thrown half-a-dozen paces clear by the impact of his fall and their eyes met momentarily, the hapless cavalryman finding nothing more in Egilhard's dead stare than the certainty of his death. He screamed incoherently as the sword swung down, the cry silenced abruptly by the severing of his head from his shoulders, and the battle-crazed warrior lifted it by the hair and turned to roar his rage at the horsemen milling around him.

'Batavi!'

The nearest rider pulled his spear back and spurred his mount forward, intent on avenging his comrade's death, but as he thrust the long blade out to take Egilhard's life, another man staggered into the path of the spear's lethal point, shuddering as the weapon sank deep into his unarmoured body.

'Father!'

Gripping the spear's shaft with his left hand, the veteran warrior grinned bloodily up at his killer and raised his ruined right arm in salute. The rider pulled his weapon free and stared down at the swaying soldier, nodding at him and raising the spear's blade

His face and hands were liberally smeared with a paste made from water, soil and lichen to soften and conceal the lines of his body. He had initially baulked at Beran's order to crumble a deer's stool into the mixture, but as the feeding animal slowly progressed through the trees to his right, almost close enough for him to have reached out and touched its flank, the Roman exulted in the fact that he was invisible to all of the animal's senses.

'Hunt slow. Like spider.'

In the days following Beran's initial sharing of his secrets of the hunt, Marius had followed the hunter in his glacially slow progress through the forest, wincing every time Beran had wordlessly raised a hand to indicate that he had heard the Roman pacing behind him despite all the careful stealth that Marius believed himself capable of, until his mentor had called him to his side and pointed to his own booted feet.

'Watch feet. I walk.'

Concentrating closely on the German's feet, he had realised that the hunter's almost imperceptible progress was not simply the result of his philosophy that a born hunter had no need to pursue his quarry, and that the animals would be drawn to him by the invisible power of their spirit bond to a true man of the forest, but the result of the infinite care with which he walked through the trees.

'I look twig or branch, not break.'

Beran, Marius realised, did not simply place his feet back on the forest floor, risking the chance of snapping a hidden twig buried in the detritus that littered the soil, but slid his boot into the litter toe first, gently sweeping any such debris aside. As the German continued forward, his pupil realised that he was picking a careful path from one tree to the next, always staying as close to cover as possible while making his slow, silent progress through the forest's half-lit greenery. And as the days had passed, and he became accustomed to the slower rhythms of his new world, the Roman had gradually adopted not just his teacher's way of moving, but also his sense of belonging in the vast emptiness of the woods. What he had not expected to pose a problem, however, had proved to be his biggest difficulty in learning Beran's skills.

'When you strike, *no* think. Only strike, like snake.'

Whilst complimentary with regard to the distance Marius could throw a spear, and the accuracy he was capable of achieving given a moment to consider the target, the hunter remained unconvinced even by his best efforts, simply shaking his head and pointing at a spot a hundred or more paces distant.

'*Heruta* run while you look down spear. Now he laugh at you from there.'

Pointing to a large knot in the trunk of a massive oak, the German had walked him back twenty paces and bid him to turn his back on the target and squat down.

'Now you turn and throw. White spot is top of heruta leg, where heart lie. You put spear in spot, you kill heruta. But you throw without wait to look and think, yes? Throw like hunter, not soldier.'

Marius's efforts to hit the target had seen most of his throws sail away into the trees, and he had quickly become disillusioned with trudging after it, often having to search through the leaf litter to find the weapon, but Beran's main concern had been with the speed with which he cast the weapon rather than whether it flew to the target or not. When, at length, he had declared himself satisfied with his pupil's ability to turn and stamp forward to sling the spear in the same movement, he had smiled knowingly at Marius, marching him forward ten paces towards the oak.

'Now you throw.'

Halving the distance had an almost revelatory effect on his ability to hit the knot, and as his confidence grew he was able to put the spear's iron head into the circle nine times out of ten, and at the end of the day Beran asked him a question to which he already knew the answer.

'So, Centurion, what you learn?'

'That I need to stay invisible to the animals I'm hunting so that I can get close enough not to miss with the fastest throw I can make.'

The German had inclined his head in recognition.

'And now is time you hunt. Have taught you all I know. Now is for you to use.'

The stag snuffled again, and Marius turned his head slowly to the left, estimating that the animal was no more than five paces away, moving slowly away as it hunted the forest floor for food. Summoning the memory of Beran's last instruction, to put his spear into the beast's body just behind its shoulder, throwing from behind to minimise the risk of the heart being protected by the big bones, he took a long, slow breath, allowing the air to leave his body in a gentle exhalation, then uncoiled himself from out of the tree's cover, standing and hurling the spear with all the whiplash speed the German had drummed into him.

The weapon's iron head sank deep into the animal's side, a good throw but not perfect, and with an expression of disgust he watched helplessly as the stag bolted, blood streaming from the wound and encumbered by the weapon's long shaft protruding from its side, but still moving fast enough that it would be out of sight in less than twenty paces. He knew from Beran's tales of frustrated hunts in his younger days that the beast could easily run for a mile or more before succumbing to the wound, with every chance that it would be lost to them, along with the precious spear, but even as he shook his head the other man rose from the trees to his right and made his own throw. The stag dropped in mid-leap as it jumped a fallen tree, hitting the forest floor with a heavy thump and lying motionless, not even twitching, such was the speed with which the German had killed it. Marius ran to the spot, vaulting the tree trunk to find his teacher grinning happily at the dead animal.

'Tonight we eat fresh meat, friend Marius! Skin heruta and butcher he. Then we cook heart and liver, take he strength to make us better hunter.'

The Roman stared in amazement at the dead beast, Beran's spear having flown unerringly to punch through the stag's eye socket and penetrate its skull, killing it instantly.

'How did you do that?'

'I learn, over many years, that spear in heart make hole in pell. So learn to kill this way.'

Marius shook his head in undisguised admiration.

'In all my years I've never seen—'

Both men turned, and Marius's hand went to the hilt of his sword, the hairs on the back of his neck standing up as the unmistakable howl of a wolf sounded from the forest, swiftly answered by several more calls. Beran shook his head in disgust.

'Wulfa. Forest gods punish me for pride in making throw. We lose kill, wulfa too strong for we. Is . . . how you say . . . ?'

'Inevitable?' Marius gripped his spear's shaft and wrenched the weapon's long iron head free. 'No, it fucking well isn't! Nothing is decided until the blood's dry, my friend. And I'm fucked if I'm going to allow some dumb forest dogs to take my first kill away!'

The first wolf came trotting out of the undergrowth, a heavily built brute of an animal, and the Roman instinctively strode towards it with his spear half raised, ready either to throw or wield in self-defence if the animal attacked, but the wolf, lacking the support of his pack, only stood his ground, lips pulled back in a fearsome snarl.

Striding swiftly towards the beast, Marius raised the spear, took a moment to pick his spot and then let fly, putting the heavy iron blade straight into the snarling face with enough force to tear the wolf's jaw from its socket and rip deep into its chest, sending the animal into a paroxysm of thrashing agony. Drawing his sword he screamed defiance at the gathering pack, the wolves taken aback by the abject state of their leader.

'Gods, Marius, what you *do*?'

Beran was alongside him, shaking his head in amazement at the pack leader's writhing agony.

'There is a time to be the forest and there is a time to be a man! And I am not just a man, I am a Roman *fucking* centurion!' He stamped forward, finishing the dying animal with a brutal hack of the sword's iron blade across the back of its neck, then turned to the hesitant pack with a roar of berserk defiance, waving the bloodied weapon at them. 'Come on then! Have some of this!'

The pack considered the Roman for a moment as he strode forward, ignoring the risk that they might still attack together, the bubbling screams of their dying leader clearly having unnerved them, their disquiet growing as Beran stepped alongside him, ready to throw his own spear. The cold-eyed male closest to the two men considered them for a moment, then turned and loped away, followed by the remainder of the pack, and Beran allowed a long breath to gust from his body as he watched their unhurried departure.

'Beran always submit to wulfa. Until this day. Now that time over.' He walked over to the dying wolf, nodding at the spread-eagled corpse. 'You not friend Mariuz now. You *brother* Mariuz. Hunt brother.' The Roman smiled wearily, suddenly bone weary in reaction to the events of the previous moments, but Beran pointed back to the stag's carcass. 'Now we got two times work. Skin and butcher heruta, then same with wulfa. Give krubjan that left to wulfa.'

'Krubjan?'

'Bone and meat we not take.'

'The wolves will eat their own kind?'

The German laughed softly.

'Every animal eat own kind, brother Mariuz. Even man. You go back to legion, you find out, I think. Now come, much work, little time. And Beran hungry for heruta liver.'

10

The Fog River, September AD 70

'What do you expect his terms will be?'

Kivilaz brushed a speck of dirt from his tunic before answering Hramn's question, looking down the length of the bridge on which he and the Roman general Cerialis were to meet. Constructed specifically for the purpose of their conference, a five-pace gap had been left in the central span, a void too wide for an armoured soldier to leap but sufficiently narrow for two men to negotiate with each other. At Kivilaz's back what remained of the Batavi army had been paraded in ordered ranks, his guardsmen closest to the bridge and the remnants of the once mighty cohorts at their rear with what was left of their tribal allies formed up behind them. The soldiers were clearly exhausted, their clothing and equipment worn to the point of destruction by months of campaigning, but their ranks were ordered and precise, and every man present stood with a straight back and a stern expression, discipline maintained to the last. The Romans were just visible at the far end in the dank, drizzle-filled air, a full legion standing in equally disciplined ranks behind the party of a dozen men who were gathered around their legatus augusti.

'Look at them and then you tell me. He's accompanied by a legion, the bloody-handed Twenty-first from the look of them, but he has three more available at the sound of a trumpet. If we fail to agree terms then all he has to do is cross the river and we'll have nowhere to run. He's burned out every farm on the Island except for those owned by our family, the cunning bastard, which means that our support has dwindled to almost nothing. The German tribes are no longer willing to stand with us, not with a Roman army eager to be at their throats and the better part of their manhood either dead or fought out after the disaster at the Old Camp. And we've fought on for three months since that fateful day when one among us betrayed our battle plan to them, but all to no effect. Our men are exhausted, and they sense the lack of will among the people of the tribe clearly enough, which only makes them less inclined to be the last men to die in a war that now has no meaning. All of which means that if we choose to fight on we'll be forced to surrender in short order, and on whatever terms they deign to allow us. Cerialis has won this war, and he knows it.' He raised a hand to gesture at the Roman general, visible at the bridge's far end among his escort. 'I am commanded to come alone to this *discussion*, but Cerialis brings lictors, secretaries and bodyguards, and even that bastard traitor Labeo if my eyes don't deceive me, all to reinforce his superiority over me. He's won, and he wants me to be in no doubt that he's got his sword at my throat.'

He sighed.

'So what do I expect from Cerialis? Nothing good. He will either order me to kill myself, here and now, or, if his master has ordered him to be merciful, he may send me to Rome to argue for my life, and possibly to be spared in return for exile from my tribe, perhaps in Rome, perhaps somewhere much farther away. Either way, today marks the end of my time leading our people. From today a new era begins, and you must face the realities of this situation without my help, the only man in the tribe with the influence to hold onto the power that remains to the ruling families. Cooperate, Hramn, play the respectful and penitent war hero. Put the responsibility for this war on my shoulders and be public with your regret for the things that war forced upon you. Deny all foreknowledge of the things that Rome will charge me with, the massacre of the Old Camp legions and the death of Lupercus. Do all of these things and with a little good fortune you will find yourself in a position of power once again.'

He paused, lowering his voice to be sure that they were not overheard.

'And on that day move swiftly and decisively to take control. Use intimidation and murder if you have to, but re-establish our family as the foremost in the tribe. If other families stand against us then do whatever you have to do to intimidate and control them. Fight from the shadows, nephew, but fight with only one aim, to be the victor. We may have lost our fight to be independent of Rome, but we can still return our fortunes to the position we held before this war was forced upon us. Don't let me down in this.'

The younger man scowled at the legion massed on the other side of the river.

'I won't. You know what I'm capable of. Who was it that put your nephew Briganticus to the spear, when he came at you like a fell-handed maniac in that last battle before we fell back to this side of the Rhenus? Whatever it takes, whoever I have to kill, I will restore our family to power. I swear this. I'll make a start with the wolf-priest, and make sure that he can never betray the tribe again.'

Kivilaz nodded.

'As you see fit, you have my blessing. And now, I suppose, the time has come to go and talk to this Roman once again, and see what fate he has in mind for his one-time friend.'

He stalked out onto the bridge, conscious that the eyes of his followers were upon him as he walked slowly down its length until he reached the point where the gap had been left in its structure. Folding his arms, he watched impassively as Cerialis made the same walk on his own side of the crossing, waving away most of his party with the exception of a pair of scribes and a hulking figure who Kivilaz recognised with a hard smile. The Roman reached the edge of his half of the bridge and looked down at the Fog River's dark water flowing beneath him, then back up at the Batavi leader waiting in silence for him to speak.

'Gaius Julius Civilis. It's been a long road to this strangest of meetings, since the last time we spoke in Rome.'

Kivilaz stared across the gap that separated the two men in silence for a moment, his face as impassive as stone under the other man's scrutiny.

'Long and bloody.'

Cerialis nodded.

'It's certainly been that. A dozen battles or more. Two legions temporarily lost to desertion and another two destroyed for ever, slaughtered almost to the last man it seems, despite your promises that they would be spared if they abandoned the Old Camp. A legion fortress razed to the ground, a fleet suborned and turned against Rome along with numerous auxiliary cohorts . . .' He paused and stared at the Batavi nobleman questioningly. 'And yet all of that death and destruction has ultimately proven fruitless. And so here we are, at the end of your rebellion, with tens of thousands of men dead, a province in ruins, and your people's survival hanging in the balance. Under the circumstances I feel constrained to ask you just what it was that you were hoping to achieve? It's not as if you lacked guidance from my father-in-law's generals, is it? You might have believed that the assault upon the Old Camp would be forgiven when he became emperor, given that you were diverting military resources that could otherwise have faced us in Italy and turned the battle in favour of Vitellius, but once that battle was won you seem to have lost your mind? You attacked a Roman fortress, an act that you knew Rome could not tolerate. Why? What was it that stopped you from quietly abandoning your revolt, once it was clear that Vespasianus was going to be emperor? Surely you know that he would have accepted you back into the empire with an equal lack of drama, had you chosen to do so?'

The Batavi shrugged.

'I was committed. Gaul rose against you, much as I expected, and I saw the chance for our combined strength to close the door against any attempt to reconquer us.' He laughed bitterly. 'If I'd known just how ineffective the Gauls would prove to be, I might have been more circumspect.'

Cerialis raised his eyebrows.

'You were *committed*? So it was all an expensive gamble. But tell me, what expectation of mercy can you really think you have now? Why would I take your hand, after all the good men you've had murdered? I'll warn you now that I've heard more than enough stories about your own bloodthirstiness to have hardened my heart against any idea that you might live out a quiet retirement in Rome, in case you have hopes of the traditional imperial indulgence to a defeated but honourable enemy. You'd have the same hard view as I do if you were in my place. Officers forced to fight their own men? Legionaries used as living targets for your son's javelin practice? Two legions herded into a trap to be hacked to death by your vengeful German allies? These are not the acts of Gaius Julius Civilis, honourable foe of Rome, they are crimes of war perpetrated by a barbarian whose infamy will rank alongside that of Arminius before you.'

Kivilaz shrugged, affecting to be untroubled by the venom in the Roman's voice.

'That will be a decision for Vespasianus, I would imagine, and not for you. I am a Roman citizen, as you well know, and I demand my day in Rome. I *demand* an imperial judgement. And who knows, you Romans do love your noble barbarians, do you not? Perhaps my one-eyed arrogance in defeat will persuade enough of you to petition the emperor that he will choose to be magnanimous and spare me? After all . . .' he grinned unashamedly, 'I only rose up at the direct instigation of Marcus Hordeonius Flaccus, Gaius Plinius Secundus and Marcus Antonius Primus, as I can prove by producing their correspondence and calling upon Plinius and Primus to bear witness to the truth of my assertions. It was only my fear of the revenge that would be exacted on my people by the returning legions, no matter who won, that convinced me to keep fighting when your father-in-law took power. As for the "crimes" you mention, most of them are lies invented by my enemies to blacken my name, and the destruction of the Old Camp legions was an unfortunate miscalculation.'

He fell silent, and Cerialis shook his head in disbelief.

'The deaths of thousands of men? A *miscalculation*?'

'Yes. You surely can't imagine that I actually intended such a thing to happen? I counted on my German allies being able to keep their warriors under control when the legions marched out in defeat, but their rage at the losses they took over the six months of the siege was greater even than I had predicted. I simply miscalculated what they would do.'

'I see. It was a *miscalculation,* was it,' Cerialis almost spat the word out, 'that cost the lives of all those men? There is a man serving with my army who will bear witness, as you put it, that it was nothing of the kind.' He gestured to Aquillius, looming behind him, his hate-filled eyes locked on Kivilaz. 'I doubt very much that Vespasianus would be minded to view *that* evidence with any predisposition to lenience. And that's before I come to consider the murder of a Roman gentleman, a war hero who resisted your attacks until he and his men were reduced to literally eating the grass that grew in the gaps between the cobbles of the Old Camp's streets. You imprisoned Quintus Munius Lupercus, a Roman senator, you shipped him across the Rhenus to your German allies and you colluded in his execution by whatever barbaric methods they use on their most hated enemies.'

Kivilaz shook his head.

'That is most assuredly *not* true. Munius Lupercus was exactly what you describe, an honoured foe with whom I fought in Britannia. He was being transported to serve a period in captivity as the servant of the Bructeri priestess Veleda, as—'

Cerialis overrode him with all the arrogance of a man used to being heard rather than forced to listen.

'Rome is aware of the woman, and her part in encouraging your rising. I can assure you that she will be dealt with when the time is right. And if you're going to tell me that Lupercus was to serve a short period of captivity before being released, simply to prove the magnanimous generosity of the German tribes in victory, you can save your breath. I've heard of your boasts that he was destined for a lifetime of slavery but I still prefer to believe that your intention was only ever for his murder, to assuage the tribes' lust for Roman blood.'

'Lupercus committed suicide! He killed my nephew Bairaz and used his sword to kill himself!'

Cerialis shook his head in firm denial.

'Nonsense. The man was as weak as a kitten from months of privation, he could no more have fought his way free of your guardsmen than you're going to be able to talk your way out of having ordered his murder.'

'There was a centurion, a man called Marius! He could have killed Lupercus! Ask him!' He pointed at Aquillius. 'He knew the man, he can vouch that—'

'Enough!'

Kivilaz fell silent, contemplating Cerialis with the calculation of a man who instinctively knew his fate was close to hand. The Roman spoke again, his voiced pitched low so that only Kivilaz could hear him over the river's ripples.

'Do you want to know what I find funny in all this, Civilis?'

'Tell me. I could welcome some humour.'

'What amuses me is the irony of your position. All those lies you've told about how the deaths of our legionaries cannot be laid at your feet? Even if they were true, nobody would ever believe them. History will say that you ordered the destruction of the surrendered legions, that you had your son throw spears at helpless prisoners and that you instructed your men to force Roman to fight Roman in the Old Camp's arena.' He pointed at the imperturbable Aquillius. 'He's the living proof of all those accusations. Your lies will be refuted and left to rot where they fall. And as a consequence, the only truth you *might* be telling – that you never intended Lupercus to die – that will be rejected as yet another lie as well. In seeking to muddy the waters over matters that Vespasianus might have found a way to forgive, or blame on others, you will die for a crime against Rome's ruling class that you might never have intended.'

'But if you think I'm telling the truth . . .'

'Why order your death on the basis that you're lying? A calculating man like you already knows the answer to that question. Rome needs to put a head on a spike, Civilis, someone to point to and say "he has lived". Someone the people can blame for this uprising, to take the focus away from the ruling class's crass mistakes of the last few years. And that head can only be yours. Your citizenship has been expunged from the record, and as you are no longer a citizen of Rome there is no need for Rome to grant you the dignity of a trial before the emperor. Instead, I have been given clear instructions as to your fate, instructions that Vespasianus agonised over for weeks before issuing the order, and finally only agreed with the assistance of his colleague Gaius Hosidius Geta, a man known to you and whom he felt he could trust to consider the matter from the perspective of a man who undoubtedly owes you his life. You will die, Gaius Julius Civilis, today. Here. Now. And by your own hand. If you acquiesce to this order your people will be treated with the greatest leniency. Our alliance will be restored. Your people's immunity from tax will continue just as it was before this unfortunate revolt. Your cohorts will continue to serve, although without their horses and never as anything more than single cohorts, or anywhere close to home for that matter. After all, you've taught us a few painful lessons as to just how to manage the military units contributed by our subject peoples.'

'And am I to presume that my former colleague, and indeed your own, for that matter, Claudius Labeo, is to rule the Batavi after my death, given his presence here? Will you disband the council of our elders and give power to a man who has broken every alliance he ever forged?'

Cerialis shrugged.

'I am yet to decide how and by whom the Batavi will be governed, but I can assure you that your family will have no part in it. For now Labeo is here to demonstrate that the decision is not for you and your cronies, but rather an imperial prerogative.'

Kivilaz nodded wearily.

'And Batavodurum?'

'Your capital will be reconstructed in a place where it cannot be fortified and defended. And a legion will be set to watch it, one of my better house-trained legions and not the Twenty-first, as has been suggested to me by men whose first priority is revenge. I have the Second Adiutrix in mind. All of these concessions to continued alliance will be granted to your people . . .'

He paused, and Kivilaz nodded his understanding.

'But I have to die. By my own hand?'

Cerialis smiled bleakly.

'Why would I deny you that one last honour? I'm not a monster, simply the man who has to enact imperial policy. Would you like some time to compose yourself?'

Kivilaz shook his head.

'I've had the best part of a year in which to make my peace with the gods. All I need is a reliable and suitably honourable man to perform the mercy stroke once I've opened my guts.' He gestured to the men clustered at the bridge's end. 'If you'll allow me to make my choice?'

The Roman inclined his head gravely.

'Of course, Prince Civilis. Take all the time you need.'

The Batavi officers waiting at the bridge's northern end watched gravely as their prince walked slowly back to them, stiffening their backs as he stopped and looked around them.

'My fate is sealed, brothers. The Romans have pledged to allow the tribe to return to their service without further punishment, under their officers and not our own, of course, and as infantry-only cohorts, which will be posted far away to prevent any further risk of uprising, but we will retain our tax exemption in return for their service. A legion will be billeted on the Island but with orders to respect our people. There will be no resettlement and no enslavement. Cerialis will keep his dogs muzzled. He will grant the tribe all of these concessions in the name of a continued alliance with Rome only if I kill myself, here and now, for all to see. I have accepted, of course, as my last act as commander of the tribe's army.'

Hramn nodded slowly.

'I will stand as second to you with pride.'

Kivilaz shook his head.

'I expected this, and I have given thought to means by which I intend to leave this world.' He turned to Alcaeus. 'You have a chosen man who goes by the tent name of Achilles, if I recall correctly? The man who captured Labeo's assassin and prevented an attempt on my life?'

The wolf-priest nodded gravely.

'Yes, my prince. He is a man whose family is of unquestionable honour, and whose father and brother died in your service, one at Augusta Trevorum, the other after the battle at the Old Camp, giving his life to save his son. There is no better man among us to stand with you.'

'Fetch him here, and warn him of what it is that will be expected of him.' He smiled wearily, patting the hilt of his sword. 'Once this blade is sheathed in my guts I have no desire to provide the Romans with the satisfaction of the slightest sign of distress, so I'll be expecting a quick and clean ending at his hands. A death with honour.'

The centurion inclined his head in a gesture of respect.

'Of course, my prince.'

Kivilaz turned away and walked towards the waiting cohorts. Hramn looked at his uncle with the expression of a man who had expected a gift that had not been forthcoming.

'You're going to ask a man with no family blood in his veins to be your second? You're going to trust a man you don't even know to give you the mercy stroke?'

Kivilaz looked at his nephew levelly for a moment before continuing.

'I must go to my grave with the least fanfare possible, if our family is to survive the storms that will batter it this winter. Better for me to choose a man of impeccable honour from the ranks of my army to give me my peace than for there to be any way for our enemies to accuse me of seeking to build a dynasty in my last moments. And besides . . .'

He stared at his nephew for a long moment.

'We started this war, Hramn, and for the most part we have avoided its hardships, while our men, especially those of the cohorts, have been bled white in battle after battle. It is important for us to be seen to be aligned with their sacrifice, to be men of the tribe and in no way setting ourselves above it. That's why I'll have the mercy stroke delivered by a man who's given everything he has in that painful, bloody retreat. For the good of our family I will be seen to seek a humble and honourable exit from this life at the hands of a Batavi war hero.' He looked out into the drizzle, nodding to himself. 'And besides that, because it is the right thing to do. History will judge me better for making this simple choice. Send him out to me when Alcaeus brings him here.'

He turned back to the bridge, calling his last words back over his shoulder.

'And remember what I told you – our family's day is not done, just as long as you have the sense to keep your head down.'

'Don't ask me to do this.'

Alcaeus shook his head at Egilhard.

'I'm not asking you to do it, Achilles. I'm not even ordering you. I'm telling you that you have no choice in the matter.'

The chosen man shook his head in bafflement.

'But—'

'I don't know what's in your mind? I have no idea what you might be capable of?' He reached out a hand and gripped the collar of Egilhard's mail armour, pulling the younger man so close that he could whisper and still be heard. 'Trust me, I *know*. I told your father before he died, and now I'll tell you. I have dreamed of this day every night for the last year, more or less, which means that I know exactly what you're capable of. And in my dream you walk out onto that bridge just as Prince Kivilaz has ordered.'

'And after that? Have you seen what follows?'

The wolf-priest nodded into his chosen man's questioning stare.

'I have. All of it.'

Egilhard looked into his eyes for a moment longer and then nodded.

'Very well. I cannot argue with the gods themselves.'

Alcaeus took the brass-bound hastile from his unresisting hands and passed it to Lanzo.

'Here. He won't be needing this.'

He led the slightly dazed soldier towards the bridge, telling him what it was that his prince would expect of him as they walked.

'This is Kivilaz's last moment in history. He knows that whatever he says, and however he dies, will be remembered by every man watching, written about in the histories and passed down for generations to come. He will repeat his justifications for leading us to war, refuse to accept the Romans' accusations of ordering the slaughter of the legions he captured when the Old Camp fell, and generally pose as a man doing what was forced upon him. And with that done he will kill himself, or rather he will take his sword to himself and expect you to finish the job with one swift killing stroke, severing his head from his shoulders. He'll be in the most appalling pain, and he will expect you to put him out of that pain as quickly as you can.'

The younger man nodded slowly, lost in thought as they reached the bridge's foot. Hramn turned from his contemplation of Kivilaz's lonely figure to face them, his furious expression revealing the humiliation he was feeling at not having been selected to grant his uncle the mercy stroke.

'He knows what is expected?'

Alcaeus nodded.

'He does. I have told him that every moment he delays will be an hour of agony for the prince.'

The big man nodded brusquely, addressing Egilhard directly.

'Do this properly and there will be a reward for you. But if my uncle suffers unnecessarily, you'll pay the same price. Do you understand?'

Egilhard nodded, holding the prefect's stare.

'Perfectly, Prefect.'

'Very well, go out there and do as you are ordered. Let's get this over and go home. This war is over, and I have better places to be.'

Walking out onto the bridge the young soldier realised that he was being watched by hundreds of men on both sides of the river. On the far bank a cohort of legionaries was drawn up in neat, orderly ranks, their armour and helmets gleaming faintly in the damp, drizzle-filled air, a stark contrast to the weary remnants of the Batavi cohorts whose equipment and clothing were rusted and threadbare from months in the field, the soldiers themselves gaunt from lack of food and beaten down by the succession of defeats they had endured since the disaster at Gelduba. As he neared the end of the bridge he saw that the Roman general Cerialis was standing on the other side of the hastily opened gap in the central span with a familiar figure. His gaze met the big man's stare for a moment, Aquillius nodding his recognition of the Batavi soldier with a directness that raised the hairs on the back of Egilhard's neck.

'You are the soldier that my army has chosen to name Achilles? The man who saw off an attempt to kill me in my own tent?'

Egilhard bowed.

'Yes, my prince.'

Kivilaz shook his head.

'There is no need for formality. I am Kivilaz, simply a warrior now, and I will shortly accept my fate and kill myself in order to spare my people the indignities of a Roman occupation in force. Your part in this is to swing that sword of yours, an honoured blade that has tasted the blood of our enemies on a dozen battlefields, if the stories I hear of your deeds are true?'

He paused, a questioning expression on his face and Egilhard nodded impassively.

'They are true. This sword has sung, both in my hands and in those of my father Lataz and my uncle Wulfa.'

'Good. Then I will be the last man to fall in this war, and to a blade whose honour cannot be maligned. When I am done you must cast the weapon as far out into the river as you can, to prevent the Romans from taking it from you and parading it through Rome to be placed at the emperor's feet, as is their way. Let it go to the river goddess and bear testimony to my sacrifice. And make it quick, one swift blow to end me and give me peace from the agony these Romans have demanded I inflict upon myself, you understand? I have no desire to spend any more time in the agony between life and death than is necessary.'

Egilhard nodded, unable to speak such was the strength of emotion running through him. Kivilaz, meeting his gaze, was satisfied. He turned back to the waiting Romans, his long hair streaming out in the fresh breeze that was whipping the river's water into waves that lapped at the bridge.

'I am ready to satisfy the terms of our agreement, Petillius Cerialis! Tell me again how you will uphold your part of the bargain.'

The Roman legatus augusti nodded, his voice booming out over the wind's thin whistle.

'I, Quintus Petillius Cerialis, the appointed representative of the emperor Titus Flavius Caesar Vespasianus Augustus, declare that, when Gaius Julius Civilis has surrendered his life to the declared sentence of the emperor, there will henceforth be renewed peace and allegiance between the peoples of Rome and the Batavian tribe! The Batavian cohorts will be welcomed back into the service of Rome, to serve as our trusted allies and safeguard our frontiers against external enemies! The terms of our historic treaty with the Batavian people will be renewed, and respected in perpetuity, and the Batavian homeland will be safeguarded from any aggression by Rome's enemies by the presence of a legion selected by myself and with orders to respect both the property and people of the Batavian tribe! Rome and the Batavian tribe will be at peace, and no penalty, financial or otherwise, will be levied for this brief period of disagreement! Gaius Julius Civilis, do you accept the terms of the agreement as I have made them clear to you?'

Kivilaz nodded, raising his arms and opening them wide as if to encompass the land on the far side of the river.

'I do! But before I go to meet my ancestors as your chosen price for this new, *golden age* of peace, I will first state my case! Let history decide on the rights and wrongs of my people's rebellion against Rome's betrayal of our alliance, but let it do so in full knowledge of the facts, when the story of these times comes to be written!'

He stared intently at Cerialis who, fully expecting his demand, simply waved a gracious hand as a signal for him to continue.

'For generations my people have been steadfast allies of Rome! We were called "the best and bravest", and granted the pride of place in the line of battle by our parent legion! When the Iceni tribe rose against Rome, destroying cities and despoiling their inhabitants, it was the Batavi who took their iron to Rome's enemy and broke the Iceni people, and yet it was the Fourteenth Legion that claimed the glory. As the years passed, our parent legion came to take our service for granted, belittling us at every opportunity, and when we expressed dissatisfaction we were chastised for disloyalty! Our cohorts won the battle that placed Vitellius on the throne, and yet our reward was nothing more than a handful of empty promises from that faithless impostor and a plan to distribute our men throughout the legions, supposedly to replace their battle losses but in truth, and all too evidently, as a means of preventing the supposed threat of our prowess on the battlefield from becoming reality! Our treaty with Rome was ripped up by the very man we had gifted with the empire, and Rome's centurions were sent to conscript our youth, abusing their power to make free with our children! What else was there for us but to rise up against this abuse of our honourable service?'

He stared directly at Cerialis, his eyes blazing with indignation.

'And what of the promises we were made? In letters from your emperor's general Marcus Antonius Primus I was offered a free Batavi homeland, to be governed as my people saw fit, offers made on behalf of Titus Flavius Vespasianus to encourage me to lead my people against Vitellius and sink a dagger into his back, forcing him to fight two wars with forces barely adequate for a single enemy! Offers reinforcing those I had already received from Vitellius's legatus augusti for Germania, Hordeonius Flaccus, may his spirit find rest after his murder by his own men, acting against the interests of his master and in the clandestine service of Vespasianus! Offers that were in turn repeats of the blandishments of Gaius Plinius Secundus, friend to both Vespasianus and his son-in-law Quintus Petillius Cerialis who now leads Rome's forces against the Batavi! The Batavi people were subjected to a deluge of promises when Vespasianus needed the Batavi's threat to distract his rival for the throne, but once his rule was secure those promises were forgotten! And what of myself and my family?'

He shook his head as if in sadness.

'My family have served Rome faithfully since the time of the first Caesar, before Rome was ever an empire! We accepted Rome's friendship and allied ourselves with her interests, never once considering any alternative until my brother Paulus's flimsily justified execution, and my own brutal arrest and transport to Rome to be tried and murdered, a murder only averted by the death of Nero. And no sooner had I returned to my homeland, sworn to live quietly for the remainder of my days, than I was arrested once more by Vitellius, to satisfy the anger of his centurions, then released as a means of keeping the Batavi quiet until such time as there was enough strength to deal with us once and forever! You accuse me of treason? Consider the mind of a man who has cheated death twice, both times by the width of a hair, and who knows that the inevitable third attempt will not fail for the lack of resolution on the part of the men holding the blades. What is he to do, that man threatened for a third time? Should he smile and accept his would-be murderers' repeated betrayal, or should he rise up against them with every ounce of his strength? I know what any Roman would do! Why should a man of the Batavi be any different?

'You accuse the Batavi of breaking treaties and betraying Rome? I say that it was Rome who inflicted the first wounds on our previously happy relationship, expecting the Batavi to smile and bear the repeated insults! You thought you could dominate us, and reduce us to a subject people! You were wrong! You accuse me of leading that betrayal, of plotting with Vindex and of desiring to make myself king of the Batavi and rule Germania? I say that all I ever wanted was to be left in peace, a peace you rudely disturbed not once but twice, executing my brother and making my own fate very clear! You thought you could sweep me aside and leave my people leaderless! You were wrong! And now you call me a murderer, and accuse me of going too far in the rebellion that you begged me to raise! You say I killed your colleague Lupercus! I tell you he committed suicide! You say I slaughtered two legions when they surrendered to the Batavi for lack of food? I say it was my allies from across the river, provoked one time too many by men like him!' he pointed to Aquillius, who stared back at him expressionlessly. 'Provoked by disfigurements inflicted on helpless tribesmen, by a refusal to allow our dead to be retrieved from the field of battle with dignity, by inhuman and barbaric means of war that left their victims between life and death. You call us *barbarians*? You are the barbarians now, burning farms and murdering their occupants! Yes, I will do as you wish and end my life, if it is the price I must pay for peace, but Rome should consider its part in this war with care, if it is to avoid inflaming other peoples with the same wanton lack of regard with which it provoked the Batavi! Let my words enter your historical record as a rebuke to every man involved in bringing about this sad state of affairs for which I will now pay with my life!'

He fell silent, staring obdurately at Cerialis, who looked back at him for a long moment before drawing breath to reply with equal vigour.

'Gaius Julius Civilis, there is a good deal of truth in what you say! Rome's relationship with your people has become more troubled than the emperor is willing to countenance as acceptable! From this moment onward Rome will manage its relationship with the Batavian people with more care. This does not, however, excuse your people's uprising against Rome becoming a war, with repeated and bloody attacks on our armies and their fortresses, and Rome's swift and entirely justified response is no less than you can have expected when you personally threw that first spear over our walls! You yourself have indeed been mistreated, but your response has been to abuse the trust placed in you by our legionaries when you starved them into surrendering, to callously murder a Roman senator and to massacre his legions almost to the last man, forcing those few captives you took to fight each other in the arena like common slaves, and using their living bodies as targets for spear practice. You have led your people to transgress the usual rules both of protest and war and now you will personally pay the price demanded of you by the emperor, the life of the man responsible for these crimes against the empire in return for the emperor's forgiveness, and his renewed favour for your people! You have accepted the terms that have been offered, so if you wish to afford the Batavian people the continued friendship of Rome you must now conduct yourself with the dignity that both Rome and your people expect and deserve, and end your life in a manner that will reflect credit upon you and your tribe for accepting defeat with grace and magnanimity! I have nothing more to say, and you have spoken to the limits of my patience! Let this be ended now, so that we can declare that you have lived, and put this matter in the past where it belongs!' He lowered his voice, speaking directly to Kivilaz. 'As do you, Julius Civilis. You are a throwback to a more brutal age and you have no place here. End your story and take your leave of a life that no longer requires your blood thirsty choler.'

Kivilaz nodded, turning to Egilhard with an expression devoid of animation, as if all of his anger had been spent in his final oration to leave him devoid of passion. Ignoring the rain, now falling with sufficient force to be audible against the iron of the soldier's helmet, he drew his sword, lowering his body into a kneeling position facing away from the Romans and placing the weapon's point against his stomach. Looking up at the young soldier he nodded, his lips tightening to a hard line as he readied himself to commit the act that would end his life.

'You know what is expected of you. A swift death, so that I may betray none of the agony I will know when this blade pierces me. Strike surely, and grant me that mercy, and you will be rewarded richly both in this life and the Underworld.'

Tensing his body, he gripped the sword's hilt with both hands, looked up to the skies and pulled it towards him with a convulsive jerk, the point punching through his stomach wall with an audible crunch as the muscles parted around the blade. Grunting with the pain, he pulled again at the weapon, wrenching it forward and stabbing the blade deep into his body, hunching forward over the sword as the overwhelming pain of the cold iron's intrusion gripped him, his voice little more than a strained whisper.

'Kill me.'

Egilhard looked down at him for a moment and then swept out Lightning, sliding one foot forward into a braced stance, ready to swing the sword high and then cut at the prince's neck with all his power to sever the agonised man's head. Ready to strike, he muttered one word, loud enough for Kivilaz to hear whilst inaudible to anyone else.

'No.'

'What?'

'No. There will be no easy death for you, Prince Kivilaz.'

The agonised nobleman hunched forward over the weapon whose blade was sheathed deep in his body, his crotch and thighs red with the blood that was seeping from the wound in his stomach, forcing his head round to stare uncomprehendingly up at the hard-faced soldier.

'W . . . what? What . . . are . . . you . . .'

'My brother didn't die easily. He coughed blood over me, stabbed through by a spear with his wind leaking out through the hole it left when the Roman who killed him tore it free. He cried for his mother as he choked out his life. When *you* cry out for your mother I will consider granting you release.'

'What's he doing?' Hramn paced towards the bridge's foot with a puzzled expression, shaking his head slightly as he wondered what it was that he was seeing. 'He should have given Kivilaz the death stroke by now.'

'Your uncle is cut from harder stone than the rest of us. Perhaps he is testing himself against the pain, showing the Romans how long a Batavi warrior can last before he calls on his second.'

The big man looked back at Alcaeus, finding nothing in the priest's face to gainsay the note of respect in his voice.

'Perhaps . . .'

*

Egilhard spat the hatred that had grown and festered within him over the hard months of the cohorts' destruction at Kivilaz's uncomprehending, upturned face.

'My father didn't die easily. He ran for an afternoon as his life bled out of an arm severed in the course of a doomed battle fought at your command, and at the end he threw himself onto an enemy spear to spare my life. He died because of you, so now you can suffer for him. And when you can't control yourself any longer, when you have to scream with the pain, *then* I might send you to join him in the Underworld!'

'What's he doing? Shouldn't he have cut off the man's head by now? Or do the Batavians have a different way with these matters?'

Aquillius shook his head at Cerialis's question.

'No different to the rest of us. He holds the death blow. Why I do not know, but there is no mercy in that man.'

'Kill . . . me . . . you . . . young . . . bastard . . .'

Egilhard shook his head, his flint-hard eyes locked on the nobleman's hate-filled and yet imploring face.

'No. You haven't earned that death. You've earned what you're getting, what you gave my brother and my father. They endured because they had no choice but to do so, and so can you because you have no choice in the matter either.'

'This is *wrong*! Your man is letting him suffer!'

Alcaeus shook his head in evident disbelief.

'Kivilaz must have ordered him to hold his arm. Why else would he . . .'

Hramn rounded on him, his eyes suddenly wide with anger.

'You've seen this, haven't you! You *know*!' He drew his sword, pointing to the two figures at the bridge's centre, one hunched over with both hands holding the hilt of his sword, the other waiting with his own blade upright, apparently ready to strike and yet showing no sign of granting his prince the release he surely craved. 'This is treachery! Batavi Guard, with me!'

He stamped forward onto the bridge with a handful of soldiers at his back, but as more men moved to follow him, Alcaeus drew his own sword and stepped into their path, raising his left hand in a gesture of denial.

'I *will* kill the next man to follow him. I have seen this in my dreams, and I know which one of you will test my resolve!'

He turned, shouting the words he had heard himself speak so many times in his sleep.

'Centurion Aquillius! Now is the moment of your sacrifice!'

Cerialis stared at the scene in amazement. Kivilaz was looking up at his second with an expression that combined supplication and hatred, while a group of his followers were hurrying up the bridge's length with their swords drawn.

'I never thought I'd see such a . . .'

'Centurion Aquillius! Now is the moment of your sacrifice!'

He frowned at the words, just audible over the wind's thin whistle, turning to look at his bodyguard only to see the big man pacing backwards from where he stood at the bridge's very end. 'What in Hades are you—'

Aquillius looked up, rocking backwards and forwards like a sprinter preparing to hurl himself at his track, his eyes focused on the other side of the severed central span.

'Step aside, Legatus Augusti. This is the moment when I must obey my oath.'

'But . . .'

The hulking centurion was in motion, his powerful thighs thrusting him towards the bridge's end as he strained every sinew in his body, and Cerialis realised that he had already been discounted as irrelevant. He stepped backwards, feeling the bridge's side against his back as the wooden surface beneath his feet shook with each thunderous impact of the big man's pounding feet. In a blur of motion, Aquillius was upon him, and the Roman shrank back as the centurion bellowed a challenge at the sky and hurled himself at the open space between the two halves of the severed crossing, leaping high into the empty air with his arms spread wide, his head thrown back to roar a single word.

'Hercules!'

Alcaeus met his attacker blade-to-blade, pushing the guardsman's sword wide and then snapping his vine stick, still gripped in his left hand, up into the other man's throat. Before his victim had time to register the fact that he was suddenly unable to breathe, the priest lunged with the sword, opening his neck to the bone, then kicked his shuddering body back into the group of his fellows crowding in behind him.

'No more of you will die today! But you *will* stand down!'

They faced him for a moment, twenty furious men confronting a lone centurion, torn between hatred for their comrade's killer and fear of the wolf's head affixed to his helmet and the absolute certainty in his voice. Then, as the boldest among them spat on the ground at his feet and raised his sword to attack, another voice spoke.

'That's. Fucking. *Enough!'*

To their rear, where a moment before there had been twenty paces of open ground between themselves and the men of the cohorts behind them, the guardsmen found themselves facing a wall of spears and shields, hostile faces staring at them with the dead-eyed knowledge of impending bloodshed. Lanzo stepped forward, his spear's point unwavering as he confronted them.

'Enough blood has been shed, too much of it ours and not enough of it *yours*! The cohorts have fought this war, and the men of the cohorts have died for the tribe by the thousand! And now the men of the cohorts are telling you to either stand down or die! Any man who raises his sword to Alcaeus raises that sword against *me*!'

Frijaz stepped forward alongside him.

'And me!'

On his other side Adalwin paced forward, his eyes blank with the promise of death.

'And me. Chose a side, you cunts, and make it quick.'

★

Egilhard shook his head at the shuddering prince, staring down into his tear-streaked eyes.

'Not nearly enough. You've a while more in you yet.'

The bridge's wooden surface began to tremble with the running feet of the guardsmen hurrying towards them, and Kivilaz turned his head to look at them, a chuckle staining his lips with fresh blood.

'Here . . . comes . . . your . . . doom . . . boy . . .'

Egilhard stepped past the kneeling figure and raised his sword, readying himself for what he knew could only be a brief and one-sided fight, then looked back in amazement as the bridge shuddered with a sudden shock behind him, recognition dawning as a hulking figure straightened up from the crouch into which he had dropped as his feet had touched down on the wooden surface only inches from the edge of the roughly hacked gap.

'You're the *Banô*!'

Aquillius drew his sword, kicked Kivilaz brutally against the bridge's side and stepped alongside Egilhard.

'Your priest told me this day would come. And that when it did I would fight alongside the greatest swordsman in your tribe. Now is your chance to prove him right.'

The guardsmen were upon them, Hramn at their head, their shields a wall of wood and iron as all five of his men stepped alongside their prefect at his shouted command.

'Leave the traitor to me! And a farm to the man who kills the *Banô*!'

They advanced with the co-ordinated expertise of long practice, step after step towards the waiting pair of swordsmen, and Aquillius grinned back at them, his voice almost conversational as he waited for his moment.

'You know the problem you people have?' Egilhard shook his head blankly, seeing his death approaching in the implacable guardsmen's eyes. 'With all that drill you do, you've forgotten how to do *this* . . .'

He lunged forward, grinning savagely as the line of men facing him raised their spears to take him down and then, as they thrust the iron-tipped poles forward into his face he dropped, rolling beneath the questing spearheads and came back to his feet face-to-face with them. Pulling down the closest man's shield with contemptuous ease, he used his superior height to stab the gladius in his right hand down into the space behind his opponent's collarbone. The stricken guardsman coughed blood and died with a look of disbelief, as the sword's blade tore a huge wound in his lungs and stopped his heart. Leaving the weapon embedded hilt deep in the dying Batavi's body, the Roman plucked the spear from his unresisting fingers and spun it in his right hand, almost absentmindedly burying it deep in the booted foot of the man to his right. The wounded guardsman screamed in agony as Aquillius whipped out the dagger from the sheath on his left hip, releasing the spear's shaft and grasping the shield to his left. Pulling it savagely down to put its holder off balance, he drove the knife's blade through the Batavi's mail once, twice, three times, each blow tearing through the iron rings and opening a rent in his chest through which blood poured. A stab of intense pain stiffened his body as another man stabbed him in the back with his spear, the long iron blade punching through the Roman's scale armour. To the guardsman's amazement the big man whipped a hand round and took hold of the weapon, pulling it free of the wound and then turned, ducking under the weapon's shaft. Wrenching the spear away from its wielder, he rammed it back into the guardsman's body with enough force for the butt spike to punch through his mail and impale him, his hands pulling uselessly at the deeply embedded blade.

Not knowing whether his wound was mortal, but feeling the wet warmth of blood soaking into the subarmalis, he looked beyond the human wreckage surrounding him to the bridge's end where Egilhard was fighting a desperate battle against the remaining three Batavi, one of them the prefect Aquillius recognised from the moment that he had been stunned and carried away to the Old Camp's arena. Wielding his sword with dizzying speed, the young soldier was nevertheless being forced back towards the edge of the timbers by the trio's combined assault and, lacking the space in which to fight, had been reduced to desperate self-defence that could only end in his defeat as he tired. Grunting with the pain, the Roman straightened his back, feeling blood running down his legs from the wound, and judged from its flow that he had only a short period of consciousness left. Tearing the spear from his last victim's body as he passed, his first step was tentative, the second less so, and with the third he was running, no more than a trot, but moving as fast as his damaged body would allow, every step taking him closer to the remaining guardsmen, whose rasping breaths and the hammer of iron on Egilhard's increasingly tattered shield and flickering sword blade kept the sound of his hobnails on the bridge's timbers from them until it was too late. Hurling the spear into the closest man's back with such force that the blade tore through the front of his mail, he spread his arms wide and sprang at the Batavi prefect with a vengeful snarl. Turning at the last moment as he sensed the danger behind him, Hramn tried to raise his sword to defend himself from the oncoming centurion only to have it pushed aside as the big man wrapped his arms around him, butted him viciously with the brow guard of his helmet and then, as they tottered at the bridge's edge, the Batavi's feet scrabbling against the side boards as he fought to avoid the drop beneath them, made one last herculean effort and pushed them both over the bridge's railings and into the water below. The water closed over both men as the weight of their armour pulled them beneath the wind-riffled surface, and as Cerialis watched in amazement, all trace of whatever was happening beneath the river's rain-beaten surface was lost.

'Can someone just tell me what happened on that bridge?'

Cerialis looked from Antonius and Pugno to Longus, and then finally squarely at Àlcaeus and Draco, who had been summoned to his presence as the most senior members of their tribe's polity and what was left of its army. The wolf-priest had been disarmed on his arrival at the command tent, and a pair of Pugno's centurions had been stationed behind him with their swords drawn until the exasperated legatus augusti had dismissed them with a growl of frustration at their first spear.

'We're at peace, Pugno, or perhaps that had escaped your notice. He's disarmed, he's showing no sign of wanting to do anything other than talk, and to be quite frank I've seen more than enough blood for one lifetime. Is that clear, or do I have to post the Twenty-first somewhere cold and wet to make my point?'

Still clearly irascible, the general looked at each man in turn, waiting for an answer.

'Is any of you going to speak, or do I have to have this priest open up a lamb to tell me exactly what I'm supposed to make of all that?'

Draco raised a hand.

'If I may, Legatus Augusti?'

'I'd be grateful.'

The veteran officer stepped forward, leaning on his staff, and gestured to Alcaeus.

'What my centurion here cannot tell you, Legatus Augusti, for reasons of loyalty to the tribe, is that the men of our cohorts have become increasingly unhappy with this war. They have come to believe that Kivilaz's nephew Hramn squandered their lives in pursuit of his own thirst for glory, that Kivilaz himself ignored opportunities to make peace, and that their lives have been spent without regard to who was actually paying the price for their collective hubris. In selecting a soldier to end his life whose father and younger brother died alongside him in one futile battle after another, Prince Kivilaz quite simply chose the wrong man to act as his second.'

Cerialis looked at him appraisingly.

'And that's why he allowed the prince to die in agony, rather than cutting the man's head off once he had the sword in his guts?' Draco nodded impassively, and the Roman looked up at the command tent's roof for a moment before speaking. 'Gods below, you people never cease to amaze me. What will happen to him?'

Draco pursed his lips.

'There are precious few men of the tribe who feel that they owe any loyalty to the royal family these days. With the losses we've sustained over the last year, and the devastation your legions have visited on every part of the Island other than their farms, I think it's fair to say that very few men consider the old families to be their natural rulers any more. Indeed, it would be my expectation that you will wish to extend Rome's hospitality to what's left of Kivilaz's family, both to remove a rallying point for those men who still feel loyalty to them and for their own protection. Once you have appointed a new magistrate, the main concern will need to be feeding the tribe through the winter, and rebuilding Batavodurum, not with the rights and wrongs of what Egilhard did.'

'And if the old families decide to make an example of him, or just to have revenge for the agony he inflicted on their leader?'

The veteran prefect smiled slowly.

'I think you can leave that to me, Legatus Augusti. I wasn't exaggerating when I told you that their day is done. Once the prince's remaining kin have been shuffled off into exile, I expect their peers will quickly realise that even a hint of any attempt to retake their former influence will result in something similar for their own families. Or worse. And I also expect that his new prefect will decide to promote him to a position in which he's effectively untouchable, once your new magistrate has decided who it is that he believes should command the tribe's cohorts.'

Cerialis nodded.

'Which brings me to the main reason for calling you here. Your people do indeed need a new magistrate, someone not effectively appointed by the tribe's Julian families, but neither can that appointment just give power to the Claudians, for all that Claudius Labeo probably expects that he'll be the man of the moment in return for risking his life on Rome's behalf. Having spoken to the man, and reviewed his actions early in the war, it's evident to me that he's not to be trusted with power. I need a neutral, Prefect Draco, a man beholden to no man, who will govern your people through what is bound to be a difficult winter, with supplies and shelter both in short supply. You can have an election next summer when everything's settled down, when your farms have been rebuilt with the assistance of legion craftsmen and hunger and cold are no longer problems, but until then I need a dependable man to shepherd your people through the winter. Do you think you're up to it?'

Draco bowed respectfully, his face betraying no surprise at the offer.

'It would be my honour to lead my people for a short time, Legatus Augusti. Am I right in thinking that it would be within the new magistrate's remit to appoint a new prefect of the cohorts?'

The Roman nodded.

'Yes. It'll be more of a ceremonial position henceforth, of course, as your cohorts will never again be allowed to combine. Each one will always be commanded by a Roman prefect from now onwards, and your men will return to the Island on leave individually, rather than as formed units, but we'll still need a good officer to take charge of recruitment and training.'

Draco nodded.

'I have a man in mind. And yes, I accept your generous offer, Legatus Augusti. I will rule the tribe in full cooperation with the legion officers you appoint to supervise our recovery from this disaster, and I will ensure that we provide as many battle-ready cohorts as possible given the number of men who have survived this unfortunate war, once my warriors have had time to recover from the last few months.' He drew himself up and saluted. 'And now, with your permission, I'll go and get about readying the tribe for winter.'

Cerialis gestured to the tent's door.

'Thank you, Magistrate Draco. There'll be a formal proclamation posted before nightfall, but in the meantime just tell your people you speak with my authority. That ought to be enough when combined with your own natural authority.'

Alcaeus paused at the door, turning back with a question clearly on his lips.

'Centurion? Is there something I can do for you?'

The priest came to attention.

'Forgive me, Legatus Augusti, I have a question regarding your centurion. Aquillius, I mean.'

Cerialis nodded.

'I was waiting for you to ask. He told me that it was you who freed him, and that you believed he had a place in the plans of the gods for your prince. Do you still believe that?'

The Batavi nodded.

'Yes, sir. It happened just as I saw it in my dreams. I was wondering if any sign of him has been found?'

Cerialis looked to Pugno, who shook his head with absolute certainty.

'Your prefect's body was found on a sandbar a mile downstream. Drowned, of course. As must also be the case with Aquillius. No man can swim any distance wearing that much iron, never mind the fact that he'd also taken a spear blade in the back, and we didn't see either of them come up for air once they were in the water. My fleet officers tell me that the river will spit him out eventually, when it gets bored with playing with his corpse.'

Alcaeus nodded.

'Thank you, First Spear, I'm sure you're right. And at least he fulfilled his destiny before he died.'

With the Batavi officers out of the tent, Legatus Longus looked at his superior with a slightly puzzled expression.

'I know the man makes a good first impression, Petillius Cerialis, but is making an enemy soldier his tribe's magistrate a wise idea, even if he is retired? Surely that position should go to one of our own, if we want to be assured of total obedience?'

The senior officer sat back in his chair with a beatific smile.

'Ordinarily I would agree wholeheartedly, but in Prefect Draco's case there's something I know that you don't. Alfenius Varus can elucidate, I suspect.'

His senatorial colleague raised an eyebrow.

'Have you and our colleague Varus been keeping secrets from your officers, Legatus Augusti?'

Varus answered, his tone light.

'Not from choice. The Legatus Augusti and I were briefed

before we left Rome, taken into the confidence of the emperor's right-hand man Mucianus on the strict condition that what he told us was to be kept strictly to ourselves, Petillius Cerialis because he needed to know and myself to brief his replacement if such a thing came to pass. But I suppose that we can trust you and your first spear. And if we can't, then both of you will be exploring rather lower strata of the military rank structure than you've become used to, won't you?'

'Magistrate. Should I bow? Presumably you'll need some of those men the Romans employ to walk around in front of them with rods and axes?'

Draco eyed Alcaeus pityingly in the afternoon's drizzle.

'I'm not Roman, Priest, I'm Batavi. And I don't need lictors to scare respect out of my brother tribesmen, I can do that myself, thank you. But since you evidently find the idea of my reluctantly agreeing to rule the tribe for a few months amusing, you clearly don't realise that the joke's on you as much as it is on me. *Prefect.*'

The centurion stared at him for a moment.

'*What?*'

'You heard me. The cohorts need leadership, what's left of the guard need some sense beating into them if we're not to have some idiot or other start summoning the memory of Hramn and Kivilaz, and all too soon we'll need to start standing up cohorts for service elsewhere in the empire. It's going to be a shock to our men when they realise just how far from home they'll be serving, and how infrequently they're going to see their families. There'll need to be a training staff retained here, of course, and every man in what's left of the army will want to serve in it and stay here, rather than being posted to somewhere we've never even heard of for years at a time, so all things considered I'd say we're going to need a man who can combine good-natured diplomacy with vigorous discipline when the occasion calls for it. Wouldn't you?'

Alcaeus shook his head in only partially-feigned disgust.

'I'd imagined that I'd be allowed a little peace, now that we're done with killing Romans, instead of which you're offering me the chance to be hated by most of the army for choosing them to go away and kill the empire's enemies in far-off places, never to see their women and children again.'

'The cohorts need leadership, Alcaeus. Not for very long because they'll be marching away come spring, probably never to return if I understand the way the Romans plan to manage their auxiliary forces in the wake of this disaster. They'll separate soldier from home, so that there'll be no sympathy with the local population of wherever it is that they're sent, and when they've been in one place for long enough to put down roots and start to feel that sympathy, they'll get moved somewhere new again. So, once you've rebuilt as many cohorts as can be formed with the manpower we have left, you can concentrate on training new soldiers and building new cohorts as our youth matures into men, but to earn that relative relaxation you're going to have to cope with all the problems that come home to roost after a war is finished.'

'Caring for the wounded. Providing for the families of the dead. Dealing with the men who go mad because of what they've seen.'

Draco nodded.

'All that. And probably more. And this isn't a request, in case you were wondering, it's an order. I can't rule without a strong prefect to keep my soldiers in hand, and you're the best man I have left.'

Alcaeus nodded, his lips twisted in distaste.

'I'll do it. But there are two conditions.'

Draco raised amused eyebrow.

'Conditions? On an order from a magistrate to his military leader? We'll see. What are they?'

'Firstly, I get to decide what I do once the cohorts are ready to march for their new duty stations. I may not want to get fat and lazy supervising the training of boys.'

Draco shrugged.

'Agreed. If you're stupid enough to want to go and be a senior centurion under a snotty-nosed, soft-palmed Roman prefect who probably doesn't know his prick from a pilum, then you'll be very welcome to do so. I'm sure there'll be a queue of men who'll be delighted to take your place getting fat and lazy, after the events of the last year. And the second *condition*?'

'It's simple. You have to admit that it was you feeding information to the Romans.' The veteran stared at him with hard, calculating eyes, one hand grasping the top of his staff, but Alcaeus shook his head with an equally uncompromising expression, his right hand resting lightly on the handle of his dagger. 'You won't need the blade you keep hidden in that stick. And if you do try to draw it, I'll have you bleeding out before the point clears its sheath. I'm not seeking vengeance, but I do want to know why.'

Draco nodded, leaning on the staff to render its threat negligible and smiling thinly as the priest allowed his hand to fall from the hilt of his sword.

'It's a fair question. How did you know? Another of your dreams?'

'I didn't know, not until I saw you dealing with Cerialis just now. I have some small gift for reading men, and you looked . . . at home with the Romans. As if you'd never truly left Rome's service. And then I thought about the disaster at Gelduba, and who was most obviously positioned to have known about the attack on their legions *and* in a position to send a messenger to warn them. And the most obvious answer was you, although it couldn't have been you because you were the man set to hunt down the traitor. And then I thought back to something you said to my man Egilhard, or at least in his presence, not knowing just what a sharp blade he conceals beneath that apparent simplicity. He told me you said that Kivilaz was always looking for glory, sometimes despite orders to the contrary, and you added under your breath that you'd always feared that he would lead us to disaster.' He stared hard at Draco, challenging the veteran to deny his accusation. 'And once I knew in my heart that it was you all along then the logic followed as easily as day follows night. So tell me, why?'

The older man pulled a wry face.

'The same Roman who came to convince Kivilaz to lead the tribe in rebellion, Vespasianus's associate Plinius, took me aside one evening and asked me, straight out, whether I believed that Kivilaz could be trusted to end a revolt when it was no longer needed. And I thought back to the times he wilfully disobeyed orders as a young centurion, when I was his prefect in Britannia. That eye he lost? He'd have gone to his grave with the two eyes he was born with if he'd followed orders at the battle that did for the Iceni. The way the old soldiers who were there told it to me, Prefect Swana gave the order for our attack to pause, and to allow the Fourteenth Gemina to pass through us and take up their share of the fight, as he'd agreed with their legatus, but Kivilaz was having none of it. He led his cohort forward instead, eager for glory, and managed to damage our relationship with the legion *and* lose an eye, and get dozens more men killed into the bargain. And so I told Plinius that no, I didn't think he could necessarily be trusted to haul on the tribe's rope when the time came, and that it was more likely he'd be the one driving us on to wage war.'

'And this Roman asked you to spy for the empire?'

'He asked me, since you keep using the word *spy*, to act as a go-between for the two sides when the time came, and to do whatever I could to reduce the damage done to our relationship with Rome, in the event that the revolt he hoped for failed to end when its purpose was at an end. The decision to do the things I did was entirely my own.'

'But *why*? I can't understand what would inspire a man of your standing to betray the tribe. I lost friends as a consequence of your message to Flaccus, good men who died needlessly. My own chosen man Banon among them.'

Draco nodded soberly.

'Yes, doubtless you did. But the thing you're not considering is how hard the Romans would have come down on us if I hadn't given them the warning they needed to defend themselves from the attack Kivilaz ordered. Just imagine if they'd been in camp when you arrived. You'd have slaughtered all three legions out of hand in the madness of battle, and put Rome's undying enmity squarely on the back of the cohorts. Instead of which, one of those legions marched south to the Winter Camp and the other two surrendered to the Gauls, and were ultimately returned to Rome more or less intact. Which means that Roman pride was spared the indignity of another Varus disaster. And no, the Old Camp legions don't count, because the histories will undoubtedly be carefully written to say that they were murdered by the tribes from across the river, not by the Batavi, in the interests of our alliance with them. We would have lost this war whether we'd won at Gelduba or not, but if we *had* won that fight the reckoning we'd be facing now would be exactly what Kivilaz feared the most. Our tribe, Alcaeus, would cease to exist. All of the usual treatment of a captured enemy who has chosen to resist Rome would have been visited on our people. Enslavement. Rape. Resettlement. Instead, we're to be greeted back into the fold like the errant sons we will be portrayed as, tempted to fight a war we could never win by a rogue prince who realised the error of his barbaric ways and manfully paid the price by falling on his own sword. I'd call that a good result, and if I had to compromise my loyalty to the tribe to save it, that's simply what I had to do. If you have a problem with that I suggest you draw that sword and use it, then face the consequences, both for yourself and our people.'

The wolf-priest stared out into the grey afternoon for a moment, then shook his head.

'What would be the point? Killing you won't bring Banon back, or any of the others. Hercules can judge you, when your time comes, not me. And who's to say you're not right in your assessment of what would have happened without your intervention. This will remain between us.'

Draco nodded inscrutably.

'Very well, Prefect. And now that you have command of the army, you can act to root out any last vestiges of Hramn's influence.'

'Yes. I'm going to remove all distinctions between the cohorts, the guard and the militia, and form new cohorts with a blend of all three.'

'And your man Achilles? Do you expect him to survive the ire of men who still loved Kivilaz at the end, for all his failures and faults?'

Alcaeus pondered the question for a moment before replying.

'The boy's risen a long way in a short time. He was a recruit not much more than a year ago, and already he's a chosen man, but I don't think he's suited to it. All that pushing and shoving at the back of the century, that's not for him. He's a front rank man, pure and simple, a leader of men, not a driver of sheep.'

'You're going to demote him back to the ranks?'

The priest laughed tersely.

'Demote him? Of course not. I'm going to promote him to centurion. There must be a dozen positions vacant, given the losses we've taken, and he's clearly born to it, now that the shyness has been beaten out of him. Of course there'll be men who'll hate him for what he did to Kivilaz, men who'll want to see him dead. By making him an officer I'll send them a very clear signal as to what will happen to anyone that raises a hand against him. We need to heal the divisions between us, Magistrate, and I can't see any better way of starting that healing than standing by the man whose actions this morning rid us of Hramn's malign influence.'

Draco nodded.

'Neither can I. I just hope he's as fast with his iron as you say, because he's more than likely going to need to be, one dark night. Very well, Prefect, you're dismissed. We have a homeland to rebuild, and the sooner we prove to the Romans we're serious about fulfilling our end of the bargain we just agreed with them, the sooner they'll be inclined to start helping us. You can go and make a start by finding me the cohorts that are buried in the remnants of the army that Kivilaz led to disaster.'

II

Germania, November AD 70

'You set on this, I think. Is true?'

Marius looked at Beran, nodding slowly at the German's question.

'Yes. I have to go back.'

'Forest your home now. Save your life.'

'And I'm grateful to you for that, but . . .'

'You not understand. Watchful tree save your life, not Beran. Forest save you life, now you belong forest. Now you hunter, like Beran. You no need for legion. And legion say you dead. New life in forest, why not? Take pell from beasts, trade with Rome, enjoy Rome horon. Good life. You got woman wait?'

Marius shook his head.

'No, there's no one waiting for me. And I understand. I could walk away from my old life and enjoy this one. Simple and clean, without the dangers of revolts and mutinies. The gods know I'd like to do just that. But . . .'

'Legion call you.'

'Yes.' The Roman shook his head with a rueful smile. 'Let me tell you a story from my world that might help you to understand.'

Beran gestured for him to continue, and Marius looked up at the trees above their campfire before speaking again.

'When I was just a centurion, before I became a first spear and led the Fifth Legion, my first spear was a man called Decimus. He really was the tenth child in the family, which meant that he was fighting as soon as he was old enough to stand. If I tell you that he was the only man I was ever truly scared of, you'll have some idea of, what a bastard he was. Anyway, when the legion's legatus, the man appointed to command it by the emperor—'

'Beran think first spear lead soldiers?'

Marius smiled knowingly.

'So did Decimus, you can be sure of that. But the legatus was a senator, one of a few hundred men who ruled the empire—'

'Beran think emperor rule empire?'

'Yes, well let's say that he can't do it all on his own, so these rich men help him. Anyway, this legatus—'

'Rich man, help emperor rule empire?'

'Yes. He decided to support his general who wanted to be the emperor. So—'

'This man challenge emperor to fight. If he kill, then he emperor?'

Marius realised that his story was going to be more difficult than he had expected.

'Not a challenge in person. He decided to march his legions and their auxiliaries over the mountains to Italy and fight a great battle. So most of my legion went with him, with Decimus as their first spear, and they fought a great battle at a place called Cremona and won the war.'

'So new emperor. What happen to other emperor?'

'He killed himself, we were told.'

Beran shrugged.

'Weak man. A strong man fights.' He yawned. 'Your story hard to understand. How this explain you go back legion?'

Marius nodded.

'You'll see clearly enough. Anyway, the new emperor marched his army to Rome and took power.'

'Many horon for him. If I emperor, I take any horon I want.'

The Roman grinned.

'And you're not alone in that expectation. Anyway, a few months later a new army marched on Rome, under the command of another general.'

'He want be emperor too?'

'Yes, and this general's officers marched their army to the same place where the first battle had been fought and challenged the emperor's army to fight.'

Beran shook his head in puzzlement.

'Fools. Why fight where enemy has already won? He know ground, he have gods' favour.'

'Not this time, it seems. The new challenger's army fought bravely, and the emperor's generals were defeated.'

'Your Decimus die?'

'Yes. And yet from the stories that reached us in the Old Camp, he had every chance to retreat from the battle with his legion in good order and his own skin intact, if he'd chosen not to stand and fight.'

'I see why you tell story. Your Decimus, he should run, but he fight and he die. This he . . . duty?'

Marius nodded.

'He did more than fight, he led his men forward against twice their own strength, against massed bolt throwers, and—'

Beran cursed, making the warding gesture.

'Machine-arrows? I see once at Rome fort. Kill ox at two hundred pace with single arrow. No way to fight.'

Marius pursed his lips, thinking of the thousands of tribesmen the Old Camp's bolt throwers had slaughtered during the fortress's long siege.

'No, it's no way to fight. Decimus was killed by a machine-arrow.'

'Kill by man he never see.'

'Yes. And he'd been asked to take off his crested helmet by his men, because it made him a target, but he ignored them. Despite knowing that he was likely to die as a result.'

'He serve he legion and ignore the danger.'

'Exactly.'

'But your legion *dead.* Slaughtered, you tell me. No man left. You legatus fall on sword. So nothing left for you. *Nothing*. You just be . . .'

He struggled for the Latin word and Marius shrugged.

'An inconvenience? Perhaps. And yet I have to go back. It's my duty.'

Beran nodded.

'Yes, you be *inconvenient.* They not want you back. And like you Decimus, you will die. I know this.'

The Roman shrugged.

'Perhaps. Although I'd hope for something better from my former brothers-in-arms.'

The German raised his open hands in a gesture of resignation.

'Tomorrow we take *pell* to great river, pay boatman to cross. We know you love you duty, we see if you duty still love you back.'

South-Western Gaul, January AD 71

'Fuck me, that's cold! Get that door shut, will you?'

The newcomers were a trio of soldiers, stamping snow from their boots and propping their shields neatly at the entrance, two of them carrying viciously barbed spears while their leader sported the crested helmet of a centurion. The speaker, a man dressed in good quality if nondescript clothing, was standing in front of the tavern's open fire, the wet puddle of snowmelt at his booted feet testifying to his own recent arrival. He turned to look at the newcomers as they shuffled in from the snow-filled night air, closing the heavy wooden door behind them. Casting a significant look at the two hulking men lurking at the table next to him, he turned his back to the blaze, luxuriating in the flames' warmth.

'Come far, have you?'

The officer, his face partially masked by his helmet, stripped off his snow-flecked cloak to reveal a shirt of scale armour before replying.

'All the way from the Old Camp, by way of here and there.'

'The Old Camp? The last time I saw that place it was nothing but wreckage and ashes.'

The newcomer nodded.

'It's being rebuilt. In stone this time, but the same size as before, by a pair of very bad-tempered legions whose men will be making life difficult for the tribes across the river for some years to come. And keeping an eye on the Gauls too, just to make sure nobody gets any more ideas about a Gallic empire any time soon.'

The man by the fire smiled.

'That shouldn't be hard, should it? The Gauls proved to be just about as hard as day-old dog shit.'

The other man nodded agreement, tossing his cloak down on the table beside him.

'And you should know that better than anyone.' He called out to the tavern's owner. 'Landlord! Wine for my men! And bring us six plates of whatever it is you've cooked for dinner, we're about to work up an appetite!'

He turned to the two soldiers behind him, nodding a silent instruction, and as one they raised their spears ready to throw, the threat freezing the two bodyguards as they rose, knives in their hands, in response to the unspoken command their client had flashed them.

'Drop the knives onto the floor, and kick them over here. Then sit down and put your hands under your arses, if you don't want me to find out what a pilum feels like when it's buried a foot deep in your chest.' He waited while the two men relinquished their weapons and did as they were told. 'Good. Stay that way and nobody needs to get damaged. Well, neither of you two at least. But as for you . . .'

The man standing at the fire stared back at him with narrowed eyes.

'I know you.'

'Of course you do. If I hadn't left the camp outside Novaesium before you turned up with your Gallic friends, you'd have had me killed alongside Legatus Augusti Vocula, wouldn't you?' He grinned as the subject of his evident ire flashed a glance at the tavern's rear door. 'Don't bother. My other three men are waiting out there, impatiently, I'd imagine, just in case you try to make a run for it. You show as much as a whisker through that door and they'll put you down and leave you to bleed out in the snow. There are better deaths.'

The man by the fire shook his head in disbelief.

'Who is it you think I am, exactly?'

'I don't think you're anyone, I *know* you're Aemelius Longinus, just as well as you know *exactly* who I am. And why I'm here.'

'Longinus? I'm not Longinus! Longinus died when—'

'Longinus died when the Picentine cavalry wing decided not to fall in with the First and Sixteenth Legions, when you cowards swore loyalty to the Gallic empire. Is that the story? Longinus died when they came across him on the road to the Winter Camp in his new centurion's equipment, and were so incensed that they showered him with spears? Apparently he did. Except I found three men happy to swear an oath to Mars that it wasn't Longinus they killed, because they saw the corpse and all three of them told me that while Longinus was hung like a donkey, the dead man was somewhat lacking downstairs. They all speculated that you must have realised you were a dead man, once the joy of putting your sword through a Roman general had faded, and that you'd found some way to put another man in your place and have the legion cavalry put him to death. After all, you had long enough in his tent to have looted his personal effects, so you were hardly short of gold. And I'd imagine that your friend Classicus made sure you were well provided for, having played your part and slaughtered Dillius Vocula when nobody else had the balls for it.'

'But—'

'No. I was there, you fool. Dressed as a chosen man, and so close to you when you killed him that I saw the look of glee on your face as you pushed your sword into him. You're Longinus.'

The murderer sighed.

'How did you find me?'

'It's ironic, really. That manhood you're so proud of? Not all of the tavern owners remembered you, but the prostitutes certainly did.' He smiled grimly at the other man. 'And, one by one, they all told me what it was that you boasted about while you were playing the big man, once you were sated and wanted to talk. They told me that you were headed somewhere warm and far away to the south, where your face won't be known and your gold can buy you a place to hide and drink and whore away the rest of your days. And do you want to know the funniest part of it? No? I'll tell you anyway. That empire you told your mates was dead and buried just before you killed the best officer I ever served under? It's back in control, Longinus, and it scares the shit out of everyone more than ever, now that it's got fresh blood on its hands. A legion centurion asking questions inspires instant and unquestioning responses. Those tavern keepers and whores gave you up in a heartbeat, no sly demands for payment, they just pointed out the way you'd ridden and scuttled back into their premises hoping we'd go away and leave them in peace. And that empire, Longinus, sent me to make an example of *you*.'

He pulled the dagger from his belt, raising the weapon to be seen in the firelight.

'See this? A beautiful thing, isn't it? Vocula entrusted it to me before he sent me away. It's worth a small fortune, unlike the sword, which is probably worth a much larger sum. It was made by one of the finest swordsmiths in the empire, and it would be a shame to sully such a blade with your blood . . .'

He paused, as if to reflect, and then the dagger's blade was buried deep in Longinus's belly, the fugitive's mouth gaping wide as he sucked in air to scream, but Antonius snapped a hand to his windpipe and choked off the scream, pulling the other man's face close to his own.

'I told Legatus Augusti Cerialis I'd have the empire's revenge for the killing of a good man. And here I am.'

Kicking the wounded man's legs out from under him, he pulled the dagger free and thrust down with the death grip on his victim's throat, pushing him back onto the fire, then stepped smartly back. Whooping for breath, the murderer shouted in pain as the flames' incandescent heat made his clothing smoulder, the moisture trapped in the fibres boiling out with a faint hiss, his limbs thrashing as he fought to escape the pain, but Antonius had taken a spear from one of his men and put the weapon's butt spike into his victim's chest, pinning him to the burning logs without any visible emotion. He watched hard-faced as the fire took full hold of the other man's clothing and hair and his body was suddenly engulfed in flames. His screams went from wounded outrage to animal fury in the space of half-a-dozen heartbeats, no longer an expression of rational anger and pain but simply the insensate distress of a dying beast whose entire being was consumed by the agony of its ending.

'That should be enough.'

Raising the spear, Antonius gestured to his soldiers. Taking a boot apiece, they pulled him clear of the fire, beating at the flames with their wet cloaks to extinguish them and leave Longinus writhing on the tavern floor. The centurion turned to the horrified tavern keeper, his expression still emotionless.

'You have a back room, I presume? I'll pay you twice the usual to put him in there and leave him to it. It'll take him a day or two to die, and I want him to know every last moment, so no putting him out of his misery. He murdered a man I considered a friend, and this is how he makes recompense. If you come between me and that revenge I'll have to put you in his place. Understood?'

The tavern keeper swallowed and nodded quickly.

'Yes, Centurion.'

Batavodurum, March AD 71

'Well done, Prefect, they're barely recognisable as the men who'd fought themselves into the ground six months ago.'

Alcaeus inclined his head in recognition of Draco's praise, flicking a glance at the three Batavi cohorts paraded on the training ground over which loomed a new legion fortress, now almost completed.

'Thank you, Magistrate. Of course, the Romans had quite a lot to do with that.'

The veteran shrugged.

'Their assistance was with the physical, Alcaeus, with the things that can be seen and understood. Armour, weapons, boots . . . but then that was only in their own interests, if they want cohorts. What you have achieved here is a good deal more than just physical. They look like soldiers again, and not the exhausted husks of men they were when we surrendered to the Romans.'

'Enough food, some respite from the constant threat of battle, the chance to see their loved ones. It all helps. They still carry the scars though, some on their skins, the others in places we can't see. Some of them still wake up screaming every night, though not as many as I'd feared.'

Draco nodded.

'My grandfather told me stories from the war against Arminius with just the same punchline – some men are haunted by what they've seen and done for the rest of their lives while others don't lose a minute's sleep over it. So what we're seeing now is just the same as it was then, and as I expect it will always be.' He looked out over the cohorts awaiting inspection with a dispassionate eye. 'Some of them will kill themselves, eventually.'

Alcaeus nodded.

'I'm busy training a new crop of priests to replace those who died in the war, but it will be another six months before I allow them into the forest to kill their wolves. In the meantime, we depend on the sensitivity of their centurions to pick out the most obviously damaged as their symptoms make themselves clear.'

'The sensitivity of their centurions? And just how well is that working out? I always thought it a rarity in my day when I met a centurion with anything more than a fleeting regard for whether his men were sane or not, as long as their spear drill was up to standard.'

The prefect shrugged.

'Some of them are still disappointingly impervious to the idea that they might give a shit for their men at all. But the younger men, the ones who started the war as junior officers or soldiers, they've got a different attitude.'

'They know what it's like in the front rank.'

'Yes. Add to that the fact that a fifth of our centurions are men of the former guard and you can see the problem. They still look down their noses at the rest of the army and resent being "reduced" in status to command mere soldiers, many of whom are effectively raw recruits. They beat their men more, which breeds resentment, which leads to more beatings . . . You know the way that goes.'

Draco nodded.

'I suggest that you pick one and deal with him just as hard as you like. Make it the worst of them, let him step over the line and then show him what it feels like to be on the receiving end. Do it privately if you like but do it soon. You still have the stones to order one of your officers to be punished, I presume? Reduced to the ranks to give the others a salutary example, perhaps, or just flogged and dismissed if he's earned it.'

Alcaeus nodded.

'I do. So it's back to the old ways, is it?'

'The old ways were usually the old ways for a reason, Prefect, so don't mistake our renewed obedience to Rome for any excuse to exchange raw meat for bread and milk. This is still an army founded on the principle that hard men know when to use their fists, and that when they use them without good cause harder men are likely to put them straight. Some things have changed though, which means that I'll need all three of these cohorts ready to march by the end of the month. The Second Adiutrix's legatus wants them to report to their new duty stations before summer's out, which means that we can say goodbye to them for a while.'

'And their duty stations are . . . ?'

'Pannonia, Raetia and Noricum. Far enough away that they'll never be tempted to rise up on behalf of the tribe, close enough to allow men to come home every now and then. Apparently once we've got back up to our previous eight cohort strength we can think about raising a cavalry wing. How long do you think that'll take?'

'We can probably recruit and train a fresh cohort every year or so, as long as we can pick officers and men out of the cohorts that are already on their duty stations to salt the fresh meat, and send some of the new boys to join the established cohorts. They'll be young but they'll be soldiers.'

'So, you'll need five years to re-establish our full strength? Good enough. And when you've achieved that target, you can think about what you want to do with the rest of your military career.'

The wolf-priest stared at him in disgust.

'Whatever will remain of it by then. I thought I was going to be allowed to choose my path once I had the first cohorts stood up?'

Draco smiled, his eyes hard, then looked out across the parade ground.

'You're going to do your duty to the tribe, Prefect. Which will undoubtedly be better than finding yourself on trial for colluding in the deliberate insulting of a tribal noble in the moment of his self-sacrifice, I'd imagine. With your accomplice alongside you.'

Alcaeus stared at him for a long moment, then shook his head in disgust.

'I wondered how long it would take you to fall back on threats to keep me in place.'

The magistrate's level stare at the paraded men did not waver.

'Threats, Prefect? On the contrary, I'm complimenting you on the fine job you've done in getting this many men ready to serve again so quickly. As I am in turn being complimented by the Second Adiutrix's legatus, and encouraged to increase our contribution to the empire's military strength as fast as possible in the most Roman of ways. More soldiers will result in more assistance in the reconstruction. A failure to deliver on the other hand . . .'

'Will result in shit flowing downhill?'

'Indeed it will. Just another example of how we're back to the old days, it seems.' Draco smiled with more warmth. 'Cheer up, Prefect, you've managed to keep your champion alive, and established him as one of your best centurions. Surely that's reward enough for your efforts? Tell me, which cohort does he serve with? I'd like to meet him again now that he's had his vine stick for a few months.'

The priest shook his head.

'I've given him and his uncle leave to go and pay their respects to Lataz and Sigu.'

Draco nodded.

'That seems fair, given that he'll be serving a thousand miles away soon enough. Send him to see me when he returns, will you? I never found the time to talk with the man who held back the death-stroke in the face of his prince's wrath, and I'd like to know how it feels to walk in those boots.'

Alcaeus shook his head, his lips a white slash in his face.

'You want to know how it feels to walk in those boots, Draco? I'd pray to Magusanus you never find out, if I were you.'

The Old Camp, Germania Inferior, March AD 71

'Here comes another pair of the dirty bastards. Fuck 'em off nice and quick before the centurion gets a whiff of them, or we'll all be pulling double duty again.'

The older of the two legionaries standing guard on the Twenty-second Primigenia's temporary fortress stepped forward and raised a hand. One of the two heavily-bearded men stopped at the command, but his companion, a man in his late middle age whose long hair was shot through with grey and whose gait, distorted by a limp, was nevertheless a good deal more confident than most tribesmen confronted with the camp's magnificent edifice, strode towards the impressive wooden gates as if he had simply failed to comprehend the unspoken order.

'What the fuck . . . ?'

Looking at his comrade with a disbelieving expression, the soldier stepped out into the road and raised his hand again.

'Halt!'

Gripping the hilt of his gladius, the threat in both his tone and deed were unmistakable, but to his amazement the German not only failed to show any of the expected fear, but simply put his hands on his hips and surveyed the two legionaries with disdain.

'Which legion?'

After a moment's astounded silence, in which the two men absorbed the fact that not only had a German tribesman addressed them in Latin but had the temerity to demand information of them in such a preemptory manner, the soldier decided that enough was enough when faced with such bare-faced disrespect. He pulled the sword from his right hip, levelling it at the German with a flourish that made very clear his complete willingness to use it if the offending native pushed him just a little harder, but as he drew breath to roar a tirade of abuse, the other man, astoundingly, beat him to it.

'Put that fucking weapon *away*! I'll have you in front of your legatus inside an hour on a charge of threatening a centurion with your sword, and you'll find yourself sitting in a boat with a coin in your mouth wondering what went wrong!'

The legionary's jaw fell, his face abruptly reddening, the sword seeming to sheathe itself of its own volition, his voice quivering as he turned to his fellow sentry.

'F-fetch the centurion. *Now!*'

As the younger of the two sprinted into the camp, the bedraggled newcomer looked about him with what appeared, to the men who had gathered on the wooden rampart ten feet above him, to be an incongruous but unmistakable professional curiosity.

'So, which legion is this?'

The answer was a moment coming, almost reluctant, the soldier feeling compelled to answer but still unable to believe his eyes.

'Twenty-second Primigenia.'

'Twenty-second Primigenia, *Centurion*.' The gaunt figure looked up at the camp's walls, nodding appreciatively. 'Not a bad piece of work, but then you've had six months to put it together. They're not rebuilding the Old Camp, then?'

'No, Centurion. They're going to build a new fortress, in stone, because—'

The legionary's centurion stalked through the camp's gate with an expression that brooked no nonsense, his vine stick held ready to dispense swift and violent discipline.

'What's this? Your idiot mate told me you had one of the long-haired bastards pretending to be a cent—'

The older man stepped forward, apparently considering himself to be on very firm ground in addressing a man whose soldiers only ever spoke to if they couldn't avoid it, so foul-tempered was his reputation. His tone was at once threatening and condescending as he pointed to the charred ruins of the fortress alongside which the legion was camped.

'See that fortress? The one that's been reduced to ashes because Rome's valiant legions couldn't get their fingers out of their arses fast enough to relieve the garrison before we were starved into submission and then massacred by the Batavians?' The officer stared at him in amazement equal to that of his gawping soldiers, knuckles clenching white on his vine stick. 'I commanded that fortress for six months, Centurion, waiting for you delicate flowers to get around to coming back north, fighting off wave after wave of barbarians from across the great river, holding out until we had nothing more to eat than grass and boot leather! So take me to your legatus, or I'll make sure you end the day as a single-pay latrine scrubber!'

The Twenty-second's commander looked up from his desk in disbelief as the man who called himself Marius, standing rigidly to attention, laid out the bones of his story, finally shaking his head in amazement when the former first spear stopped talking and waited for a response. His own first spear stood behind the newcomer in the corner, expressionless and imperturbable.

'So, you want me to believe that you're the former senior centurion of the Fifth Alaudae? A man who's known to have been taken north of the river in the company of—'

'Legatus Quintus Munius Lupercus. A man whose heroism in the service of Rome deserves to be told, Legatus.'

The Roman sat back.

'A man, First Spear . . . if you are who you say you are . . . who surrendered two legions to the enemy. And who was brutally murdered on the road into captivity. Were it not for the rash actions of some unknown enemy warrior, Lupercus would by now be enslaved to a German priestess, his honour and that of Rome forever traduced by his lack of resolution to fight to the end. Come in!'

His clerk, having tentatively knocked at the office door, escorted in a soldier whose face was at once familiar to Marius, last seen on a dark, moonless night a year before. Taking one look at the prematurely aged first spear, he snapped to attention with a vigour that raised the eyebrows of the watching officers.

'First Spear Marius, sir! We were told you were dead!'

The gaunt figure nodded gravely.

'Not everything you've heard is true. Or, I suspect, fair.'

The legatus pointed at Marius.

'This is really an officer of your previous legion, soldier?'

The legionary nodded confidently.

'I'd know First Spear Marius anywhere, Legatus! I was there that night he got that scar . . .' He pointed to the line of puckered tissue bisecting Marius's right eye. '"Get that fucking ladder off my fucking wall!" Do you remember that, sir?'

Marius nodded slowly.

'It seems to have happened in another life, but yes, I do.'

The legatus dismissed the soldier, one of the few who had been released by the Batavi to spread the word of the Old Camp's surrender, waving to the seat in front of his desk.

'Sit down, First Spear. I was dubious as to whether your story could be true, but now that there can no longer be any doubt I suppose you'd better tell me what really happened.'

Marius recounted the tale of the fortress's besiegement, the multiple German attacks and the garrison's surrender and slaughter, but it was only when he reached Lupercus's fate that the legatus took a close interest.

'He really took his own life? All of Rome believes that he was murdered in the most barbaric of manners by the German tribes.'

Marius nodded.

'The truth of it is that he fell on a sword taken from Civilis's nephew, Bairaz. He died with honour, Legatus, and his family deserve to know that.'

The Roman pondered for a moment.

'Perhaps they do.' He raised a hand to forestall the other man's protest. 'I know, you served the man for a year, you shared his travails and you were there with him at the end. You may even have been instrumental in his suicide.' Marius stared at him expressionlessly, sensing that the senior officer was searching for any sign, for the slightest hint that Lupercus's death had been assisted. 'I see. You're not going to provide me with any clue as to anything other than Munius Lupercus having died with spotless honour, are you?' He waved a hand dismissively at the centurion's impassive anger. 'I understand, and don't mistake me as not caring, but the whole matter of the man having died with dignity, as you're assuring me was the case, is out of my hands.'

Marius frowned.

'Out of your hands, Legatus?'

'Yes. Are you aware of what happened to Civilis when he finally agreed to surrender and end the war?'

Marius shook his head.

'No, sir. I spent the winter in the forests north of the Rhenus. I was wounded escaping from the Germans, and my life was saved by a hunter, a man whose life kept him far away from the German tribes, and it was only when the spring thaw came that I was ready to walk south to the great river. My knowledge of the war's end is minimal.'

'I see. Well the quick version is that the new emperor decided that Civilis had to die. That he was too great a threat to the empire to spare because it would be too much of a risk to allow a man who had thrown a spear into a Roman fortress to be seen to survive. Of course, there were some, men looking to score points against the new emperor, a man sufficiently open-minded to allow such comments to be made, men who were ready to argue that it was our own fault that Civilis whipped his people up to war because he did so at the express request of the emperor's own supporters, although of course that's been flatly denied by all concerned. That we had betrayed them in the first place by breaking our treaty with them, and that on top of the provocation of his needlessly having been accused of treason, and the execution of his brother on the same charge. Why was it, they asked, that the Batavians have been taken back into the empire without punishment, other than the loss of their horses, but Julius Civilis was ordered to kill himself to expiate their crimes? And you can see their point, to a degree. Which is why, like the good politician he is, and predicting just such criticism, Cerialis quickly fastened onto the story that the Germans had murdered your legatus on a bloody altar as all the justification he needed for ordering Civilis to commit suicide. He argued that it had never been Civilis's intention to imprison Munius Lupercus with this Bructeri witch Veleda, but rather to present him to his allies, with his sacrificial death to be staged for the pleasure of the tribes on Bructeri territory, and that Civilis's story of Lupercus's suicide was an invention, intended purely to deflect the blame for the murder of a Roman senator onto the man himself. This is the accepted version of events, First Spear. And any challenge to it may not be . . . wise.'

He fell silent, watching Marius while the centurion nodded slowly, comprehension dawning on him.

'You're telling me that the news that Munius Lupercus took his own life will not be welcome in Rome. And that if a man were to be responsible for that news becoming widely known . . .'

'Exactly. The last thing the emperor will want is any hint that Civilis was telling the truth when he insisted that your legatus was found beheaded, bent over a sword, which he had thrust into his own guts. The story of his slow and horrible death has become the accepted version of events, and that suits everyone concerned very neatly, First Spear. Everyone that matters, which that means that voices from the past with new stories to tell will not be welcome. A man of my status who failed to suppress such voices would find himself in a very uncomfortable position.'

'And Lupercus's honour is of no account?'

The legatus shook his head.

'His honour is unblemished, First Spear. Vespasianus, a man with a good deal more of that commodity than most of his predecessors, it has to be said, has been careful to praise Lupercus's family for his evident dignity in defeat, and to declare that his death can only bring pride on their name, as he clearly remained steadfastly loyal to his city and people to the end. His wife and children have been placed under the protection of the imperial household, and his boys will doubtless find themselves with a good start upon the *cursus honorum* when the time comes. I doubt that even they would be delighted to have the accepted version of events altered to accommodate a story of suicide, rather than that of glorious defiance to the last breath, which has brought them so much imperial favour. So you can see the problem that your unexpected arrival gives me.'

He gestured to the centurion waiting silently in the corner, and Marius nodded, his expression bleak, not looking around as the man behind him paced slowly forward, the faintest hiss of oiled iron against the centurion's scabbard throat reaching his expectant ears.

'I'm sure it does. But one that's probably easy enough to solve.'

The legatus stared across his desk, his face softening in sympathy.

'You should never have come back, First Spear Marius. When military reality and political necessity meet, there is usually only one victor.'

'Yes.' The veteran centurion rose to his feet slowly, raising his hands so as to give the man behind him no reason to strike prematurely. 'Although I like to imagine that if I were ordered to murder a brother officer I would have found the courage to refuse.'

'That's easy for the man on the wrong end of the sword to say.' The voice behind him was bone-hard, and Marius knew beyond any doubt that his death sentence was being pronounced. 'But when a legion commander orders the death of an impertinent tribesman who doesn't know when to keep his mouth shut, a man either plays his part or pays the price.'

'And better me than you.'

'Yes.'

'Very well. You know how to do this quickly? I'd hate to—'

The gladius's point punched through his unarmoured body, its cold intrusion shocking him into silence, his blood spraying across the legatus's desk and arms. Marius coughed a bubbling laugh as the man behind him put a hand on his shoulder and pulled the sword free, staggering as his body spasmed with the abrupt agony of the blade's removal. He slumped forward onto the desk, staring unblinkingly at the legatus facing him.

'Appropriate . . . my blood . . . on your hands.'

The senior officer shrugged.

'It will wash off.'

Marius struggled back to an upright position, his sight dimming, and the legatus raised a hand to forestall another blow.

'He's dead on his feet. Let the man die with dignity.'

Feeling the taste of blood in his mouth the veteran centurion grinned, then spat crimson spittle into the other man's face.

'Fuck dignity . . . and if . . . you think . . . this is bad . . . wait until . . . my comrade . . . Aquillius . . . hears . . . of . . . this.'

The legatus wiped his eyes, shaking his head at the tottering centurion.

'Your friend Aquillius is long dead. He drowned on the last day of the war.'

Marius stared at him, swaying on his feet, laughed through another mouthful of blood and fell full length to the wooden floor. The centurion knelt beside him for a moment, then looked up at his legatus.

'He's dead.'

'A shame. He was a good officer, from what I've heard. Dispose of his body, and have that legionary who identified him join him in whatever pit you throw him into.'

'As you command, Legatus. And the German he walked in with?'

'I don't think you need me to tell you how to ensure that this matter is buried here, today?'

'Legatus.'

Wiping his sword on the dead man's tunic, he sheathed the weapon and turned for the door, looking back as the legatus spoke again.

'The one thing I don't understand is why he laughed when I told him that Aquillius is dead.'

The centurion stared at his superior for a moment before replying.

'When I agreed to kill this man, Legatus, I did so in the full and certain knowledge that his colleague Aquillius is a man—'

'Is?'

'Yes, Legatus. *Is*. I've talked with more than one officer who served under him, and I quickly came to understand that his reputation for being indestructible was well earned. He was written off as dead during the war with the Batavians but found his way back to the army with no more concern than if he'd just taken a stroll down to the latrines, having killed an entire tent party of auxiliaries and tortured one of them to death just to remind the Batavians that not all Romans considered themselves beaten. And so when I agreed to this . . .' he gestured down at Marius's sprawled body, 'I did so knowing that if this man Aquillius is still alive, as I suspect is likely, then I'll probably be meeting him when I least expect it at some point in the next few years. As might you, Legatus. Killing the man who identified him won't avoid his hearing this story at some point, it'll already be all over the camp by now.'

The legatus shook his head in disbelief.

'This man Aquillius was a centurion. What does a man of my rank have to fear from a *centurion*? Any man laying a finger on me would die in the most agonising manner, and . . .' He frowned at his subordinate's expression. 'What?'

The senior centurion shrugged.

'From what I've heard, Legatus, Aquillius would happily murder an emperor if he felt himself, or anyone close to him, sufficiently wronged.' He drew himself up and saluted. 'I respect your courage, but I can assure you that I'll be watching my back with the greatest of care having killed this man. From now until the day I depart this life.'

The senior officer stared at him for a moment in silence.

'I see. Well in the meantime you can go and deal with his German friend. If that's not too much of a risk?'

Saluting briskly, the centurion stalked out of the headquarters building with two trusted men in his wake, walking swiftly to the tavern outside the fortress's walls to which his men had followed the hunter. Pausing on the threshold, he drew his dagger, indicating to his men that they should follow his example.

'Let's make this quick, eh? The poor bastard didn't do anything other than make friends with the wrong man, so there's no reason for him to suffer.'

Finding the tavern empty except for a pair of disconsolate veterans clearly used to making a beer last an afternoon sitting in one corner, he called for the barman, who pointed at the stairs without having to be asked.

'Your lads said you'd be along.'

The centurion nodded brusquely.

'Where is he?'

'First room on the right at the top of the stairs. Don't damage the merchandise, eh?'

Nodding with an amused smile, the officer led his men up the wooden stairs, ignoring the quiet creaking of the treads, which was barely audible over the apparently delighted female cries of pleasure coming from the room in question. He readied himself to open the door, lifting his dagger in readiness.

'The dirty bastard didn't take long to get his prick wet, did he?' He grinned at the two soldiers knowingly. 'Let's go and rescue him from all that fake enjoyment, shall we?'

'You think that's faked?'

The centurion nodded.

'I can tell. That's not passion, it's just acting. Come on!'

He pushed the door open, bursting into the room with his dagger held ready to strike, only to freeze as the woman lying on her back, alone on the bed, screamed in terror. Turning back to the door he was knocked across the room by the body of one of his men, the soldier's gasping, silent entreaties for help punctuated by sprays of blood from the rent in his throat that jetted across both the woman and the bed she was lying on, redoubling the intensity of her screams. The man he had been sent to kill came through the door in the wake of the dying man, his hunting knives dripping blood as he levelled them at the reeling officer, the horrified groans of a man who wasn't yet dead but soon would be issuing from the corridor behind him. He gestured to the woman to leave, and waited in silence while she scrambled past him, the legion officer regathering his wits and raising his dagger again.

'I was going to make it fast, but you can take your time dying now, you cunt!'

The German grinned.

'I tell my brother Mariuz, some men talk, some men act. I got no time talk, forest call me home.'

'I'll fucking—' Abruptly, with no warning other than what seemed to be a gesture by his opponent, something hard and cold was lodged in his gut, and he looked down to see the handle of one of the hunter's knives protruding from his belly. 'Fuck . . . I . . .'

Gasping for breath, unable to move from where he lay slumped against the wall, he could do no more than watch as the German pulled off his bloody tunic, quickly donning the clothes he had worn when he had walked through the gates an hour before. Using the blood-soaked garment to prevent any further blood spray, he pulled his knife free, wiping it clean on the wool and sliding it into its sheath as his victim sank onto the floor. Still looking down at him, the other man picked up his small pack.

'You kill Mariuz, yes?'

The centurion nodded, his eyes slitted in pain.

'Yes. He was . . .'

'*Inconvenient.* He teach me that word. Not wanted by legion he love. I tell him even men sometimes eat their own kind, he not listen. You make it quick for him?'

'Y-yes. It wasn't his fault.'

The hunter cocked his head on one side, studying the Roman for a moment.

'Not your fault either. You and he same, serve legion. And legion a jealous *horon.* Live long Centurion, if you not be *inconvenient.*'

He turned and was gone, leaving the legion officer to slump back against the room's wall, unsure whether to curse his fate or thank his luck while he pondered the German's last words with a feeling of dread.

Colonia Agrippina, Germania Inferior, March AD 71

'What can I get you, big man?'

The hulking stranger shook his head, leaning forward to speak quietly into the tavern owner's ear, the hard-etched lines that rendered his face skull-like freezing the barman where he stood.

'I'm not here to drink. I'm looking for a woman.'

'Well you've come to the right place! We have all sorts of women, and for a small fee any or all of them will—'

The babble ran to a halt under the newcomer's cold stare.

'I'm looking for one woman in particular. She was the friend of a man I served with. I was told that I would find her here.'

'Ah.' The tavern keeper nodded knowingly. The war that had raged across Germania and Gaul over the previous year had reduced many women to having to sell themselves to feed their children, a state of affairs that, while unpalatable given the nature of his clientele, was something he was powerless to prevent. 'What's her name?'

'She was the woman of a chosen man called Petrus.'

The barman pointed across the room at a small group of drinkers clustered in one corner, a single woman perched on the biggest man's lap. As the stranger turned to look at them she wriggled in apparent discomfort, the man in whose grip she was captured reaching round and pawing at her barely concealed breasts, pulling at a nipple to provoke a fresh protest. The big man turned to face the as-yet-unaware group, his gaze flicking across them in a swift appraisal, then put his shoulders back and flexed his spade-like hands. Feeling a pull at his sleeve he turned back to look at the barman, plucking the offending hand from his garment with a grip that, the gulping tavern owner realised, could have broken every bone in his hand with a swift squeeze.

'You won't start any trouble, will you?'

A smile breathed life into the big man's face but to the barman's dismay it was threat rather than pleasure that animated the newcomer's features.

'I cannot promise that violence will not occur. But I can assure you that it will be brief.' Turning back to the corner where the woman was now being groped by all three men, he nodded decisively. 'Damage will be paid for.'

Three strides had him standing over them, looking down at the woman and completely ignoring her tormentors.

'You are the woman of Petrus of the Fifth Legion?'

She looked up at him, her body jerking as the man to her left pulled the nipple again.

'Yes.'

'Oi, you can fuck—'

The big man raised a hand and to his own surprise the drinker who had the woman on his lap found himself silent under the brooding stare.

'I'm talking to the woman. Be silent and nothing bad will happen.'

'Hah! You can—'

As the man to his right started to rise, reaching for the knife at his hip, the big man pivoted with fluid grace, snapping out a hand and grasping his neck, then extended the arm with contemptuous power to bang his head off the stone wall just once. Glassy-eyed, his victim's face split in an idiot grin, uncomprehending as his captor pulled the knife free from its sheath and smashed it down through the wood of the table at his side, the blade's length protruding through the wooden plank's underside. Frozen in their places by the speed and brutality of the one-sided fight, the other two sank slowly back into their places, and the stranger nodded.

'A good choice. Stay seated and nothing bad will happen.'

He offered the woman his hand and she took it, pulling herself upright and closing her tunic's open flap to cover her breasts, her face betraying the unease she felt under his gaze, and the likelihood that her former customers would hold her responsible for his actions.

'What do you want?'

He nodded.

'I have something for you.'

Reaching into his purse he took out a small leather bag, placing it into her hand and closing the fingers around it.

'I don't understand.'

'It is gold. Enough gold to start a new life. Here, or perhaps somewhere else where you are not known. This sort . . .' he gestured at the goggling men, 'may presume that your former weakness remains an opportunity once I have left this place.'

She stared up at him, still not completely comprehending the change in her circumstances.

'Why? Will you expect me to—'

'No. The money is a gift. Use it as you see fit.'

Still baffled, the woman opened the bag and peered inside.

'But this is . . .'

'You lived with a man. A soldier named Petrus.'

'Yes.'

'He died when the Old Camp fell. I saw him die.'

She nodded sadly.

'I'd guessed as much.'

The dazed man started to rise, staring in puzzlement at the sight of his knife buried in the table before him, reaching out a hand and pulling ineffectually at the weapon's handle. The big man raised a hand to excuse himself for a moment, bending to look into his unfocused eyes but speaking loudly enough to be heard by the tavern's astounded customers.

'The next man who tries to pull a knife on me will die on his own blade. Now take this fool away before he falls over and hurts himself some more.'

He stood and turned back to the woman as the other two men dragged their comrade away, leaving his knife embedded in the table.

'You went to the army and asked for his money?'

She nodded.

'They laughed at me. The centurion on duty said I had no

right to as much as a copper coin, seeing as soldiers are forbidden to marry. Said there was no money to spare to pay off soldiers' whores. And then he offered me a denarius to let him fuck me there and then, in the guardroom.'

'And you needed to eat.'

'I needed to feed my son.'

He shrugged.

'It's an easy path to fall onto at a time like this, and a hard one to leave with men like these around you. And nothing to be ashamed of.' He looked around the silent room, shaking his head slowly with clenched fists. 'These are the people who should feel shame.' He shrugged, pointing at the bag of gold coins in her hand. 'But there was money to spare. There is always legion gold to be had, if a man knows where to look and how to lay his hands upon it. And there it is. A year's wages for a legionary, yours to spend as you wish. A new life, if you choose.'

The woman nodded.

'Yes. But . . . *why*?'

The big man shrugged.

'I made a promise to your man, to bring you the news of his death. When fate placed the opportunity to repay you for his loss, and others like you, I decided to listen to the counsel of a priest I met on the darkest night of my life. I was a centurion, feared by friend and enemy alike. Now I am simply an instrument of the gods, bringing light to lives I had some part in making dark.'

'You're him!'

A man across the room had risen from his seat and was pointing, his expression incredulous. 'You're the *Banô*! The centurion who killed all those legionaries in the Old Camp arena to save himself!'

Aquillius nodded sadly as the woman shrank away from him, the realisation of just who he was evident in her shocked expression.

'Yes. I was Aquillius. And yes, they called me the *Banô*. And yes, your man died in the Old Camp arena when the Germans set him and his comrades against me. It was kill or be killed. So now I do the only thing that will earn my spirit a little peace in the afterlife.'

He turned to leave, stopping as the woman reached out and put a hand on his arm.

'For killing my man, you have my hatred. And for saving me from this life, you have my gratitude.'

The big man bowed his head.

'And somewhere between the two I will, perhaps, find some measure of peace.'

The Old Camp, Germania Inferior, March AD 71

'Here we are then. There's the altar, which means that this is where the Romans buried them all.'

Egilhard nodded silently, and behind him Frijaz and Lanzo shared a glance. The rest of the tent party were waiting at what was intended to be a respectful distance, although the sound of bickering between Adalwin and the oldest of the new recruits was clearly audible over the wind's shrill moan. As a former guardsman, Hanu had little tolerance for the veteran soldier's disdain for his former unit, while Beaky, combat hardened and untroubled by the prospect of violence, clearly still bore a grudge.

'Oi! Start showing some respect for my fucking brother or I'll put you both on your arses!'

The two men fell silent, both glowering at their new leading man whose unofficial rank and privileges they had both coveted before his unexpected promotion by the century's new chosen man. As Lanzo had told his centurion on declaring the decision, waving away Egilhard's protestation that it would look like favouritism, the choice was made and his friend could like it or simply ignore it.

'We're not having a guardsman in charge of them, he'll have them all cleaning his boots before you know it. And Beaky couldn't find his own arse with both hands and a hunting dog. So it's Frijaz, whether you think it'll look bad or not.' Patting his *hastile*'s brass-bound end he had smiled evilly at his comrade. 'And the first man to say it was favouritism can spend a day getting the dents out of his helmet, once I'm done with him.'

Egilhard shook his head, his face desolate at the sight of the mass grave.

'It's not right for him to rest here. He wanted to be buried in our own soil. And I promised him . . .'

Frijaz nodded his understanding, putting an arm round his nephew's shoulder.

'When your uncle Wulfa died in Britannia we buried him where he fell, more or less.' Frijaz stared at the distant half-built shell of the new Old Camp fortress, its hard stone walls a visible message to the tribes across the river that Rome's long reach had re-established its vice-like grip upon them. 'Which is to say that we laid him to rest in the forest nearby, with the locals all chased away while we buried the dead and made sure that only we could ever find them. Mother complained, of course, said we'd denied her the chance to say goodbye, but the old man quickly put that to rest. Gods below, but he was a flint-hearted old bastard, he talked to her about what rotting corpses look and smell like after a few weeks until she burst into tears and told him to hold his tongue, but he'd made his point by then. So, do you really want to dig up whatever's left of him? Are you sure you want to see him with worms hanging out of his mouth? Because I don't think I do.'

'I promised . . .'

Lanzo stepped forward.

'It's none of my business, so forgive me for having an opinion.'

Egilhard turned to look at him.

'Which is?'

'More of a question, I suppose. Who is it, do you think, that suffered the most out of everyone in your family from that idiocy?'

The young centurion shrugged.

'That's easy. Our mother.'

'Exactly. Lost her youngest son, lost her man. We think we had it hard, but you try having the baby you fed at your breast killed, and the man that helped you make him as well, and see where that leaves you? Your mother, Egilhard, has been through agonies that we can only guess at. And now she's starting to get over it, I'd imagine. Considering her life without them both, and with you a thousand miles away in another province, and working out how to make the most of it. The last thing she needs is to have those wounds opened up again, if we could have found him and took him home.'

Egilhard stood in silence looking down at the cairn that marked his father's resting place.

'And you think that would have been too much for me?'

His chosen man smiled sadly.

'No, my friend, far from it. But I think it would have been another layer of scar tissue that you don't need to inflict on yourself. You've been a bit more lively of late, noticing the girls and even joking with their mothers.'

'I only told that woman to look out for Frijaz, when he was about to—'

'And thanks for that, nephew.' Frijaz shook his head in disgust. 'It used to be my brother who made a profession of sabotaging my chances with the ladies, but you're doing a pretty good job in his absence.'

'My point *is* . . .' Lanzo waited for both men to show that they were listening before continuing. 'My point is that you deserve some *life*. You're *Egilhard*, for fuck's sake! The man whose kills in battle are beyond count! The man who killed the giant at Cremona! The man who captured the tribune at Gelduba!'

'He escaped!'

'It doesn't matter! You're the man who had the stones to deny Kivilaz an honourable death because he hadn't earned one! You're *him*!'

'And your point is?'

Frijaz nodded.

'Yes, Lanzo, apart from giving me a hard-on for the boy, what is your point?'

'The point, farm boy . . .' he swayed backwards with expert

timing to avoid Frijaz's attempted cuff, 'is that the last thing his reputation needs is any further embroidery. The man who dug up his father's rotting corpse and took him back home for burial? It'd go with the image, I suppose, but you don't need your reputation to be any harder than it already is. Forget any idea of digging through a mass grave in search of him, leave him where he lies, tell your mother we stood no chance of finding him, and do the same for your brother. They lie where they fell, and that's all any of us can ask, isn't it?' He raised a hand. 'I know, a warrior should end his days on a pyre, or at least that's the theory. Well just this once, let's ignore that. He's long since across the river and drinking with his father, wherever they both are. Leave him in peace, eh?'

Frijaz nodded silently, his lips pursed in approval, and the men of the tent party, having shuffled closer to listen, quietly muttered their respectful agreement. After a moment the centurion turned to face his friends with an expression that combined relief and something akin to disappointment.

'If you think it's for the best.'

His uncle nodded again.

'Your mother will be a little disappointed, but she'll be a lot more relieved than you might expect.' He looked down at the grave. 'Do you want to say goodbye to him properly? Then we can go and find somewhere to get hot food and something to drink, and perhaps something else that's w—'

He thought better of completing the sentence, patting his nephew on the shoulder and then turning away to join the rest of the party, leaving Egilhard standing in silence. After a moment the young centurion went down on one knee, taking off his crested helmet and laying it on his cloak to avoid unnecessarily spotting the gleaming surface with moisture.

'Well, Father, here I am. They promoted me, as you might have noticed. Mainly to stop men who still think the revolt was the right thing to do from trying to kill me, I think. It's worked this far at least. And my cohort will be marching south in few weeks, so I might not be able to come and see you for a while. Which means that I probably need to say a few things that I didn't have time for the day you died.'

He looked up at the scudding clouds above for a moment.

'You probably told me not to be a hero every other day of my life from the moment I was old enough to hold a wooden sword. And I listened, Father. I swore not to be that man you warned me not to be, the one with the swagger and the awed tent mates, so full of himself that he didn't see the blade that took his life until it was sticking out of his back. And I succeeded. But . . .'

He smiled, ignoring the trickle running down one cheek.

'You weren't telling me not to be a hero, were you? You knew what was in me, some mix of you, Wulfa, Frijaz and grandfather, and you knew what I'd become. What you were warning me off wasn't following that path, because you knew I couldn't *not* follow it. What you were trying to tell me was how to wear it. And in that respect, Father, you succeeded. I see that now.'

He wiped the tear away, smiling down at the ground under which his father slept the deep, dreamless sleep of the dead.

'And I know something now, something I wish I'd known before you died. Sitting round in barracks with nothing to do for six months gives a man time to think, and to come to fresh conclusions. You had a hero in you too, didn't you? I only ever beat you with a sword by inches, but you kept all that ability under your helmet and played the simple soldier, because for a while you were happy to live that potential life through Wulfa and then, once he was taken by the gods as the price for his bright flame, you realised that you had a choice. And you made it. You kept your head down and soldiered, never accepted promotion and never showed your true skills, because by then you had me and Sigu, and you knew that you had to bring us up in a way that let us avoid your brother's mistakes. And I love you for that more than I ever realised while you were still alive. Which means I owe you something.'

'Are you going to be there on your knees all day, boy? There are beers to be drunk and women to be romanced!'

He raised a hand, waving away Frijaz's good-natured complaint, understanding what it was the veteran was trying to do.

'Just a little longer.'

Taking a deep breath he looked down at the grave again.

'So here's my promise. I'll find a woman before I leave the Island. The gods know that Mother's already put enough of them in front of me to form a decent harpastum team. And if I have sons I'll raise them to your rules and in your name. And I'll come here every time I pass, going south to serve the Romans or coming north to see my family, and tell you the stories of my life and how my sons are growing up, so that you can see that I'm keeping that promise. And to tell you that I love you.'

He stood, smiling through his drying tears, raising his voice to be heard by his men.

'Right, let's go and see what sort of welcome we find in the Old Camp, shall we? I suspect that Frijaz's rather original approach to "romance" means that he'll end up spending the night with the wrinkled old lady and her five daughters, but that would be nothing new, would it, Soldier Frijaz?'

Lanzo saluted and shouted for the tent party to form up, and while he strode up and down their short column checking that their equipment was suitably clean for them to make an appearance in a legion camp, the young centurion took one last look back at the forlorn altar that showed where his father lay.

'Sleep well, Lataz. You've earned that much.'

Historical Note

Researching the *Centurions* trilogy was a fresh challenge for a writer who has, over the course of writing nine previous stories in the *Empire* series, become a little blasé about the historical background, events, military units and tactics, weapons and armour and just about anything else you could care to name about the late second century. To find oneself suddenly over a hundred years adrift of one's chosen period of history was in one respect easy enough – after all, not that much changed in that century in many ways – and yet a bit of a head-scratcher from several other perspectives. The revolt of the Batagwi tribe is on the face of it a simple thing – Romans upset tribal mercenaries, who then rise up and teach them an almighty lesson as to how to manage subject peoples and their armies – and yet the history, and the story that can be teased out of those dry pages left to us by the primary sources Tacitus and Cassius, is far more complex than anything I could have predicted.

To start at the beginning, the Batagwi – Batavians to the Romans – were one of the German tribes subjugated by Caesar in the wake of his rampage through the Gauls, and quickly became a firm ally of what was to become the empire. Providing Rome with a military contingent that sounds like it would have been the match of any legion – eight part-mounted five-hundred-man infantry cohorts and a cavalry wing – they were a powerful blend of German ferocity in battle with Roman equipment and, to some degree, Rome's military ethos and tactics. In return for this disproportionate contribution to the imperial forces, they paid no taxes to Rome, an indication of just how valuable their contribution was deemed to be. Their role, to judge from the relatively scant sources, was in the long tradition of shock troops that has continued into the modern era in formations like the Parachute Regiment and the US Marines, hard men trained to high levels of physical competency and tactical aggression and, by consequence of both that conditioning and their collective underlying social backgrounds, lacking some of the instincts to self-preservation that can hamper soldiers from risking everything in pursuit of victory in the moment of decision that occurs on all battlefields. The best equivalent for us to consider with regard to the Batagwi tribe's contribution might well be the Gurkhas, Nepalese soldiers who have fought with great honour and bravery for the British empire and its post-colonial army, and whose bloody reputation has resulted in their mere presence in the order of battle proving fearsomely intimidating to Britain's enemies on many occasions.

Parented for decades by the Fourteenth Gemina Legion, it seems that the Batagwi cohorts did a good deal of the initial dirty work on one battlefield after another, as at the battle of the Medway in AD 43. Their sneak attack at dawn across the seemingly unfordable river seems to have destroyed the British tribes' chariot threat before the battle commenced, and allowed the Fourteenth, under the improbably young Hosidius Geta, and the Second Augustan, under the future emperor Vespasianus, to establish the bridgehead from which victory would eventually result. Incidentally, for those readers with an interest in the cursus honorum and its age restrictions, the historical record is a little confused with regard to Geta, and the legatus in question might have been an older brother, although age restrictions on command tended to be relaxed by a year for each child born to a family, probably to encourage fertility among the ruling classes – so we can consider legion command at the age of twenty-four (it was usually no younger than thirty) as improbable but eminently possible under the right circumstances. The most startling aspect of all this is that on more than one occasion the Batagwi used an organic amphibious capability – and by organic I mean without the assistance of any third party such as a naval unit – to cross rivers and narrow coastal straits and turn an enemy flank by appearing where they were least expected. How did they do this, swimming while wearing their equipment, which, weighing around twenty-five kilos, would obviously overwhelm even the strongest of swimmers before the encumbrances of having to carry a shield and spear are taken into account? It's possible that the latter were carried by means of some kind of improvised floatation device, but we cannot discount the possibility that fully equipped infantrymen were carried across the water obstacle and straight into battle by means of the cohort's horses being used to literally tow them across. This seems to have been what Cassius Dio is describing in *The History of Rome:*

> *The barbarians thought the Romans would not be able to cross this* [the River Medway] *without a bridge, and as a result had pitched camp in a rather careless fashion on the opposite bank. Plautius, however, sent across some Celts who were practiced in swimming with ease fully armed across even the fastest of rivers. These fell unexpectedly on the enemy . . .*

This was probably as innovative and disruptive to an unprepared enemy as massed parachute drops were in the twentieth century, and the Batagwi seem to have been viewed as Rome's best and bravest shock troops, capable of doing the impossible and turning a battle to Rome's advantage by their unexpected abilities. For a long time this guaranteed them the highest possible status as an allied people, ruled not by a governor but instead by a magistrate voted into office by the tribe's most exalted citizens, the *noblissimi popularium* (the ruling class, literally 'most noble countrymen'). This tended to mean, one suspects, that they were pretty much guaranteed to take a Roman perspective on the behalf of a self-interested ruling class of families, themselves granted citizenship in perpetuity by the early emperors, in the pursuit of a Roman foreign policy that sought to ensure an alignment of the empire's ambitions with those of the tribe's rulers.

This relationship went even further than the battlefield, for in 30 BCE Augustus recruited an imperial bodyguard from the

Batagwi and the other tribes that dwelt in the same area: Ubii, Frisii, Baetasii and so on. Where the Praetorians guarded the city and in particular its palaces, the *corporis custodes* protected the emperor himself, and were trusted for their impartial devotion to the task of ensuring his safety and deterring assassination attempts that might otherwise have been considered by the praetorians themselves (and for which they later gained an unenviable reputation). Disbanded briefly at the time of the Varus disaster in AD 9, they were swiftly reinstated when it became clear that the tribe had taken no part in Arminius's act of outright war, and the Batagwi played a full role in the suppression of the tribes to the north and east of the Rhine that was to follow. They remained at the side of a succession of emperors until late AD 68, when the new emperor Galba made what appears to have been the fatal mistake of dismissing them for their loyalty to Nero, thereby leaving himself open to assassination by an improbably small number of praetorians.

It is important to understand just what this meant to the Batagwi, and why they took the dismissal quite as badly as they undoubtedly did. The Bodyguard were, of course, a source of enormous kudos to the tribe and their local neighbours, and a significant source of income to boot, but the importance of their place in Rome went deeper than simple national pride – the influence of their position close to the throne on the tribe itself cannot be ignored. Exposed to Rome, the hub of empire and meeting point for dozens of nationalities and cultures, it was inevitable that the guardsmen would have had the blinkers of their previous existence removed to some degree, and that they would have been eager to share their new experiences and learning with friends and families. Anthony Birley argues in *Germania Inferior* (in an article entitled 'The Names of the Batavians and the Tungrians') that many guardsmen would have been likely to have been given new Latin or Greek names on their entry into service, as their own names might be unpronounceable for a Roman. The perpetuation of these names into the Batagwi mainstream as proud parents sought to rub a little of a brother or an uncle's fame off on their new offspring must have been inevitable, which is the reason why some Batagwi characters in *Betrayal* have apparently anachronistic Greek names that are in fact entirely valid for their time and place. The guard effectively came to define the Batagwi's significant status within the empire, a source of enormous prestige at least within the tribe itself. This in turn justified the degree to which they had subjugated their culture to that of Rome, including the incorporation of their religion into the Roman framework, their god Megusanus, as was so often the case with local deities, being deftly spliced with the Roman version of Heracles/Hercules to create a new and mutually acceptable deity. The guard had come to define the Batagwi to a large degree, and when they came home for good late in AD 68 it must have seemed as if the tribe had been cast aside by the previously doting parent regime, with immense impacts on both the Batagwi's own self-esteem and indeed their relationships with the other local tribes who were equally impacted by this inexplicably sudden and shocking change of fortunes.

Of course, the split with Rome was more complex than just the overnight loss of their prestige. It went far deeper than the sudden thunderbolt of late AD 68, and had been growing ever more obvious to those with eyes to see it over the previous years. The Batagwi and their allies the Cananefates, the Marsacii and the Frisavones had to some degree, if the Roman commentators are to be believed, simply got too big for their own boots. In effect, it seems, they had made the age-old mistake of believing their own propaganda (or at least that of their Roman allies who called them the 'best and bravest', in itself possibly a play on the Germanic origins of the tribe's name, Batagwi, which might well have meant 'the best'). They had taken, we are told, to strutting around telling anyone who would listen how important they were to Rome, had fallen out with their former parent legion the Fourteenth Gemina – possibly because the legion was lauded by Nero as his most effective after the Battle of Watling Street and the defeat of the Iceni, while the Batagwi had presumably gone relatively unrecognised – and had thereby contributed to the increasing disenchantment with what was later portrayed as their overbearing behaviour. Rescued from internal exile of a sort by the onset of war between the German army of Vitellius and Otho's loyalist legions – having previously been posted on garrison duty standing guard on the Lingones in eastern Gaul, ostensibly to prevent a recurrence of the Vindex revolt – they had immediately (if we believe the primary sources who were of course propagandists with their own agenda) taken up where they had left off, telling all and sundry how they had mastered their former parent legion and how critical they were to the success of the war against Otho. It is doubtful if they were much loved by either legions or generals, but rather tolerated for their ability to turn a battle given the chance to do so.

In late AD 68, and at about the same time as the returning men of the Bodyguard, Gaius Julius Civilis ('Kivilaz' in the book, this being my own invention albeit at the learned encouragement of Jona Lendering, and therefore quite possibly accurate, but in no way attested by any source) returned from captivity, trial and acquittal in Rome. Civilis's Roman name identifies him as the son of one of the tribe's original noble families – a prince and successful military commander, but he was a man with an unhappy recent past. Charged with treason for having allegedly participated in the Vindex revolt, a failed uprising that had ultimately led to Nero's suicide, his brother Paulus had been summarily executed and Civilis himself sent to Rome to face the same charge. Freed by Galba – who had after all benefited hugely from Vindex's apparent folly in rising up without an army worthy of the name – he went home and was promptly rearrested by the army of Germania Inferior under the emperor-to-be, Aulus Vitellius, on the same charge. Freed once more, by a canny emperor who realised the risk posed by potentially hostile tribes in his own backyard while his armies were for the most part far distant in Italy, Civilis seems likely to have discerned the inevitability of a third attempt to make the charge stick, once Vitellius had no further need to tread softly around the Batagwi at the war's end.

And if the quasi-judicial murder of his brother and the threat hanging over his own head weren't enough to motivate him to revolt against Rome, the opportunity to seize power in a political system that must have seemed to be sliding away from the *noblissimi popularium*'s control, as more and more men of common rank achieved citizen status through their military service, may also have been too strong a temptation to be passed up. Whatever the reason, Civilis roused his people to revolt and the bloody events that run to their completion in *Retribution* came to pass.

And what of the military situation at the point that *Retribution* takes up where *Onslaught* left the story? On the face of it the odds were fairly evenly balanced at the end of AD 69. On the Roman side, underwritten by the empire's usual single-minded focus on the restoration of power over their former German subjects, legions were being put back into the field fresh from the fighting that decided the last act of the Year of the Four Emperors at Cremona, with orders to return north over the Alps and deal with the tribal revolt that threatened Rome's grip on the province. And nor was the Rhine army, which had been ordered to return to its home province, the only threat that Rome could muster. From the periphery of the European empire, battle-hardened legions were being summoned to march to the fight, posing the Batagwi with a complex threat on several axes of advance, which only the rebel main force could hope to fend off. Properly coordinated, the oncoming legions would present Civilis with a threat whose defeat would be almost impossible unless they would obligingly present themselves to be beaten one at a time.

The Batagwi, however, were far from defeated even if their master-stroke at Gelduba late the previous year had gone from triumph to disaster in minutes, with the unexpected arrival in their rear of cohorts from Northern Spain just when it seemed that victory was in their grasp. Despite losing about half of the cohorts' fighting power at that one battle, they still had significant numbers, both their own remaining soldiers and the tribesmen who had flocked across the Rhine to join them in the hope of conquest and plunder. And Civilis had another trick up his sleeve. The Gallic tribes neighbouring the Batagwi homeland, Treveri,

Lingones and Nervii, were in the final stages of planning their own revolt, not in the Germanic model so aptly illustrated by the rebellion to their north, but in the hope of emulating Rome's civilised political model with an 'empire' of their own. Encouraged by the civil war, if perhaps a little late to the party, they were plotting to join with Civilis's army and, at the right moment, expel the last of the legions from Gallia Lugdunensis and then march south to prevent Rome's army from leaving the foothills of the Alps, securing rebel control from the mountains to the sea.

The two forces were, therefore, probably more or less evenly matched in January AD 70. How long they would stay so would ultimately come down to a struggle for superiority between two men, Civilis and Cerialis. Both flawed, both ruthless and both capable of military masterstrokes. It would be a contest fought with all Rome's implacable will and every bit of the Germans' unrestrained ferocity. And so the stage was set for *Retribution.*

As usual, your comments and criticisms are very welcome, whether via my website's comments page or social media. I endeavour to answer all posts quickly, but writing and work sometimes get in the way, so please continue to show the usual patience and don't be afraid to nudge me if I'm slow responding. And now I'm off to start work on *Empire* book 10.

EMPIRE

In 2019, Anthony Riches returns to the world of Marcus Aquila in his next novel

THE SCORPION'S STRIKE

The tenth novel in the *Empire* sequence

In Anthony Riches' new story, one of the most important incidents mentioned in Retribution *comes to life . . .*

'Death Ride' was first published in July in the limited edition artwork collation Centurions: Codex Batavi *– available for a brief time from www.anthonyriches.com*

DEATH RIDE

The lone rider came down the road at a full gallop, heedless of his horse's flagging stamina or his own safety, reining in his foam-mouthed mount at the last moment and submitting to the scrutiny of Briganticus's bodyguard at spearpoint. If a single rider hadn't already been enough to catch and hold the attention of the men of the Ala Singularium, the exhausted beast beneath him only served to emphasise the irregularity of his being alone, where despatch riders usually rode in pairs to make sure their message was delivered should a horse go lame. Rising up in his saddle he raised a message container, his eyes searching the cavalry wing's ranks in search of the man for whose ears his message was intended.

'I know that man! Let him through!' The heavily-bearded tribune beckoned the rider to him, smiling slightly as his escort's leader turned his own horse and trotted behind him with his spear held ready. 'Gods, Obcasus, the man's delivered a dozen messages to us in the last month!'

The decurion nodded in recognition of the point, but his eyes remained fixed on the courier with the intensity of a hunting wolf, the point of his spear unwavering a foot from the messenger's back.

'You know that your uncle would pay a hefty price to have you sleep in the mud.'

'How could I not know this, since you remind me of it several times a day. Usually adding that this will only happen if you and your brothers of my bodyguard are already ready for burial.' Briganticus turned his attention to the courier. 'What news do you have for us?'

'Nothing good, Tribune!' The Roman turned in his saddle and

pointed north to the smoke-stained horizon. 'The Batavians and their allies have mustered every man they have left and attacked at Grinnes and Vada, with such strength and fury that our forward outposts were overwhelmed and put to the sword! No mercy was shown!'

'Nor can we expect any.' He looked around at the men of his bodyguard with the light of certainly in his eyes. 'This is a fight to the death, and it is a fight I am happy to accept, if it will afford me the chance to end the disgrace of my people's rebellion. Tell me, messenger, what other news do you carry?'

'The cohorts defending the outpost forts are lost, Tribune, scattered before the Batavian attack. I am sent to warn you that Julius Civilis himself is advancing in this direction with what is left of his cohorts, and to instruct you to fall back as planned by Legatus Augusti Cerialis in the event of such an attack. The Legatus Augusti is riding to confront the traitor with his full force of cavalry, and you are to join with him at the pre-ordained location in preparation for an attack.'

Briganticus nodded slowly as he digested the messenger's report, shaking his head at the men of his bodyguard.

'I told you it would come to this. What started as a rebellion against the empire's iniquities has become what the Romans call a war of attrition, with victory to the last man standing. My uncle Kivilaz, to the eternal dishonour of our family, has put our city of Batavorum to the fire. He realises that he cannot hope to deflect the legions from their mission to re-assert Rome's control over our people. So he has chosen instead to scorch the earth before us, and even to divert the course of the river Rhenus to block our path, making it clear to Rome that this is a fight which it can only win by smashing all resistance. Yes, this is a fight to the death, with only one possible ending. And now he has chosen to come at us, rather than sit behind the Rhenus and postpone the day of his reckoning. One last flourish of his blade in Rome's face before he either does the honourable thing and sheathes that sword in his own guts or lays it at Cerialis's feet like the coward I know him to be.'

The Batavi noble shook his head, visibly angered at the messenger's suggestion of retreat.

'But any idea that he might stand and wait for Cerialis to muster his full strength and come for his head is wide of the mark. He will make a demonstration, burn out a few forts, and hope that it will be enough to keep us from hunting him down before winter closes in and freezes this war until the spring thaw. He knows just as well as we do that Rome's army will be forced to retreat to barracks and wait out the cold days huddled around their fires, unable to take advantage of his weakness. And who knows what might change in that time, and lead Rome to call its legions home? No, this might be the last chance that we have to defeat him in battle, and to demonstrate that the only reward for betrayal is death!'

Flexing his thighs to stand in his horse's saddle, he shouted at the riders gathered around him.

'Men of the Ala Singularium! My brothers from a dozen different provinces, raised by the emperor Vitellius to form his bodyguard when he took power in Rome, you were chosen from the best horsemen in the empire that rules the world! And yet, despite our prowess, at every battle we have been ordered to wait patiently while other men have taken the glory that we crave! Our excellence has made Cerialis see us as his last and most potent reserve, but that in turn has denied us our chance to fight! And now we are bidden to withdraw and make way for our general to lead his cavalry to victory over my treacherous uncle, if that cowardly dog chooses to wait for Cerialis's blow to land! Doubtless with our spears detailed to wait behind the line once again.'

He pointed at the horizon, and the thin, dirty grey columns of smoke rising from burned out forts.

'*There* is the battle! *There* is the enemy! Are we to meekly turn away, or should we accept this gift from the gods and take our spears to them, at the very moment they decide that victory is theirs and before they turn to flee, as they inevitably will?'

A chorus of voices was raised in response to his challenge, the men of his ala demanding their moment of glory exactly as he had expected. Obcasus nudged his horse in close, fixing his tribune with a hard stare.

'Cerialis has kept you in reserve because you are of your tribe's royal blood, a potential successor to your uncle when this war is done with, and because he knows that your choler runs hot enough for you to do exactly what you propose, and throw your life away in pursuit of Kivilaz's head. You know that this will be the death of you, and of every man who loves you? You realise this, and still you intend to ride at them?'

Briganticus returned his stare unblinkingly.

'You write our epitaphs too quickly, brother, even if you are named for death and ruin. One perfectly flighted arrow can turn a battle where a thousand spears might fail, if it flies true and finds its mark. I know my uncle all too well, and his kin, and I know that I will find him at the head of the bloody path that we will carve into his remnant of an army. I will put my spear into his throat, and laugh in his face as he chokes his last breath. And when Kivilaz dies, trust me, this pitiful revolt will die with him!' He leaned forward, putting a hand on his friend's shoulder. 'Ride with me to the glory that is ours, brother. Ride with me, and feel the joy of your horse floating across the ground towards a cringing enemy once again. We will take our iron to these cowards who hide behind rivers, only coming out to fight when the odds are with them. And you men of my bodyguard – sword-brothers Adamus, Martinus, and Parmenion – sword-brothers, will you join me in the glory of riding at the point of our spear?'

They nodded in proud silence, and Obcasus nodded, pursing his lips at the challenge.

'It *will* be the death of us all, I know that in my heart. But I can no more deny my destiny than I could renounce our friendship . . .' he looked around at the other men of his tribune's bodyguard '. . . our brotherhood. So yes, we will ride with you, Briganticus, and leave a tale for those men who survive to tell their sons' sons when their beards are grey with age, proud to tell them "I rode with Briganticus"'.

He lead his men forward at a trot, giving orders for the four hundred riders of his ala to spread out across the farmland and form an arrowhead formation with his own squadron at the point, the men of his bodyguard forming a ring of iron about their tribune at the point of their spears as the Singularium advanced steadily in the direction that the messenger had indicated before spurring his horse away to the rear.

'There!'

Parmenion raised his hand to point at the ground before them. A line of well-disciplined infantry was advancing out onto the flat ground before them, the banner of their rebellion raised above a tightly packed group of horsemen marching behind them.

'Kivilaz.'

The Batavi tribune's voice was a soft growl as he raised his spear's pale blade, its polished and honed iron pointing at the oncoming line of rebel infantry. He rose in the saddle and pointed the weapon at the enemy army before them, undaunted by the increasing numbers of soldiers advancing out onto the plain bordered by the newly-liberated Rhenus.

'Now we have him! Our enemy's leader is before us, my brothers of the Ala Singularium! At last he comes to war like a man, with little more than a line of his guardsmen between his sword and my own! We strike now, my brothers, and we strike fast, before they have time to bring their own horsemen back to protect them! With me to victory!'

He looked to Obcasus, who nodded and raised his spear in the command the entire ala was waiting for, bellowing a command into the total silence that had fallen with his tribune's final call to battle as he swung the weapon down to point at the enemy formation.

'Singularium, at the canter, *advance!*'

The horsemen spurred their mounts forward, the rolling thunder of flying hoofs forcing Briganticus to shout to be heard.

'Straight through them, Obcasus, scatter their line like chaff and put me alongside my uncle! This . . .' he raised the spear high above his head in an extravagant gesture of purpose 'will finish this rebellion for Rome!'

The decurion nodded grimly, scanning the Batavi line intently for any sign of doubt or weakness, any slight gap in the line into which he could lead his squadron as the spear point of the ala's flying advance. The enemy infantry were two hundred paces distant, their shields a mismatched scatter of different colours and shapes which in itself was testament to the bitter war they had fought up the length of the river, as Kivilaz's revolt had initially led them to the brink of victory and then subjected them to defeat after defeat at the hands of Rome's legions, their tattered ranks equipped with the spoils of those initial victories, now rusted and battered by long months in the field.

'*There!*'

Briganticus pointed at a section of the enemy formation close to the flag underneath which Kivilaz and his bodyguard's horses stood, the otherwise unbroken line of shields and helmeted heads suddenly disturbed by a flurry of movement. A Batavi infantryman had discarded his shield and turned to run, his struggle to escape momentarily distracting the half-dozen men around him as they fought to put him back in his place.

'*At the gallop!*'

The decurion's command was instinctively swift, spurring his mount at the fleeting opportunity with his comrades at either shoulder, all three men roaring their battle cries at the cringing enemy line as the men around the terrified soldier realised that his action had made them the target for a hundred onrushing lances and more. Briganticus bared his lips in a feral snarl as the vengeful enemy soldiers thrust their hapless tent mate out in front of the line without either shield or spear, the hysterical soldier raving soundlessly into the thunder of the ala's headlong charge as the horsemen spurred their mounts to one last glorious spurt of effort. In the last instant of his life the doomed man stared helplessly at the onrushing wall of horseflesh, then vanished beneath Martinus's horse with a wailing scream that was abruptly silenced by the pounding hoofs that would tear him to pieces. An instant later the charge reached its objective, the still unsettled men whose line had been disturbed by their comrade's panic,

Obcasus and his comrades driving their horses deep into the Batavi ranks, the terrible impact sending armoured soldiers flying.

The line broke into two under the charge's shock, men on either side being forced further back as each successive squadron of horsemen entered the fray, but reinforcements were hurrying to join the fight from the unengaged ends of the Batavi formation, throwing themselves into the fight with the determination of men who knew that if their defence was broken, the cavalrymen would pursue them back to the river, picking them off at their leisure as the exhaustion of defeat slowed them to a staggering walking pace. Already the ala's initial success was becoming mired in a gradually increasing tide of reinforcements, and as Briganticus watched Obcasus's horse was felled by a spear-thrust that dropped the beast to its knees. The decurion himself leapt out of the dying beast's saddle with the grace of a born warrior and swept his sword up in an arc, splitting the spear-wielding Batavi's chin and nose to leave the enemy soldier tottering with both hands holding the bloody ruin of his face. Knowing that the moment of decision was upon him, Briganticus bellowed a fresh challenge at the men crowding in behind him, the press of iron-clad warriors on all sides placing the tribune and his bodyguard at the very heart of a brutal melee that would determine their fates.

'*Into them! Victory or death! We do this the old way!*'

The tribune jumped from his horse, knowing that to remain mounted so close to the enemy would only result in his being speared by some anonymous soldier, hurling his spear into a Batavi guardsman's face and drawing his sword, looking to either side to find his closest comrades at his shoulders and behind him. Obcasus was already in motion in front of him, a twisting, stabbing god of war carving his way into the enemies before them. Briganticus instinctively hurried forward to stand at his shoulder, Martinus to his left and Parmenion on his right, the four men driving forwards towards the flag flying over the men they were striving to kill, with Adamus in his customary place at their backs. The decurion staggered as a spear blade punched through his mail and deep into his side, recovering from the shock of its penetration to wrench the sharp iron from his body and kill its wielder with a stroke of his sword that almost decapitated the man, mustering his strength to attack again, hunched over the wound as blood ran down his right leg but still fighting, still killing, as the blades of the men gathered behind him raged against their disconcerted enemies. The enemy guardsmen were stunned by the nerveless courage of the handful of men driving into the gap in their broken line, savage in their rush to confront their own deaths and heedless of the threats gathered on all sides as they fought and slew the Batavi soldiers in flying arcs of blood.

'*One last effort! To the flag!*'

The small party advanced into the thickening ranks of the enemy, almost totally cut off from their embattled comrades as the ala's riders were slowly but surely driven back by the rush of reinforcements on either side, horses screaming and dying as the guardsmen, no strangers to cavalry fighting, took a terrible toll of the helpless beasts, and with a grim lurch in his guts Briganticus realised that he and his bodyguard were isolated from the remainder of his command. But even as Obcasus took a spear through the mail that covered his back and arched in his death spasm, the tribune realised that his companion's fearless charge had taken them to the brink of victory. Before them, surrounded by a handful of his own bodyguard, his uncle Kivilaz was advancing towards the men who had broken his elite guardsmen's line.

'*I have you now, traitor!*'

Stalking forwards, Briganticus patted his friend's shoulder as he stepped over the dying decurion's body, looking down into the stricken man's eyes.

'Wait for me, brother. I will join you soon enough.'

Taking the lead, limping on a leg slashed by a blow he had not even registered as he had killed the man who had wounded him, he felt the presence of Martinus and Parmenion at his sides, both men fighting for their lives while the desperate exertions of Adamus at his back were equally evident from the clash of iron blades, but his only thought was for the one-eyed man stepping forward to confront him with a drawn sword.

'You know that I will kill you!'

Kivilaz nodded soberly.

'There is that risk, nephew. You always were good with a blade. But I cannot hide behind my men, not if I am to hold my head up among the men of the Batavi.'

He stamped forward and attacked with the strength and speed of a man whose blade was not yet blooded. But even as Briganticus parried the first blow and stepped out of the path of the second's vicious swing he knew that a man twenty-five years his senior would not be able to best him, even wounded as he was. The Batavi gathering around their contest stayed their blades, as if recognising their prince's need to prove his manhood unaided, but as the fight between the two men raged to and fro Briganticus caught momentary glances of his comrades falling against the overwhelming numbers gathered around them. Martinus stabbed through front and back with a spear, holding the bloodied pole as his eyes rolled upwards in death. Adamus beaten down by the swords of three men but still managing to put his dagger into the throat of the closest of them as his life ebbed from savage wounds carved by their blades. And Parmenion, hobbling with one leg hamstrung from behind, tottering with a line string of bloodied spittle hanging from his open lips, eyes uncomprehending as the guardsmen around him savaged his failing body with repeated thrusts of their long spear blades.

'Was it worth their lives? Was it worth the destruction of your command?'

His attention flicked back to his uncle, swaying back out of the hissing path of the older man's sword as he swung it down two-handed, then jumped forward on his good leg to put his shoulder into his uncle's chest and send him sprawling. His sword-point found Kivilaz's throat before the prince could rise, its cold iron bite freezing him where he lay as Briganticus stared down at him dispassionately.

'You were a fool to offer me battle, Uncle, and *more* of a fool for meeting me blade to blade. I will —'

He stiffened as a spear punched into his back, feeling the cold iron carve deep into his body in a wave of searing pain that clenched every muscle in his body simultaneously and emptied his bowels and bladder with the immensity of its agony. The shock of its sudden removal was as bad, leaving him tottering as the blood released by his ruined organs ran down his legs, barely able to stay on his feet as the spear's wielder stalked around him and held out a hand to pull Kivilaz to his feet.

'I told him as much, but you know our uncle, he listens to nobody once a thought is in his head.'

'*Hramn!*' Briganticus shook with the effort of staying erect as his sight began to dim. '*You . . . honourless . . . dog . . .*'

His killer shrugged.

'What would have been the point in allowing you to kill him? Your cavalry wing is broken, its remaining men in full flight, what few there are of them. You *lost*, Cousin.'

Briganticus staggered, falling to his knees before the two men and staring up at them with the detachment of a dying man. Hramn smirked down at him.

'How apt. See, Uncle, your nephew gives you his respect at the last. Even if unwittingly.'

Drawing the last of his strength he spat a mouthful of blood across their chests.

'My sight . . . fades . . .' Briganticus coughed, spitting blood on the ground at their feet. *'But . . . I . . . see . . . your . . . death . . . Kivilaz.'*

Hramn whipped out his dagger and stepped in, punching the foot-long blade into his cousin's chest.

'Just *die*, Briganticus. Go to Hades with all the good men you killed today.'

Writhing against the knife's fresh agony, the younger man shook his head slowly from side to side.

'*You . . . will . . . die . . . alone . . .*' He dragged in a final breath, feeling something tear within his body *'And . . . at . . . your . . . own . . . hand.'*

He slumped backwards, the last light leaving his eyes as Hramn stepped back and shook the blood from his dagger.

'A pointless sacrifice.'

'Was it?' Kivilaz stepped forward to stand over the hunched corpse. 'I think not. He stopped us here, prevented us from finding some better position to hold against Cerialis when he advances to push us back into the river. All that's left now is to turn back and seek the safety of the other bank before that happens. Give the order.'

Hramn nodded and turned away, leaving his uncle staring down at Briganticus's corpse.

'Thanks to you all that's left now is to run, and sue for peace if I get the chance. And pray that your last curse proves unfounded.'